THE TRACKER'S SECRET

INGRID SEYMOUR

PenDreams • BIRMINGHAM

Published by PenDreams
Cover design by "Covers by Juan"

Manufactured in the United States of America

ISBN-13: 978-1-736061213

CHAPTER 1

I was a freaking werewolf.

My whole life my mother had lied to me, and I wasn't just a tracker, a human with magic in her blood. But, I was also a shifter.

Double Skew, and triple fucked.

Mom had promised me creamy tortellini, and instead, she'd sprung a cloak-wearing mage on me, and he hadn't been creamy at all. In fact, he'd been a total asshole. With a sneer, he'd tried to put a spell on me, except it didn't work.

"It's too late, Amalia," the mage had said. "She's already shifted. Renewing the spell is impossible."

That was when all hell broke loose, when I found out my mother was a big fat liar.

"What the hell?" I staggered back, glancing from the copper-eyed mage back to Mom. "What is he talking about? What is this?"

"Oh, God. Oh, God. Oh, God!" Mom lost it and got stuck in a loop that offered no explanation. Maybe she needed a *thump* on the head.

I walked up to her and shook her. "Mom, what's going on here? What was this man trying to do to me? And what did he mean by 'renewing the spell'?"

"For all the witchlights. This can't be!" she exclaimed, turning to the mage, who stood stoically off to the side. "You have to try again, Damien."

The mage shook his head. "I warned you that there would be no turning back if this happened. It's too late. I'm sorry, but there's nothing I can do."

"Too late for what?!" I demanded, taking a step in his direction, even though the mage scared the crap out of me. He was a Copper Mage, his eyes gave that away, and I didn't want to make him angry. If I pissed him off, he might decide to turn us into a couple of squawking parrots—though, maybe Mom deserved it.

She'd been lying to me about something, but what?

The mage shrugged and headed out of the kitchen without an answer.

"Get back here and explain," I roared, my voice a loud grumble that shook the knickknacks on Mom's shelves.

Mom squeaked. I cleared my throat.

What the hell?

The mage nonchalantly glanced over his shoulder, his gaze going from my face to my hands, which were shot out ready to strangle him. Thick, rope-like claws tipped my fingers.

I was already freaked out, but this grisly sight pushed me to the brink. I trembled, seeing red.

"Watch your temper, girl," the mage said. "You could hurt yourself, or worse, your mother." He gave Mom a sad look. "I'll be in the next room to make sure she doesn't eviscerate you. It seems an explanation to your daughter is in order."

"Eviscerate." Now, that's a word that will sober anyone. Shaking, I sat at the kitchen table and watched the claws retreat into place, leaving behind jagged nails with cracked polish. I shook all over from shock.

Claws, I'd sprung claws!

The same had happened last night. I remembered it now. At the repair shop, I'd seen Bernadetta Fiore's driver, Bertram, along with that Fae female who sneaked out of the Lucciola van. Then I'd chased her, matching her gazelle-like speed and thinking it was all a glamour. Then the claws came, but after that, my memory was a blank.

She's already shifted. She's already shifted, the mage's words rang in my ears.

Fear thrilled down my spine, a cold blade that made me shiver. I glanced over at Mom, who stood with her back against the refrigerator as if she could melt into it and disappear. Her eyes wouldn't meet mine, and her lower lip trembled. Tears wavered in her eyes. Mom was a strong woman. I could count on one hand the times I'd seen her cry: the day my brother, Leo, left to travel the world, and the day my father died.

My heart shrank to the size of a shriveled pea. Whatever explanation she owed me, I didn't think I wanted to hear it—not if it brought tears to my tough mother's eyes.

And yet, how could I not demand an answer?

My body tingled and itched all over, my skin feeling three sizes too small. My fingertips ached, and my throat felt tight. When I spoke, my voice was a few octaves lower than it should have been.

"You'd better start talking and explaining what this is all about," I said.

Mom's dark eyes finally met mine. The tears spilled down onto her cheeks as she blinked and swallowed hard. "I don't know where to begin."

"Rip off the Band-Aid, Mom. I had a hell of a surprise already. Maybe that means I'm strong enough to survive whatever else you've got," I said, my voice ripe with anger.

I had never talked to her like that, but it was clear she'd been lying to me and would've continued to do so if the mage had been able to "renew the spell," which meant it wasn't the first time he'd done it. Mom had been insisting I come to visit her for days, but I'd been too busy and had avoided her insistent calls. Now, it turned out she hadn't been desperate for my charming company.

With one shaking step, Mom came away from the refrigerator. Her hands were clasped in front of her as she wrung them together nervously. "I only wanted the best for you. I didn't want this to happen."

A low rumble started in my chest. Mom cowered, pushing her back against the refrigerator again. I pressed a hand to my breastbone. I sounded like I had swallowed my Camaro's engine. What the hell was up with that?

"What is happening to me?" My voice had gone back to normal, but it rang with fear.

"You're changing." Mom's words sounded like some sort of curse, like something I should be terrified of.

Changing into what? That was what I needed to ask, but Mom wasn't the only coward here. It seemed I'd inherited the trait from her, because, instead, I avoided the question.

"And that mage," I pointed in the direction of the living room, "he was here to…?"

"He was here to stop it, like he's done every year since you were born."

Since you were born.

I glanced under the table, considering the possibility of hiding there for the rest of my life. I wouldn't lack shelter or food. Mom was a great cook. It wasn't a bad idea at all.

Changing into what? I still shied away from the question that mattered most, but Mom finally grew a pair and shot the elephant in the room right between the eyes.

"You're a werewolf, Antonietta."

I'd known it was coming. Yet, I couldn't accept it.

"NO!" I shouted, though deep inside, I knew it was the truth.

Even as I shook my head, a part of me bristled at the news, feeling acknowledged as if, all along, it'd been waiting to be *seen.*

"What kind of joke is this?" I demanded, letting my denial take the wheel. "I can't be a werewolf. I'm… I'm…"

I stared at my hands where claws had been just minutes ago. They were still there under my skin. I felt them like tiny beating hearts at my fingertips, pulsating, pushing, aching to be released.

Mom exhaled deeply, and wearing a resigned expression, she approached and sat across from me. She looked like someone who had given up a well-fought battle, someone who hated to lose but, at the same time, found relief in knowing the struggle was finally over.

"I have been lying to you and everyone else for over twenty years," she said, her eyes growing dark and distant as if she'd been transported to a different place and time. "I'm not proud of my mistake, of everything I kept from you and your father."

I know what she is going to say. I know what she is going to say.

No, you don't. It's not *possible.*

As she spoke, I shook my head over and over, wishing I had come to lunch when she first asked me so that none of this would have happened, so I wouldn't have to let her words break my heart into more pieces than I thought were possible.

"Antonietta, you… you aren't Peter's daughter."

No!

Dad. A sob escaped me.

"I had an affair. It didn't last. There is no excuse, but your father and I were going through a rough patch, and I was still young and foolish. It was over as soon as it began, but even though he broke things off and he went away, you remained."

He broke things off, not her.

What the fuck kind of bitter pill was this?

I jerked out of the chair and stared down at Mom, fists shaking at my sides. She must've seen something in my expression because she flinched and pressed her mouth into a thin line, turning her lips white. Without a word, I turned my back on her and walked away.

"Toni, please let me finish," she begged.

But there was nothing else I needed to hear. It hurt too much to even look at her, so I walked out and faced the mage. He was sitting in the living room, reclined on the sofa, his legs crossed as he hummed a tune I didn't recognize.

When he saw me, he stared at me from under his round dark glasses and said, "Impressive."

I frowned at him, unable to make a reply. My mind was too jumbled up with anger and pain to cobble up a proper insult.

Damien Ward, that was what Mom had introduced him as, stood up, his cloak oscillating behind him. Slowly, he reached into his breast pocket, pulled out a business card, and offered it to me. "You will have questions once you relearn how to form words again. Here's how you can reach me."

I stared at the card as if touching it would make furry ears spring from the top of my head.

The mage huffed and set the card on the coffee table. "I would suggest that, for the time being, you avoid getting angry, anxious, nervous, or sexually aroused. At least until you learn to control the shift. You wouldn't want to get a SUD. It's a bitch having them on your record. Much worse than a DUI."

As if he'd suggested the exact opposite, blind fury flared in my gut and those gnarly claws made a reappearance, along with a set of major fangs. Shifting Under Duress be damned!

Damien cocked his head to one side and regarded me with pursed lips. After a moment, he waved a hand in the air and a sweet aroma saturated the room and filled my head and lungs with a cloying warmth that made me feel heavy and woozy. My claws and fangs retreated. I blinked several times, feeling disoriented.

"Do you remember shifting?" the mage asked.

Huh? What?

I thought about the question from every angle. Suddenly, the conversation I'd had with Mom came rushing back like a boomerang on steroids. Tears pricked in the back of my eyes as her words played inside my head.

You're a werewolf, Antonietta. You aren't Peter's daughter.

"You shifted," Damien said. "That's the reason my spell won't work anymore. The animal is free. Do you know when it happened?"

I should've known. The thought flashed through my head, reminding me that I hadn't been feeling right lately. My skin had been itching, feeling too small for my body. And my sense of smell… it had always been too keen.

"I… I think so," I said, trying to keep my anger at bay. This man was saying things I needed to know. "But I don't remember anything."

Damien nodded as if that were normal. "This won't be easy, but you'll have to learn how to control it. You need someone of your own kind to teach you."

Your own kind.

My ears started ringing. All my life I'd believed I was something I was not. My entire world was a lie, and my true self something… unknown and terrifying.

"Is there someone who can help you?" the mage asked.

Immediately, my thoughts went to Jake. He was a werewolf. He could teach me. Suddenly, the words he'd told me just yesterday came rushing back to me. *"I didn't want to leave, Toni, but I had to. I made a promise. I owe it to my father, my grandfather, and Neil to pass on our legacy, and with you… that would be impossible."*

My stomach flipped and flopped like a fish. A part of me felt elated. I was a werewolf, which meant I could be with him. There were no obstacles. I could give him children and help his family continue their legacy.

Yet, another part of me shied away from the idea. I wouldn't know how to raise werewolf children. I didn't even know if I wanted to have them. Besides, I wasn't a proper werewolf. Jake wouldn't want me. He would want someone strong and able, a mate who could stand alongside him to uphold his traditions, and I had no idea how to do that. I wouldn't make a good mate for him. And I didn't like the idea of becoming nothing but a puppy factory.

And why the hell was I thinking about Jake right now?!

I pushed the thoughts aside. They were too much to digest, especially when I hadn't processed the extent of my mother's betrayal, and when every time I thought about dad my heart ached. He wasn't my father. Someone else—some man I didn't know, who might be dead or alive—was responsible for creating me.

And there was more… I was a tracker *and* a werewolf. How? That was impossible, wasn't it?

My head pounded as all these ideas swirled around, crashing into each other like balls on a pool table. I pressed my palms against my temples, trying to make it stop.

The mage glanced off to the side and said, "Amalia, do you know someone who can help her?"

I glanced back. Mom stood behind me. I took a step toward the front door, the anger in my gut rekindling. "How could you?!" I demanded.

"I'm—"

"No! Don't talk to me. You ruined everything. I would have rather lost you than Dad."

An injured expression etched her face. "Don't say that."

"I wish he was here and not you. I wish… I wish…"

Suddenly, there was only one thing I wanted, and it was to be as far away from Mom as possible. I took another step toward the door and was about to bolt out of the house when I remembered the mage's business card.

Merely on instinct, I leaned over and snatched it from the coffee table. At that moment, I didn't quite understand why I took it. But later, I would be grateful. He was the only one who could explain the spell that had kept my wolf caged.

And sooner or later, I would need those answers.

CHAPTER 2

Lying in bed in the spare bedroom of my best friend's condo, I shook my head as the memories kept spiraling out of control, bringing back yesterday's events with so much vividness that I could almost see the sneering mage staring at me over the edge of his round, dark glasses.

Fury surged as the image of Damien and Mom standing in that kitchen flashed before my eyes. My skin began to tingle, and my fingertips and gums grew tight to the point of bursting with claws and fangs.

I sat up and clutched the edge of the mattress, staring at myself in the full-length mirror that hung from the wall. I tried to will the anger away by breathing slowly and focusing on my face. Something was different about it, though I couldn't say exactly what. Some subtle changes had honed my features, turning them… wild. It seemed my cheekbones and my nose were sharper, and my mouth protruded slightly forward.

God, don't let me shift. Rosalina is in the next room.

She was getting ready for work. Her makeup routine took her a while. She was a genius with eyeshadow and concealer. As I thought of my friend, the tingling in my skin subsided a little, so I squeezed my eyes shut and thought more about her and our day ahead at the office.

We had a new client coming in today. Someone Celina Morelli had recommended to Sunder's Mate Tracker Agency, which meant Rosalina and I were well on our way to turning our clientele to the most exclusive in St. Louis. The business goals we had set out for ourselves were coming to fruition. With this new type of client, we would be able to charge more for our services, and we would do more than stay afloat.

With a deep breath, I opened my eyes and stared at myself in the mirror again. My face had gone back to normal. It was rounder and *not* wild.

Thank the witchlights.

I could do this. I could keep it together. I didn't need someone of *my kind* to help me and teach me. I didn't need to ask that mage any questions, for all I knew Mom would convince him to keep me in the dark again. At once, the anger returned and started bubbling like an already-boiling pot set back on the stove.

Forget about the mage. Forget about mom.

Forget about the mage. Forget about mom.

Forget, forget, forget.

Except all the chanting in my head only made things worse. A rumbling built in my chest, and I fell in front of the bed on all fours, my back arching, my muscles spasming, and my face twitching. I stared at my fingers as they started shrinking, and brown fur sprang at the knuckles.

No, no, no!

Let me out, a separate voice seemed to yell inside my head.

No, go away!

A knock came at the door. "Ready to go? Aaron Blackridge will be in the office at eight sharp."

I opened my mouth to answer, but afraid of what would come out, I closed it again and begged my body to relax, and my spine and fingers to go back to normal.

"Hey, Toni The Tiger, are you in there?" Rosalina's voice acquired an edge of worry.

Please, stop. Please, I begged, staring at the disgusting hair that had sprung over my forearms.

It's not disgusting, that other voice said. *It's just as it should be.*

Shut up.

I didn't need the wolf making things worse. I was supposed to be Little Red Riding Hood, and instead, I'd turned into the big bad wolf like in that movie *Red: Werewolf Hunter* where the protagonist gets bitten and turned into a werewolf.

"Toni?" Another knock.

I hadn't told Rosalina what I was. She was my best friend, but I still didn't know how to confess that I was a werewolf, one who knew nothing about being a shifter and could, with one wrong move, screw up everything we'd worked so hard to attain. *Crap!* Just when everything was looking up, when we'd accomplished what we'd set out to do, I couldn't be counted on.

Hell, I shouldn't even go into the office—not when my butt could spring a tail out of nowhere, and my wolf might decide to eat one of our clients for supper. We needed to cancel all our appointments until I figured this shit out.

The door opened and Rosalina stepped into the room. "Toni?" A pause. "Where did she go?"

I heard her step further into the room. My breath froze. I squeezed my eyes shut, begging the wolf to butt out.

"What are you doing?" Rosalina asked as she came around the bed.

I opened my eyes and stared at my hands and forearms. They were normal. No nasty hair all over them. Slowly, I glanced over my shoulder. Rosalina stood behind me, frowning at my behind, which stuck up in the air, as I was on all fours. She didn't look freaked out, just annoyed, which meant I didn't look different from any other morning.

"Um, I dropped my pen," I said lamely.

Yeah, right, my wolf said.

Pipe down, Red!

My wolf bristled at the name.

"Well, leave it," Rosalina said. "We're going to be late."

"Right." I jumped to my feet and smoothed my Navy blue slacks.

Rosalina narrowed her eyes, staring at my chest. I tensed. Had I grown two more pairs of boobs? Because wolves worked like that, right?

"Nice blouse," she remarked. "New?"

I breathed a sigh of relief. "Yes. I bought it a couple of weeks ago and haven't worn it." It was an elegant blouse with flowing sleeves and a V neckline. It looked professional with slacks, and I could dress it down with jeans.

"You're acting weird." Rosalina gave me a raised eyebrow. "Ever since you got back from your mom's yesterday, I don't know, you haven't been the same. Did something happen?"

My shoulders slumped forward. I couldn't keep this from her. "Actually, something *did* happen, but it's kind of a long story. Maybe we can talk about it tonight?"

"O-kay," she said slowly. "Should I be worried?"

"Maybe. A little." She probably needed to worry a lot, but it wouldn't be nice to ruin her day by telling her that. And maybe between now and then, I would come up with some genius idea to help me keep the animal inside me under control.

She huffed, not pleased with my answer. "Fine then. We'll talk tonight. Now, let's hurry or we'll be late. Wanna grab breakfast on the way?"

"Definitely. I'm starving. Let me feed Cupid before we go." I was determined to be more diligent about feeding my betta fish his yummy pellets. He waved his colorful tail as he gulped his food. I would need to change his water soon. It was starting to look clouded.

On our way to the agency, we got tall cups of coffee and gooey bear claws at a small pastry shop near her condo. The food distracted me for a bit, and when I finished licking my fingers I did my best not to think of anything but our next client.

We still didn't know much about him except that his name was Aaron Blackridge and that he was a popular Skew DJ that went by the name of Slice. He was a werewolf from a well-known pack. The Blackridges had been in St. Louis for generations. Today, we would create a file for him, go over the contract, and hopefully get some heartfelt tears out of him to start a tracking potion.

We arrived at the agency with ten minutes to spare. Rosalina parked her red Scion in front of our door and we got out. I hurried inside the office, afraid of running into Jake. Without Damien Ward's spell on me, I was afraid he would be able to detect a change in me, and I wasn't ready for anyone to know, much less Jake. Even the idea of talking to Rosalina tonight scared me. I didn't know if I would ever accept myself, and I was afraid others might not accept me either. Though in Jake's case, I worried that he would instantly receive me with open arms and for reasons that had too much to do with my damn uterus.

The badass Cupid artwork that hung on the wall greeted us as it did every morning, and I allowed my shoulders to relax. I had avoided Jake. For now.

Rosalina quickly took a seat at her desk and fired up her laptop. She handed me the folder she'd prepared for our new client, and I was about to go into my office to settle in when the door behind me opened, and the person I least wanted to see came waltzing in.

"Good morning," Jake said, inclining his head.

I turned to face him, meeting Rosalina's eyes with a quick wince as I did.

He stood framed by the door, tall and broad, his hair and beard perfectly styled, and the scent of fresh soap drifting from him. He wore a pair of dark jeans, black biker boots, a gray T-shirt, and a bomber jacket. His silver eyes twinkled with the overhead lights, and my heart did that weird, irregular drumming it always did when he unexpectedly appeared and I hadn't braced myself to face his mouth-watering hotness.

Red licked her lips at the sight. I did, too.

Coming back to my senses, I took a couple of steps away from him, afraid he might be able to capture a new scent coming from me. He frowned as I retreated, cocking his head to one side. His nostrils widened, and I feared there would be no hiding this from him, but he dismissed my attitude as I put on an annoyed expression.

Disappointment washed over me. It was stupid. Logically, I didn't want him to know what I was, but my heart had always been a dumbass when it came to Jacob Knight.

"Sorry," he said, "I won't interrupt your workday for long, I simply had a question about our landlord."

Jake's PI agency sat next door to ours. Only ten days ago, though it felt like a lifetime, he had shown up out of the blue after being away for one and a half years. Shamelessly, he had rented the vacant office space right on our street and had managed to drag me into an ordeal of screwed-up proportions.

Now, all I could hope for was that, since he had no more use for me, he'd decided to vacate the premises. A girl could only hope.

"Ask away," Rosalina said.

"There are a few things that need his attention before I can officially open for business, do you know another way to contact him besides his email address? He hasn't answered any of the messages I've sent him."

Nope, he hadn't decided to leave. Instead, he was making himself comfortable and was on the verge of opening for business. He had been doing repairs to the space. Maybe he had finished getting things the way he wanted them.

Slowly, I backed away toward my office. "I think Rosalina has his phone number, don't you?"

She nodded, then picked up her cell phone and started scrolling through the contacts.

"I've got to get ready for a client. He'll be here any minute." I hooked a finger toward my office, then quickly disappeared through the open door. Once inside, I heaved a sigh of relief. It didn't seem as if he'd detected anything different about me, but I couldn't be sure it would remain that way. Maybe the mage's spell hadn't completely worn out, and as soon as it did, Jake would know.

The skin around my fingers began to itch. I scratched it absentmindedly, and when I realized what I was doing, I stopped and shook myself. Taking three deep breaths, I calmed myself. The annoying itching passed. Man, if I didn't know better, I would say that my *werewolfness* came with mange.

Stupid, shifting urges!

Eager for a distraction to keep my mind off my traitorous body, I sat behind my desk and set the new customer folder in front of me. I had work to do.

ꙮ

Rolling my shoulders, I took a couple of pens from a holder and placed them next to Aaron Blackridge's folder. Quickly, I checked myself in the small mirror I kept in my desk drawer and made sure I didn't look wolfish. Somehow I doubted that "deranged, uncontrollable shifter chick" was the kind of look that would put customers at ease.

A moment later, Rosalina appeared at the door and announced our client.

"Mr. Blackridge is here," she said in her pleasant, businesslike tone.

I stood and shook his hand as he walked in. He was an African-American man of around twenty-five. His dark hair was arranged in locs that fell to his shoulders. He was dressed all in black except for a pair of entirely red, high top sneakers. One diamond earring pierced his right ear, and a gold chain with a heavy pendant in the shape of a treble clef hung from his neck. He offered me a warm smile that immediately made me like him.

"Good morning, Ms. Sunder," he said in a friendly voice.

"Good morning, Mr. Blackridge. You can call me Toni. Please sit down." I gestured toward the chair in front of my desk.

"In that case, call me Aaron." He took a seat, and I followed suit.

"I am so glad you could see me this morning."

"You come highly recommended by my friend. I have never seen Celina happier. She and Vincent are perfect for each other."

"It makes me happy to hear that. I hope I can do the same for you."

"I hope so, too."

I picked up one of the pens and clicked it. "Let's get started."

Over the next few minutes, I filled out his intake form and went over the contract with him. He didn't seem worried at all about our terms or the deposit, which was a breath of fresh air. The less affluent clients we'd worked with so far had refused to pay for our services unless they saw results. Clients like Celina and Aaron, however, splurged on far less important things all the time. Paying up-front for romantic happiness had to be easy when Starbucks trips on a private jet were the standard.

Still, I couldn't help but feel like a greedy person. Others needed to find happiness with the right partner, too, and it wasn't fair for them to suffer through loneliness or the wrong person because they couldn't afford someone like me. Rosalina and I had bills to pay and clothes to wear and meals to eat, so I tried not to beat myself up about it. Maybe, when things got easier and we built up our savings and paid off our business loan, we could do a little pro bono work. It would certainly make me happy. I would definitely have to run that by her.

After Aaron signed on the dotted line, I gathered all the papers and lined them up neatly. "Great. Now that this is out of the way, I should explain that in order to find your mate, I need to craft a potion that will allow me to locate her."

"Actually, it should be *locate him*."

"Oh, I'm sorry. I shouldn't have assumed."

"It's okay. It's not common among werewolves."

I knew this to be the case, though I didn't know the reason. It wasn't something Jake and I had talked about during our time together. I'd been too busy drooling over him and tracking missing people to worry about much else.

Aaron's warm expression grew somber. "If I wasn't a gay werewolf, I would already have a partner. My kind marries young, as you may know. Passing on our legacy is important."

I knew all too well about that. The man I loved was the last in a long line of Knight werewolves, and his legacy was more important than our feelings for each other.

"My parents are very disappointed as you might imagine. They keep telling me I won't be able to find another gay werewolf." He grimaced, clearly afraid to prove his parents right. "That's why I've come to you. As hard as I've looked, I've never met one."

"Do you mind me asking, since bearing children won't be an issue, why a werewolf? Your mate could be Fae, human, another type of shifter."

"I hope it doesn't appear like I'm discriminating against anyone, but I really hope you can find another werewolf. I do hope we'll be able to adopt, and it would be easier if my partner understands our kind and knows how to advise his own children. There is much to teach a young werewolf."

Such as not Shifting Under Duress and ruining one's entire criminal record. Something I was trying hard to avoid at the moment.

"I never thought about it that way," I said, wondering if the reason Mom had chosen to lie to me was because she'd had no clue how to raise me like a proper werewolf. I knew my next question would sound weird to Aaron, but I couldn't help myself. "So… how would someone who wasn't raised by werewolf parents learn proper werewolf skills? There isn't a place where they offer… lessons, is there?"

Aaron laughed, putting a ringed hand on his chest and throwing his head back. "Oh, I'm sorry," he said, sputtering. "That's just funny. No, I've never heard of a place like that. There aren't many shifters who grow up without that kind of guidance. It would be hard to survive, I would imagine."

I swallowed. "But you're hoping to adopt, so there must be… shifter orphanages? And people to teach them those skills."

"Um," he considered, pursing his lips. "Maybe so. But why are you so interested? Do you know someone who needs to learn how to be a *proper werewolf*?"

I froze, unsure of what to say.

"Because if you do," Aaron went on, "I would be glad to help. If you find me a mate, I would do anything for you, even kiss the ground you walk on."

I laughed nervously, heat building up in my cheeks.

Aaron narrowed his eyes, and something told me he saw right through me. "At any rate, you have my number, so call me if you find yourself in dire need of werewolf advice."

I smiled. "Thank you, but I was just curious. Sorry for distracting you and taking too much of your time. We should get back to business. Like I said, the next step is creating a potion, and for that, I need a batch of heartfelt tears from you."

"Yes, Celina warned me about this. But I doubt I will be able to cry in front of you. Nothing macho about me. I just haven't cried in a long time. I'll get one of my buddies to punch me in the gut."

"Sorry, but, like I said, they need to be *heartfelt.* Tears caused by physical pain won't work."

I pulled out a small vial from one of my desk drawers and handed it over. "You may go to the restroom or come back later after you fill this up. Just keep in mind that the sooner I get this ingredient, the sooner I can start the potion and find someone for you."

He stared at the vial with a frown. "I think I'll probably need to come back. Would onions work?" He smiled crookedly.

"Sorry. Nope."

"Why did you have to make this so hard, Toni? How about a tearjerker book or movie?"

I smiled. "Not really. You need to dig deep and find your most sincere emotions. That's the kind of tears the potion needs."

"Damn!" He mock-punched a closed fist into his hand. "There goes my plan."

We both laughed. He was so lighthearted. I really liked him and would surely do my damnedest to find a mate for him.

CHAPTER 3

After Aaron left, I handed Rosalina the hefty check for his deposit. Her eyes grew as wide as tennis balls when she saw the number on the check.

"Wow, I never thought we would be able to charge this much," she said. "A few more clients like this and we would be able to pay off our loan."

"I know. It feels awesome, doesn't it?"

"Damn awesome." She waved the check in the air.

"Shopping trip this weekend?"

"Yep, there's a pair of boots I saw the other day, they have my name written all over them." We fist-bumped each other and went happily about answering phone calls and screening new potential clients. I even had a little time to go upstairs to the loft and pack a few more of my things. I would close on Tuesday, then be able to move into my new place in less than two weeks. I felt all glowy inside when I thought about it, so much that not even the latest events could dampen my excitement. Just four more days to sign the contract and get the keys to my first home!

And since, after paying all the bills, there would be a little money left, I had plans of going furniture shopping this weekend. Not much, just a few pieces, but I was psyched all the same. Of course, I would miss Rosalina. Staying with her these past few days had been amazing, but we both needed our privacy. Besides, if it turned out that my wolf shed, I doubted she would appreciate fur on her carpet and sofa.

I was still packing things up in the loft when Rosalina poked her head in. "Hey, Toni, someone is here to see you."

I glanced back, frowning.

"Stephen Erickson," she mouthed.

Crap! I had forgotten I was supposed to have lunch with him today. I jumped to my feet, dusted off my pants, and rushed to the mirror to check my hair and makeup.

"You look hot, don't worry," Rosalina mock-whispered.

I pressed a finger to my mouth. "Shh."

Honestly, what was I doing? It didn't matter how I looked. Plus, I didn't want Stephen to get the wrong idea. I was only going out with him because I hadn't been able to tell him no when he asked. He'd been in a hospital bed, recovering from the awful ordeal of being kidnapped, of being locked inside a dark van for eleven days. He was probably craving normalcy. I planned to go out with him only once. No romantic shenanigans. I would not let his dreamy blue eyes put a spell on me again. Nope.

I sighed. One good thing: at least now I understood my dumb attraction to werewolves.

Taking a deep breath, I followed Rosalina downstairs, nervously wondering if Stephen would notice anything different about me. He stood admiring the black and white photographs on the wall as well as the cool Cupid that dominated the room.

When he saw me, his handsome face lit up, and he drew me into his arms, wrapping me into a tight, warm embrace. He gave no signs of smelling wet dog on me, and I was grateful for it.

Rosalina walked to her desk, meeting my gaze over his shoulder, fanning herself as if the room had grown hot all of a sudden. I rolled my eyes at her and pulled away from Stephen.

"So good to see you out of that hospital bed." I scanned him up and down. He wore gray slacks and a white T-shirt under a black trendy jacket with metal buttons. His red hair was a little long and tousled. Very stylishly. He still looked thinner than usual and a bit pale, but he was improving quickly.

"And I'm sure glad to be out and about." He gestured toward the Cupid illustration above us. "She looks like you."

"You think?"

"Well, the pink-tipped hair matches."

"I guess that actually means *I* look like *her* 'cause she was the one who inspired me to color my hair this way."

"Cool." He nodded approvingly. "The place looks great. Very warm and inviting. And it puts you in the right romantic mood." He pointed toward a picture of a man proposing to his sweetheart on one knee.

His words made me go even *glowier* inside. Rosalina and I had put a lot of thought into the décor, and it was nice to hear that it accomplished its purpose. It didn't escape me that Jake had never said one nice thing about the agency.

The self-interested asshole!

"So what are you in the mood for?" Stephen asked. "Anything your heart desires. Just speak the word and I will make it come true."

Behind Stephen, Rosalina fanned herself a little more and drooped down in her chair, acting as if she was about to faint. I walked toward the front door, passing Stephen and forcing him to turn in Rosalina's direction. Stephen frowned at her wet noodle impersonation.

Reacting quickly, she let out a big, fake yawn and mumbled, "I didn't sleep good last night. I might take a nap while you two go for lunch."

I smirked. *The little imp!* She'd been quick with the lie. She, herself, had a lunch date with a college friend who was in from Austin where he worked at a big tech company. She wasn't taking a nap.

"To be honest," I said with a grimace, "I had forgotten you were coming, and I have an appointment with a prospective client at one o'clock. If we drive somewhere, it will cut our lunchtime short, so if it's okay with you, we can go to Giovanni's across the street. They have the best pizza. You won't regret it."

"It sounds perfect to me. I don't care where we go. It's the company that matters." He smiled, showing his perfect white teeth while his baby blues twinkled with something like delight.

This time Rosalina didn't fan herself, but her green eyes were expressive enough to show me that, inwardly, she thought the room was on fire. But no! I would be the fire hose if things got that bad.

Stephen opened the door for me, and I stepped out onto the sidewalk. My first instinct was to stare straight ahead and ignore Jake's office, but that would have seemed petty of me, so instead, I gestured in its direction.

"I'm sure you noticed Jake's PI firm."

"I did. I'm so glad he's finally doing this. He has talked about it for a while."

I started walking in the opposite direction, toward the restaurant. We crossed the street as Stephen commented on some of the other stores and suggested we get ice cream at Mootown

Cones after lunch, which sounded like a perfect idea because I loved their salted caramel gelato.

The familiar rumbling of an engine sounded down the street, and Jake appeared at the corner, riding his badass Harley, and as usual, wearing no helmet. As he checked left before turning, he noticed us. I caught the surprise in his eyes, which he quickly concealed. Instead, he put on the same congenial expression he might've used if he'd just run into his grandma.

Likewise, I put on a smile and waved at him. I would've liked to avoid any awkwardness, but too late.

Stephen followed my gaze and brightened when he saw his friend. "Jake, my man!" He exclaimed in his usual warm manner.

Jake turned and drove his motorcycle in our direction, meeting us halfway down the street. He stopped close to the sidewalk and put out a hand, which Stephen clasped in both of his.

"We're going for some pizza as a thank you for saving my life." He laughed at the disparity. "Wanna join us?" he asked, surprising me.

This was a good sign. If he was willing to invite Jake, it meant he wasn't treating this like a date. I felt my shoulders relax as the pressure eased off.

"Thanks for the invitation, man, but I've got work to do, and I actually ordered some stuff that'll get delivered any minute. You guys enjoy."

His eyes flicked in my direction for a quick instant, long enough to give me a glimpse of something that looked very much like disappointment. Shifting gears, he drove his bike the rest of the way, parked right on the sidewalk in front of his office, and walked inside without a backward glance.

"So what do you recommend in this place?" Stephen asked as we walked into the restaurant.

We sat at one of the booths, and within minutes, we had placed our order. Stephen steepled his fingers, elbows on the table, and peered at me. I noticed the stump of his ring finger. It looked healed.

He smiled sheepishly and pulled his hands under the table. "I've found someone who says they can grow my finger back."

"Really?!" That was almost unheard of. Only a very powerful witch or mage could do that. Ah, the things money could buy.

"Um, this is awkward, but I think it should be mentioned. I asked Jake if he would be all right with us… doing this." He flicked a hand, pointing at me and then at himself.

My hackles rose, and I felt a growl building in my throat. Although both Red and I didn't seem to have a choice when it came to Jake, I liked to think that I did. I wasn't some object they could pass around between them. I tried to not snap at Stephen, but really he'd just pushed a big button of mine. I slid into bitch mode.

"I'm sorry, but the only permission you needed for *doing this* is mine. Jake doesn't have a say."

Stephen ran a hand through his red hair and rubbed the back of his neck, looking sheepish.

Ha! Bitchy Toni was my hero. I wondered if she was twins with Red. Or maybe they were one and the same and always had been.

"You're right," Stephen said. "My apologies. It wasn't my intention to make it sound like that. I guess what I meant was…" He sputtered, unsure of what to say. "Really, I guess my question to him had nothing to do with you, and everything to do with a friend I don't want to piss off."

"So what are you saying… that if Jake had told you he wasn't okay with it, we wouldn't be here?"

He raised his eyebrows, considering. "Um, I'd like to think so," he answered, sounding a bit unsure.

I chuckled, my anger dissipating. "I can appreciate your honesty, and I guess I should be honest with you, too."

He winced. "Oh, no, you're not going to tell me this is just a friendly lunch and not a date, are you? Because I really had my heart set on the latter, even if it's just pizza and not what I had in mind. Toni," he reached across the table, grabbed my hand, and pinned me with his intense gaze, "since I broke things off at my dad's insistence, not a day has gone by that I didn't regret listening to him. I keep thinking about how it could have been, you and me, together. And I can't help but feel it would've been amazing if I hadn't screwed things up."

Biting my lower lip, I pulled my hand out of his warm grip and slid it under the table away from his electrifying touch. There had always been attraction between us, but to my regret, it didn't compare to what I felt for Jake. It had to be a werewolf thing, though I wasn't sure. Maybe if I'd been raised properly, I would have a name for the way he affected me, but I had no clue.

"I'm sorry that it was so difficult for you," I said, measuring my words. "I've wondered the same sometimes. It could have been amazing like you said, but that's in the past. I've changed. I'm not the same person you met. I'm not looking for a relationship, though I would value your friendship. You should know that."

He cocked his head and sighed. "I was so afraid you'd say that."

He leaned forward, his gaze drilling into mine once more, so intensely that I had to turn away. I peered through the window at a car driving by. It was gone in a second, leaving the street empty and revealing a man standing on the other side of the street. He was staring straight at us, his hands glowing bright red as he waved them around in what could only be a spell.

I blinked in a panic, adrenaline pumping through my system,

bursting into my chest. The urge to run possessed me. The magic in the man's hands grew to the size of a basketball. It crackled like electricity, getting larger and larger. Then he held it in one hand and pulled his arm back like a pitcher at a Cardinal's game.

"Look out!" I yelled.

Leaping forward, I grabbed Stephen by the shoulders and knocked him to the floor. An instant later, the window exploded, and the restaurant filled with cries of fear.

CHAPTER 4

Shards of glass rained on top of us like tiny knives, cutting into our skin.

My ears rang, and my left side stung as if someone had poured acid on it. Stephen squirmed underneath me and reared up, glancing around. I curled into a tight cocoon, wincing at the pain. White lights flashed before my eyes, and I struggled to focus. I blinked, staring at my arm to see what was causing such terrible pain. When my eyes finally cleared, and I stared at my arm, horror struck me.

The skin from my wrist to my elbow looked like angry-red bubble wrap. Blisters oozed blood, popping as they swelled. I growled in pain, my teeth bared, my stomach churning at the sight. Panicked cries from the other customers filled the room.

"Someone call the police," a waitress yelled.

Stephen turned to me, and seeing my arm, winced. "Oh, Toni. You shouldn't have. You'll be all right. I promise."

He rose to his feet, and staying low, dragged me across the room to a safe corner behind an empty table. I gritted my teeth against the pain that shivered down my entire left side. I didn't dare inspect the rest of my body, but from the way it felt, my imagination pictured it like a slab of ground meat.

Stephen turned away from me, his blue eyes shining with their own light, his body quivering as he prepared to shift. "Stay here."

Like I could go anywhere.

There was a loud bang followed by a crash. I peeked from behind the table to find our attacker bursting in through the front door. Patrons shrieked and pulled back into their hiding places.

"Damn Skews!" a man to my right exclaimed as he pulled out his phone, presumably to dial 911. He threw me a dirty look as he waited for someone to answer. I would've given him the finger if my body didn't hurt so much. One Skew shouldn't give all others a bad name. If I judged all Stales by Jeffrey Dahmer, where would that leave them?

My gaze snapped back to Stephen as he let out a guttural growl. The back of his jacket and shirt split down the middle revealing powerful, furred shoulders. His pants went next, and as he shook his tattered clothes off, a magnificent brown wolf was left behind. He'd shifted so quickly and gracefully, I barely perceived his limbs morphing from human to animal. The creature was massive, almost as big as Jake's wolf.

He growled at the mage who stood by the door. Our attacker was whirling his hands again, readying another sizzling spell. He had spiked red hair. His eyes glowed blue, marking him as a mid-level mage. A worn leather cloak hung heavily behind him. I recognized him immediately. He was the mage who attacked me in Elf-hame.

Without waiting for another attack to come, the wolf lowered his head and leaped toward the mage, covering the distance between them in a couple of wide gallops. I held my breath as

Stephen soared through the air. Even as the bigass wolf flew at him, the mage stood his ground without blinking, and in the last instant, released a new magical attack, thrusting it right at Stephen's chest.

"No!" I cried out as the spell struck him and sent him flying on top of a table. His fur burned down to the skin, releasing an acrid smell that quickly filled the air and overpowered the scent of spices and tomato sauce.

Stephen whimpered and trembled, sliding off the table and hitting the floor with a *thud.* His limbs and tail twitched as he lay there, and his now-bare skin began to blister.

Oh, God.

I wished for my gun, so I could shoot the mage bastard, but it was tucked in a drawer in the office where I had left it, hoping I wouldn't need it again. Talk about wishful thinking. It seemed Stephen's kidnappers weren't done with him, and now they'd sent someone to kill him.

Smirking, the mage walked in Stephen's direction, sending chairs and tables out of the way with a flick of his wrist. He glowered at the twitching wolf with disdain, then twisted his hands into another spell, the killing blow.

I glared at my hands, willing my claws to come to the surface. If I could shift now, I would be able to help Stephen. But despite my anger and frustration, nothing happened.

Really, Red? All morning you've been itching to come out and now you chicken out? Why?!

The mage's mouth twisted with contempt as he prepared to unleash death on Stephen.

I struggled to my feet, teeth clenched against the pain, and limped out of my hiding place.

"Leave him alone, you coward," I spat.

He surveyed me, appearing annoyed. "'Coward isn't a word the weak have a right to use on the strong," he said.

Clearly, he had forgotten about the ass whooping I gave him in Elf-hame. I was surprised he wasn't singing soprano after I punched his balls into his throat.

He pulled his crackling hand back and, with a quick flick of his wrist, released the magic he'd prepared for Stephen and sent it flying in my direction.

Screams rose all around me. Time slowed to a crawl as I stared wide-eyed at the fiery ball of magic whizzing toward me.

I'm dead.

That was the only thought that crossed my mind, though my instincts flexed of their own accord, and I ducked out of the way, never taking my eyes off the swirling energy.

I stared in wonder as it passed by a few inches above my head. The magic slammed against the wall, destroying a picture of two juicy tomatoes on a cutting board. I staggered sideways and held onto a nearby table as bits of the wooden frame exploded outward.

My head snapped back toward the mage. His expression let me know how pissed he was, though he didn't seem surprised that I'd evaded his attack. I, on the other hand, stood in shock, my jaw hanging open. How the hell had I moved so quickly?

With a dismissive grunt, the mage turned his attention back on Stephen and prepared a brand-new attack.

"No!" I yelled as he unleashed it.

Out of nowhere, a shape slammed against the mage, knocking him to the floor and diverting the blazing magic, which hit the register and set it on fire.

Two shapes struggled on the floor. I limped closer to get a better view and found Jake on top of the mage, his clawed hand wrapped around the man's throat.

With a predator's rumble in the back of his throat, he said, "If you want to test my speed against yours, go ahead. I'll be glad to rip out your throat at the least little provocation."

Relief flooded me, burning away the adrenaline that had been coursing through me and keeping me upright. The next thing I knew, my strength abandoned me, and I collapsed to my knees. My vision blurred, and my spine rippled with pain. Weakly, I crawled towards Stephen and laid a hand on his furry neck.

"Hey," I croaked as I felt for a pulse. I released a pent-up breath when I felt it. Gazing in Jake's direction, I gave him a reassuring nod, then slumped next to the brown wolf, the pain from my burns getting the best of me.

In the distance, I heard sirens approaching. The police would be here soon, and hopefully an ambulance with a healer.

"Toni," Jake called out.

I couldn't see him as I lay there, eyes focused on the upturned legs of a wooden chair.

"Hey, Toni, talk to me," he said, concern dripping from his voice.

"I'm alive," I mumbled incoherently, which seemed enough to pacify him.

Tires screeched outside the restaurant, then came the sound of people shouting and running all around, barking out orders.

"Hands up," a voice boomed.

The patrons yelped and whimpered but did as they were told.

More people rushed into the restaurant, a pair of polished shoes appeared in my line of sight.

"Hands up, I said," the voice boomed again.

"I'll let him go," Jake spoke loudly and clearly, "and I will raise my hands very slowly. But this man here is a mage, and he's the one responsible for the attack on this establishment."

"It's true," I tried to say, but my voice wasn't strong enough to project.

Thankfully, others raised their voices to say the same thing, including the owner from behind the counter. I relaxed, assured the police weren't going to try to arrest Jake.

I thought of sitting up, but it was so comfortable lying next to Stephen's warm body, and I was so tired. Something touched my arm. I blinked my eyes open and met the unfamiliar face of a woman.

"Hey, hon," she said, looking me over, her smile holding despite the unpleasant sight of my roasted arm. "I'm a paramedic. My name is Lola. I'm going to make some of this pain go away. Okay?"

She laid a cool hand on my forehead that made my eyelids flutter with relief. Her lips moved quickly as she mumbled what could only be a spell. Immediately, a tingling sensation spread from my forehead to the rest of my body, and I exhaled in relief, ready to melt into the floor.

When she removed her hand a moment later, a smile spread over my lips. "Lola, you're so pretty. Do you have a boyfriend? I can get you a boyfriend."

She chuckled and shook her head. Another paramedic came up behind her. He had a halo around him. I stared at it in awe. "An angel. I've never seen an angel before."

"You see, Lola," he said. "I've been telling you I'm an angel, but you don't want to believe me."

Lola patted my arm. "You're gonna feel a little dopey for a while. It's just the effects of the pain spell. It dulls the senses."

I grinned and snuggled against Stephen. "Do you like my teddy bear?"

"He's not a teddy bear," Lola said. "That's a big bad wolf." She peered up at her partner. "Randall, can you move her so I can take care of this other guy."

"On it." Her partner put his hands out toward me, focusing intensely, and I started floating away stiffly as if I were lying on top of an invisible board.

I grinned at the tables and chairs that passed under me. "Woohoo, I'm flying. I'm Superwoman."

Jake—standing off to the side, his hands high up in the air—glimpsed at me as I drifted past him on my way to the door. He scanned me from head to toe, a deep frown etching his forehead.

"Hey, there," I said. "Now, that's a big bad wolf, not the other one."

His eyes narrowed as he glanced at the paramedic who was floating me away. "Is she going to be all right?"

"Yeah, for sure, man."

A police officer walked up to Jake. "You can put your hands down. We'll need to take your statement."

I scanned the area where the mage had been, but he was already gone. I had one last sobering thought before they stuffed me in an ambulance and took me away.

I hope that mage bastard rots in jail.

CHAPTER 5

At 5 PM that afternoon, I sat next to Stephen across from Detective Tom Freeman at the police department. He had fully recovered from the donut explosion and was even regrowing his trademark, graying goatee, which they'd shaved off due to the numerous surgeries he underwent. Apparently, it had interfered with the oxygen mask.

After that maniac mage attacked us, Stephen and I had both been taken to the hospital and healed by practiced hands. Since the injuries had been caused by magic, the healers had been able to reverse the effects with ease. Damage caused by natural causes was much harder to heal, and good healers knew counterspells to all sorts of magical attacks.

I kept staring at my arm, remembering how it'd looked, pocked with liquid-filled blisters and angry raw flesh. My stomach flipped, making me forget how hungry I was. We'd never eaten our lunch, and from the looks of it, dinner might be a few hours away still.

"Did you get a good look at the attacker?" Tom asked Stephen.

Stephen shook his head. "Not really. Toni noticed him first. Through the window, I think. She knocked me off the booth. Saved me, really." He glanced sideways at me, his blue eyes gentle, grateful. "Then I was too busy shifting, and when I went for an attack, he hit me right away."

Tom turned to me. "What about you?"

"I did, and I recognized him. He was the same mage that tried to abduct me in Elf-hame."

He nodded approvingly. "You think you could pick him out from a lineup?"

"Of course."

"Good. Let's go then." He turned to Stephen. "Stay."

We left the room. The detective closed the door behind us. Out in the hall, he stopped me with a heavy hand on my shoulder and gently turned me to face him.

"Are you all right?" he asked in his fatherly tone.

"I am." I put on a smile, lying to him. Physically, I'd been healed and set right, but emotionally, I couldn't shake the terrifying idea that one second had made the difference between life and death, that, if I hadn't turned to glance out the window, my family would have received a dreadful call, and I would have died while still mad at my mother.

I didn't know how to feel about that. On the one hand, I couldn't just get *unmad* after what she'd done, but on the other, almost dying and leaving unresolved shit like that would suck. I guessed that meant I had to forgive Mom, but how? Just the thought of her lies made me angry enough to want to shift.

Tom let out a heavy sigh, his dark eyes glittering with some emotion. "Toni, I'm worried about you. Lately, your life has taken a turn for the dangerous."

I lowered my gaze to his polished shoes, his protective concern reminding me of my father. A painful pang filled my chest. And the reminder that there was someone else out there who I could call "father"—even if only for his contribution to my DNA—distracted me from what Tom was trying to say. I didn't want to know who the man was, though. It felt like an awful betrayal to Dad.

Tom went on, unaware of my internal struggle. "I can't help but blame Jake and now Stephen Erickson for this unfortunate change."

I couldn't disagree there, but I still had nothing to say about it, and all I could do was wince.

"You're a smart girl, Toni, and if you know what's good for you, you'll stay away from those two."

"I didn't go looking for them, Tom," I said, my voice quiet.

Tom huffed. "Well, that's all I'm gonna say about it. You're the captain of your own ship. C'mon."

He marched down the hall, gave one quick knock on the next door, and opened it without waiting for an answer. Inside, the room was dark and a man stood to one side, his arms crossed over a broad chest.

"Toni, this is Detective Frank Archer. He's my new partner."

"Nice to meet you, Ms. Sunder," he said with a slight bow of his head. He was a beast of a man, probably six foot seven or more. His hair was cropped short in a military style, giving his head a squarish appearance, kind of like Rosalina's Scion. He was in short sleeves and wore a thin black tie. His nose was wide and slightly crooked as if it had been broken once. I could definitely see him getting into brawls, but I couldn't imagine the type of guy it would take to injure him. Maybe he'd fought The Hulk. Yeah, that would explain it.

We stood facing a wide window into a brightly lit room with a small platform and black lines and large numbers painted across the back wall.

Tom pressed a button on a console and said, "Okay, we're ready."

A door opened off to the side in the one-way-window room, and five men dressed in casual, clean clothes filed in and positioned themselves under the numbered spots. They all wore glowing handcuffs, charged with a spell to block magic.

I recognized our attacker immediately, and I almost started pointing at him, but I stood still. The men turned in our direction, staring blankly. Tom pressed another button, and one by one, asked them to step forward while I examined their faces carefully.

Two of the men were of the same height and hair color as the mage, but the others were blond and taller. I vaguely wondered how they picked this bunch. Were they all criminals?

When number four stepped forward, I had to clench my fists and resist the urge to pound on the window, shouting a couple of colorful insults at him.

His face looked as pleased as if he'd just come back from a trip to the beach. *The bastard.* He was full of smugness, like someone without a worry in the world, someone who expected to be out of here in the next minute. I seethed, a phantom burning sensation running up my side. I would gladly put the asshole mage into a frying pan to give him a bit of his own medicine.

After all the men had taken a step forward, Tom turned to me. "Is your attacker among these men?"

"He is," I said between clenched teeth.

"Under which number?"

"Four," I said without hesitation.

"Very well."

We left the room followed by Detective Archer, who handed Tom one of the five folders he held in his large hand. "Here, his name is Jenson Boyle. He has a previous record."

"Of course he does." Tom opened the folder. A picture of the mage rested on top, held in place by a paper clip. Tom flipped through the rest quickly, his frown growing deeper and deeper the more he read.

"What is it?" I asked, a nervous tingle running up my spine. My skin began to itch all over.

No, no, no. Not now, Red!

I took a deep breath to calm myself down. After what I've been through today—almost being burned into a crispy piece of bacon—this stupid urge to shift would return now?! How useless! I had to force a few more slow breaths before the itching stopped.

Tom closed the folder. "Stephen may be able to explain better. Let's go back."

Huh? Why?

We went back into the room where we'd left Stephen. He sat waiting patiently, hands interlaced in front of him, resting on the table. He glanced up when we walked in, a worried frown on his forehead.

I took the chair next to Stephen, and Tom sat across from us, opened the folder, and unclipped the picture from the rest of the documents.

"His name is Jenson Boyle." He pushed the photograph in Stephen's direction. The mage had a shaved head in this picture, but his smug face was unmistakable.

Stephen froze and let out a pent-up breath. He licked his lips and started to shake his head but froze again, making his confusion plain.

At last, he said, "I know this man."

"You do?!" I blurted out.

Tom leaned forward. "Can you tell us about him?"

"He works for my father."

I gasped, my mind reeling with that piece of information.

Tom leafed through the documents, his inquisitive dark eyes going through the material with methodical care. "Do you have any idea why he would try to kill you? Any personal grudges between the two of you?"

Stephen shook his head. "No. I barely know him. We've never even spoken past a simple greeting."

"Do you know what kind of work he does for your father?"

"I don't. I've seen him a few times at my father's office but only in passing."

"I hate to ask you this next question, Stephen, but I have to." He paused. "Do you think your father has anything to do with the attack?"

Stephen shook his head adamantly. "No. No. No."

The fact that he said it three times wasn't helping his cause. Once should have been enough, if he really believed it. I was reminded of the cufflink Ulfen had given me to help me track Stephen. He'd said they'd found it in Stephen's car after he was kidnapped, that it must have come loose in the struggle. But when I gave it back to Stephen in the hospital, he'd been surprised to see it and to learn where I'd gotten it. In his recollection, he'd had both cufflinks with him while trapped in the van. Though, he'd doubted his own memory because of the abuse he'd endured during his captivity. They'd beaten him over the head, and he'd had some difficulty keeping things straight.

And now this? It was too much damning evidence pointing at Ulfen.

I touched Stephen's arm to get his attention and catch his gaze. I glanced toward his wrist pointedly, trying to remind him of the cufflink. He understood me. I saw it in his expression of incredulity, and in the way he shook his head, still trying to deny what seemed to be getting more obvious by the minute.

"Is there something you two are not telling me?" Tom asked, not missing a thing.

I pressed my lips together. I didn't have any tender feelings for Ulfen, and I would have gladly told Tom my suspicions, but it wasn't my job. Not right now, anyway. Maybe later, if Stephen didn't come clean. For now, I needed to give him an opportunity.

For a long moment, Stephen stared at the mage's photograph, and I started to wonder if he would decide to protect his father, but in the end, he told Tom about the cufflink.

"Why hadn't either one of you mentioned this?" Tom asked, clearly peeved.

"I forgot," I said, which was the truth.

There had been a lot dumped in my lap these last few days. I had at least told him about Bernadetta Fiore's chauffeur, and I made time to work with a sketch artist to come up with a likeness of the Fae driver, all while dealing with Mom's dandy news. What else did he want from me? The promise of my firstborn?

"You forgot," Tom repeated as if he didn't believe a word of it. "And what about you, Stephen?"

"The kidnappers roughed me up. I couldn't trust anything I remembered—much less something as minor as a cufflink. Still, none of this makes sense. My father wouldn't try to kill me. He's been trying to convince me to get more involved in the family business, to take my responsibilities more seriously. Why would he do that if he wanted me dead?"

Tom inclined his head to one side. "But you haven't been listening to your father, have you?"

"Not for some time," Stephen agreed. "But since the kidnapping, I'm seeing things differently. He and I have had a few meaningful conversations. Things are changing between us. I'm coming to see his side of things, and he has been more understanding."

Tom and I huffed at the same time.

Stephen's gaze went from Tom to me then back again. "It's true. This makes no sense. There has to be something else going on. Maybe Bernadetta Fiore hired Boyle." He stabbed his finger at the mage's photograph.

Tom sat back, looking skeptical.

"Fiore has done worse things." Stephen's voice rose a few notches. "And we know her chauffeur was involved in my kidnapping. He was there."

"How do you know that?" Tom glanced at me. I had testified in private, and Tom had asked me not to tell anyone what I'd seen. He wanted to keep such facts out of the news, which always tended to pollute police investigations.

I shook my head slightly to let him know I hadn't spilled a word of it.

"I have my sources, and I know there was also a Fae involved," Stephen said, standing abruptly and pointing a finger at Tom's face. "So before you start trying to accuse a man of attempting to kill his own son, you'd better look more carefully into Fiore's involvement."

Without another word, Stephen whirled on his heel and stormed out of the room. Tom and I stared at the door as it slammed against its frame and shook the walls around us.

"Damn," I said.

A muscle jumped in Tom's jaw. "I don't like any of this. You need to stay away from the Erickson family, and let's not forget Jake."

It was what I wanted to do, but it was easier said than done. I hadn't gone looking for any of this. My past had come out of nowhere to slam headfirst into my life. And it was more than just Jake and Stephen. It was my entire freaking life, which had been a lie from the moment I was born. Now it turned out I was a werewolf—an incompetent one that couldn't shift to save her life—but a werewolf all the same. And maybe even if I tried to run from all the things that kept rushing in my direction as if I were a magnet, I would still be unable to escape. Sticking my head in the sand wouldn't help, not when, even now, my bones felt on the verge of twisting into a shape that would make every cute outfit in my closet completely useless.

"Sure, I'll try to stay away from them," I said to pacify Tom.

My life had turned into a whirlwind of bad, and something told me that things would get much worse before they got better.

CHAPTER 6

As I walked out of the police department, Jake and Rosalina rushed in my direction. They'd been waiting by her car and peeled away from it as soon as they saw me.

"Toni!" Rosalina wrapped me in her arms and checked me up and down. "Jake said you were hurt."

"I'm fine now," I said. "They healed me right up. It didn't even take long. See." I spread my arms out to show her I was safe and sound. I didn't want her to worry. I could easily put myself in her shoes. If something happened to her… I didn't want to think about it.

"How did it go in there?" Jake asked.

"I picked out the perp from a lineup. It wasn't hard."

Jake raised a thick eyebrow, waiting for more, but I had no idea if I should tell him anything since it might pull him into danger. Already Ulfen didn't like him. He thought Jake was a bad influence on his son and blamed him for Stephen's defection to New Orleans. Though, if Ulfen was really trying to hurt his son maybe he didn't like Jake for other reasons.

Though, wouldn't leaving Stephen alone in New Orleans, or wherever else he decided to go away with Jake, be better than trying to kill him? If that was even what was going on here. I honestly didn't know. Stephen had been adamant about defending his father, and he wasn't the kind to be easily deceived. At least I didn't think so. Only God knew how deep this rabbit hole went and what kind of surprises were buried in it. I surely didn't want to be the one excavating that lovely treasure.

Tom was right. I needed to stay away from Stephen and, by extension, Jake if I didn't want my life to be turned on its head again. Though, with my *werewolfness*, life was already upside down. So maybe the guys could turn it back on its ass, like two wrongs making a right. If only.

"Anyway," I said, ignoring Jake's desire for more information. "I'm tired. I want to go home."

Rosalina took my hand and started pulling me toward the car. "Then home it is."

Suddenly, Jake gripped my other hand and started a tug-of-war with Rosalina. I glanced back and forth between them, too stunned to say anything. This hadn't happened to me since elementary school when I brought a loaf-sized Twinkie for lunch.

Realizing the ridiculousness of the situation, Jake let me go and quickly said, "Toni, can I have a moment?"

Rosalina gave me a questioning glance, and I nodded to indicate it was all right. She rolled her eyes and got in the car to wait for me.

"What is it?" I joined Jake, stepping back onto the sidewalk.

"I know the man who attacked Stephen," he said, surprising me. That was not what I had expected him to say.

He peered at me in a peculiar way. His nostrils widening as he sniffled. "Are you sure you're all right?" he asked.

"Um," I hugged myself, feeling self-conscious, "yeah, I'm perfectly all right. Why?"

"I don't know." He paused. "You seem… different."

Crap! Was he smelling my wolf? I turned my head to the side and surreptitiously tried to smell myself, but I couldn't tell any difference.

"Maybe it's the… healing magic they used at the hospital," I said, quick on my toes.

He considered, frowning. "Yeah, maybe." He didn't sound convinced, but it was better than nothing.

God, I needed a way to keep this a secret from him. I wasn't ready for anyone to know what I was—not even Rosalina. Though with her, I didn't really have a choice. I couldn't lie to my business partner and roommate. That would be all kinds of wrong.

He shook his head. "Anyway, that mage, he works for Ulfen."

"We know. Stephen never got a good look at him in the restaurant, but he recognized him as soon as Tom showed him a picture of him. He asked Stephen if he thought his father had sent the mage. Stephen wasn't happy about that. He stormed out. Didn't you see him leave?"

"I didn't. I went inside to use the restroom. He must've left when I was in there. Shit, this is bad. Clearly, he's not safe."

"No. Maybe he should leave St. Louis again."

"That's not going to happen. He's bent on staying."

"Then he's staying at his own risk."

Jake held my gaze for a long moment, without saying anything. My skin tingled as if his eyes had the power of touch and were caressing me as they roved over me.

"Well, I should…" I took a step toward Rosalina's car, but Jake put a hand on my waist and held me in place.

If his gaze had awakened my body, his actual touch immediately made me catch on fire. Heat rose up my neck and into my face. He moved closer still, his silver gaze like a tether that kept me immobile.

"I had to restrain myself not to rip that mage's throat out," he said.

"Um, I'm glad you did. That would have landed you in a prison cell."

"When I ran into the restaurant and saw you… injured, I almost lost it."

My chest went so tight with a host of confusing emotions that I was unable to say anything. What was this? He'd told me why he couldn't be with me, and now he was… doing what?

"If anything were to happen to you—"

I stepped backward, away from his touch, from his words. "What are you doing?"

He appeared at a loss for an instant, then he lowered his eyes, embarrassed. "I'm sorry." His fists clenched, his embarrassment morphing into frustration. "This isn't easy for me, Toni."

"Then stop making it harder."

"You're right. You're right." He paused, then went on, his manner growing detached. "I'm glad you're safe. That's what I was trying to say."

"Thank you for that and for saving both Stephen and me."

"Don't take this the wrong way, but maybe it would be best if you don't go out with Stephen anymore."

I blinked incredulously, anger replacing every other emotion that still whirled inside my chest. "That's your advice?"

He frowned at my question.

"Then here is mine, maybe it would be best if you don't stick your nose in my business and if you stop pretending to care."

I climbed into Rosalina's car, slammed the door, and stared fixedly at the dashboard. I knew that what I'd just said was unfair, but the last thing I would stand for was Jake Knight telling me what to do.

Rosalina started the car and got us on the road in a couple of seconds. She didn't say anything until we were almost home, and I was grateful when she spoke of work and not Jake.

"I canceled this afternoon's appointments and told them that we'll reschedule as soon as we know your availability."

"Thank you. I'm sorry that lately, things have been so… unstable."

"It's not your fault, and don't worry, Triple T, we'll deal with things as they come."

"I should probably cancel my kick-boxing membership. I didn't get to go. Again."

But that was the least of my worries. The world I had carefully constructed around me since Jake left was falling apart one piece at a time. I made fists on my lap as my fingertips began to feel tight. I took several deep breaths, closed my eyes, and rolled my shoulders, inhaling deeply.

"Are you all right?" she asked.

"Not really. There's something I need to tell you."

"Is it what we talked about this morning?" she asked in a quiet voice.

I nodded. "I'm afraid it might make things worse than they already are."

She sighed. "Well, whatever it is, we'll deal with it like we always do. Together."

A warm feeling spread inside of me, relaxing me right away. The pressure at my fingertips went away, and I was able to breathe more easily. No one could have a better friend.

"Let's get home," she said. "We'll eat some dinner, and then we'll talk over a cup of tea, how does that sound?"

"It sounds great."

During the rest of the way home and while we ate dinner, I felt calm and capable of telling Rosalina my secret without losing my cool. But as we sat down in the living room with matching cups of tea—Rosalina on the sofa and me in the armchair to her right—my heart started hammering and that awful itching started all over again.

"All right, I'm all ears," Rosalina said, then took a sip of her chamomile tea and set the cup down on the coffee table.

She'd changed into comfy flannel pants and had put her black hair up in a messy bun. Her gentle smile told me that no matter what I was about to tell her, she was behind me one hundred percent. I had no idea what she was imagining, but one thing was certain: there was no way any of her notions came close to the truth.

"Um, you know how I went to see my mom yesterday?" I started.

She nodded.

"And how she'd been desperate to have me over?"

Another nod, then she pushed to the edge of the sofa, her elbows resting on her knees as she leaned forward attentively.

The pressure in my fingertips came back abruptly as if someone had flipped on a switch. I shot to my feet and walked behind the armchair. I grabbed the headrest and stared down at my friend, whose green eyes shone with concern.

"It's okay," she said. "You know you can tell me anything."

My heart pounded as the words formed inside my mouth. I wanted to explain everything calmly and from the beginning, but my vocabulary seemed to, in an instant, have been reduced to only one phrase.

I'm a werewolf.

I searched for more inside my addled brain, but it had gone blank.

My hands tightened over the headrest, and my arms trembled as I dug my fingers into the upholstery. There were several pops as the fabric ripped under the pressure of my nails. Rosalina blinked in surprise and frowned at my hands.

"Did you just…?"

I swallowed.

Shit, I'd just ruined her new armchair.

"Oh, my God! I'm so sorry," I blurted out, plucking my fingers out of the holes I'd made. They came out one by one, strips of cottony stuffing stuck to my gnarly, disgusting claws. Shame washed over me as if someone had dumped a bucket of cold water over my head.

"Oh, no!" I exclaimed, mortified. I glanced up at Rosalina, feeling lost and helpless.

"Um, what's with the claws?" she asked in a trembling voice. "Is that like some sort of Fae glamour you got from Yalgrun?"

"No, Rosalina. It's not a glamour. The thing is… I'm a werewolf."

CHAPTER 7

"You got hit in the head during the attack, right?" Rosalina asked, staring at me as if I'd gone certifiable.

"Nope."

Now that the secret was out, my shoulders relaxed, and as my desperation and fear dissipated so did the threat of shifting. I breathed a sigh of relief and collapsed back in the armchair.

"I'm so sorry about the chair, Rosalina," I said. "I'll get you a new one."

"Who cares about the damn chair? You need to see a shrink. Maybe you even need to be locked up in the psych ward or something. Toni, you're not a werewolf. Yeah, something really weird is going on…"

She pointed in the general direction of my hands, which now looked normal, just a little fuzzy with puffs of cotton still stuck to the fingernails. I started picking the last bits off, finding the task relaxing. Since it was Rosalina's turn to freak out, it seemed I could be calm.

"… But the fact that you grew claws," she went on, "doesn't mean you're a werewolf. Maybe this is some sort of prank, or a spell that lunatic mage put on you during the attack. Or maybe a side effect of the attack and healing magic combined. Or maybe—"

I glanced up at Rosalina and interrupted her. "I'm afraid you're rambling."

She blew a raspberry and sank into the sofa, her arms limp to her sides as if she was exhausted. "Wait, I get it. This is just your idea of a joke," she said, sitting up again.

"I wish that was all, but no. Yesterday, Mom didn't feed me creamy tortellini. Not at all. Instead, she told me that my dad wasn't my dad." As I uttered that last sentence, an awful sadness descended over me, making everything around me feel pointless.

Dad, I'm sorry. It doesn't matter what she says, you will always be my father.

Always.

"You're not joking, are you?"

"Not in the least. Get this… Mom had a mage waiting for me in the kitchen, the same one who, since I was born, has been putting a spell on me to prevent me from shifting. Except, the night we found Stephen, I did shift. I don't remember it happening, but there's these few hours I don't remember at all. I blacked out, and the next thing I knew, I woke up entirely naked on top of our building. You remember that lovely situation. I'm sure."

"Holy shit. Holy shit. You're telling the truth."

"Yes, I am."

"You're a freakin' werewolf. You're a freakin' werewolf." She stood and started pacing in front of the sofa.

I followed her with my eyes, my heart starting to pound again. "I think you'd better calm down. You're starting to make me nervous, and nervous isn't good for me right now." I glanced down at my hands, then at the holes in the back of the armchair.

"Calm down? Calm down?! How can you ask me to calm down? You're… a… werewolf. Aren't you freaked out?"

"Of course I am. I've been trying not to shift all day. I don't know how to control it, so I need *calm.* Can you do calm for me? I mean, unless you want your nice leather sofa to be next."

This seemed to sober her up. She sat back down on said sofa, leaned her cheek on the back rest, and caressed it. "Don't listen to the big bad wolf. You'll be alright. I promise. I can do calm. Just for you."

I gave her an incredulous look. "Who's crazy now?"

"I'm sorry. I'm just having a very hard time processing all of this." She sat up straight, her expression growing serious. "How are you holding up?" she asked in a sweet voice.

And that was all it took to undo me. I started crying like a baby, sobbing and hiccupping, and for the first time, allowing myself to feel the pain of Dad's loss. My father. My sweet, sweet father. It was what hurt the most. Not that Mom had lied to me, but that from now on, anytime I thought of Dad, I would wonder about that other man.

And my sisters and brother, what about them? What if they started seeing me differently? Like we didn't quite belong together anymore? *One of these things is not like the other.* Guess which one? *Me!*

Gah! I knew better than to think this way. I would love all three of them no matter what. They would always be my siblings, one hundred percent, but I couldn't stop the stupid thoughts from driving through my head.

When I finally stopped crying, I found that I was on the sofa with Rosalina, surrounded by her warm embrace as she smoothed my hair with tenderness. She passed me my cup of tea, which soothed my scratchy throat and helped slow down my breathing enough so the sobs passed.

After that, I told her everything in detail. She listened carefully, her mind working behind her sharp green eyes. She was a woman who, when confronted with a problem, immediately thought of solutions. She might have a little meltdown at first, but in the end, she always had good advice.

When I finished, I asked the inevitable question. "What do you think I should do?"

"One thing is for sure, you can't try to figure this out on your own. You need help."

I was reluctant to get help. I certainly didn't want to have anything else to do with Damien Ward, and the only werewolves I knew were not the ones I wanted to take advice from.

"I know you probably won't like this idea," Rosalina said. "I wouldn't like it much either, considering what he did, but I think you should talk to that Copper Mage."

I shook my head adamantly. "No. I don't want to deal with that creep. 'Cause he's gotta be a creep, right? Only a creep could do what he did. Twenty years, Rosalina. That's how long he has been messing with…" I waved my hands around my body and head, unsure of what part of me he had tampered with.

"Yes, but he's the only one who can answer all the questions you have."

I couldn't argue with that. He *was* the only one who knew exactly what the spell had done to me. And maybe he knew of something that could help me control my random urges to shift.

"I'll go with you," she offered. "You don't have to do this by yourself. I'll do anything I can to help you."

"I'm afraid, Rosalina. What if I hurt you?"

"You won't."

"How can you be so sure? My wolf… it's untamed, and I don't even know what I do when I shift. I've had a couple of weird dreams since that night. They're just flashes of fangs and teeth and blood, but I have a feeling they're real. Something happened that night. Bad stuff, and I can't remember."

"If that's the case, then even more reason to talk to the mage and get your questions answered. You've managed not to shift today despite everything that happened. You're strong. You'll figure this out. I know you will, but you need help."

I nodded, trying to soak in her positive, supportive words. It wouldn't do to wallow in negative thoughts. I *had* to get this under control. There was no other alternative.

"Okay," I said. "I'll call Damien Ward."

CHAPTER 8

The next morning at 7 AM, Rosalina and I found ourselves driving downtown under a sky thick with gray clouds. We had tried to get Damien Ward to meet us in a public place, but he refused to do that, insisting that he was in no mood to leave his home and if I wanted to see him, I had to come to him. According to the creepy mage, he had done enough for me and my mother already. I almost told him to go to hell, but Rosalina snatched the phone from me and set up the appointment.

His "house" turned out to be a five-story building on a corner lot, located on Olive Street. It was made of dark brick with veined marble arches that rose from the ground level to the third floor. The roof was flat and two honest-to-god gargoyles flanked its corners. It looked to have been built in the 1800s and had a Goth feeling about it that made me think of haunted houses and old horror films. It had a crumbly appearance as if, at any moment, it might fall to pieces.

As I parked my Camaro across the street, my phone rang. It was Mom. I ignored it, doing my best not to get angry.

"You'll have to talk to her sooner or later, Toni," Rosalina said. "You can't keep ignoring her forever."

"Are you sure about that? I might just as well block her."

She shook her head. I knew she was right, but I wasn't ready to talk to my mother, and I had no idea when I would be.

Rosalina and I got out of the car and walked shoulder-to-shoulder toward Damien's front door. She folded her hand in mine, which let me know she was also getting a weird vibe from the house. My shifting symptoms began as soon as I laid eyes on the place and grew the closer we got. I had to stop to take a few deep breaths before reaching the door.

Slowly, I lifted my hand to knock, but before I could, the door slid open and Damien Ward appeared on the other side.

"Hello," he said with a smirk, his ink-blotch pupils shrinking with the sunlight. "I'm delighted to see you are on time. I hate tardiness."

I stared open-mouthed. He was wearing jeans, a T-shirt and an apron stained with what looked like tomato sauce. He wasn't wearing his dark glasses, his ridiculous top hat, or his cloak, and if not for his coppery eyes, he would have looked like any other guy in full domestic bliss.

"Follow me," he said, turning on his heel and walking through a lavish foyer that absolutely did not match the outside of the house.

Rosalina and I stepped inside, and the door automatically closed behind us, which we barely noticed since we were glancing around with our jaws unhinged. The interior was the epitome of modern. The décor, the materials, the furniture, they all screamed rich asshole. The walls were painted a light gray with white trim. The furniture was angular with straight lines and metal accents. The art on the wall was contemporary and contained in simple black frames. The huge marble staircase that led up to a wrap-around landing was ornate and from another era and should've clashed with the rest of the scheme, but it seemed to fit right in.

What the hell? This mage was confusing, a little walking contradiction.

"What's up with his pupils?" Rosalina asked in my ear.

"No idea," I whispered.

"Are you two coming or not?" His voice came from deep down the corridor through which he'd disappeared.

We followed the sound, still staring at everything in confusion. Past an arched doorway, and the sight that greeted us—a massive, industrial-looking kitchen—only added to our bewilderment.

Caged lights hung from a tall ceiling, illuminating a wide island with polished concrete countertops. The cabinets were plain, painted gray, and had no handles. A large window sat above a steel farmhouse sink the size of a bathtub. Images of a fairy forest played on the window's surface, some kind of mirage spell, for sure. Open shelves on the wall were filled with implements that looked like they belonged in a lab and not a kitchen.

"Take a seat wherever you want," Damien said from his place in front of a huge, stainless steel gas range fit for a restaurant.

We picked tall stools in front of the wide island, which featured a normal-sized sink and built-in cutting board.

"Nice place you have here," I said, watching him stir the contents of a pot as tall as a toddler.

He grunted in response, too intent on his cooking to acknowledge me. If his idea had been to put me at ease with his domesticity, he had accomplished his goal. It was a genius plan, really, because I couldn't muster any fear for a man wielding a ladle and wearing a dirty apron.

My nose twitched as I tried to identify what he was cooking, but there were no scents in the air. Odd.

"There," he said, making a racket by beating his ladle on the edge of the pot. "Now, it just needs to simmer for a bit." He covered the pot, lowered the heat, and finally turned to face us.

His coppery eyes focused on Rosalina. He raised a thin eyebrow, which made me notice, for the first time, that they were completely white, like his hair.

"Um, this is my friend, Rosalina," I said.

He quickly removed his apron, placed it on a hook near the stove, and came around the island. We were forced to turn in our stools to face him.

With a smile he extended a hand toward my friend. "Nice to meet you, Rosalina." No smirk, no smugness, just genuine interest.

She lifted her hand hesitantly as if she were afraid Damien might bite it off. But he only squeezed it gently and deposited a slow kiss on her knuckles, his strange eyes never deviating from hers. Color rose into her cheeks as she mumbled a reply.

Really? The creep was flirting with my best friend. What the hell? Maybe shifting and killing someone wasn't entirely out of the question.

"Can I offer you anything to drink?" he asked after finally releasing Rosalina's hand.

"No, thank you," we both said in unison. We had agreed not to drink or eat anything that he might offer. Mages could be tricky like that, and we already knew this one couldn't be trusted.

"Mmm." He scanned us carefully, judging, understanding the full meaning of our response.

I shifted in my stool, feeling uncomfortable. We were practically accusing him of trying to turn us into toads—or whatever evil mages did to their unsuspecting victims.

To my relief, he simply shrugged and said, "Your loss." He walked toward a fancy espresso machine and began grinding coffee that smelled heavenly. "I figured you would eventually come. Shifting involuntarily when you least expect it can't be any fun."

"I actually haven't shifted again. Just the once," I said.

Damien turned from the machine and faced me. "You haven't?"

I shook my head.

"That's… interesting." He pronounced the word interesting as if he actually meant "weird" instead.

We sat quietly for a moment while he considered, only the bubbling of the pot filling the silence.

"What do you mean?" Rosalina asked at last.

Damien's attention shifted to her, and his coppery eyes seemed to sparkle, becoming more vivid. "Because it would take a reasonable amount of strength to prevail over a wild animal that has been caged for twenty years. Though, my spell hasn't completely worn off, and it's still keeping the wolf somewhat in check. But I would be lying if I hadn't expected to read about some awful massacre in the newspapers this morning."

"What?!" I said indignantly. "You mean I could have gone on some sort of rampage and you just let me go as if…" I waved my arms around at a loss for words, then turned to Rosalina. "What is wrong with this guy?"

"I normally don't involve myself with werewolf matters," Damien said. "I only did it with you to help your mother. You know, she and I had a thing back in college and—"

I put a hand up. "Hold your horses. I don't want to hear about any of that."

That was just disturbing, especially since I kept forgetting that he and Mom had been classmates in college. Despite his white hair, he didn't look a day older than thirty. I wondered how old he really was, though, and how many spells it took to keep him looking so young.

"Fine," he said, rolling his eyes, then went back to his coffee machine and pressed a few buttons. Soon the entire kitchen filled with the unique scent of coffee.

As if he'd forgotten we were there, Damien went about the kitchen gathering plates and utensils, then pulled out several containers from the six-foot-wide refrigerator and started preparing breakfast.

My stomach growled at the sight of bagels and cream cheese and jelly. I had already eaten breakfast, but lately hunger had been assaulting me even more often than before. Mostly, I was hungry for meat, though, and couldn't seem to have enough of it. I'd eaten an entire package of bacon this morning, while Rosalina watched me over the rim of her mug.

He placed a bagel inside a toaster oven and crossed his arms, waiting.

Rosalina elbowed me and nodded toward the mage, encouraging me to ask my questions. His comment about expecting to read about a massacre in the papers still rang inside my head. I didn't think I would be able to stop myself from shifting for much longer. I could feel the pressure mounting. My wolf felt like a ticking bomb, and the explosion would not be pretty.

Cocking my head and tapping my chin, I stared at the mage. If I was going to go on a rampage, it might not be a bad idea to start here. It would teach him a lesson for doing unnatural things to people. Or at least, I could get him to blast me with a killing spell and take me out of my misery.

"Is there no way you can help her?" Rosalina asked, since I'd become enthralled by the idea of sinking my claws into Damien's willowy ass.

"I'm afraid not, love," he said.

"Each year," he continued, without turning from the oven, "that I applied my spell on Toni, it grew increasingly more difficult. Amalia was supposed to keep a close eye on her daughter to catch any symptoms that indicated the magic was wearing out. I warned her that if Toni shifted, it would put an end to the subterfuge. You see, the spell has kept the wolf confused. Um, how can I explain?"

He finally turned to face us, making a flourish with one hand as if to draw an explanation from the air. "The wolf was trapped inside a labyrinth that didn't allow it to see the exit, the light. Every time she got close, the spell would have created a diversion, guiding her away from the surface. But now that the wolf has figured out the exit and has gotten a taste of freedom, there is nothing that can stop her. Nothing that will keep her caged for much longer. Except, of course, Toni herself by learning how to control the shift, a particularly difficult task in cases like hers. If she doesn't do anything soon, things could reach critical mass."

"How can she learn to control it?" Rosalina asked as I struggled to process everything he'd said.

"I already told her. She needs to find one of her kind who can guide her. Somebody willing to put themselves through the ordeal."

"Put themselves through the ordeal?" I echoed.

"Oh, yes. It won't be an easy matter. It could take weeks, months even."

"Months?! I don't have that kind of time. I have a life to live, a business to run."

"Take that up with your mother, love. I'm not to blame for any of this."

I stood up abruptly and slapped my hands on the counter. The stool scraped the floor and teetered, though it didn't fall.

"That's bullshit." I growled. "You're almost as guilty as she is. You enabled her, allowed her to lie to me, to my father. You could have said no."

He shrugged. "She was pretty convincing."

He got the bagel out of the toaster oven and, turning back toward us and placing his breakfast on the island, proceeded to apply a thick layer of cream cheese on each slice, followed by grape jelly. Then, he took a hefty bite. He wasn't going to tell me anything.

"Why the hell did you leave your card behind if you didn't plan on talking to me?"

"Um," he lifted his index finger as he slowly chewed. "Yes, indeed," he mumbled, taking a Mason jar from one of the open shelves and walking to the pot on the stove.

With the ladle, he scooped some of whatever he was cooking and poured it inside the jar. Chunky, brown liquid splattered inside. When he was done, he gingerly transferred the hot jar to the island and set it in front of me.

"This will help," he said.

I stared at the steaming contents, wrinkling my nose. An awful smell wafted from the jar and quickly filled the room.

Rosalina leaned in to peer at it. "What is it? It smells delicious, and it's so pretty."

Huh? I gave her a sidelong glance. Was her sniffer broken? It smelled like shit. Literally. Looked like it. too.

She hopped down from her stool and walked closer, her hand reaching for the jar. I grabbed her wrist and held her back.

"Appearances *and* smells can be deceiving," I said with a pointed look.

Rosalina snatched her hand back, looking freaked out. "I'm so stupid," she blurted out, shooting death rays at the mage.

He gave her a disarming smile that made her frown disappear. *Oh, God.* This wasn't good. My friend couldn't buy into this guy's antics.

Pushing those fears aside, I focused on Damien.

"Why would you give me… poop?" I demanded.

Damien laid a hand on his chest as if injured. "That, young mutt, is a powerful potion."

Young mutt?!

That was it! Anger sizzled through me like fire, and the next thing I knew my claws broke the surface. I growled and felt my wolf bursting with satisfaction. I was going to tear the fucking mage to pieces.

CHAPTER 9

For once, I was glad for my fangs and claws. Mage or not, I would gut him and hang his intestines around his neck like a Christmas garland. I licked my lips with relish.

Uh, wait a minute! What's wrong with me?

Nothing. Absolutely nothing, the wild part of me shot back.

My stomach turned at the bloody, non-festive image that materialized inside my head. I had never, in my entire life, wished to kill anyone, much less in such a gruesome way. I took a step back, grabbing my head between my clawed hands. The Toni that had always been me fought against this new, emerging one that seemed bent on erasing me.

"Toni, what's wrong?" Rosalina reached a hand in my direction, and I slapped it away. She brought it back to her chest, looking injured and scared.

I was losing it, and this time I would not be able to stop the transformation. I had to get out of here before I hurt someone. My head snapped from side to side, searching for an exit. I felt trapped, ready to detonate.

With an annoyed sigh, Damien walked around the island and marched toward me.

"Stay away from me." My voice was the deep growl of a three-packs-a-day dude with thick hair on his chest.

Despite the scary voice, Damien didn't stop and kept coming at me with determination. I crouched, ready to slice him open and turn him into a gruesome holiday ornament. He stopped a few paces away from my reach and shook his head with pity. My anger redoubled.

"Oh, God!" Rosalina exclaimed, her tone almost unrecognizable with fear and horror.

Instinct took over, and I went for him, aiming for his softer middle. In my mind, I almost felt my claws tearing into him, cutting through skin and organs, but it was only wishful thinking because he moved easily, faster than I was able to track, and laid a punch across my jaw that snapped my head backward. My neck whiplashed, sending a jolt of pain down my spine. I cried out, my face throbbing and ears ringing.

"You beast," Rosalina yelled, coming up behind me and cradling me in her arms as I went down. She eased my fall, setting me on the cold floor.

White stars flashed all around my head.

"Why would you hit her?" she demanded, smoothing hair away from my face. She peered down at me, her green eyes full of concern, none of the horror I'd heard in her voice left in her expression.

"She's back to normal, isn't she?" Damien walked away nonchalantly, straightening his T-shirt.

I lifted my hands and stared at them. The claws had disappeared and so had the feeling that I was about to become a fur coat. I rubbed my jaw, wiggling it around. It hurt but not nearly as bad as it should. The ringing in my ears subsided quickly, and the pain across my back did, too.

Rosalina helped me stand, hanging around me like a mother hen, dusting my backside as if I were a toddler who had fallen in the playground. I gave her a sheepish smile of thanks as embarrassment washed over me. She had been horrified by me. What if I had hurt her? I couldn't keep putting her in danger.

"Thank you." I moved back, putting some distance between us, then turned to Damien.

Before I could even ask anything, he spoke. "Pain will keep you human. Remember that."

Pain?!

Of course. That was the reason I hadn't been able to shift in the restaurant, despite the danger.

"It should do the trick," Damien said. "Most of the time. Hopefully."

"Well, that's not very helpful?" Rosalina said.

"It's better than nothing, love. Anyhow, you two have already taken enough of my time today, and I have things to do."

Pausing, he seemed to consider what to say next. After a moment of deep consideration, he sighed, pulled a drawer open, and took out two envelopes. He kept one to himself and put one next to the jar of stinky poo.

"This is an invitation to a very exclusive party tonight. Lucky for you, I happen to have two of them, so you can have that one."

He fanned himself with the envelope and winked at Rosalina, who both glowered and blushed crimson.

I wanted to roll my eyes, but I had more pressing things to worry about. "Please, explain why the hell you would give me a jar of shit and a party invitation when what I need is help *not* shifting into an unpredictable animal?"

Damien huffed. "The *moonfable*," he gestured toward the jar, "is so that you can pass for human among werewolves. It will mask your werewolf scent without disturbing your human smell, the same way my spell has done so far. Just dab a little bit like perfume every morning, and you'll be safe."

"Safe?" Rosalina and I echoed at the same time.

I was in danger from other werewolves?

"Yes, once the effects of my spell completely wears out, other werewolves will be able to take in your scent and know you're a weakling. An omega, most likely, given your lack of experience. That would be a very bad thing. A pack could take you and make you their… bitch. Weak shifters don't do well. Anyone stronger than you, which pretty much will be anyone at this point, will seek to subdue you, make you do whatever they want. It's a dog eat dog world out there."

"Lovely." I swallowed thickly and protectively pulled the jar toward me. It seemed the most valuable poop was now in my possession.

Damien made a satisfied noise in the back of his throat, glad that I understood. I didn't know much about shifters and their customs—they were secretive—but everyone understood what could happen to a runt.

"As for the invitation," Damien said, "the werewolf throwing the party is an acquaintance of mine. He owes me a big favor. I will cash it in tonight by asking him to help you, to teach you how to control the shift and hopefully save you from a lifetime of *poop perfume* as you would call it." He twirled a finger and pointed toward the jar.

I stood speechless. He had decided to help me? After all his posturing? I'd really thought he would wash his hands of me, but he'd just given me the two things I needed most at the moment. As realization hit me, I darted a glance in his direction. He stood haughty, his pointed chin up in the air, one white eyebrow cocked. Yet, I saw through his puffed up exterior.

"You *do* feel guilty," I said.

"*Pshaw*!" he exclaimed, facing the stove and turning the knob to the off position. "I've never felt guilty about anything in my life. I do what must be done. That is all. Now, go on. Like I said, I have much to do."

Rosalina and I exchanged wary glances. I needed to know more. I was sure there was a lot Damien Ward could tell me, but I couldn't press my luck—the moonfable and the promise of a werewolf who could teach me were more than I'd been expecting out of him. So, deciding to take this as a win, I started on my way out. Rosalina followed me, but before we left the kitchen, Damien cleared his throat. We turned and found him standing right behind us.

He snatched Rosalina's hand in his and inclined his head. "I will pick you up at nine," he said with a sexy smile that made me do a double take and sent another blush to Rosalina's cheeks. "I have two invitations, as I said, and would love to show you a good time."

My mouth opened and closed several times before I finally said, "No way!"

At the same time, Rosalina said, "I would be delighted."

"Grand." Damien straightened, turned on his heel, and went back to his bagel.

Rosalina hooked her arm in mine and led me out of there in a hurry. When we made it outside, I blinked at the sunlight, disoriented. The clouds had parted.

We got in my Camaro, and I placed my potion securely between my legs. I started the engine and as it rumbled to life, I asked,

"What is wrong with you? Why would you agree to go out with him?"

"There's no way in hell I'm letting you go to that party alone," she answered, her tone righteous and protective.

Yet, I knew there was more to it than that. She liked Damien Ward and was excited to go out on a date with him.

CHAPTER 10

When we got to the agency later that morning, I rushed into the potions alcove with my poop perfume and applied it generously to my neck, wrists, crook of my elbows, and behind my knees. The stench that rose from the jar made me gag a few times, but I managed to hold on to my breakfast. When I was done, I capped the jar, sure I would end up smelling like a freaking sewer, but after a few minutes of wincing and heaving, the awful smell passed.

I exhaled in relief, walked back out, and stood right behind Rosalina's chair as she typed an email on her laptop. After a few beats, she glanced over her shoulder.

"What?" she asked.

I shrugged one shoulder.

Her nose twitched. "God, you smell good. Do you think moonfable could harm a Stale? I wouldn't mind if you shared some with me."

She had a thing for all beauty products and implements, but this went beyond her preening passion. She was out of her mind.

"Trust me, if you got a whiff of how that stuff really smells, you wouldn't be asking."

She was about to reply when her eyes drifted to the front door. I glanced in that direction just as the door opened and chimed.

Daniella and Lucia—my older and younger sisters—walked in, which could only mean one thing: Mom had told them the truth about me. My first impulse was to run up to the loft and hide under the bed. I wasn't ready to face them or the fact that the bond between us was lesser than we'd imagined.

I wasn't even a Sunder.

That half of me had been stolen, leaving behind a huge question mark.

A lump formed in my throat and tears burned at the corners of my eyes.

"Hey, Toni," Daniella said.

Lucia toed the hardwood floor, hands stuffed in her hoodie's big pocket. "What's up, Sis?" she said, her eyes meeting mine just briefly.

"What… a surprise," I said.

The last time they were here was the night before Rosalina and I opened for business. We had hosted a little inauguration party and invited only our closest friends and family. They'd visited a few other times, but not together.

They stood shoulder to shoulder, both beautiful with their long, brown hair and dark eyes. No one could deny we were sisters. We all looked like Mom. To my surprise, Lucia stood slightly taller than Daniella, which meant she was also taller than me since Dani and I were both 5'7". I had no idea when that had happened. She had grown in the blink of an eye.

Daniella wore beige slacks, a black sweater with glittery trim at the neck, and red flats. I could imagine her with her healer's coat over the cute outfit, a stethoscope around her neck, and a Children's Hospital badge to complete the look. In contrast, Lucia wore ripped jeans, a tie-dye hoodie, and skater shoes.

"It's good to see you, Rosalina," Daniella said.

Rosalina smiled. "Same here."

Lucia bobbed her head at my friend. She could be so eloquent sometimes.

"We wanted to talk to you?" Daniella cautiously glanced at Rosalina

"No worries. Rosalina knows," I paused for a beat, then blurted out, "Did Mom send you?"

"No," Daniella said, "but she talked to us yesterday and told us everything."

"Everything?" I asked.

They nodded.

"Even the werewolf bit?"

Daniella nodded. "Yes."

"Quite the big reveal, huh?" Sarcasm rode heavily in my tone.

Daniella took a step forward. "Are you all right, Toni?"

"Sure, I'm fine."

Another step closer. "Are you sure?"

Her brown eyes were gentle, concerned. She'd always been great at comforting us—the most nurturing and kind. I still remembered her carrying Toddler Lucia around, changing her diaper, and feeding her with such patience.

I melted under her gaze, and all my emotions came rushing out. Before the first tear splattered onto my cheek, Daniella wrapped me in a tight embrace and squeezed me so hard I hiccupped. Lucia rushed over and snuggled right between us.

"Guys, you're killing me," Rosalina said, then joined in the hug.

They held me until I stopped crying. Embarrassed, I pulled away, drying my tears.

"We're so pissed at Mom," Lucia said.

"I can't believe she lied to you like that." Daniella shook her head. "All these years."

Lucia sniffed. "She'd better never act all holier-than-thou from now on. If you want us to, we'll never forgive her." She sounded so serious, it made me laugh.

"You don't have to be mad at her for my sake," I said.

"I was already mad at her anyway. She took my phone," Lucia said.

Daniella and I exchanged a glance. Lucia was always getting into trouble because of her phone and social media shenanigans.

My older sister drew herself up. "I don't think this needs to be said, but I'm going to say it anyway. We're the Sunder sisters, and nothing and no one can ever change that."

"Thank you, Dani," I said.

"I'm sure Dad would agree," Lucia put in, and as soon as she said it, I knew she was right. Dad wouldn't have cared. He would have loved me just the same, and even if everything else changed, this one truth would remain the same.

I was Peter Sunder's daughter.

CHAPTER 11

Later that evening, Rosalina and I sat in front of the vanity in her bedroom, getting ready to go to Damien's party. She stepped away from me, tiny brush in hand, and let her eyes rove over my face as if it were a canvas.

"Yeah, now, it's perfect."

She hadn't approved of my makeup job. I thought I had done all right with it, but to her standards, it was seriously lacking. I turned to face the mirror—a large, rectangular piece with tiny, clear light bulbs going all around its frame—and stared at myself in surprise.

I looked *ah-mazing*! My jaw dropped.

"See?" Rosalina jutted a shoulder out, putting on a smug expression. "Now, that's how you do makeup."

She had spent five minutes removing what I'd put on and fifteen more applying everything from scratch. I had to admit my skills, which I'd acquired in high school during a quick instruction from Daniella, left a lot to be desired.

Rosalina had applied a primer, foundation, concealer, blush, eye shadow, eyeliner, falsies, setting powder, and who knew what else. She had given me a rundown as she worked, but it had been so many things that I'd lost count. I'd been afraid it would be too much, that I would look unnatural, but what she'd done had simply enhanced my features. No more, no less.

I blinked at the mirror, turning my face in different directions, completely in awe of her talent. "Shit, Rosalina, you could probably work on Broadway or Hollywood or something."

"Yeah, if our agency doesn't pan out, that's my plan," she joked.

She opened the drawer to my left. Glass clinked inside. The space was full to the brim with perfume bottles of different colors and made me think of a pirate's treasure chest full of glittering jewels. She ran her fingers over them, picked a red bottle, and sprayed herself generously.

"I'd better change. Damien will be here soon," she said, walking toward the bed and picking up the dress she'd selected out of her closet.

I went to my room to change, too. It was eight forty-five, and my nervousness had mounted. I felt like a young teen going to her first dance. I'd never been to a werewolf party. I preferred to party with Stales in mostly benign, public places. I had never even been to The Scourge—the Skew party district—because I knew it could be dangerous for people without considerable power. Shifters, vampires, powerful mages, and witches partied at a whole other level, which was not safe for Stales or weaker Skews like me. I didn't feel at all like going, but I didn't have a choice if I wanted to quickly tame Red. On top of that, I had to worry about Rosalina and hope Damien would keep her safe.

I slipped into my dress—an off-the-shoulder, knee-length number with slits running up both legs. Its fabric was flowy and plum-colored with a bit of glitter. After slipping into a pair of strappy kitten heels, I walked out of the bedroom and sat at the edge of the couch, tapping my fingers on my bare knee.

My back began to itch. I pinched my arm as hard as I could.

"Ow!"

I hate you, Red growled.

The itching went away. Not a pleasant method but effective.

A moment later, Rosalina came out of her room, filling her dress as only a curvaceous woman can. She looked gorgeous in her bodycon dress. It was light blue with a swooping neckline. Her long black hair tumbled in perfect locks around her shoulders and her toned, bare arms glittered slightly as if she were some sort of water nymph.

It was obvious why Damien Ward had set his eye on her, but I didn't like it, especially since it'd been a while since I'd seen Rosalina this excited about a date. She had no shortage of them, and most of the time, she kept her expectations low. Tonight, however, there was a twinkle in her green eyes that scared me. I didn't want her getting involved with a Skew—much less someone like Damien Ward. That guy had been tampering with me for twenty years, which didn't speak highly of his moral backbone. If he'd done that, what else was he capable of?

As Rosalina sat next to me on the sofa, I took her hand and clenched it tightly. "I wish you would stay."

"I already told you, I'm not letting you go alone."

"I can tell you like him, Rosalina, so don't pretend that's the only reason you want to come."

She didn't try to deny it. She just shrugged.

"I don't trust him, and you shouldn't either."

"Who said I did? I'm not stupid. I may not be a Skew, but I'm no stranger to them. You know that."

It was true. Rosalina's family was mixed. Her Abuela Esperanza was a witch who, in her youth, had specialized in exorcising demons. Rosalina's mother hadn't inherited any skills and since she had married a Stale, Rosalina and her sister had no skills either. However, several of her uncles, aunts, and cousins did.

"Don't worry." She squeezed my hand back. "I've got a few hexes in my bag. You know I always carry them, and I won't go anywhere with him. We already agreed on that."

We were going to drive separately—me following Damien in my Camaro—but the plan was for Rosalina to come back with me afterward.

When the knock came at the door, I jumped, and my heart started pattering at a million miles per hour. Rosalina walked calmly to the door.

"Ow!" I exclaimed before she opened it.

She glanced back over her shoulder. "What?"

"Nothing." I smiled, rubbing at the spot on my arm where I'd pinched myself again. I was probably going to have a bruise by the end of the night.

She pulled the door open, revealing Damien Ward standing on the other side. My friend's sharp, green eyes took him in. He wore a three-piece suit. The jacket had velvet lapels and a gold-embroidered pattern. The vest underneath it was tight around his slim middle, and the shirt was open at the collar, revealing a smooth chest. For all intents and purposes, he looked like a world-class supermodel. Everything about him was utter perfection. His perfectly trimmed white hair, the smoothness of his jaw, the trim of his suit, the slight tilt of his shoulder as he stood casually, smirking. His copper eyes flashed with amusement.

"You look as stunning as I knew you would," he said. "May I come in?"

He didn't wait for an answer and took a step forward.

Both Rosalina and I held up our hands and waved him back, but it was too late. He hit my mother's protective spell, which crackled and sizzled as soon as he tried to cross the threshold. Stunned, he yelped and jumped back.

He cursed and blinked very slowly, looking mad at himself. "You'd think I would know better. Of course, Amalia would protect her daughter with her best spells. She was always good at making them undetectable." He blinked up at us. "Well, don't just sit there staring at me. Let's go."

I met Rosalina at the door.

"He has a temper, huh?" she said, a slight smile stretching her lips. She liked them stubborn and fiery—her words not mine.

Men like him represented a challenge to her. Someone to tame and keep her interest. Most of the time, she didn't have a second date with the men she went out with. They bored her that quickly. I suspected this was one of the reasons she didn't want me to track her mate. She was afraid he would be a mellow man, the kind you settled for because he would make a good, compliant husband. And she wasn't ready to settle. Not by a long shot.

Oh, this doesn't bode well.

We followed Damien to his car, which turned out to be a two-seater black Mercedes. Clearly, he hadn't planned on giving me a ride.

I tugged on Rosalina's arm and whispered in her ear. "Maybe you should ride with me."

"It's fine. It'll give me a chance to talk to him and get the scoop about this party."

She didn't fool me. She was aching to be alone with Damien. Why did dangerous men have this effect on women? I thought about my own dangerous man and wondered what he was up to.

Red perked up as I thought of Jake. My wolf definitely had the hots for him. No surprise there.

As the mage opened the passenger door for Rosalina, I rushed to my Camaro and started it. The engine roared to life. I patted the dashboard. "Good, baby."

It was still running in tiptop shape. Dad and I had done an excellent job fixing it up. Still, I should take it for a general checkup before long. Old cars needed extra TLC to keep them going.

Damien sped out of the parking lot like a bat out of hell. I stepped on the gas and caught up with him, determined not to let him lose me, if that was his intention. Thirty minutes later, however, we ended up at the address spelled out on the invitation, an affluent neighborhood in Ballwin.

The mansion was one of the most modern I'd ever seen. It was three stories tall, built of concrete and glass, appearing more like an office building than anyone's home. The party was taking place on the second floor, judging by the purple strobe light that refracted through the glass walls. Dark, dancing silhouettes blinked to life with the light.

We parked in the massive circular driveway and walked up to the front steps. They ran along the side of the house, flanked by concrete planters with well-kept flowers and shrubs, and led to the second floor and a thick glass door that slid open as we stepped in front of it.

A mean-looking guy with a chest as wide as Damien's refrigerator took our invitations and examined them closely. After pressing them against a UV reader, he scanned us up and down, giving me the feeling that he could see right through our clothes. I squirmed on the spot, biting my lower lip. His inquiring eyes combined with the loud music and strobing lights made my entire body feel like an overfilled water balloon, thin-skinned, and ready to burst.

Damien bore the man's scrutiny with irritation, but he waited until the man gave us the go-ahead, then strolled forward, Rosalina's arm tucked under his. I followed behind like the scaredy-cat that I was.

We went around a long wall hung with abstract art set in dark metal frames, then came out on the other side into a large room surrounded by glass walls on three sides. The area was set up more like a club, not a home. In the center of the room, a dance floor filled with people drew my eye. It was hard to miss, considering the large disco ball twirling above and the spotlights dancing in erratic patterns. The bass of dance music thudded in my chest.

Couples in all states of ecstasy and *disrobement* danced in suggestive ways, grinding their hips together and flat-out making out as if it was the end of the world and all the fun had to be had right then and there. Heat warmed up my cheeks as I stared at a sexy couple pawing each other in the most intimate places.

I jerked my gaze in the direction of the bar at the end of the room. The counter appeared to be made out of ice. It shone with blue light from within and had sculpted ends in the shape of swans. Bottle-filled shelves lined the back wall. I started drifting in that direction, wanting to touch it and, of course, get a drink, when Damien put a hand on my shoulder and whispered in my ear.

"I'll talk to my friend, then I'll introduce you to him. Make yourself comfortable for now."

I nodded and glanced around nervously, wondering who this mysterious friend could be, but I had no clue since Damien was being cagey. Either way, the only thing that could take the edge off right now would be something strong to drink, and I intended to get it.

Rolling my shoulders as if I were going to battle, I walked toward the bar. As I went, I caught the attention of two men standing with their backs against the bar top, whiskeys in hand. I held their gazes for an instant, acting way braver than I felt. They were werewolves, I could tell from their musk and some other instinct that hadn't been there before.

With my new scent disguised, they would assume I was a Stale, which was nearly as bad as them knowing I was a runt. I made sure to send all the stay-away-from-me vibes that I could, and found an open spot at the bar, far away from them.

I laid my hands on the clear counter, expecting it to be cold, but it wasn't made of ice. It was glass. I had no idea how something like that could be constructed. It was impressive. I ran my hands over the smooth surface and the intricate edge, which looked like a flower chain. I'd never seen anything like it before.

I waved one of the bartenders over. There were three of them, all working furiously, blurring back and forth as they prepared drinks using their preternatural speed. One noticed me and sped over.

"What would you like?" she asked, flashing pointed fangs encrusted with tiny diamonds. Beautiful vamp bartenders were common. They were easy on the eye and worked fast.

"A whiskey sour, please." I wanted something strong that would dull my sharpened senses quickly.

The drink appeared in front of me in the next five seconds, then the vamp was gone to serve another customer. Damn, she was efficient. The bad thing was that Skews could drink the stuff as fast as she could make it, especially werewolves who could metabolize alcohol almost as if it were water.

Oh, shit!

I stared at my drink with a frown. Were my tipsy days already over? I hadn't even turned twenty-one yet. Great! I took a gulp of my drink. It burned on the way down and I winced, welcoming the warmth in my chest and stomach. I turned to face the crowd, hoping the drink would kick in soon.

A vamp dressed in a tube dress with strategically torn holes down its length staggered in the direction of the bar and settled herself next to me. She was swaying on her feet, clearly drunk or high. I raised my eyebrows as I examined the dopey expression on her face.

Whatever she was drinking, I needed some of that. A strange sour scent wafted from her. It rivaled my poop perfume. I wrinkled my nose.

The same bartender who had fetched my drink came to her. She frowned at the new customer, obviously displeased. I'd seen that look on bartenders before. This vamp had been tagged as a potential troublemaker and was probably close to losing her bar privileges.

"Another *raybow*," she said. "Positive."

Raybow? Rainbow, maybe? What the hell was that?

The bartender heaved a sigh. "This will be your last one," she said, then moved away in a blur.

"Um, hi!" I said.

The vamp turned her head in my direction as if in slow motion. She blinked several times, trying to focus. "Do I know you?" she slurred.

"Not yet." I put my hand out to shake. "I'm Toni Sunder."

She dropped her chin to her chest as if her head were too heavy and stared down at my hand, but made no attempt to shake. I shrugged it off and pulled my hand back.

"So… what's a *raybow*?" I asked.

She gave a goofy laugh, throwing her head back. "It's the best thing to ever happen. That's what."

I watched with interest as the bartender returned with a shot glass filled with a green shimmering liquid. Oh, so it was some sort of magical drink with colors like in a rainbow. Skew mixologists were always coming up with new interesting combinations that sort of worked, though I had never seen anything affect a vampire like this. She was really high.

The vamp went for the glass, missing it on her first attempt, then clutching it tightly and lifting it to her mouth slowly as if afraid to spill even one drop. When it reached her lips, she downed it in one gulp, throwing her head back in ecstasy and letting out a moan like someone reaching a climax.

"Wow, that's hot," I said, without thinking.

The bartender huffed. "No, it ain't. It's disgusting."

Surprised at her comment, I turned to look at her but she disappeared again, the *whoosh* of her rapid retreat rustling my hair.

A moment later the stoned vamp staggered away from the bar, her high heels twisting inwardly with her every ungraceful step. I frowned, my curiosity mounting. A drink that could truly intoxicate vampires, and a bartender who didn't approve of it.

I stared down at my drink, realizing that it had never kicked in. Not one bit. Damn!

"Well, that's no fun," I mumbled, then downed what was left in the glass. The raybow was definitely starting to sound like an option right about now. I raised my hand to get the bartender's attention.

She came back and offered me a smile. "Another whiskey sour?"

"It's not doing the trick tonight. How about one of those raybows?"

Her smile dropped immediately. "No can do. They're only for vamps."

"Huh?" That was stupid. "How come?"

"Because if you drink one, it will kill you."

I blinked and stared at her wide-eyed. "You're kidding, right?"

"Nope." She sped away and a moment later, she was back with another whiskey sour, which she smacked down on the counter. "Raybow's poison. If you have any vamp friends, tell them not to touch it," she warned, then sped away once more.

Questions multiplied exponentially inside my head. The party scene was certainly changing. I'd been so busy working that I'd missed it. I had to find out what this was all about. I wondered if Damien knew.

I turned to face the crowd again, my eyes scanning for the white-haired mage, but instead, I spotted the last person I thought I would see here.

Jake Knight.

CHAPTER 12

Jake was standing off to the left, reclining against one of the glass walls and talking to a blonde in shoes with pencil-thin heels. She was medium height and athletic, her blond hair falling mid-back like a straight silken sheet. She wore a loud red dress that stopped at the edge of her butt and left her back bare. She was talking animatedly, her hands moving in front of her like erratic birds, while Jake listened with a half-smile. He was holding a beer and taking distracted, small sips. After she said something and laughed, his smile deepened, but it didn't quite reach his eyes.

Jealousy burned me like acid. My hand tightening around my glass, and I carefully set it down on the counter, afraid to break it. My entire body rippled with a shiver. A low rumble built in my chest and images of tufts of blond hair flying across the room filled my vision. I dug my fingernails into my palms and glanced in the opposite direction, trying to calm my agitated breaths.

My chest swelled with anger. The emotion was more intense than anything I'd felt in a long time. I squeezed my eyes shut.

Holy shit! I had to get out of here before I went super-nuclear on somebody.

"Toni?" The voice cut through my anger, chilling it immediately.

My eyes sprang open, and I found Jake standing in front of me and frowning deeply.

"What are you doing here?" he asked, his tone critical.

I couldn't answer. I was trying hard not to slap him and demand what he was doing here with *that* blonde.

He snatched my glass from the bar and smelled its contents. "Whiskey sour," he said with relief. He leaned closer. "Are you here alone?" He glanced around the room. "Is Stephen with you?"

"No, I'm not here alone," I said, finally finding my voice, the pissed-off version of it, anyway.

"Who did you come with?"

"That's none of your business."

He cracked his neck and blinked slowly as if to calm himself. Then, obviously failing, he grabbed me by the arm and pushed toward the far corner of the room. "You shouldn't be here. These types of parties are not for…" He searched for a term.

"Weak Skews," I said in a sardonic tone.

"Exactly."

I jerked out of his grip, still digging my fingernails into my palms. "I told you already, Jake, quit acting like you care. It's getting tiresome."

"Damnit, Toni. Do you have a fucking death wish?"

"Maybe I do."

"Don't be stupid."

"And you shouldn't be an asshole, but you don't seem able to help it either."

He took a step closer, barely leaving an inch between us. My shoulders hit the wall as I tried to pull away, but there was nowhere to go. He leaned closer, his nose almost touching mine, his breath hot on my lips. Those silver eyes roved around my face and stopped when they reached my mouth. I felt my anger melt and quickly morph into something else.

"Leave me alone," I said, but my words carried no authority whatsoever.

"I should."

"Go back to your blonde." I hated to let the jealousy show, but I couldn't help myself.

"Green looks good on you," he said with one of his crooked grins.

"You should check your eyes. The dress's color is plum." The hell if I was going to admit I was jealous of that pasty blonde.

"My eyes work perfectly fine." His strong hand wrapped around my waist and pulled me against him.

His solidity felt divine as my torso molded to his like a puzzle piece finding its match. He buried his nose in my throat and inhaled deeply. "What do you do to me?" he growled against my skin. "I can't stop thinking about you."

My entire body filled with butterflies, and that awful feeling that I was about to go postal on the world disappeared. In its place, heat and want built up, and before I knew it, my hands were on his chest, exploring, enjoying the feel of his perfect body.

He inhaled sharply at my touch and let his lips glide along my jaw while his other hand slid behind my neck and held me in place.

Desire surging through me, I pulled away, grabbed his face in both hands, and pulled him in for a kiss. Our lips touched. A pang of heat thrilled its way straight to my core. His velvety tongue slipped inside my mouth, insistent and possessive. His strong arms wrapped around me, crushing me against him.

We can *be together, Jake. I'm not what you think I am.*

I'm what you need me to be.

The words sprang into my mind, unbidden. I could tell him what I was, and we wouldn't have to fight this anymore. We could have a future together. I could be the one to help him fulfill the promise to his father. I could be the one to help him continue his legacy.

Our attraction was inevitable. It had always been. Maybe, somehow, he'd known what I was. And maybe I had, too.

His right hand found the slit in my dress and caressed my inner thigh. I let out an involuntary moan. He hooked his hand behind my leg, hitched it to his waist, and settled between my legs. He deepened his kiss, savoring me, letting his own desire run rampant, quickly meeting mine.

He pulled away. "I'd better stop." Breathless, he rested his forehead on mine. His upper lip shivered.

I opened my mouth, irrational words ready to spring forward, to let him know how I felt about him, but they dried up as quickly as they formed because I noticed the blonde standing behind him. Looking annoyed, she tapped him on the shoulder.

Jake took a step back and glanced over at her. She put a hand on her waist and jutted out her hip, demanding an explanation with her mere posture. I could tell immediately that she was a werewolf.

His expression gave nothing away. He didn't look surprised or sorry to have been discovered.

"You have to admit, our date wasn't going too well," he said.

Really? Oh, my God. What a bastard!

Why did I fall for this man? He hadn't just met her. He had brought her here on a date, and this was how he treated her?

The blonde glanced at me, looking at a loss for words. She didn't seem angry at me, which was as it should be. She wasn't here on a date with *me*, so I didn't owe her any consideration, but Jake did, which made him a son of a bitch.

"Can you believe this guy?" she asked me, looking truly disappointed as if she'd expected more and had received a negative value instead.

I shook my head. I'd thought Jake to be better. He had been better with me, at least for the few months we dated after I graduated. But maybe, this was the Jake everyone had warned me about in the beginning. What was to prevent him from treating me this way at some point? Scratch that, he'd already treated me like garbage. He'd already lied and abandoned me. Falling for him again was like shooting myself in the foot with a bazooka.

"Good riddance," the blonde said, appearing relieved to have discovered his douchebaggery in time. Gracefully, she whirled on her pointed heel and walked away.

Jake scrubbed at his face, appearing exhausted.

I thought of saying something biting and hurtful, but being around Jake got me all tangled up inside. I lost my mind around him—exhibit A: our recent make-out session—and forgot all the promises I'd made myself. The best thing I could do was avoid him, so I skirted around him and walked away, too.

"Toni, I didn't mean to." He went for my hand, trying to grab it, but I snatched it away.

"Stay away from me, Jake."

"I—"

I lifted a hand to stop him from saying anything else. "You already told me that *this*," I pointed at him then back at myself, "wasn't possible, so you need to stop acting like it is."

My words were all kinds of wrong. The reasons that had made our relationship impossible had disappeared, and all I had to do was tell him the truth. What he thought was an obstacle didn't exist anymore. In fact, it never had. But now, more than ever, I felt I couldn't open up to him. Jake had destroyed my trust, and he wasn't making a good case in rebuilding it. On the contrary, his actions were nothing but a flashing warning sign to keep away.

And not just that. There was too much I needed to learn. I didn't know *me* anymore, didn't know my limits, my strength, my character. Everything was changing, so how could I be with anyone when I didn't even know myself. I would not become anyone's accessory out of convenience. I would not join my fate with someone else's without understanding the consequences.

Did I need a pack? Would being with Jake mean I was joining one? He'd been a lone wolf when I met him, but now he was talking about building his legacy. I didn't understand enough about being a werewolf, and I needed my head clear to be able to make the best decision possible. That definitely meant staying the hell away from Jacob Knight.

"I have enough problems as it is," I said. "Don't add more to my list. Do you think you can do that? Because I can surely help you with your promise and legacy problems. I'm trying to let you be, to move forward." I swept a hand over the room to indicate the party. "You see, this is me trying. So let me."

I waited for an answer, but he just stood there staring at me, his eyes dark, his expression guarded. I felt what he felt. It was plain in his features. He shared my pain, and it tugged at my heart. But I had to be strong. I had to look further than today. He and I couldn't have a future together if there was no trust.

At last, he spoke, "You're right." He took a step closer and lowered his voice. "I'm trying, but it's not easy. You have a hold on me that I can't understand. It's like…" He shook his head and pressed his lips together, unwilling to say what he thought. "I know you feel the same. It's been like this since that first time."

I held his gaze, unable to deny any of it. We were like two open books to each other. The dumb attraction was mutual. We were a pair of fools who lost all reason whenever the distance between us was less than a few hundred miles. God, maybe Rosalina was right about moving to China.

"Why can't you understand I just want you to be safe," he continued. "If something happened to you…"

I took one of his large hands in mine and squeezed it. "You have to let me go, Jake."

"Don't friends have a right to worry about each other?"

"We can never be friends. You know that." I let go of his hand and retreated a step. "Friends don't…" I gestured toward the corner where we'd just made out.

"Then maybe we should…" He let that hang, eyeing me suggestively.

Wait?! Was he trying to say that we could be lovers while he found someone else to fulfill his other needs?

I narrowed my eyes at him. "Don't you dare say what I think you're going to say."

"I'm sorry. I don't mean to insult you. I guess I can be a selfish asshole sometimes." He paused and considered for a moment, then added, "It wouldn't do for me either. I want to give you everything."

My chest squeezed painfully. I wanted everything with him, too. God, this was so painful. The back of my eyes stung, and I turned away before tears made their appearance.

"There you are!" Rosalina came running toward me. "Damien's friend is ready to meet you." Noticing Jake standing behind me, she came to an abrupt stop, looking surprised.

"Hi, Jake." She gave him a little wave.

"Hello," he said.

Her sudden presence brought my onslaught of tears to a halt, for which I was more than grateful.

"Oh, good," I said, putting on a cheery voice. "I was starting to get bored. Let's go."

Damien appeared next, weaving through the crowd. "C'mon, Eric Lone waits for no one. Hurry up!"

What? Eric Lone? That was Damien's friend?

Eric Cross—or Eric Lone as he was known in St. Louis—was an infamous werewolf that had almost become a sort of urban legend. The rumor went that fifteen years ago his wife and daughter had been killed by the leader of a rivaling pack. They said that when he heard the news he was stricken with grief and tried to take his own life. His pack stopped him and when the bulk of the pain passed, he vowed to avenge his loved ones.

He parted from his pack, becoming a lone wolf, and a year later, every trace of his enemies had been erased from existence. Eric Cross had killed every single one of them, down to the last descendant, erasing their legacy forever. Ever since, everyone knew him as Eric Lone, and his name inspired dread and curiosity in all Skew circles.

My insides shivered at the thought of meeting such a legend. And not only that, Damien intended for him to teach me how to be a werewolf. That didn't sound like a good idea at all.

"Well," Damien said, "are you just going to stand there and waste everyone's time?"

Mechanically, I took a step forward.

"Wait, Toni." Jake put a hand on my shoulder.

Damien scrutinized Jake with a frown.

"What business do you have with Eric Cross?" Jake asked.

There he went again, sticking his nose in my business as if we hadn't just had the most painful conversation ever.

Really? We'd just gone over this.

He was such a thick-headed, possessive, over-protective, irresistible jerk!

The sad part was that if he hadn't said anything, I might've thought twice about getting involved with Eric Lone, but since Jake didn't want me to do it, then by God, I was going to jump right in. And while I was at it, I would learn everything Eric could teach me, even how to exterminate entire packs.

Taking a deep breath, I spoke in a cool tone. "We just finished establishing that my business is not your business, so please, butt out."

"Cross is dangerous," he said. "Are you bent on getting yourself killed? What is this all about?"

"It's nothing that concerns you, and I swear if you don't stay out of my business, I'll file a complaint against you. Tom can help me make sure it sticks."

"You wouldn't."

"If it'll take a restraining order to keep you away, I swear I'll get one." Gritting my teeth, I turned and walked away, determined to move on once and for all.

I wasn't going to let Jake or anyone else interfere with what I needed to accomplish. I would tame my wolf.

CHAPTER 13

Stomping angrily, I weaved through the partygoers, following Damien around the bar toward a door on the opposite end. I resisted the urge to glance back at Jake and squeezed Rosalina's hand hard when she reached for mine. As always, she knew I needed her support, and I was glad she'd come because I could borrow a little strength from her. Besides, she helped me keep my eyes on the goal and away from what should have remained in my past.

Another man dressed all in black waited by the door. He opened it for us as he noticed Damien and let us through, then immediately closed it behind us.

Damien led the way down a wide hall decorated sparsely with the same abstract paintings as in the front. After a couple of turns that led us deep into the house and away from the thumping music, we reached a mahogany door that seemed at odds with the rest of the décor.

The mage knocked, and without waiting for a response, walked in. I squeezed Rosalina's hand harder while I bit the inside of my cheek, drawing blood. The heavy door eased closed behind us, completely shutting away all the sounds from the party.

Rosalina and I peered around the room, then exchanged a perplexed glance. If the wooden door had seemed out of place, this room seemed like it belonged in an entirely different house, one built in a different time and place.

We were in a study or library, flanked on every side by floor-to-ceiling shelves filled with hundreds, if not thousands, of books. Worn Persian rugs rested on top of each other barely giving us a peek of the hardwood floors underneath. A sitting section with leather loveseats and sofas formed a square around a round coffee table laden with open tomes.

A fireplace sat in the center of the left wall and made me think of winter nights reading by a warm fire. A beautiful oil portrait of a statuesque woman and a little girl sitting on her lap hung above the mantle. I held my breath as I realized who they must be, and I would have gone on staring if Damien hadn't urged me to walk further into the room.

Letting go of Rosalina's hand, I padded silently over the rugs and faced a massive, carved desk like a naughty little girl waiting to be chastised. The high back chair on the other side of the desk was turned around, completely hiding its occupant.

Damien cleared his throat and pushed me forward. I staggered to within inches of the desk and froze. The chair swiveled slowly. I held my breath and pinched my arm, struggling to keep my cool.

When Eric Cross faced me, the first thing I noticed about him was his intense blue eyes. They held me in place and seemed to speak a thousand silent words.

You are nothing. You are weak. You don't belong here.

My shoulders caved in, but I stood my ground even though I wanted to run. Was feeling like this what it meant to be an omega?

He stood up slowly and rested a hand on top of the desk as he assessed me. A large silver ring in the shape of a wolf's head covered half of his index finger. I stared at the tiny wolf's jeweled blue eyes, avoiding Eric Cross's own sapphire gaze. After a short moment, he huffed as if he found me lacking in every respect.

Anger flared in my gut. I met his eyes, defiantly. Who did he think he was? He wasn't so impressive himself. He was at most 5'10" and slender, almost wiry. He had a crooked nose with wide nostrils that kept twitching like mine often did. He wasn't exactly ugly, but he wasn't handsome either. The resting bitch face certainly didn't help.

"You owe me, Eric," Damien said as the werewolf made a face.

"And this will clear our score? Forever?" Eric asked between clenched teeth.

"Forever," the mage answered.

Eric heaved a huge sigh and rubbed his jaw, considering, looking as if someone was asking him to sit his bare ass on a bed of hot coals.

At last, he threw a hand up in the air and said, "Okay, I'll do it." He looked at me with narrowed eyes. "Be here Thursday morning at 4 AM. We'll train for three hours. If I don't see progress in three days, I'll stop."

4 AM?! What kind of torture was this? I opened my mouth to protest, but he went on.

"If she gives me lip, I'll stop. If she's late, I'll stop. If she doesn't try hard enough, I'll stop. It could take a lifetime to teach her what it is to be a werewolf, but I'll only give her five days."

"Five days?!" Damien said incredulously. "That's hardly enough. It doesn't seem a fair exchange considering what you owe me."

"Take it or leave it."

Damien sighed. "We'll take it."

"Good. Now, go." Eric made a dismissive gesture toward the door.

I stood motionless, feeling like a cheap trinket everyone kept passing up at the flea market. I wanted to spit in his face as I stared at him, hatred building inside me at record speed. Honestly, I'd never gone from zero to I-hate-your-guts so quickly in my life.

My claws sprang out, and I took a step toward the lone wolf. Before I knew it, he had me by the throat, his own claws digging into my skin. He snarled, baring sharp fangs and releasing his hot breath straight into my face. His blue eyes glowed with iridescent light and bore into mine, digging deep into some animal instinct I didn't know I possessed.

Fear and submission unfurled inside of me. I felt the need to curl into a tight ball on the floor and whimper. My shoulders shook slightly, but I fought the urge to cower, and instead, let out a baby growl.

Eric's eyes widened in something like surprise, then he dug his claws deeper into my throat and snarled again, louder this time.

My claws slipped back of their own accord. Gone in a jiffy. I curled inwardly and wrapped my arms around my stomach. He let me go, and I staggered backward into Rosalina's arms, who held me protectively against her body and smoothed my hair as I trembled.

"Leave," Eric repeated.

Damien and Rosalina helped me out of the room.

I didn't straighten from my submissive position until ten minutes later. All that time, Rosalina soothed me, and Damien paced up and down the hall with impatience, muttering to himself. At last, we left the party, though the time between my short meeting with Eric Cross and Rosalina helping me to bed was a blur.

I felt weak and ragged as if I'd just come out of a tracking trance and went to sleep shivering, despite the many blankets Rosalina draped over me. All night, I dreamed of snarling faces and shook in fear to my very soul.

CHAPTER 14

Saturday morning, I woke up late and dragged myself out of bed. I fed Cupid, then shuffled into the kitchen. When a strong cup of Columbian coffee didn't wake me up, I took a cold shower. I shivered all the way through it and felt happy to be alive afterward, which was a great improvement.

"Do you still feel up to going out?" Rosalina asked as I came out of the bathroom, rubbing my wet hair with a towel.

We had plans to go furniture shopping for my new place, and since Aaron Blackridge had stopped by the office to drop off the tears and I'd started his potion, we were also supposed to go by the agency to pick it up. We'd decided to do the tracking trance tomorrow, so we could set DJ Slice on his path to bliss. However, just the thought of going under made me tired to the bone. If only I could track people's mates by devouring their Cheetos or something, I would chomp at the bit.

We had been excited about selecting furniture for my apartment, and though I felt like curling up on the sofa to binge-watch Netflix or take a nap, I put on a smile and told myself that getting out would be good for me.

"Yeah, I need a distraction," I said, sounding as chipper as I could. "Plus, I, at least, need a bed and a sofa before I move in. I close on Friday, and I'll get the keys right away."

Rosalina returned my smile and looked relieved to see my enthusiasm. I didn't want her to worry about me and my upcoming appointment with the Werewolf from Hell, Mr. Eric Cross. He seemed to live up to his heartless reputation, but he had agreed to teach me what I needed to know, and it wasn't like I had many options. I could tough it out.

A knock came at the door just as we were leaving. Looking through the peephole, I saw my mother. My anger popped like a jack-in-a-box.

I turned to Rosalina. "Tell her I don't want to talk to her."

"Who is it?"

"My mother."

Rosalina cocked her head and gave me a worried look. "I'll do it, but are you sure?"

"Yes. I need some breathing room. I'm not ready to deal with her." Tears pooled in my eyes.

"All right." I went into my bedroom and waited, fidgeting as I sat on the bed.

Rosalina peeked her head in after a few minutes. "She's gone now."

I nodded. "Thank you. I'm sorry for—"

She waved a hand. "No need. I'm with you. You need time to process. So…" she hooked a finger over her shoulder. "What do you say we get out of here?"

I hopped to my feet. "Let's go!"

I drove the Camaro with the top down, enjoying the cool April breeze. Soon, the summer heat would come, and our brains would fry like eggs if we did this, so we needed to enjoy the weather while we could.

Our first stop was a chain furniture store where I found new stuff for a comfortable price. My bed and sofa would be new, but for the rest of my furniture, I planned to hit some antique and thrift stores for cheaper options. The pieces would have character and I could refurbish them if needed. I wasn't shy about getting my hands dirty. Dad had taught me how to be handy.

After a couple of hours browsing, Rosalina and I picked a bedroom and living room set. They weren't exactly fabulous, but I couldn't complain. The bed was better than the one in the loft, which would now go to the guest bedroom, where I looked forward to hosting Rosalina every once in a while, just the way she was hosting me.

We grabbed a couple of burgers on the way to the office and ate them at Rosalina's desk. When we were done, I packed Aaron's potion in a tight container, and we headed back to Rosalina's apartment. It wasn't until we were on our way there that she brought up the topic of my werewolf teacher.

"Eric Cross," she pronounced the name like a curse. "Do you think it's smart getting involved with him?"

I didn't think it was, but I couldn't see any other choice. "I'll be careful."

"He's a monster. The things people say he did, and the way he manhandled you. Aren't you scared?"

I nodded. "Of course I am. I'm terrified, but I'm also terrified of not being able to control myself, of hurting you, or my sisters, or anyone. It's an awful feeling." We stopped at a red light as a jumble of feelings unpacked itself inside my chest. "There's an entire night

I can't remember. I don't know what I did. I just have flashes of awful things. I'll learn as much as I can from Cross in five days, and then it'll be done. I don't think he'll hurt me. He's paying a favor back to Damien, so that means he has some kind of honor."

Rosalina rolled her eyes as I stepped on the gas and crossed the intersection. "Honor." She laughed. "He killed an entire pack."

"We don't know if that's true. They could never prove anything."

"I can tell you've made up your mind. Just be careful, Toni. Werewolves are strange creatures."

"Um, thank you."

We both laughed.

"You know what I mean," she added.

I did know, and it scared me more than anything to think that I would change and then Rosalina would think I was strange just like the rest of them. What if in the end, she wanted nothing to do with me? What if *I* wanted nothing to do with her? What if a year from now my life was nothing like I'd dreamed it would be? I didn't want to lose myself inside a pack, give up my independence. Did that mean I would have to be a lone wolf? Was that a guarantee for a miserable life? I had no idea, hopefully a week from now I would know better.

That afternoon, I took a short nap and went to bed early at Rosalina's insistence. The plan was to do the tracking trance early the next day, and considering how wiped out it always left me, rest wasn't a bad idea at all.

Sunday morning, I cooked cheese omelets for Rosalina and me, and we ate in front of the TV, watching old cartoons like two little girls. My favorite was The Roadrunner, and Rosalina's was Daffy Duck. They only played Bugs Bunny reruns, though, but we still laughed at his antics.

When we finished eating, I prepared the potion and set it on my night table. It smelled of fresh strawberries and honey, either Aaron's or his mate's favorite flavors.

Casting away my weariness, I dipped my hands in the potion, lay in bed, and got to work. The trance came over me quickly, and I rushed through the motions as much as I could.

I activated my sense of smell next, and after only a few seconds, a rush of pleasant smells assaulted me. Pistachio, raspberry, peach, sugar, Oreo cookies, milk. A strong memory hit me, and I thought I knew the place, but I had to be sure.

Quickly, I released my next sense. My ears revealed the sound of many voices, a jumble of words that, at first, I couldn't identify. There was also the sound of a whistled tune I didn't recognize, then I started to pick up a few of the words, which repeated over and over: concrete, crunch, and cookie.

Got it!

I snapped out of the trance, smiling from ear to ear.

Rosalina squeezed my hand, looking surprised. "Already?" she mouthed, pronouncing the word slowly so I could read it on her lips.

"Yes, this was the easiest trance ever."

She nodded vigorously and held one finger up, which meant I'd only been under for one minute. I lay back down, relieved. I felt exhausted down to my bones, but I would get my sense of smell and hearing back in an hour. I could sleep it off, and after that, Rosalina and I would go stalk Aaron's mate because I knew exactly where to find him.

ꕥ

That evening, once I'd regained my strength and senses, I drove us to Ted Drewes Frozen Custard, one of my favorite places in the world. Ted's was a landmark in St. Louis, a place with the best frozen treats in the city. Every year locals and tourists lined up outside to get their preferred flavors. My mouth watered as I thought of mine.

"I hope we find him," Rosalina said as we approached the parking lot.

"We will." I felt certain.

The scents had been so clear that they'd immediately taken me to Ted's. I'd been there many times as a kid with my family, and I still went as often as I could, craving the flavors and atmosphere. So it was no surprise I'd identified the location right away. One good thing, this was the only open location this time of the year. He would be there.

"I think today I'll get a Dutchman," Rosalina said. "What about you?"

"Hmm, good choice."

The Dutchman had chocolate, butterscotch, and pecans in it. I knew all their flavors.

I thought about what my choice would be for a moment, recalling all the scents. "I'll have to go with a Twisted Caramel." Caramel was my weakness.

Rosalina moaned. "It sounds delicious. Gah, I want them all."

"We'll buy a pint to take home. How does that sound?"

"Perfect!"

I parked in one of the few available spots. We got out of the car and walked toward the serving windows. A line of people stretched along the sidewalk. We went to the back and tried to peer at the attendants, but the glare at the windows prevented us from seeing anything.

As people walked away with their treats and huge smiles on their faces, my nose twitched with all the scents, and my mouth watered, desperate for a taste.

"This is torture," I whined.

"I know."

Finally, it was our turn to order. Young college and high school kids bustled around inside, dispensing custards, malts, and shakes, and topping them with all kinds of goodies. I quickly peered at all the guys working behind the counter, but none of them fit the bill. They were all Stales and on the young side.

I glanced at Rosalina and shook my head. Her mouth turned downward but went right back up as I handed over her Dutchman. After paying, we pulled aside and shoveled spoonfuls of custard into our mouths like two savages.

We made indecent sounds, licking our spoons and tasting each other's flavors. An old woman walked by and gave us a disapproving look, but we didn't care. She'd probably forgotten what ecstasy felt like, the poor thing.

Oddly, there was nowhere to sit, so we just stood there, hoping to catch a glimpse of Aaron's mate, as people came and went. After we finished, we got back in line to order our take-home pint. We agreed on Brennan Blend for the flavor because… more caramel. Yum!

Suddenly, a strange sensation came over me. It was like a thrum rippling through my body, alerting me, telling me to pay attention. I straightened my back, eyes roving all around.

"Something the matter," Rosalina asked.

"He's here," I said.

"You smell him?"

I shook my head.

Rosalina frowned. "Then how do you know?"

Slowly, I turned to face the parking lot.

A young man was walking toward the employee entrance. He was dressed in a khaki bottom and a yellow T-shirt like the rest of the workers and carried an apron in one hand, and a large open umbrella in the other.

I elbowed Rosalina. "That's him."

Her green eyes darted in his direction. "Ooh, he's cute."

He really was cute with his disheveled hair, smooth complexion, and intense dark eyes. He smelled of strawberries and sugar, Ted Drewes's scents.

As he got closer, he started whistling the tune I'd heard in my trance. My heart leaped in excitement. Yep, we'd found him! Aaron would be so happy.

Rosalina scratched her head. "Uh, why is he carrying an umbrella? It's not even raining."

The umbrella was massive, one of those UV-blocker numbers with a reflective lining that went for over two-hundred dollars at the mall.

"Oh, no," I said, a sinking feeling descending over me.

"Oh, no, what?" A little panic had entered her voice.

"He's… he's a vampire."

Why, oh, why?!

I should have known.

Vamps didn't have a scent of their own. They simply picked up the smell of things and people that surround them, and for Aaron's mate that consisted of Ted's sweet treat. *Dammit!* I'd been so overwhelmed by all the delicious aromas that I never stopped to think why I hadn't picked up a distinctive personal smell for him or much of anything else.

"How do you think Aaron will react?" Rosalina asked.

"Oh, I don't think it'll go over well."

Vampires and werewolves didn't mix. They barely tolerated each other, and a vamp was definitely not what Aaron was looking for.

"I knew it was too easy," I said. "Maybe I should call the furniture store and cancel my order. I can sleep in my old bed and sit on a plastic bin."

"Oh, Toni. I'm sorry. Why don't we wait and see what Aaron says? Maybe he's the most open-minded werewolf to ever live."

"Yeah, right."

"One can hope."

Of course, there had to be a fly making itself comfortable in my ointment. If things were ever easy, I wouldn't know what to do with myself.

Heaving a sigh, I turned to leave just as a breeze picked up almost flipping the vamp's umbrella on itself. He huddled under it, hiding from the sun. The wind carried his scents in my direction, giving me a full whiff of sun-drenched strawberries and sugar. Except this time, another scent came along. My nose twitched, grappling with the hint of a sour tang. I recognized it. I'd perceived it before at Eric's party. The stoned vamp had smelled just like that, except way stronger. How odd.

"What is it?" Rosalina asked.

"Nothing." I shook my head.

Most likely, raybow Vamp and Aaron's mate had picked up that scent from some popular vampire hangout. But whatever. That didn't matter. I had bigger things to worry about such as convincing Aaron that vampires and werewolves didn't have to be mortal enemies.

Make love and not war, Aaron. Om.

I wondered if that line would go over well.

CHAPTER 15

On Tuesday, I strutted into the office, jingling the new keys to my condo.

Rosalina looked up from her laptop and beamed up at me. "That's my girl," she said and got up to give me a hug. "It's a great feeling, isn't it?"

"Yes, it is. I had to sign a gazillion papers, but it was worth it. I can't wait to go and check it out, even if it doesn't have any furniture."

"They'll deliver it in just a few days."

"Gah!" I jogged in place like a little girl.

"Once you're all settled in, we'll throw a housewarming party."

That sobered me up a little. I always imagined my mom there, celebrating with me. When Daniella got her place, part of the event was for Mom to do her protection spells and test them to make sure everyone who was welcomed could get in the house. We had such fun following Mom around in single-file and chanting silly tunes while she tried to concentrate on the spells. I would also love to have my brother there, but who knew when I would see him again.

Rosalina rubbed my arm, her eyes growing sad. "I'm sorry. Maybe we can wait until you and your mom…"

Man, Rosalina knew me so well. It was as if she could read me like a book.

I shook my head. "That might be years, and by then, there would be no point in having a housewarming party."

"Don't say that. Things will change. You'll come around."

"Fat chance." I walked away from her, wishing to change subjects. "Did you find out Aaron's mate's schedule?"

Rosalina sighed, abandoning that side of the conversation reluctantly. She turned toward her desk and reached for a piece of paper. "I did. He'll be there this afternoon. His name is Josh Rice."

I nodded in appreciation for her detective skills. She always had a way of getting information out of people. I didn't know how she managed, but after I located the mates, one of her jobs was to do research to get their names, addresses, and any other relevant information to get in touch with them and make a meeting between them and our customer happen.

"Okay, that's great." A nervous thrill ran through me at the possibility of Aaron meeting his mate today.

Since I'd been doing this, I had never seen two mates *not* fall for each other right away. As soon as I brought them together, the attraction was immediate and inevitable, and it was both physical and emotional. But with these two I feared that their prejudices about werewolves and vampires might be too ingrained and more powerful than whatever else they felt.

I checked the time on my phone. It was almost 10 AM. "Aaron will be here anytime now."

"Actually, he's here." Rosalina pointed through the window at the black Jaguar parking across the street.

Aaron got out of the car and headed our way, a swagger in his step, and a slight smile on his lips. I told him I'd found a mate for him, but I hadn't gone into any details. I had invited him here this morning to explain.

"Good luck," Rosalina said, sitting back at her desk, a frown going across her forehead.

She seemed worried, too. If Aaron decided he didn't want to meet Josh, we would have to give the deposit back and forget about receiving the rest of the payment. We had already gone over our finances, taking that money into consideration, and the numbers had looked really good for our business's future. We would certainly breathe a lot easier if we could set aside some money for our monthly loan payments.

I took a deep breath and rolled my shoulders as Aaron walked through the door. Today, he wore baggy jeans, a pair of unlaced military boots, and a red, yellow, and blue gym jacket. He took off his diamond-studded shades and greeted us with a warm smile and a happy "good morning."

Rosalina and I greeted him back, and I invited him into my office, my heart skipping around restlessly.

After we sat down, Aaron said, "Give me the good news, Toni."

I gave him a tempered smile, which caused his excitement to die down a little.

"Something wrong?" he asked.

"There is a slight… hitch."

He heaved a heavy sigh. "What? He doesn't want to meet me?"

"Actually, we haven't talked to him yet. I wanted to talk to you first. His name is Josh Rice. He's about twenty-one years old and very good-looking, but he doesn't meet all the requirements you specified."

"He's not a werewolf," Aaron said, guessing where I was going with this.

"No, he isn't. But that's not all, he's actually a vampire."

Aaron sprang to his feet. "A vampire?"

"I understand it's not exactly the type of mate you were looking for, but I can assure you that the two of you *will* be compatible."

His eyes searched the room, then he sat back down slowly, looking lost. He didn't appear angry, which I had been afraid of. Instead, he seemed tired and extremely disappointed.

"I'm sure you're right," he said. "I would probably fall madly in love with him, but I have enough problems as it is. I can't invite more."

"Whatever decision you make, Aaron, I will understand it. I know how complicated things can get in our world. All I will say is that you shouldn't let fear stop you from looking for happiness. Besides, you wouldn't be alone anymore. You would have someone by your side to help you weather whatever storm comes your way."

He shook his head. "I can't. I just can't. I'm sorry."

Pain shaped his features as he stood up again and walked out of the office. I walked after him, stopped by Rosalina's desk, and watched him exit.

She sank in her chair. "I guess that was a no."

Outside, Aaron reached his Jaguar, but he didn't get in. Instead, he laid his head on the roof of the car and just stood there as other vehicles drove past him. After a long moment, he pulled away from the car and turned around to face our building. Rosalina and I exchanged a glance.

I held my breath, expectantly.

Aaron squared his shoulders and walked over with firm steps, a determined expression on his face. He pushed the door open and reentered the office.

"You're right, Toni. The hell with being afraid. I want to meet him."

ꕥ

I waited outside of the ice cream shop minutes before Josh's 2PM shift. I was slurping on the last bit of a vanilla milkshake when the young vampire parked his car at the very back of the lot and walked over, his reflective umbrella in hand.

Besides the trance, this was another part of the process that I found difficult. As easy as it would have been to schedule an "accidental" meeting between two mates who would inevitably fall in love, making my life a lot easier, I couldn't do that.

Not everyone was ready to meet their soulmate. Rosalina was the perfect example. She didn't want that kind of commitment and simply wasn't in the right place for something so serious and permanent. I hoped one day she would be, but I understood that she might not. Some people never were. I just hoped Rosalina and Josh weren't among the latter.

Josh walked slowly, his eyes set on the pavement. He sported the khaki and yellow uniform that all Ted's employees wore. He didn't look like someone who particularly felt like going into work.

I took a step forward into his path, waiting for him to notice me. That same sour sent I'd detected on the vamp at Eric's party wafted from him, making me curious once more. He got very close to me until he noticed my shoes and glanced up. A forlorn expression shaped his face, making him look like a sad puppy dog. But when he caught my eye, he smiled and greeted me.

"Good afternoon." He had a boyish voice to go with his young features.

He started to skirt around me, but he stopped when I returned his greeting. "Hi, Josh. I would like to talk to you about something important."

He blinked in surprise, his shoulders tensed. "How do you know my name?"

I held my palms up. "Oh, it's nothing bad, on the contrary. My name is Antonietta Sunder." I handed over my business card. "I own a tracker agency."

"*Mate* tracker agency," he elaborated, frowning as he read the card.

"That's right. I will not interrupt your day further. I know you have work to do, but I wanted to give you this." I handed over a cardstock envelope with the name of the agency embossed in the corner. "Please, read it when you have a chance. I hope you will find it interesting and decide to follow the instructions at the end of the letter. Have a good day, Josh."

He whirled as I walked away. "Wait." Stretching out his hand, making sure it didn't go past the reach of his umbrella, he offered the envelope back.

My heart sank. He wouldn't even give it a chance. I took it back, feeling terribly sad for Aaron. I started to put it away in my purse when Josh spoke.

"Would you read it for me, please? It's hard for me to read in the sunlight, and once I get inside I won't have a chance."

I smiled in relief. "Of course, I'd love to read it for you."

Opening the envelope with care, I took the letter out and unfolded it.

Dear Josh,

There is someone for everyone. Love isn't a path on which we must struggle. Companionship and happiness are possible when the right people come together.

You may think these words are designed to deceive you, to fill you with hopes that are never fulfilled, but I assure you they are not. My tracking skills are true. I have brought many couples together who have found their "happily ever after."

I don't expect simple words to convince you. So instead, I want to invite you to meet the man who hired me to find you. His name is Aaron, and he is very eager to meet you.

If you have ever felt that everyone you've met isn't quite right for you and are ready for a deep and fulfilling relationship, come to the address below today at 6 PM, and find out what you've been looking for. We will wait for you, but if you don't come, we will understand. The choice is yours.

Antonietta Sunder

I gave back the letter without reading the address and scanned Josh's face, searching for a reaction that might let me know if he would come, but he just looked confused.

"Um, I know it's a lot to process. Maybe a hard decision," I said, taking a step back. "So I'll let you get to work."

A smile stretched across Josh's lips, changing his face so completely that I hadn't realized how deeply sad his expression had been. "Not hard at all," he said. "I'll see you at six."

ဢဣ

Aaron was pacing in the agency's waiting area across from Rosalina's desk. He had changed from his jeans and colorful jacket to a shiny gray suit with a white shirt and purple tie. He looked very handsome and extremely nervous.

I had gone across the street to get coffees for everyone, except Josh who, being a vampire, couldn't consume any food. Aaron's coffee sat untouched on the side table, and I had started eyeing it since mine was almost gone. I tended to eat or drink too much whenever I was nervous.

Rosalina seemed to be the only one keeping her cool. She was more level headed about matters of the heart, whether they involved her or others.

When the clock struck 6:10 PM, I started to get worried.

"Do you think he changed his mind?" Aaron asked just as I started wondering the same thing. "Maybe it's for the best." He sat on the small sofa, staring at the floor. He was clearly disappointed but trying to find some silver lining where there was none.

I opened my mouth to say something when the front door abruptly opened and a figure rushed in and stopped on a dime.

It was Josh Rice, his skin smoking slightly, his hair in disarray.

He hissed, shaking his hands. "Shit, that hurts." Noticing us, he went rigid. "Um, sorry. The sun is almost down, and I didn't want to look stupid with… my umbrella." He trailed off as he focused on Aaron.

The werewolf stood up slowly, his brown eyes fixed on Josh. He looked like somebody who had forgotten how to breathe and blink.

"Hi, Josh, I'm so glad you could make it," I said. I perceived a hint of that strange sour scent on him, but it was disguised by the smell of sweet, ice cream treats.

With difficulty, he glanced away from Aaron. "Sorry, I'm late. Traffic was bad."

He scanned Aaron from head to toe, and self-consciously straightened his yellow T-shirt. Josh was too handsome to be insecure, but he was certainly worried about first impressions, considering that he'd risk getting burned so he wouldn't look dorky with his reflective umbrella.

"It doesn't matter," I said. "If you remember, I'm Antonietta Sunder, but you can call me Toni. That over there is my partner, Rosalina López. And this gentleman is Aaron Blackridge, our client."

Aaron extended a hand toward Josh. "Nice to meet you, Josh."

Josh hesitated for a bit, then took Aaron's hand. I felt electricity spark between them as they touched, and all my concerns about them accepting each other dissolved into a giddy, happy feeling. It happened every time I brought two mates together. The chemistry was immediate and undeniable. It was easy to see in their interlocked hands and gazes, and in the way they lingered on each other longer than should be comfortable.

Josh smiled up at Aaron who was a head taller than him, and that sadness that I'd perceived in him seemed to become something imagined, something that had never been there.

"You work at Ted's?" Aaron said. "I love that place."

"Um, it's just a temporary job until I finish school. I'm studying graphic design," Josh said.

"You are?"

Josh nodded, excitedly. "I love manipulating images. Photographs mainly."

"You'll have to show me some of your work," Aaron enthused.

Rosalina handed me an envelope, another of our embossed cardstock. I took it and offered it to Aaron, who had a hard time glancing away from Josh.

"We took the liberty to make a reservation at one of the best restaurants in The Hill," I said, handing over the envelope. "The details are in here, and all the expenses are taken care of. We thought you might want to spend some time getting to know each other."

This particular place served cold and warm drinks for vampires, elixirs that contained a combination of human and animal blood, all licensed and organic.

"Great idea." Aaron took the envelope and turned to Josh. "Tell me you're hungry."

Josh nodded a bit shyly.

They left after saying their goodbyes, smiling hugely and casting furtive glances toward each other. When they were gone, Rosalina and I practically squealed like we were back in grade school. It just felt so good to make people happy.

Our work here was done. Another lucky couple guaranteed to stay together for life.

CHAPTER 16

The dreaded day came, and the alarm blasted like a banshee screaming in my ear. I batted at it and sent it flying across the room where it kept going, taunting me from a safe distance. I groaned, slid out of bed and onto the floor, and crawled toward it. I poked the snooze button, collapsed on my stomach, and went back to sleep drooling on the carpet.

The banshee screamed again. My eyes sprang open and stared straight at the red numbers. 3:40 AM.

Shit, shit, shit!

I jumped to my feet, adrenaline punching me right in the chest. Without looking, I pulled some of my kickboxing workout clothes out of a drawer, stuffed my feet into my new tennis shoes, snatched my car keys, and ran out of the condo. I got in my Camaro and drove like a maniac through the empty streets, headed west.

A quarter moon hung in the sky. My skin itched at the sight of it.

Great, the mange was moon-activated.

At a red light, halfway to my destination, I took off my pajama shorts and put on the cropped yoga pants I'd snatched. Next, I stuck the sports bra over my tank and pulled the latter out by sneaking my arms out of the straps and almost getting tangled in the mess. The shirt I'd grabbed was made of lace—something to wear to a club, and not a workout, or whatever this was supposed to be—so I opted for my PJ tank. I sped toward Eric's house the rest of the way, ignoring the red lights and praying a cop didn't spot me.

I made it there with three minutes to spare, and ran up the stairs of his slick house, taking them two at a time. I stopped in front of the glass doors, panting. They were closed but slid open as soon as my face flashed in the security monitor.

Warily, I walked inside, feeling like a thief. It was still dark, and I didn't belong here.

I came around the artsy wall that fronted the door to find the area that had held the party looking nothing like it had the other night. There was no dance floor and definitely no disco ball and dancing spotlights. The glass bar was gone as well as the bottle-filled shelves.

Tasteful, modern living room furniture filled the space instead, creating several sitting areas to read, lounge, or receive visitors. More abstract, contemporary art hung on the back wall, and a twisted metal sculpture that resembled chewed taffy separated the area in two.

My eyes roved around as I tried to decide which way to go. Back to the study? I started walking in that direction when a voice boomed overhead, startling me.

"Not that way," Eric Cross grumbled through unseen speakers. "Go to your left, take the steps to the bottom floor, walk to the end of the hall, then take a right."

Good morning to you, too.

I found the staircase, a slick piece of architecture of polished wood trimmed with metal, and a banister made of tension cables. I rushed downstairs, ran down the hallway, took a right into a large room, and skidded to a stop.

Eric stood facing me, his back to a mirrored wall, his hands interlaced in front of him, the wolf ring prominent on his right index finger. He wore loose sweatpants and a sleeveless T-shirt. His arms were slender, yet muscular. Judging by the sweat stains down his gray top, it looked like he'd been working out for hours already. He didn't have the kind of bulk that Jake or Stephen did, but there was no doubt in my mind that he was in excellent physical shape.

He glanced over at a digital clock on the wall, which read 4:00 AM. "You like to live on the edge, don't you?"

My first instinct was to say that I was sorry, but I bit the words back. I hadn't been late. I had nothing to apologize for.

He huffed when I didn't say anything, then encouraged me to move closer with a "come here" gesture. I took two steps in his direction and stopped. He beckoned me again and again, until I stood three steps away from him, too close for comfort.

"How many times have you shifted?" he asked, going straight to the point.

"Once," I answered curtly. If he wasn't going to be friendly, I didn't see why *I* had to be.

He narrowed his eyes. "Damien said he should have applied his spell a couple of weeks ago, which means your wolf has had ample time to make an appearance more than once. This either means that you're strong or that she's weak. I vote for the latter."

Damn! He was good. He'd just insulted me even though he'd called me strong. Whatever, I had no time for this man's dick ways.

I was here to get answers and learn to control this constant desire to burst into fur.

I asked my first question. "Why do you talk about the wolf as if it's separate from me? I thought they were one and the same."

"Yes and no," he answered without elaborating.

Gee! So very helpful.

"Have you had any urges to shift?"

"All the time."

He raised his eyebrows. "So you're fighting them?"

"Yes. I'm afraid to lose control. I don't remember what happened when I shifted."

He paused, considering for a moment.

"Is that common? Not remembering, I mean."

"Not common, but it can happen when… the wolf is powerful. Though, I doubt that is the case with you. There's no telling what Damien's years of spells have done to you. Your wolf was repressed for a very long time, and I wouldn't be surprised if it's broken beyond repair."

"What do you mean?" I asked, panicked.

"Never mind. There is no point in speculating. Let's just find out." He crossed his arms and kicked a foot out, striking a careless pose. "Go ahead and shift."

"Um, what?"

"Shift. Turn into a wolf. You're a werewolf, right?"

I blinked slowly. "I thought you were going to teach me how *not* to shift."

"How *not* to shift?" Eric snorted with exaggerated amusement. "Let me make this clear. Without Damien's spells, *not* shifting is not an option anymore. If he hadn't tampered with you, shifting would have been part of your life since the moment you were born.

If you want to learn to control the wolf, you *have* to shift. You have to let her… be."

I shook my head. "I can't. My life is not that of a werewolf. I don't understand what I'm supposed to do anymore, who I'm supposed to be."

"I'm sorry, but this is not a therapy session. So you either do what I say, when I say it, or we call it a day."

I wanted to argue, but the hardness in Eric's blue eyes told me there would be no point. He felt no sympathy for me, none whatsoever. All he wanted was to clear his score with Damien, and I was just the pesky inconvenience that would allow him to do that.

Despite all of that, I had no reason to doubt what he was saying. He didn't strike me like the kind of man who would lie. On the contrary, he seemed to like telling the truth, especially when it hurt.

I wrung my hands together, digging my fingernails into my palms. Eric watched me with the same irritated expression he'd worn since I'd met him, but he waited patiently until I took a deep breath and spoke.

"Okay, how do I shift?"

"You know how," he said.

"No, I don't."

"C'mon, you've been fighting it all along. I can see it. Just stop, and the wolf will thank you."

I nodded, relaxed my fingers, and let my hands hang limply at my sides. I closed my eyes and rolled my shoulders.

It's okay. It's okay. You can let go.

I waited for a long minute. Nothing happened.

I opened my eyes and peeked at Eric. His mouth was twisted in a sneer, and he was tapping a finger against his jaw, looking disgusted.

"I'm waiting," he spat.

I tried again, closing my eyes.

There's nothing to be afraid of. It's the most natural thing for a werewolf to shift, so just do it. You need to—

A deafening roar filled the room, so loud and strong that I felt its rumble in my chest. My eyes sprang open, and I found a monster standing in front of me, his mouth wide open, his long canines gleaming with saliva as he bellowed in my face.

A wave of energy surged from deep in my gut and washed all over me, causing every inch of my body to come alive like never before. The feeling of release and freedom was unlike anything I'd ever felt, and this time, I didn't try to fight it. I simply welcomed it, invited it, and rejoiced as it spread through my every atom, shaping me into something I should have always been. As the animal took over, I felt exalted and relieved, then it all changed in an instant, and I was pushed aside and tossed down a cliff from which I plummeted into oblivion.

CHAPTER 17

I was shivering. My teeth clicking together like flamenco castanets. I hugged my naked arms and curled tighter into a ball. It did no good. I was still cold as hell. There was a tiny blanket on me and I clutched it closer, tight to my chest, but then my legs got uncovered, so it was hopeless.

I continued to shiver for a while longer until my brain realized that if I wanted to get warm I had to see why the hell my blanket had shrunk. Slowly, I opened my eyes and blinked at a door jamb and the textured carpet on the floor. I was lying on my side, the carpet's fibers scratching my cheek.

When did Rosalina change her carpet?

This one was Berber, for sure, and neither one of us had enough money to afford that.

I rolled over onto my back, which was when I noticed someone looming over me. I scrambled backward on my ass and pressed my back against the wall, clutching what turned out to be a towel and not a blanket. I was naked.

Eric peered down at me, his gaze appearing less icy than I remembered.

"W-what happened?" I asked in a scratchy voice. My throat felt itchy and gritty as if I'd drank a glass full of beach.

"You shifted." His voice, like his eyes, was somewhat softer. He leaned down and placed a stack of clothes on the floor next to my outstretched legs.

My eyes roved around the room until they found the shreds of the clothes I'd been wearing. My brand new tennis shoes looked like they'd been through a paper shredder.

Oh, no! I'd really liked that pair. They weren't cheap either.

"Get dressed," Eric said. "I'll wait for you upstairs."

He walked out and left me staring at the torn shoes. A feeling of loss clawed at my chest that had nothing to do with the shoes, even though I was trying to convince myself that it did.

I snatched the T-shirt from the little pile and slipped it over my head. Then I grabbed the pants, a pair of navy-blue sweats with white stripes down the sides, and found a pair of flip-flops resting underneath them. I tossed the towel aside, got dressed, and stuffed my feet into the overlarge flip-flops. The clothes were baggy, but not too much.

Before I left the room, I glanced over my shoulder at the clock on the wall. It was almost 7 AM. I blinked and squinted at the numbers to make sure I was reading them properly. Three hours had passed, and I had no memory of them.

Heart hammering, I walked out of the room, down the hall, and up the steps. Eric was standing in the middle of one of the sitting areas, cell phone in hand, his thumb scrolling. I stopped at the edge of the rug that delineated the sitting space. I noted he was wearing the same clothes he'd been wearing earlier. Had he not shifted?

The morning sun had started seeping through the thick glass walls. Eric scrolled for a little longer, then pressed the off button and set the phone on an end table. For the first time, I noticed there was a scratch along his left biceps.

"I'll see you tomorrow. Same time," he said, his eyes flicking toward the exit.

"Wait, you're not going to tell me what happened?"

"You shifted."

"I know that."

He huffed as if suggesting I was clueless.

"Okay, I may have no memory of shifting, if that's what you mean, but unless you went to the trouble of ripping my clothes off, I have to assume that's what happened."

Eric's mouth twisted. Clearly, he hadn't liked my "ripping off my clothes" comment, but if he was going to be a smartass, I could be one too.

"Don't push your luck with me," he said.

Something trembled inside me at his words, something that was all new, and I didn't like it at all. Eric was an alpha, and I suspected that my meekness was due to an instinct of self-preservation forcing me to submit to his higher rank.

I gritted my teeth, hating the feeling. I didn't like to submit to anyone. I liked using my voice and being heard. Why should I obey him? If what people said was true, then Eric was nothing but a monster and a murderer, someone who didn't need to be anyone's leader, and who clearly used his strength and ruthlessness to prevail over others.

Pushing through the servile instinct, I said, "I'm here to learn, am I not? So how am I supposed to do that if you won't tell me what happened?"

To my surprise, Eric smiled. It was the first smile I'd seen on his face. It was nothing to write home about, but it changed his face enough to let me see past his hardened exterior. Maybe once, his smiles had come easily, but I could tell they didn't anymore. I'd just met him, and I knew this was a rare moment for him, so rare that when he realized he was smiling, he quickly went back to being serious.

"You're strong, Sunder," he said, using my name for the first time. "And your wolf is too."

I didn't know what to say. Earlier, he'd insulted me with similar words, and now…

He sighed deeply, and his shoulders slumped a little. He looked tired, like someone who had seen too much and had lost all interest in seeing more.

"There are things," he said, "that words can't explain. I need you to be patient and do as I say. Don't question me. I could try to explain but it would be a waste of time. Suffice it to say that your wolf holds the answers you want, and once you're able to remember, you'll know everything, and any words I could waste now trying to explain, would pale in comparison to reality."

I found myself nodding, accepting his explanation because it made sense. If I tried to explain to anyone how the tracking trance worked, my words couldn't come close to describing that shimmering darkness that enveloped me, and the way smells and sounds and sights assaulted me as I involved my every sense.

"Good," Eric said when he saw I understood.

"But I have so many questions," I said.

"Our time for today is up, but you can ask your most pressing question."

This was so unfair. Why didn't he leave time to answer my questions? But I knew why, I was a beggar stealing his time, and the best I could do was to content myself with his scraps. All right… my most pressing question. It jumped to the forefront without me even trying to find it.

"Damien told me to use pain to stop the shift. It works, but just barely. Is there a better way? I'm terrified of hurting my friends like… I hurt you." I pointed at his arm.

He threw a careless glance at his arm, which was already healing.

"You don't have to worry about that today," he said. "Your wolf will be content. Now, go. I have a long day ahead of me."

He picked his phone up and rushed out of the room in the direction of his study.

I headed toward the front door, telling myself not to be dissatisfied. He'd said my wolf would be content today, and he sounded certain about it, so I had to trust him. He was the expert, after all. This temporary reprieve was more than I could ask for from someone who didn't owe me anything.

I walked with my head down, deep in thought, and reached the front door. It slid open on its own to let me out. I took a step forward and, too late, noticed a figure standing outside. Startled, I halted and gave a yelp of surprise. Then the figure lunged forward—claws extended, fangs dripping—and attacked.

CHAPTER 18

The creature smashed into me, wrapping its arms around my waist, and pushing me against the wall that faced the entrance. My back banged painfully against it. Paintings fell from their hooks and crashed to the floor. I crashed down too, the creature falling on top of me, its sharp claws at my throat.

"Where issss it? Give it to me," it hissed.

I cringed, trying to shrink and melt into the floor. I stared at its disfigured face, terrified. The features were drawn back, made sharp and savage. The eyes were all black, huge voids ready to swallow me whole. The lips were pale and thin, set in a gray face that appeared cracked, like ancient stone.

Vampire!

The word hit me like a fist to the chest. I was dead. There was no way I could survive a vamp's attack. Something about the creature seemed familiar. I knew this vamp, but I couldn't remember from where. An overpowering scent wafted from her, something like rot and death with a sprinkle of sourness.

"Give it to me," she hissed again. "Or I'll drain you dry."

Okay, Red, right now would be a great time to show yourself.

My body began to tremble all over, my skin rippling strangely.

Good girl. Now, shift!

Nothing happened. Not even my claws came out. Really?

Bad time to take a freaking holiday, you erratic bitch!

Well, this was going to have to be a groveling kind of task. "P-please don't hurt me," I begged. "I don't know what you want."

"Liessss," the vamp hissed, and lowered her head, angling her mouth toward my neck.

Turning my face away, I pushed against her chest with all my strength, but she was like a slab of marble. I squeezed my eyes shut, resignation and fear mingling in my gut. Yep, I was dead.

Suddenly, her oppressing weight was gone, and a loud crash followed.

My eyes sprang open. I caught a glimpse of Eric standing over me before he bounded away. I sprang to a sitting position like a Jack-in-the-Box, my back smarting with pain. Eric landed next to the fallen vamp and grabbed her by the throat. With one powerful arm, he slammed her against the thick glass wall and held her in place.

"Who are you?" he demanded. "Who sent you?"

The vamp writhed and spat and hissed but didn't answer. Instead, she clawed at his arm, cutting into his skin. Yet, he didn't falter, didn't even flinch from pain.

I scrambled to my feet. "What do we do? Call the cops?"

"No!" Eric shot back.

He lowered the vampire just a bit. Slowly, his features turned wolf-like, fur springing over his arms, ears growing pointed, nose elongating, and terrible fangs unsheathing. Still, he remained mostly human, a trick I was suddenly envious to learn.

"Who sent you?" he repeated in a deafening, blood-curdling roar that made goosebumps ripple across my skin.

I took a step back, fighting the urge to hunker low against the wall like a tiny rodent in the presence of a lion—or worse a freaking dragon. But I managed to stay on my feet, even if I had to hug myself, and my shoulders caved inwardly to help me disappear. The vampire's face twitched, losing its sharp edges and reverting to a more human semblance.

I blinked at her, recognizing her face. "I've seen her before," I blurted out, without thinking.

Eric's pointed ears swiveled in my direction, and without taking his eyes off the vamp, he demanded, "Where?"

"Here, at your party the other night."

He snarled and pulled away from the vamp, letting her go immediately. She crumpled to the floor in a heap and lay there, spent, looking very much like a corpse, except she was a vamp, so that was normal.

"Damn it all to hell!" Eric cursed, stomping around the room, his werewolf features retreating slowly.

"That smell," I asked. "What is it?"

Eric's head snapped in my direction. "What smell?"

"That… toxic rot. I don't know how else to describe it. There's also that sour tang she had the other night, but it's overpowered by the rest."

He looked confused or surprised. I didn't know which. At last, he said, "Most can't perceive that sour smell, not even werewolves."

"My sense of smell has always been good, thank you very much," I said, annoyed that he kept underestimating me. "But what is it? Do you know? I've smelt it on someone else."

"Wherever you've smelled this before, you can expect death to follow."

I rolled my eyes. "Do you always have to be so cryptic? Can't you for once just make sense?"

He huffed, and I thought he might yell at me, but he took a step closer to the vamp and regarded her crumpled body with an upturned lip. "That sour smell, like mothballs in a closet, is the harbinger of death in one who shouldn't have a semblance of life in the first place."

"You mean like… she's sick."

Eric nodded.

I opened my mouth, then shut it again. That was impossible. Vamps didn't get sick. Eternal health came with the territory. Their causes of death belonged in a very short list among cutting their heads off, leaving them out in the sun, and stabbing them with pointy, wooden things right in the ticker.

Except, Eric wasn't the kind to joke—that much I knew about him.

Suddenly, I thought of Josh smiling up at Aaron. He carried the same scent. Did that mean he was sick, too? Questions filled my head, climbing on top of each other, trying to jump to the front of the line. I shook my head, scattering them around and chasing away all possible words.

"She's dying," he added. "Slowly and painfully."

"B-but how is that possible?" I finally managed.

"Raybow," he answered, his eyes fixed on the pitiful creature.

"You mean that shimmering drink you were serving at your party?" I whispered, afraid my question would sound like an accusation.

"I *had* to serve it. Didn't really have a choice, but my bartenders had orders to limit it."

The fact that he had given me an explanation surprised me. He wasn't the kind to offer much in the way of anything at all, but he was unsettled—I could tell by the way his eyes darted around the room as if searching for answers—and that seemed to have loosened his tongue.

The question was… why would someone like Eric Lone say he "had" to do anything. He didn't seem like the kind who could be forced into compliance. Though, Damien Ward *had* forced him into helping me. Maybe Eric just owed a lot of people a lot of favors.

Fearing he would snap out of his shock before he went back to answering in huffs and puffs, I hurried to ask, "What is raybow? The bartender said that it was only for vampires."

He cracked his neck and glanced in my direction. His blue eyes were full of coldness again. I shivered and figured he wouldn't answer my question, but to my surprise he did.

"Raybow, spelled R-H-A-B-O, is a new drug that hit the market a couple of months ago. And yes, it's only intended for vampires. It kills anyone else."

R-H-A-B-O. So nothing to do with "rainbow" as I'd imagined at first.

"A vampire drug," I repeated numbly. It sounded impossible. Drugs didn't quite affect vampires and shifters. The former were dead, and the latter had metabolisms that ran too high to be truly hindered by intoxicants.

The vampire girl stirred and moaned a little. Eric stepped closer, watching her carefully.

I swallowed hard. "And it really kills vampires?"

My thoughts went to Josh again. Was he dying?

Eric nodded. "To them, it's much more addictive than heroin is to Stales, and a hundred times deadlier. Once you smell that sourness. It's already too late."

I gasped. "Oh, no."

He peered at me curiously for a moment, but then turned away, without another word.

"Where is this drug coming from?" I asked.

"I don't know," he said dryly.

Bullshit, he'd been serving the poison right here, helping kill this young vamp, so he had to know the source.

Eric stared at a shaft of sunlight that was quickly inching toward the vamp. There was ill intent in his expression. If the sun hit her, she would disappear in a cloud of ashes that he could later vacuum up with his Roomba, leaving no trace of proof that someone had died here.

"We should call an ambulance," I snapped. "Maybe the healers can do something for her."

Eric huffed. "Fat chance."

He stepped closer to the girl, the same look in his eyes, the look of a cold-blooded murderer.

I had just opened my mouth to say something I would surely regret when Eric slipped his cell phone out of his pocket and dialed three numbers.

"9-1-1 what is your emergency?"

I heard the dispatcher's voice as if she'd been standing right next to me. My hands jerked to my ears.

What the hell?

Standing frozen, I listened to Eric's exchange with the operator. I heard every word she said without difficulty, feeling like a sneaky eavesdropper. From this distance, I shouldn't be privy to what she was saying. Being able to listen to things I wasn't supposed to seemed like a recipe for trouble. As soon as I had that thought, my ears popped, and suddenly, I could only hear Eric. I tried tuning in the operator again, and there she was saying that an ambulance was on its way.

Wow!

I was still grappling with this new skill, when Eric disconnected the call and said, "You'd better leave. Unless you want to be questioned by the police."

Leaving felt wrong, but I had things to do at the office, and police reports would only tie me up. More importantly, I didn't want any record of my involvement with Eric Cross.

"Um, I have a busy schedule today." I hooked my finger toward the exit and walked backward. "Lots of clients to see and potions to make."

I grinned like an idiot while he stared, looking annoyed. Dying vampires, illegal drugs, the police. Nope, I have enough with trying to whip Red into shape.

"Toodles." I wiggled my fingers, turned tail, and ran out of there.

CHAPTER 19

"Holy shit. That sounds intense," Rosalina said as I finished telling her everything that had happened during my visit with Eric earlier that morning. "I don't even know what to say."

I sighed, feeling exhausted. We were at the office, Rosalina at her desk while I sat across from her. After I'd left Eric's, I'd gone back to her place to shower and change. She'd still been in bed, so I'd avoided any questions until we got in my Camaro and drove here. It took me the length of our commute to tell her everything, sparing no detail. Now, I felt much better, though worry and guilt were building quickly.

"I have to talk to Aaron and Josh. I have to tell them that…" I couldn't say it.

"Any chance Eric might be wrong?" Rosalina asked.

I shook my head. "No. The man doesn't talk much, but when he does, he means it."

"Poor Aaron," Rosalina said. "He seemed so happy."

"God, I feel like shit. I mean, Aaron is going to be devastated when Josh…" I couldn't say it, so I just stopped.

"It's not your fault, Toni."

"Isn't it, though? If I had known about rhabo, about what that smell meant, I would have never introduced them. I would've told Aaron that I hadn't found anyone for him."

"Toni, this could happen to anyone. People meet all the time in all kinds of different ways. There are no guarantees that they'll be healthy or decent or anything at all."

"It's different, and you know it."

She sighed and nodded sadly. No matter how much we tried to rationalize it, we both felt responsible.

"I'll call him," I said, feeling dread just at the thought of that conversation. "We'll give him a refund."

Rosalina shook her head, her brow furrowed. "I can't believe there's a drug that can kill vampires."

"Eric said it was worse than heroin."

"That's wild."

But something didn't feel quite right about it. A lot of ideas and questions were bouncing in my head, though one stood out. "Someone must've gone through a lot of trouble to come up with it, don't you think?"

Rosalina considered, then nodded. "It would've required someone smart and a lot of trial and error."

"Yeah. And it wouldn't have been cheap."

We exchanged worried glances.

"Are you thinking what I'm thinking?" I asked.

"That someone wants to purposely kill vampires?"

I bit my lower lip. "Is that crazy? Too *conspiracy-theory-ish*?" I made air quotes.

"The way things have been going lately, I don't think so."

"Maybe I should ask Tom about it."

"Sounds like a good idea."

I rubbed my forehead. "What about Aaron and Josh?"

"Let's find out more, and when we have a better handle on the situation, we'll talk to them."

With that agreement, we got to work, meeting with a middle-aged woman who'd just had her third divorce and wanted to make the fourth husband stick, and after that, screening a couple of new clients. I was sitting in my office, ready to tackle today's mail when I heard Jake's voice in the lobby.

I groaned, burying my face in my hands. I didn't need anything else to worry about, and Jake seemed to always come with a trunk full of problems. A light knock made me lift my head toward the open door. Jake stood at the threshold, almost filling the entire space with his wide shoulders and 6'2" height.

"Hello," he said in his deep, rumbling voice.

His intoxicating smell hit me, and I had to force myself not to inhale to avoid getting drunk on him.

"May I come in?" He had a large paper bag with him that also came with its own delicious smell.

"Well, you've brought food." I gestured toward the back. "Anthonino's burgers, if I'm correct. So yeah, you can come in." I was *that* easy to bribe. One big fat bacon cheeseburger and I would agree to anything.

He smiled one of his crooked smiles, and inevitably, my heart went all squishy and weak, and I forgot how angry I was at him for constantly sticking his nose in my business, even if he'd made it very clear that, despite our dumb attraction, I was not what he needed.

He wore a gray shirt, with the top two buttons undone, revealing a triangle of smooth, golden chest. The sleeves were rolled up to his elbows, and the muscles in his strong forearms rippled as he set the bag on the table and proceeded to take the food out. After handing over a wrapped burger and a box of fries, he ripped the paper bag open and laid it over the desk so we could eat on top of it. He went back out and returned with a couple of drinks.

"I left them on Rosalina's desk," he said apologetically as he took the chair across from mine. "I brought her a burger, too. I just didn't know how she liked it, so it had everything in it. I hope that's fine."

I nodded and smiled. Jake could be so thoughtful, and yet such an asshole. Why couldn't I just find the perfect guy? Both Jake and Stephen had great traits but also such big flaws.

I unwrapped my burger and peeked inside.

"No worries," Jake said. "It doesn't have any onions, but it does have extra pickles and mustard."

There he went, remembering exactly how I liked things. A breath shuddered out of me of its own accord. He glanced up from his fries and met my gaze.

After a moment of silence, he whispered, "I wanted to apologize about the other night."

I said nothing.

"You see," he went on, "I wanted to let you be as I promised I would, but I… I just can't. This is why I don't like promises. They come back to haunt you. When I see that you're in danger, a protective instinct takes over, and I can't help myself."

I huffed.

"Haven't you ever done exactly the opposite of what you intended to do?" he asked.

I almost burst out laughing. I'd *done* him. I still wanted to *do* him, even as my brain screamed that it was the stupidest thing I could possibly do.

"Nope, I wouldn't know about that." I stuffed a fry into my mouth and stared at the ceiling.

He chuckled, knowing perfectly well I was lying. "Things are bad out there, Toni. This brewing war between vampires and werewolves is reaching a boiling point. You know Stephen and Ulfen are at the center of it, but you may not realize that Eric Cross and Damien Ward are also involved."

I froze, poised to take a bite of my burger. Slowly, I set it down and met his gaze. "They are?"

He nodded.

"How?"

"There's this new drug. It came onto the market no more than a couple of months ago, but it's already wreaking havoc. It's at the heart of the conflict in the Skew community."

I swallowed thickly and spoke almost involuntarily. "Rhabo."

His eyebrows went up in surprise. "How did you hear about it?"

"Um, Lucia told me. She heard about it in school."

Jake nodded, satisfied with my lie. High school kids are always in the know, and my sister was one of the "in" kids. She was always up to speed on everything. It was kind of scary, actually.

"But… she didn't know much about it," I added. "What is it exactly?"

"No one knows, but it's clearly the creation of some witch or mage. There's definitely magic in it, some toxic chemicals, too. It's highly addictive, and vampires are dropping dead like flies. As you can imagine, vamp leaders are in an uproar and very focused on finding the source. Bernadetta Fiore blames werewolves. She thinks that whoever created this drug works for them, and she may not be far from the truth. Vampires are out every night, looking for dealers and killing them. Most of the time, they turn out to be werewolves."

"Shit," I cursed under my breath as the magnitude of the problem became evident. "I had no idea."

He gave me a "do you see why I want to protect you?" look, though really, it should have been more like a "do you see why I've been acting like an ass?" kind of look.

"How do Eric Cross and Damien Ward fit into the picture?" I asked, afraid of the answer.

"There are people who think Ward might have had a hand in creating rhabo."

I thought of the large pot on his stove and the lab glassware on his shelves, and it wasn't hard to imagine him brewing rhabo in his fancy kitchen. My moonfable and Jake's inability to smell the wolf in me were proof that the mage had the skill.

Oh, shit! Rosalina would be so disappointed. She was still pretty excited about the mage and even had another date with him in a couple of days.

"And what about Eric?" I asked.

"He was serving rhabo at his party, so he clearly has a connection with the supplier."

Whether or not Eric had been forced to serve the drug, this was an undeniable truth.

I thought of Damien, of how he'd coerced Eric to help me. What if he'd also made him serve rhabo? Eric had supposedly owed him a favor, but what if that had been a lie? What if there was more to it?

"So now you see why I'm worried about you?" Jake asked.

I nodded, if a bit reluctantly. I ate another fry, deep in thought. The news should have killed my appetite, but it was alive and kicking, turned up a notch by whatever had gone on this morning during my "training."

"Rhabo… what a stupid name." I mused.

"It's aptly named, actually. Rh stands for the rhesus factor in blood, and A, B, and O stand for the blood types."

"Oh, that never crossed my mind." I felt really stupid. It seemed obvious now.

"The vamps say that it tastes like blood, except a thousand times better. They say it slithers hot over the tongue and down the gullet. They say it makes them feel alive."

"Wow, no wonder it's addictive."

"It's certainly a hit with those that regret having become vampires and miss that *alive* feeling. They can even order it positive or negative, depending on their taste preference."

"God, this is so messed up." *Poor Josh!* "What about rehab?" I asked.

Jake shrugged and shook his head. "They're dying too fast even for that. One taste seems to be enough to cause an addiction."

"That's insane."

"It really is more like a poison. It feels like there should be an antidote or something," he mused.

We exchanged a glance, his sudden idea seeming quite valid.

"Someone must already have thought about that," I said. "Maybe they're even working on a solution. Don't you think?" My chest filled with hope for Aaron and Josh.

Jake nodded. "It sounds reasonable."

If such a thing existed, I needed it. But how could I find it?

Jake held out his hands, palms up. "Will you listen to me now? Will you stay away from Damien Ward and Eric Cross?"

To pacify him and get him off my back, I wanted to say yes, but the word wouldn't come out. For some reason, I couldn't lie to him.

"Toni, what's going on? What could you possibly have to do with those two guys? I don't understand. Are you tracking someone for them? Because if you are, I doubt it's a mate. Eric became a monster after his family died and remains loyal to their memory. So I know he doesn't *need* a mate. And Ward… he goes through women like… like your sister goes through boyfriends."

For a second, I thought about telling Jake the truth. The words burned at the tip of my tongue, itching to be released. In some ways, maybe Jake knowing would make things easier. Maybe I could tell Eric to buzz off, and I could learn everything from Jake instead. But the fear that stirred in my heart at the thought of what could happen made me bite the truth back. I had no idea what Jake would do, what it would mean to be his mate. Maybe he would expect me to close the agency and focus on building his lineage. Not that I wouldn't enjoy all the sex, but still I needed to know more before I got swept up in the frenzy of a revelation that might alter my life forever. But, despite all my reservations, the next thing I knew… my mouth got ahead of my brain and took it upon itself to ask a stupid question.

"Would you want me if I was a werewolf?"

Jake's eyes widened in surprise, and he looked as blindsided by my words as I felt. My heart skipped a beat as I took in his expression. It seemed to spell N-O in capital letters.

"Never mind." I waved both hands in front of my face. "Stupid question. Erase that. Forget I even asked."

He pushed to the edge of his chair, his gaze drilling into mine, waking up a passion that lay dormant, like an ember that only needed his attention to ignite a roaring fire.

"It *is* a stupid question," he said. "Because you shouldn't need to ask. You know the answer very well." He stood up slowly and leaned closer, one hand pressed against the desk. For an instant, I thought he would haul me over the desk to pull me into his arms, but instead, he took a deep breath and stretched to his full height.

"I don't know why I broke the promise I made you, and I can't bring myself to break the one I made to my father."

I rose to my feet, too, wanting desperately to reach for him, realizing, for the first time, how hard this was for him. Once more, I almost told him that I could be the one to help him fulfill his promise, but again, fear of the unknown stopped me.

"I would never ask you to break that promise," I said. "I shouldn't make things harder. I'm sorry."

He smiled sadly, his chiseled lips tipped to one side, making me ache for a kiss. "I will always love you, Antonietta Sunder," he said, sending my heart into a frenzy. "Please, be careful." With that, he turned and walked out of the office.

CHAPTER 20

Jake and I had never said the "L" word.

Never.

And he'd just dropped that bomb on me and left.

I collapsed on my chair, staring blankly ahead, my heart slamming against my chest so hard that I could hear it with my new, enhanced ears.

I will always love you, Antonietta Sunder.

The words flashed inside my mind in huge block letters.

Jake loves me.

I wasn't alone in this feeling. It wasn't only attraction and passion and instinct. It was more.

More than ever, I wanted to tell him the truth, this secret that should've never been a secret. And yet, despite knowing how he felt about me, I was still scared. My need for answers grew more desperate. If I could understand how my life would change, what it would mean to fully embrace being a werewolf with Jake by my side, then I might be able to tell him everything.

Tomorrow. Tomorrow I would ask Eric everything I needed to know. He would tell me because I wouldn't take no for an answer.

Rosalina appeared at the door. "What did he want?"

I shook myself out of my thoughts. "Uh," I held up one finger, quickly pulled out my phone, and started the music app in case Jake was trying to eavesdrop. "He wanted to apologize about the other day at the party," I said as Freddy Mercury belted "We are the champions."

"You mean for getting you all hot and bothered?"

I narrowed my eyes at her.

She laughed and sat in the chair Jake had just vacated. "You guys didn't eat much, huh?" She gestured toward the burgers and fries we'd barely touched.

I sprang to my feet and began picking up all the wasted food, wrapping the torn paper bag all around it. I threw it all in the garbage can and pushed it away from the desk. Later, I would take it outside and throw it in the dumpster. The smell of food wafting from under my desk always bothered me, plus I didn't want to accidentally leave it overnight to rot. *Ew!*

I sat back down, wringing my hands. "He said… he said 'I love you.'"

Rosalina's mouth dropped open. "Holy crap, Triple T."

"I know."

"So did you tell him you're a… you know. Does that mean you guys…?"

I shook my head and spoke in a whisper. "I need to know more before I take that leap. He still wants to keep the promise he made to his father, and I'm not sure I'm ready to become a puppy factory." I heaved a sigh. "I can tell it's hard for him. I hadn't really seen that before. Maybe I didn't want to admit it."

"God, what a heart job!"

"Huh?"

"You know, like when you say 'what a mind job' but in this case, it's a 'heart' instead."

"O-kay."

"Never mind. It sounded cool in my head."

Trying to forget about the "heart job" and all the other "jobs" that sprung to mind too, I changed topics and told her what I'd learned about rhabo. She listened with rapt attention, her green eyes getting wider and wider with every new bit of information, and they almost popped out when I shared what I'd learned about Damien.

"Maybe you should cancel your date," I said tentatively.

"Like you're going to cancel yours with Eric?"

"Touché."

"I, at least, have to give him the benefit of the doubt. I like Damien, Toni." She bit her lower lip, looking embarrassed and worried by the admission.

"Of course you do, what is there not to like?"

"Right?" She pondered for a moment, then asked, "Do *you* believe he created the drug?"

An idea occurred to me, but immediately I felt like a jerk for coming up with it.

"What?" she asked, noticing my change in expression.

"Nothing."

"I know it's not nothing."

"It's just a stupid idea."

"Spit it out."

I wiggled in my chair. "What if Damien did create rhabo? And what if he has an antidote? Maybe you could find out."

"You mean spy on him?"

I shrugged one shoulder. "I told you it was a stupid idea."

"Maybe it isn't," she said, though not without a hint of dread in her tone.

"I know I should call Aaron and Josh, but what if Damien knows a way to make Josh better? What if we can save him, and they can be together and be happy?"

She half-smiled. "It would be great. It really would." She paused, then added, "I'll do it. I'll keep my eyes open."

"Are you sure?"

She nodded.

"Okay," I said, cracking my fingers as if that would help me build some courage. "Then I'll ask Eric more questions, see what else he knows. If he's involved, like Jake thinks, he might have all the answers we need. And even if he isn't, he certainly knows more than you and me."

Rosalina tapped her crimson-tipped fingernails against my desk, thinking. Finally, she said, "I'm failing."

"Failing?"

"Yeah, you asked me to keep you on a straight path, out of crazy schemes like this, and instead, I just joined your bandwagon. I hope you realize that."

I winced. "You're right. Oh, God. Have I corrupted you?"

"We're screwed."

"Pretty much."

CHAPTER 21

Later that afternoon, I was in my potions alcove inventorying my ingredients to figure out when I needed to schedule another trip to Elf-hame, when my phone rang. I picked it up absentmindedly as I finished typing a couple of numbers into my laptop, which rested on my worktable.

"Hello?"

"Toni Sunder?"

The voice sent a chill down my spine. I thought I recognized it, but it couldn't be. "Yes, this is Toni."

"Ms. Sunder, it's Ulfen Erickson."

Crap. It was *him.* I took a step away from the computer.

"How may I help you?" I asked, a part of me curious about the call, and the other itching to hang up.

"I will be brief. I only have a couple of minutes for this call. I've been arrested."

The what?! Arrested? Why? And why the hell was he calling me *of all people?*

"I'm sorry?" I said, but it came out as a question.

"There's no need for civility. I know well how you feel about me. But this is nothing personal. This is strictly business. I wish to hire you to track someone for me."

"Um, unless you need a new mate, I'm afraid I can't help you, Mr. Erickson."

"I'm willing to pay you fifty thousand dollars to find this person. Upfront."

Holy shit! That was a lot of money, but the right thing was to say no—even if it hurt a little. Well, a lot, really. Fifty grand would pay for a big chunk of our business loan.

"It's not a matter of money," I said. "I'm sorry. I'm afraid you'll need to find somebody else to help you."

"One hundred thousand dollars, Ms. Sunder," he counter-offered.

I almost choked. Rosalina and I would be set up for a while if I did this. I hesitated for too long, and he took advantage of it.

"Come see me, and we can talk about it. I'm willing to offer you a bonus if you succeed." He quickly gave me the details of where he was being jailed. It was Tom's precinct.

I was still trying to find my voice when he hung up. I walked out of the alcove like a zombie. I expected to find Rosalina working at her desk, but she wasn't there. She'd probably gone across the street for some coffee or next-door for ice cream.

Mechanically, still shocked by the call and the colossal money offer, I found myself walking into Jake's office. He was shirtless, kneeling on the floor, tapping a narrow board against another as he laid hardwood flooring. I hadn't been in his office in a few days, and I was surprised by the progress. He wasn't done yet, but he was close. He'd already painted all the walls light gray, finished all the trim, and installed industrial-looking overhead lights that hung from thick cables.

He dusted his hands and stood up, his expression turning to worry as he noticed my lost stare. "Everything all right, Toni?"

"Ulfen Erickson just called me."

He frowned. "Did something happen to Stephen?"

I shook my head. "No. He called me from jail. He's just been arrested. He wants to hire me to track someone for him."

His face twisted in confusion, making him look exactly how I felt. He ran stiff fingers through his hair as he considered.

"Why was he arrested?" he finally asked.

"I don't know. I was so surprised I didn't think of asking, and he didn't say."

He walked to a sawhorse where he'd hung the gray button-up shirt he'd been wearing and stuffed his muscular arms through the sleeves. "What do you want to do?"

"I don't know. He's offering me a lot of money to do this for him, and it's really tempting, but I don't want to get involved," I blurted out, all in one breath.

"I understand."

"You pick *now* to be reasonable. Whatever happened to 'stay out of it, Toni'?"

"This is different. I can go with you. After you find out why Ulfen was arrested, you can decide if you want to help him. You could just hear him out. Maybe he'll tell you something that can help Stephen. His life's still in danger."

"Unless Ulfen is the one trying to kill him, in which case, there's nothing more to worry about."

"True."

I sighed. If I could keep Stephen safe from maniac mages, a short conversation with Ulfen would be worth it.

Jake buttoned his shirt up and took the motorcycle keys out of his pocket. "So?"

"Let's go."

We walked out, and I climbed on behind him, wrapping my arms tightly around his waist. He started the engine, and we took off. Ten minutes later, we were at the police department. Jake decided to wait outside, while I walked in and told the receptionist at the counter that I needed to see Tom Freeman. A moment later, Tom came out of his office and greeted me with a warm hug.

"Hey, kiddo, how are you?"

"I'm good." I smiled, then went straight to the point. It was rude as hell but I was too anxious to hold back. "Ulfen Erickson called me. He said he wants to hire me to track someone for him. He asked me to come."

Tom's brow furrowed. He glanced around, then inclined his head toward his office, asking me to follow. We went in, and he closed the door behind us.

"I wouldn't suggest you take him up on his offer, whatever it entails," Tom said. "The mage that attacked you and Stephen plea-bargained and now he's out on bail. He swore under oath that Ulfen Erickson paid him to kill his son."

"What a bastard! Who would do that to his own son?"

"Who do you think he wants you to track?" Tom Asked.

"I've no idea, but maybe I should talk to him. Maybe he'll tell me something that will bury him deeper." Now, I wanted to spit in his face. That mage almost killed me, too.

"He's not allowed visitors right now. Sorry, kid, I don't think it's smart for you to get involved. Just stay out of it. Go back to tracking mates and staying safe."

That sounded great, but, suddenly, I started wondering if it would be that easy.

"What will happen when they let him go?" I asked. "I'm sure he'll make bail, too. If I refuse to help him, he might take offense and come after me. Maybe if I just talked to him and played nice, he'll leave me alone."

"If he comes after you, I'll kill him." The tone in Tom's voice left me no doubt he would do it.

"I appreciate that, Tom, but you can't be with me twenty-four seven. And Ulfen has plenty of people he can send after me."

Tom winced. He knew I was right. Still, it went against his integrity as a cop to bend to a criminal's demands. After a long moment of consideration, he said, "I guess it can't hurt if you hear him out. Just don't agree to anything, okay?"

I nodded.

"Wait right here," he said and walked out of the office.

He came back ten minutes later and led me down a narrow hall. He opened the last door on the right, and we walked in. Ulfen was handcuffed, his wrists fastened securely to the table, which in turn was bolted to the floor. He also wore a thick electronic collar around his neck, a device designed to impede shifting. His dress shirt looked crumpled, and his red hair stood on end.

I stopped a safe distance away from him. Tom closed the door and stood a step behind me.

Ulfen inclined his head. "Thank you for coming, Ms. Sunder. I had my doubts you would."

"Well, I'm here. What do you want?"

"I already told you. I need you to track someone for me."

"Who?"

Ulfen smiled coldly, then said. "Blake Foster."

I blinked and exchanged a confused glance with Tom. Blake Foster was dead. Ulfen and I, along with a bunch of other people at his charity function, had seen Blake's body hanging from a rope with the word WAR carved in his chest. Why would he want me to track a dead man? Had they misplaced his body?

"You're wasting my time," I said. "I don't track dead people. It's not very pleasant."

"Blake is not dead."

"Curious," Tom said, "because I recall his body lying in the morgue and the physical examiner's report listing the cause of death as strangulation."

"That was not Blake," Ulfen said.

"Even you, at the time, positively identified his body. Did you not?" Tom scoffed.

"I made a mistake," Ulfen said between clenched teeth.

I scanned his hard face, searching for any signs of manipulation, but I didn't see any. Ulfen truly believed Blake was alive.

"What makes you think he's not dead?" I asked.

"Because I saw him." Ulfen lifted his chin and pointedly met my gaze.

"Where? When?" Tom asked.

"It doesn't matter," Ulfen answered. "Just track him for me. A hundred thousand dollars upfront, no strings attached. You can keep the money either way, but if you find him, I'll double that."

Holy shit!

With that kind of money, Rosalina and I would be able to pay our loan outright. And not just that, there would be some money left for advertising, better security, a helper. Hell, there were a million things we could do.

Except, taking money from someone like Ulfen was wrong.

"Maybe you saw someone else," I said. "Someone who looked like Blake."

I expected him to say something like "I know what I saw," but instead, doubt flashed across his blue eyes. I peered back at Tom. He was frowning and looked as confused as I felt.

Why would a man like Ulfen grasp at straws this way, asking me to find a man that everyone knew to be dead—a man whose death Ulfen, himself, might have ordered if he was responsible for Stephen's kidnapping?

It didn't make any sense, unless… Ulfen was innocent. Well, no, he could also be trying to muddle the situation, but I didn't think so. He would've come up with something less moronic than this if that were the case.

"What game are you playing, Erickson?" Tom asked. "If this is meant to be some sort of diversion, it won't work."

"It's not a diversion," Ulfen said, his voice rising in anger. "Just find him, so we can figure out who's behind all of this. I didn't kidnap my son, and I sure as hell didn't order that mage to kill him. Someone's trying to frame me, and I think Blake Foster is involved. He's not dead. He's very much alive, and he may be working with my enemies."

Ulfen took a deep breath, reigning in his emotions, and flexing his neck around the collar as if it pained him.

"Now, will you help me?" he asked, turning to me. "Or will you help those who want to get rid of an innocent man because he stands in the way of their goals? What will it be, Ms. Sunder?"

I shook my head, at a loss for what to say. "I… I don't know. I need to think about it."

Ulfen nodded. "Good, at least you didn't say no. Text my assistant, and she'll get you the item you need to track Blake." He rattled off a number, which I memorized. "If you find out that he's dead, then you prove me wrong. But if he's alive, you'll understand that there's more to this than what some would have everyone believe. The city is changing. I've felt it. You've felt it. Someone is pulling the strings, trying to gain control. And whoever they are, they don't care about the citizens of St. Louis. They only want chaos."

A shiver ran down my spine. I knew in my bones that what he was saying was true. I could see it in the news every day, and this new drug, it only spelled disaster.

Despite the awful foreboding that trickled down my spine, I took a step back and maintained my resolve. "I'll need to think about it."

Ulfen didn't look happy, but there was nothing he could do to force me to change my mind—not here anyway. Though, I doubted he would have acted so restrained if he wasn't cuffed to the table.

"One more thing, Ms. Sunder," Ulfen said. "Please, leave my son out of this. Keep this between us. I don't want him to worry."

ഗ്ദ

Tom and I left the room and walked down the hall in silence. Before exiting into the lobby, we stopped.

"Do you think Blake's alive, Tom?" I asked.

"No," he said without a doubt. "I think Ulfen believes it, but I saw the man's body, and he was quite dead."

"Could magic have been involved in making another body look like Blake's?"

Tom shook his head. The medical examiners work in teams. Both Stales and Skews do autopsies in tandem. There are procedures to tease out that type of subterfuge. Spells are used to ensure that what lies on the table is a body and nothing else. No glamours. No spells. Nothing of that nature."

I had known this in the general sense, but hearing it from Tom seemed to put the nail in the coffin of Ulfen's theory.

"Still, I could try to track him," I said uncertainly. "Ulfen isn't a stupid man. What if he's right?"

Tom frowned disapprovingly but said nothing.

"I wouldn't take his money, though," I added quickly, fearing his judgment. "I don't want his dirt on my hands."

"That's up to you, kiddo," he said. "You know well how I feel about it, but I'm not gonna tell you what to do, and I won't judge you either." His tone was fatherly, and his brown eyes full of understanding.

I smiled, a warm feeling in my heart toward this tough man who could also be so gentle when he needed to be.

"Your opinion will weigh heavily on my decision. I appreciate it," I said. "If I find out anything of importance, I'll let you know."

"Be careful."

"I will be."

"At least Jake's with you. He'll protect you." He chuckled as he walked away back to his office.

I shook my head and smiled sadly. Jake had tried to stay out of sight, but Tom still knew he was here. The walls in this place surely had eyes and ears and even noses.

A minute later, I met Jake back outside. He was reclining on the wall, one boot propped up on the brick. He pushed away and met me by the door.

Just then, a black car screeched to a stop in front of the building and Stephen Erickson jumped out. He rushed in our direction, barely registering our presence.

"Toni. Jake," he said, blinking in surprise. He looked disheveled as if he'd rushed here without first taking a look in the mirror. "What are you guys doing here?"

I opened my mouth to answer, but Stephen cut me off.

"Actually," his eyes darted toward the door, "I can't talk right now. I'll see you all later." He hurried inside, a frantic quality to his rushed steps.

For a long moment, Jake and I stood staring at the door after it closed behind Stephen.

"Do you think we should go with him?" Jake asked, sounding doubtful.

I shook my head. "I don't think we can be of any help."

"Yeah."

"Let's go somewhere," I said. "I need a drink. Badly."

CHAPTER 22

Jake took me to a pub called The Cat's Fiddle. He ordered a whiskey sour and a draft beer for himself. We sat at the farthest booth away from the bar. He watched me closely as I took several sips from my drink.

I licked my lips, enjoying the tartness. I knew there would be no buzz, but at least it tasted good. When I was ready, I told Jake everything Ulfen had said. He listened without interruption until the end and pondered for a long moment before speaking.

"I wonder if Stephen knows about Blake," he said, rubbing his index finger against his closely trimmed beard.

"No, Ulfen warned me not to tell anyone, especially Stephen. Of course, I already told you so…"

"I won't tell anyone. Don't worry."

I didn't trust Jake with my heart, but I definitely trusted him with this. He wouldn't put me in danger. On the contrary, like Tom had said, he would protect me—even if it meant cramping my style everywhere I went.

"Let's assume that Blake is really alive," Jake said.

I liked playing this game. Jake always looked at things from every angle no matter how crazy. He was great at thinking outside the box. *"Even stupid ideas can give birth to genius,"* he'd once told me, and I agreed.

I straightened and pushed my drink aside. "All right, let's assume."

"You're first."

"Hmm, okay. So Ulfen thinks that if we find Blake we'll find the real culprit, the one who kidnapped Stephen and hired Jenson Boyle."

"Which would mean Blake faked his death. Very successfully, I might add."

I nodded. "So successfully that he fooled the medical examiners."

Jake thought for a moment, then his eyes lit up. "Maybe he didn't fool them."

"What do you mean?"

"I mean maybe it was a lot easier than that. Maybe he paid them off."

I gasped. Why hadn't I thought of that? With all the spells and magic and glamours in existence, people tended to forget there were far simpler ways to accomplish things. The good ol' American dollar could work its own magic.

"Yes," I agreed. "That would have been very easy to do."

"Now, the question is why? Blake was, or is, loyal to the Ericksons. He's worked for them for years."

"Since Stephen was little, I'm sure."

"Why would he turn on them?" he asked.

"Money?"

He shrugged indifferently. "Yes, that's always a possibility, but I don't think so. Blake wouldn't risk becoming Ulfen's enemy just for money. There must be something else."

"Extortion? Maybe someone has something on Blake. Or maybe they threatened his family if he didn't do it."

"Could be."

"Does he even have a family?"

"Dunno."

"Or maybe the Ericksons pissed him off."

Jake shrugged and rubbed his forehead, looking at a loss. "Also a possibility. And if he's working with someone, could that be Fiore? Would a well-respected werewolf align himself with a vampire?" He didn't seem to expect any answers to these questions. He just seemed to be talking out loud, which was a good thing because I had no clue, and I was starting to get a headache thinking about it.

"I can do some digging around," he added. "Find out if Blake has any family or friends, talk to them if I find them."

"Don't you have a case you're working on?" I asked.

"Not at the moment. I haven't officially opened for business. I'm still working on finishing the place. Plus there's been a lot going on." He glanced away, looking preoccupied.

I had to remind myself that he'd only arrived in St. Louis a couple of weeks ago. Though, considering everything that had gone on, it felt much longer than that.

"What will you do?" he asked. "Will you track Blake?"

"I haven't decided yet." After our conversation, I was leaning toward doing it, but I wanted to discuss things with Rosalina first.

"Let me know if you do. I'd like to offer whatever help I can."

"Sure, though there isn't anything you can do to help." I gave him a sardonic smile. His help had always come afterward, once I'd homed in on a location for my mark, and we needed to physically track them.

"I wish there was." He held my gaze, narrowing his eyes with distrust. "I wish you would tell me everything about how your skills work."

I made a dismissive gesture with my hand. "It's nothing special. Boring as hell."

"I don't think anything about you is boring, on the contrary."

"Oh, yeah, I'm oodles of fun," I said with a sigh.

He rested his chin on his hand and regarded me with amusement. "You certainly are, especially in bed."

I felt the heat climb from my neck straight into my cheeks like fireworks exploding in all shades of crimson. How dare he bring that up?

Cheeky bastard!

Did he mean it, though? I really wanted to know. God, I hated myself. But I couldn't help it. This man could turn my g-string inside out with only one look. Still, I couldn't let him disarm me like this. Two could play at this game.

I shrugged, trying to appear indifferent to his comment. "And I was just getting started. I'm much more fun now."

It was Jake's turn to turn red, except in his case, it wasn't from shame but anger. His nostrils flared. He pulled his hands under the table as they balled into fists. His teeth ground together. I legit heard them with my enhanced hearing. I waited for him to turn green with jealousy, but maybe that was too much to ask.

Brimming with satisfaction, I placed a tip on the table and stood. "We'd better go. I have work to do and a decision to make, which I need to discuss with my partner."

CHAPTER 23

"That's a screwed-up mess," Rosalina said as I finished telling her what had happened. "You can't get mixed up in that, Toni."

I cringed inwardly at this. I'd been afraid she would say that, which made me realize I'd already made up my mind that I *would* get involved.

"Yeah, it would be stupid," I said, battling with myself, wanting both to convince her *and* to distract her mind so she wouldn't guess my inclination.

Wake up, Toni! Nothing good can come out of lying to Rosalina.

She narrowed her green eyes and examined my face carefully, but a chime on her phone distracted her. She glanced at the screen.

"It's Damien," she said, excitement clear in her voice. "He wants to move our date plans for tonight. He says something has come up, and he can't go tomorrow." A smile spread across her glossy lips.

Knowing I shouldn't, I took the opportunity to distract her further. "He can't tomorrow? I don't think that's the reason. I bet he just can't wait to see you."

She brightened up. "You think?"

"Oh, I definitely think."

I walked away to let her make plans, and as soon as I entered my office, I texted the number Ulfen had given me.

"I'll do it," I typed. "Please drop the item off in the mail slot after 5 PM."

The reply came five minutes later. "Message received."

I quickly put my phone away, feeling dirty, but I rationalized that if I told Rosalina now, I would spoil her date.

A quarter to five, we headed to her condo. As soon as we got there, she busied herself with picking an outfit, showering, and doing her makeup all over again. When she was done, she looked like a billion bucks. She wore a black strapless dress with a sparkly pattern in the shape of roses. Her dark hair fell in perfect locks around her tan, naked shoulder.

"Fancy," I said. "Where are you two going?"

"Dinner at Vicia."

"Wow! He's bringing out the artillery."

When her phone dinged, she grabbed her glittery clutch. "He's waiting outside. See you later."

"Don't do anything I wouldn't do," I called in a singsong voice.

When the door closed behind her, I sat quietly for a moment, feeling like a rotten egg.

Don't do anything I wouldn't do? The worst thing to say considering my plans. I sighed, then went into my bedroom and changed into a comfortable pair of yoga pants, my old sneakers, a tank top, and a light jacket over it. I also packed a small duffel bag with a change of clothes.

"Here you go, buddy." I dropped Cupid's pellets in his bowl. He swam to the top and ate one but ignored the rest. "Oh, so we're in one of *those* moods, huh?"

I rushed out of the complex in my Camaro and snatched two lamb gyros and a large order of fries at a drive-through. I hadn't had a proper lunch, and my stomach had been growling uncomfortably for the last couple of hours.

I parked the car around the block and hurried into the office keeping my head low. I didn't want Jake showing up if he saw my car in front of the agency.

When I made it inside unnoticed, I found a yellow envelope lying on the floor. My hand trembled as I picked it up. It was small but heavy. I took my food and the envelope upstairs to the loft. I focused on my food first and placed the envelope aside on the dresser. I sat on the bed, slurping orange soda, and drowning my fries in ketchup. The gyros hit the spot, and my stomach finally quieted.

After a few moments browsing my phone, I sighed, walked to the dresser, and picked up the envelope. Inside, I found a gold, five-pointed star medal with a woman's profile in the middle and the words "The United States of America" encircling her. It looked like some sort of military decoration. The Medal of Honor, perhaps? I really didn't know.

I didn't like this item for tracking. Not at all.

Would I be searching for an honorable, dead man who should be left in peace?

I shivered, remembering that body hanging over the miniature model at Ulfen's party. If Blake was truly dead, I feared the emptiness I would encounter during the trance. I didn't know why, but it scared the hell out of me. Maybe because I hoped there would be more to the afterlife than a bunch of nothing. I didn't like to think that, after death, everything was over. I preferred to imagine that we moved on to something else, something better. It gave me hope.

But that wasn't the only thing I feared.

I also was afraid of finding that Blake was alive. If he was out there, it meant that things were more complicated than we had imagined. It meant that he was a bad man, and Stephen would have to learn that someone he trusted had betrayed him.

Either way, I had to do this.

Knowing the hard truth was always better than believing a harmless lie.

With the medal tight in my grip, I lay on the bed and, without delay, went into the trance. Darkness welcomed me. I hesitated for just an instant before opening my sense of hearing. When a loud cacophony of sounds flooded me, I realized with dismay that I'd been hoping for a whole lot of emptiness.

Instead, Blake was, indeed, alive.

As I sifted through all the sounds, dismissing them one at a time, I focused on a wet and muffled thudding. It came rhythmically, accompanied by grunts of pain. At first, I couldn't tell what it was, but when my heart started racing, I realized that my instincts knew exactly what the sound meant.

Quickly, I released my sense of smell. I recognized the first scent that hit me immediately. It was coppery and tangy, and it sharply overpowered every other scent.

It was blood, a lot of it.

I shuddered, already knowing that I had to use my sight to pinpoint a location. What I'd gathered so far wasn't enough.

Overwhelmed by panic, I fought to release my last sense. It took a few seconds longer than it should have, and in the end, I only engaged my vision because I feared to lengthen my recovery on the other side of the trance. What I saw when I finally opened my eyes turned my blood to ice.

Blake was standing in front of a man, who was tied to a chair. Blake looked different than I remembered, broader, and with less hair. His face was honed in sharp, wild angles and rage. He wore a blood-splattered, white shirt rolled up to his elbows.

The man across from him was unrecognizable, his face a mangled mess of blood and bruises. His head dangled limply to one side.

Blake's fist shone red as he pulled it back and delivered a vicious right hook to his captive's face. The man's neck and head snapped back with a crack, and a stream of blood shot out of his mouth and sprayed the concrete floor. He moaned and mumbled something unintelligible. Blake smiled, pleased with his work. He cracked his knuckles and delivered another strike, this time to the gut.

Dark blood trickled from the man's mouth as he bent forward. Blake sidestepped, cursing, the drops narrowly missing him.

Horror gripped me at the gruesome sight. Blake was torturing the man and enjoying it. But for what purpose? The man was beyond being able to share anything Blake might want to know, which made me think this wasn't an interrogation, but a spiteful act.

As Blake pulled his fist back again, his eyes full of glee, he delivered an upward punch that collided with the man's nose and sent his entire body backward. The strike contained so much power that the chair tipped and fell, carrying the man down.

I watched with alarm, dimly aware of the ticking seconds as they piled on top of each other, promising a high price for my recovery.

Blake reached for the chair's front legs, ready to right it and continue his savage assault. But just as he started to pull it up, the man started convulsing, his body twitching, his head and tongue lolling to one side, and his eyes rolling into the back of his head.

My stomach roiled, twisting with disgust and distress. I had never seen such brutality, never witnessed the damage one person could inflict on another, never imagined the pleasure a heartless individual could derive from a gruesome death.

Ending the trance abruptly, I reeled back, shutting off my senses to the vile spectacle. I came to, panting and sobbing like a child. Deaf and blind, I curled up in my bed, my eyes squeezed tightly, my hands pressed over my ears as the wet thudding of Blake's strikes echoed inside my head.

Trying to muffle my sobs, I pressed my face to the pillow, rocking back and forth, willing the horrific images out of my mind, trying to think of other things: my car, the home where I grew up, the blue sky, Jake's face.

My breathing slowed, and I calmed down by degrees. Finally, I stopped crying, and I lay on my side, breathing more easily. Without Rosalina to let me know, I had no idea how long I'd stayed in the trance, and how long it would take me to regain my senses. All I could do was lie there, trying to sleep with the sole purpose of shortening my misery.

I fought desperately to drift away, but it was impossible. My mind was working at a thousand miles per hour, images and thoughts flying by one after the next. Questions humping each other and giving birth to more.

Something touched my hand.

Panic gripped me, and adrenaline flooded my system. I almost jumped out of bed, screaming and punching blindly, but something about the gentle touch as it slid up my arm let me know who it was.

Jake.

His fingers caressed my cheek, pushing hair away from my face. I imagined him talking, asking me what was wrong. I rolled over, turning my back on him, and started crying again. The bed dipped, and I felt his body align with mine. I knew it well, and it fit perfectly. He pulled me to him, tightly, protectively. His hand caressed my arm from my shoulder to my wrist and then back again. My breathing eased, and I stopped crying.

In his arms, I finally slept.

CHAPTER 24

When I woke up, the alarm read 2 AM. My senses were back. I breathed a sigh of relief and slowly turned and faced Jake. He was lying on his back, asleep, breathing peacefully.

I watched his handsome profile, feeling a raw ache inside my chest as I resisted the urge to kiss him. His eyebrows twitched, and he stirred a little as if he could tell I was lying here, longing for him.

Suddenly, his eyes sprang open and darted to meet mine. He shifted to his side and rested a large hand on my cheek.

"You scared the fuck out of me," he said. "Are you all right now?"

I nodded.

A worry line appeared between his eyebrows. "You couldn't see me or hear me."

I lowered my gaze, feeling mortified. I hadn't wanted him to know about my side effects, and this was the worst possible way he could have learned about them. Could a tornado please whisk by and scoop me up? Was that too much to ask?

"How come?" he asked. "I think I know, but I want you to explain."

I scooted to the foot of the bed and sat up. There was no point in trying to hide any of it now.

"It's the side effects of using my tracking skills," I started. "I told you already how I can use my senses while I'm in a trance. Well, I can choose to use my smell, hearing, sight, or any combination of the three. But it doesn't come without a price. For every minute I'm under, I lose whatever senses I activated." I shrugged dismissively. "It's no big deal."

The bed shifted, and Jake joined me, sitting next to me. He stared straight ahead at the floor.

"Why didn't you ever tell me?" he asked.

"I thought you would want me to stop tracking. It's a lot easier now. I can handle things better, but I didn't do so well back then. It took me longer to recover and it affected me emotionally. Rosalina has helped me a lot. She has a great calming effect on me and makes things easier."

"This is what you meant when you told me you had lied to me when we were together, isn't it?" He turned and met my gaze then.

I nodded. "I'm sorry. That was a cheap shot."

"I wish you would've trusted me."

I huffed. "Like you did?"

"Fair enough." He heaved a heavy sigh. "Are you sure you're all right? The side effects are all gone? There's no chance it could become permanent?"

I shuddered at that. I would be lying if I said I didn't worry about it. My nonna, who trained me, had reassured me there was no risk of that happening, so I chose to trust her. Our tracking abilities worked differently—she experienced nothing more than fatigue after using her skills—but in her experience and knowledge of other trackers, she believed that using my skills would not permanently diminish my senses.

"Yeah, I'm fine," I said, feeling and sounding certain thanks to Nonna.

"I'm sorry I wasn't there for you when you needed me," Jake said, placing a hand on my shoulder and steering me gently until I was facing him.

After a moment, his gaze fell to my mouth. My body responded with a shiver. Involuntarily, I licked my lips, and that was all it took.

"Fuck it!" He leaned in and kissed me, his strong hands falling to my waist and hoisting me upward until I lay in the middle of the bed.

One of his hands slid up my side while I planted both of mine on his hard chest and returned his kiss. He pulled back from our desperate kissing, and we stared into each other's eyes. His pupils were wide with want. His other hand sneaked under my tank top, moving tentatively, almost unwillingly, as if he were having second thoughts already.

He wet his lips and inclined his head so slowly that it made me ache right in my core. I closed my eyes, anticipating the warm pressure of his mouth on mine. He teased me, the tiniest brush of his lower lip on mine. I reared up and caught his lip between my teeth.

With a groan of pleasure, he settled his weight on me, fitting perfectly between my legs. A thrill ran up my belly as his hardness came to rest on me. He slid a hand under my leg and pulled it up for a better fit. A wave of pleasure rolled through my body. I threw my head back, ready for so much more.

Jake's mouth found my neck. His tongue darted out, licking, sending electricity into every corner of my being. In one motion, he pushed up and removed his shirt. His fine, smooth muscles rippled. My legs trembled with desire. I reached a hand up to caress him, but he snatched it, pulled me to a sitting position, and slowly, enjoying every second of it, removed my tank top. My skin quivered with chills.

Hungry, silver eyes examined my chest. My breath caught as my body responded to his expression of wild hunger. He bit his lower lip, pressed a hand to my shoulder, and pushed me back down. My head hit the pillow. Jake lowered himself on top of me, his erection pressing firmly to my middle. A moan escaped me as he rocked his hips.

Without breaking eye contact, he let his fingers travel up my naked stomach to the edge of my bra. He pushed one strap out of the way and kissed my collarbone. I wrapped my hands around his neck, digging in my nails.

He hissed in pain and pulled back, surprised.

Oh, no! Not my nails. My claws!

I clenched my fists tightly, hiding the evidence, and pushed against Jake's chest. He rolled off of me, and I jumped out of the bed, snatching my discarded shirt, and dug my claws into the palms of my hand. The pain sobered me. I rushed into the tiny bathroom and slammed the door shut. Frantically, I ran my hands under cold water and revealed the half-moon wounds I'd made. I pumped soap into them and hissed at the sting that followed, but that bit of extra pain made the claws retreat.

A stream of blood washed down the sink. I watched in awe as the wounds closed, leaving smooth skin behind without a trace of what I'd done.

Holy witchlights! That was a new one.

I splashed cold water onto my hot face. It hardly felt like enough. I needed an ice bath to put out the heat and desire that was coursing through my body. I wanted to stay locked in the bathroom, but I gathered my courage, slipped on my tank top, and walked back out.

Jake was sitting at the edge of the bed, his head buried in his hands. His shirt was also back on, which sent a pang of regret into my heart.

God, I wanted him so badly, but I didn't have the answers I needed to understand the werewolf world.

"I… I'm sorry," I said. "It suddenly occurred to me that maybe having sex wasn't such a good idea—even if my entire body disagrees with my brain."

He glanced up, straightening. He ran a hand behind his neck, then looked at his fingers, rubbing his thumb over his index finger, peering at the tiny bit of blood I'd drawn. He stood and walked to me, his eyes intense, his desire still simmering.

Crap, if he kissed me again, I didn't think I would have the strength to stop him, and he would find out the truth.

"Um, we shouldn't… you know… it's a bad idea." I wrung the front of my tank top, twisting it like an old rag.

Part of me, like 99.99% of it, wished he would argue and say "to hell with it," but he didn't. He just watched me closely for a long moment, then nodded in agreement.

"I don't mean to complicate things or make things harder for you… and me. It's just," he paused and pushed a strand of hair behind my ear, "I lose my head whenever I'm around you."

"Ditto." I smiled sheepishly.

He smiled back, his eyes tender and full of love. My heart ached, twisting on itself so intensely that I gasped for breath.

The words "I love you" perched on my lips, but I held them back. Right now, they wouldn't make any of this easier, and maybe, once I knew what I should do, I would be glad I'd held them back.

If I decided that I didn't want to be with him, not saying them would be for the best. But if instead, I decided to be his mate, then I would be able to tell him without any concern about what might happen next.

He took a deep breath, his broad chest expanding. "I think it's better if I leave."

I nodded.

"I'll be right next door if you need me." He walked toward the steps, then paused with his hand on the railing. He shook his head and gave a derisive laugh. "This goes to show you how you affect me and make me forget everything, but… did you find Blake? Is he alive?"

I matched his derisive laugh because I had also completely forgotten about the awful experience, and now that he brought it up, the horror of what I'd witnessed hit me all over again, and all I could do was nod, as I squeezed my eyes shut and tried to put the images of that mangled face out of my mind.

"Fuck, so Ulfen was right." Jake forgot about leaving and walked back. "Do you know where to find him?"

I shook my head. "No. I couldn't come up with a location. Um," I searched my memory for something other than the blood and Blake's gleeful expression, "he was in some sort of warehouse, I think. He was beating a man to a pulp. I believe… I watched him kill him."

"Oh, Toni. I'm sorry. That must've been awful."

"It was. He was enjoying himself so much, beating him with his naked fists."

"Did you recognize the man?"

"No. His face was destroyed."

Jake winced. "I hate that you had to see that."

"I always thought Blake was a good man, but no good man could do what he was doing. I wish I'd been able to see more, so we could find him."

"Don't beat yourself up about it, okay? You did what you could. Just call Tom and let him know what you found out. He can tell his men to be on the lookout. I'll see what I can find out, too. Earlier today I made a list of people I can ask and places Blake was known to frequent. Maybe I'll find him."

I stepped forward and snatched Jake's hand. "Don't. Please, don't look for him. He's a monster. I don't want you to get hurt."

Jake gave me an amused smile that seemed to say "Don't be silly, little girl. No one can hurt me." Oh yeah, he thought he was such a big bad wolf, and no one could harm him or ever get the drop on him, but he hadn't seen Blake's savagery, that terrible hunger to cause pain and see his victim's suffering.

"I'll be fine. You don't worry about me."

I narrowed my eyes at him. "I've been asking you not to worry about *me*, but you don't listen, so why should I?"

"That's different. I'm a werewolf, Toni. I can rip a man's head off if I want to. You, on the other hand, are vulnerable."

If he only knew. Though I still had to learn how to control the shift, then maybe I'd also be able to rip someone's head off—not that it was something I looked forward to doing.

"Are you sure you'll be all right? I could stay. There." He pointed toward my papasan chair.

I would have loved for him to stay—in the chair, or preferably, on top of me—but we'd already determined that was a bad idea. And more than that, I had to get up in a couple of hours and go to Eric's place for my second training session.

"I'll be all right. I'll scream bloody murder if I need you."

"I'll lock up on my way out." He backed away, nodding, and went downstairs taking slow, reluctant steps. With a mind of its own, my mom's protection spell had started allowing him in, so there was no keeping him out.

The bell chimed as he exited, and then there was silence. I went back to bed and tried to sleep, but before I could catch a wink, the clock struck 3:30 AM, and I jumped out of bed and drove to my second meeting with Eric Cross.

CHAPTER 25

Eric was waiting for me in the same, bottom-floor room of his modern mansion. Like yesterday, he wore sweaty clothes that told me he'd already been through an intense workout of some kind. He stood with his hands behind his back.

I set my duffel bag down on the floor and greeted him.

He ignored my good morning and got right to business. "Any urges to shift since I last saw you?"

"Yeah," I admitted with a wince.

"What caused it? Anger? Fear?"

"No. Um, it was… lust."

He raised an eyebrow. "That'll do it."

Coming closer, he brought his hands forward, holding a strange contraption in one of them. I frowned at it. It looked like some sort of metal circlet with spikes on the inside.

"What the hell is that?" I demanded, taking a step back.

"Something that will help you remember what happens while you're in your wolf form. Give me your wrist."

It was my turn to put my hands behind my back. "No way. That looks painful."

"That's exactly the point." His blue eyes twinkled with amusement.

"Nope. Not doing it."

"Then our agreement is over. You have to do what I say."

Shit, that *was* one of the conditions.

"Fine, but I want you to answer some questions first."

"*Pshaw*, you don't set the terms, little wolf."

"Oh, yeah? Then I'll tell Damien you're not preparing me properly, the whole point is to train me to be a proper werewolf, and in order for me to do that, I need to understand stuff, so I have questions, and I need answers now."

His chest rumbled and his upper lip twitched, flashing one fang. My heart skittered, and I fought the instinct to submit to him. I defiantly raised my chin and puffed my chest.

Eric held my gaze for a long moment, a blue light flashing in the depths of his pupils, his chest rumbling without interruption like a truck engine.

At last, he threw his hands up in the air. "Okay, fine. Ask your stupid questions." He sank to the floor, crisscrossing his legs and setting the bracelet from hell on the carpeted floor.

I blinked down at him, then awkwardly sat, also crisscrossing my legs and resting my wrists on folded knees.

He waited with an expression of annoyed boredom. "Well, let's get this over with."

"Um, all right, my questions mainly pertain to… mates."

"But of course." He rolled his eyes, looking disgusted. Not his favorite topic, it seemed, but I wouldn't let him embarrass me. If he was a sourpuss about the subject, that was not my fault. Not everybody was an embittered sociopath.

Sheesh, Toni! The man lost his family, have some sympathy.

"What is the role of an alpha's mate?" I asked.

He frowned and cocked his head to one side, looking curious. "You just found out you're a werewolf, and you already have your sights set on an alpha male?"

"You're supposed to answer *my* questions, not the other way around."

"You're infuriating, you know that?"

I shrugged. "I've been told that once or twice, but I really don't give a shit what people think."

He sniffled and let out a little exhale through his mouth as if to calm himself down. *He* infuriated *me*, so I was glad to repay the favor.

"Wait a minute," he narrowed his eyes at me, "I saw you with Jake Knight at the party. That's the alpha you're referring to, isn't it?"

I clenched my teeth, refusing to answer.

"Fine," he snapped when he realized I wasn't going to say anything. "An alpha's mate's main duties would be to help him continue his lineage by providing strong and healthy offspring. If this alpha leads a pack, it will also be the mate's responsibility to provide support to his rule, and to ensure that he puts his pack first, all the time, above anything else, including his own family." Eric's jaw clenched tightly as he said the last few words, making me wonder if putting *his* pack first had resulted in the death of his family.

"Is that all?"

"Hardly, an alpha's mate must always obey without question, something I don't believe you would be capable of, given your personality. Walter Knight's pack is quite old-fashioned, and their females are supposed to behave according to many outdated values."

Walter Knight, Jake's grandfather who I'd met only a few days ago, was the pack's leader from the sound of it. Was he expecting Jake to take over?

"Females are expected to stay at home, raise the children, and ensure that their mates and the pack have everything they need."

"That's stupid," I huffed.

"It is what it is," Eric said. "The Knight pack has a certain reputation. It has been weakened for some time, but in the past few weeks, there have been rumors. Things are changing. They're recruiting, increasing their numbers. Jake is expected to replace his grandfather soon." He paused and a smile of satisfaction stretched his lips as he added, "As soon as he picks a mate, that is. His grandfather has put the word out. He seeks an alliance to strengthen his pack."

"You mean Walter is pimping Jake out to other packs for power?"

Eric nodded.

My heart sank. I didn't have a pack that Walter could use to prop his numbers up, so the fact that I was a werewolf would mean nothing to him.

"I can tell you've done the math," Eric said coldly, not an ounce of sympathy in his tone. "Maybe you should consider yourself lucky. Pack life isn't all that it's cracked up to be. Besides, it wouldn't be easy for someone like you. You wouldn't understand the way they do things. You weren't raised that way. If you want my opinion, you would be better off as a lone wolf."

"Do you get off on being mean?" I blurted out, trying to hold back the tears that stung the back of my eyes. Except, I was unable to, and they spilled forward along with my shame. I didn't want to cry in front of this cruel man. I jumped to my feet, angrily wiping my face and squeezing my eyes tightly.

He rose with me. "Don't cry." His request was curt as if I had no right to spill tears in front of him and make him feel like the asshole that he was.

I inhaled sharply and held my breath, fighting the emotions that whirled inside my chest like raging tornadoes. So much had happened in such a short time. I'd found out I was a werewolf. I had tracked a mate for Aaron, but he was dying. Jake had told me he loved me, but we couldn't be together because, even though I was a werewolf, I still didn't amount to enough.

Biting my lower lip, I tried to reign in my feelings, but they all came loose, tumbling down in a shower of tears.

"I… I'm sorry," Eric said. "I don't deal well with matters of the heart. I haven't stopped to think about such things in years. I didn't mean to hurt you. Please, stop crying." His voice grew low as he spoke until it was only a whisper that rang with sincerity.

I glanced up, blinking through my tears. He was staring at the floor, looking embarrassed and even regretful. I saw no pretense in his expression.

I dried my face and found that the urge to cry was suddenly gone. "It's not your fault. You were just telling me the truth."

"The truth that *I* understand, anyway. I don't really know Jake Knight. We've been introduced, but that's it. For all I know, he doesn't care about the same things that his grandfather does, so just ignore me. At any rate, you're not here for that kind of advice. You're here for this."

He held out the metal bracelet. Up close, I could see the fine points of each spike inside of it. They looked very sharp as they gleamed under the overhead lights. Part of me wanted to shrink away from the terrible contraption, but Red felt quite different.

"Let's do it," I shot back.

Eric raised his eyebrows, surprised, then he nodded and undid the band's clasp. A small hinge kept the two halves together as he opened the circlet. Fearing I would lose my courage, I thrust my wrist forward and turned my face away, like I did whenever they drew blood on my yearly check-ups.

But he gave me no time to think about it twice and quickly snapped the bracelet around my wrist, sending its many spikes cutting through my skin. I howled in pain as the needles embedded themselves deeply. The scent of blood filled the air.

Jerking back my arm, I desperately tried to undo the clasp. Blood made my fingers slick and obstructed my view.

Eric slapped my hand away. "No! Feel the pain."

"I do. I fucking do. Now, take it off."

He shook his head and smiled crookedly. "No."

Instead, he snatched my wrist, wrapped his hand around the bracelet, and squeezed it tightly, causing the spikes to dig deeper. A growl of pain rose up my throat, and I tried to yank my hand away, but Eric held me in place, the struggle only making the pain worse.

"Shift," he ordered.

I shook my head. "I can't. It hurts too much."

Pain kept me human, grounded. I could think of nothing else but the terrible agony of those needles embedded in my flesh, and the streams of blood running down my fingers. What if I bled to death? The needles had cut into my veins, piercing right through them.

"Take it off, please," I begged.

"Fight through the pain. Focus on changing, on the power that stirs in your chest. Can't you feel it?"

I couldn't feel anything but the agony at my wrist, and the only thing I could focus on was taking the bracelet off.

"Let me go," I growled through clenched teeth.

"No!"

Still holding my wrist, Eric jerked me toward him, causing the bracelet to shift. The pointed spikes cut across my flesh. More blood poured out.

Another cry of agony tore through my throat, but as it reached its peak, it turned into a roar. Eric finally let me go and, grabbing my shoulders, forced me to face the mirrored wall.

"Look at yourself," he said, pushing me closer.

I did, and my entire body shuddered in shock. What I saw in the mirror was not me.

CHAPTER 26

The image in the mirror was unrecognizable.

Its eyes were glowing with a faint yellow light. Inch-long fangs had sprung in place of the four canine teeth, crowding the mouth and making it impossible to close it. Its cheekbones had elongated and dark brown fur rippled over the neck.

I shook my head in denial. That wasn't me. Not me. I dropped to my knees, fighting the change, searching for the thread of my pain. I had let it go, and I couldn't find it. Taking a page from Eric's book, I clasped my hand over the circlet and, shutting my eyes, squeezed it hard. I waited for the pain to flash through me, but nothing happened.

My eyes sprang open and stared at the bracelet. Now, it encircled, not my wrist, but a large paw tipped with razor-sharp claws. As I watched, my other hand shifted, the fingers shortening, curling into themselves and springing thick fur. I watched in amazement, thinking that the transformation should hurt, but it didn't. Instead, it felt good. Though "good" wasn't the right word.

I searched for another, then realized there was no way to describe what I was feeling.

The wealth of sensation encompassed too many things. It felt natural, overdue, right, liberating, and damn thrilling.

Giving into the rightness of it all, I forgot about the pain and watched as my body changed in one smooth, unerring ripple.

My ears elongated. They stood tall and proud and twitched as a layer of soft fur spread over them. My clothes ripped and fell away as my muscles thickened. I should have felt horror when my knee joints changed directions and my legs shortened several inches, but I only felt delight and admiration for their perfect shape and strong muscles. Not even the furry tail that sprang at the tip of my spine fazed me. Instead, as soon as it was out, everything around me seemed to become perfectly balanced, making me wonder if before the world had been off its axis.

When the transformation was complete, I cocked my head, watching the beautiful wolf that stared back at me from the mirror. I stepped closer, nose twitching, eyes roving all around the strange creature.

A whimper sounded in the back of my throat, and I took a step back, lowering my head growling slightly.

Eric moved closer, drawing my attention. "You're beautiful, don't you think?"

I glanced back at the mirror, unsure.

"Don't be afraid. It's just you. Doesn't it feel right?"

It did. It felt… incredible—the way a fish must feel when it's thrown back in the water after being caught.

"Here, let me take this off." Eric knelt by my side and carefully leaned down to remove the band that still clung to my paw. When he unclasped it and opened it, the spikes slid out sending a flash of pain up my leg.

I jumped back with a yelp and snapped my teeth at Eric, who pulled back immediately, putting some distance between us. I limped away, holding my injured paw up. Without thinking, I started licking the blood off, my long tongue lapping over the many tiny wounds. A metallic taste filled my mouth. Some small part of me cringed in disgust, but the lapping motion was incredibly soothing. When I was done licking it clean, I realized that the wounds had disappeared. I set my paw down and found that it didn't hurt anymore, and I could walk without limping.

I peered up at Eric, who was watching me with interest.

"Ready to run?" he asked after a moment.

Smoothly, he shifted, his hands falling to the floor and changing to paws before he touched down. The rest of his body rippled with the transformation. It was done in an instant, like a graceful bird taking flight—nothing like my clumsy change, which seemed to have happened in stages.

Almost in the same motion, the tawny wolf ran out of the room. He was only slightly bigger than me, but the power that emanated from him made me feel much smaller. I tried to follow after Eric, but my steps were clumsy like a baby deer.

What the hell?

I stopped, wobbling, feeling I would trip all over myself if I tried to run.

I blinked at the long hall, looking for Eric, but he was gone. I took another few steps, but stumbled and slammed against the wall. Eric came around the corner and glanced at me down the length of the long corridor.

He jerked his head as if telling me to hurry. Pressure built in my temples, like a headache trying to push its way through. I shook my head, my ears flapping. Another push came, then words formed inside my head.

"Don't think too much about it. Let the wolf take over."

Huh? My eyes darted to Eric's.

"C'mon," the voice said, "you had no trouble running yesterday. Let your wolf take the reins."

Eric was talking inside my head! My hackles raised. Literally. Because now I had them, which was weird to think about.

"How?!" I demanded. "How are you doing that?"

"I'm an alpha. Only alphas can push thoughts into other werewolves' heads. We can also hear everyone's thoughts back," he said in explanation. "Now, run." He disappeared again, giving a bark of encouragement.

Wow, that was wicked. Alpha's were telepathic, and Jake never told me. *What a dick!*

Pushing that thought away, I stared down at my paws and moved them one at a time. My back legs responded in unison.

Don't think about it, Toni. Just do it. Just go!

I inhaled deeply and let my mind go blank. Without hesitation, as soon as my human instincts were out of the way, Red took over and I sprang into a run.

When I turned the corner at the end of the hall, I searched for Eric, sweeping the open area. At the back of the room, he stood next to an open window, and as soon as he saw me, he leaped through it and disappeared. I rushed after him and, still six feet away from the opening, jumped and sailed smoothly through the air and out the window. On the other side, I hit the ground running, my paws welcoming the earth's supple feel. A wall of thick trees welcomed me.

My nose twitched as I lifted my muzzle up in the air and caught Eric's scent. I went after him, following up a tree-dotted, steep hill. I leaped over fallen logs and rocks, my sharp eyes set on Eric's darting figure.

Catch him! Catch him!

The instinct to hunt him was strong. My legs pumped under me, kicking back dirt and dead leaves. Tree trunks blurred at my sides as I sped by them. Up ahead, Eric stopped and glanced back as if taunting me. My instinct redoubled, and I ran faster still.

He turned tail and started running again. Somehow, I sensed his surprise as the distance between us shrank. I gave it all I had. I would not let Eric with his arrogance and rude behavior show me up. He had no idea who he was messing with.

I was Antonietta Luna Sunder. I never gave up.

Energy thundered through my legs as my resolve grew. In a minute, I cut the distance between us in half. I snarled, letting him know I was close. He shifted directions on a dime, and I turned abruptly, narrowly missing a tree as I changed course.

My breaths came hard and even. My claws tore the ground as my powerful limbs strained to the max. Then I was on him. His tail an inch from my snout. I snapped my teeth, narrowly missing him.

Eric stopped and whirled on me, his fangs bared as he growled with savage anger. I snarled back, circling around him, teeth snapping, paws clawing at the ground.

"Heel," Eric's voice resonated inside my head, trying to break through my anger.

"No!" I shot back, my teeth snapping as I lunged forward, intent on tearing a chunk off his smug face.

"HEEL!" This time, his voice roared inside my head, while his growl nearly rattled my every bone.

Fighting my wild instincts, I lowered my head, gnashing my teeth together as I submitted to the order. It went against every fiber of my being. It sucked being an omega.

Gratefully, the small voice of reason inside my head prevailed.

He can tear you to pieces, Red. You're nothing but a pup compared to him.

The wild anger that raged inside gradually passed. My breaths slowed, and after a moment, I found that I had no reason to fight the other wolf. It had been stupid to think I was hunting him when he was not prey.

I lifted my head and sniffed the air.

Eric relaxed and turned away. He walked over to a large boulder and sat next to it. I joined him and settled by his side. We were at the top of a gentle slope that dived into a small, gurgling creek. A quarter moon hung high in the sky, and a cool breeze rattled the tree branches above us.

The tawny wolf howled, stretching his neck up, his voice mournful and compelling. Before I knew what I was doing, I was howling, too, feeling as if I were releasing years of pent-up frustration and unfulfilled dreams—dreams that my wolf had thought would never come true.

But now…

Here she was, free at last, and no one would ever leash her again.

ᢀᢁ

Back in Eric's house, he shifted from one step to the next, clothes appearing in place as he did so.

Huh? How?!

"Shift back," he ordered, his back to me.

I had only one second to wonder how I could go back to my human shape, when my body elongated, my claws and fangs sheathed themselves, and my fur disappeared. I snatched my spare change of clothes from my duffel bag and put them on in a hurry.

"You're going to have to teach me how to keep my clothes on," I said, stuffing my arms into my T-shirt.

He scoffed. "There's nothing to teach. In case you haven't noticed, I wear a shifter ring."

I slipped on my pants. "Shifter ring?"

Eric turned to face me and held up his right hand. "A witch made it for me, its only magical purpose is to spare my clothes every time I shift.

"Neat! Where can I get one?"

"I doubt you could afford it. They don't come cheap."

"How much?"

"Five hundred thousand dollars."

I choked. "You're right. I don't have that kind of money. Naked it is."

Eric took a step closer, his blue eyes holding a question. "Well, do you remember yourself? Your wolf?"

"I…" I stopped, unable to answer as a landslide of memories suddenly washed over me all at once.

I saw myself in this room, yesterday, shifting, going wild. I'd attacked Eric, but he'd run out of the room, forcing me to chase him back into the woods. There, I managed to scratch him once, but he mostly stayed ahead of me, issuing orders that I wouldn't heed. Instead, I had run until I tired myself out and passed out from exhaustion. Interesting!

After that, different images of Damien and Mom's face flashed before my eyes. Damien looked the same, but Mom kept getting older in each of them. It took me a moment to realize I was seeing all the times that the Copper Mage had put his spell on me.

Next, I was at the repair shop the night Jake and I rescued Stephen. I remembered turning and fighting a massive shifter in the shape of a gorilla. Then I'd helped Jake. He was injured. Two vampires were on him, and I…

Oh, God!

I took several steps back, a hand flying to my mouth as horror washed over me.

"I take that as a yes." Eric stepped closer. "Are you all right?"

"I killed someone," I said, my voice trembling. "The first time I shifted, I killed someone."

He frowned but didn't look concerned. "Did they deserve it?"

"What?!"

"Did they deserve to die?" he repeated.

"That's not the point. The point is that… I'm a murderer."

He shrugged. "Then do us all a favor and turn yourself in."

My breath shuddered as I inhaled. I started backing away.

"Um, actually, don't turn yourself in." Eric scratched the back of his neck. "That was a joke."

I ignored him and kept walking, a feeling of terrible anguish building in my chest. I had killed someone. How could I live with myself knowing that I'd ended someone's life? I grabbed my duffel bag and headed out of the room, feeling lost.

Eric joined me. "Who was it?"

I didn't answer for a long moment and kept walking down the hall, but suddenly the tremendous need to tell someone, to unload the awful guilt that had suddenly dropped on my shoulders, took hold of me.

"It was a vampire. I…" I paused, wanting to omit the details, but I pressed forward. "I snapped his head off with my bare teeth."

"You what?!"

Bile rose up my throat as I remembered the bitter taste of the creature's blood in my mouth.

"Two vamps had cornered Jake," I said. "They were going to kill him. I couldn't let that happen. I had to help him. He was already injured and—"

"It sounds like you had no other choice," he cut me off. "But you don't have to explain yourself to me. If you killed a vampire, all I can say is *good riddance.*"

I whirled on him, anger fizzing up like a chemical reaction. "How can you be so callous? Just because you can go about eradicating entire packs doesn't mean that others have no scruples." Too late I realized what I was saying and snapped my mouth shut.

Eric's eyes narrowed, and his upper lip twitched. His blue gaze grew colder than I'd ever seen it. For a second, he struggled to restrain himself, clenching his fists and quaking on the spot. But then he lost it, and in a flash, he was on me, his hands around my neck as he pushed me against the wall.

He spoke between gritted teeth. "Don't you dare talk about things you don't understand."

"I'm sorry," I said in a raspy voice.

Sheesh! Did I have a death wish? Yeah, go ahead and piss off the vengeful wolf. Very smart, Toni.

He released his hold a tiny bit, enough for me to catch my breath.

"I was out of place," I managed to say.

Disgusted, he let me go and stormed away.

"Wait," I called out, panicking. "Can I come back tomorrow?"

He grunted and kept going, which I assumed meant "yes" since he hadn't responded with an angry roar. Now that I knew what I was capable of, I needed to learn how to control myself more than ever.

Then, I remembered I was supposed to ask him more questions about rhabo, but I'd totally forgotten, and now he was mad at me. *Way to go, Toni.*

CHAPTER 27

My mind heavy with remorse after having lied to Rosalina about tracking Blake, I keyed the lock to her condo and walked in. My heart jumped in my throat as she stormed in my direction and wrapped me in her arms.

"Oh, thank the witchlights you're okay!" Her hold on me lasted for only a second, though, and in the same breath, she pulled away and demanded, "Where the hell have you been?!"

"Uh, at Eric's."

She scowled. "Before that. The rest of the night, I mean."

I winced. Lying never paid off. Sooner or later you got caught.

"I was at the office, um…"

"Don't you dare try to come up with a lie." She pointed a finger straight at my nose. "Never mind, I know what you were doing." She whirled and headed into the kitchen.

I scrubbed at my face, feeling terrible. I followed after her and stood by the kitchen table, watching her set the coffee maker.

"I didn't want you to worry," I said.

She huffed, her expression telling me she had worried anyway.

"I had to do it. I had to find out." I waited for her curiosity to get the best of her and ask me if I'd found Blake, if he was still alive, but she walked toward the refrigerator and pulled out a carton of eggs and a container of Greek yogurt without as much as a peek in my direction.

"Ulfen was telling the truth," I blurted out, hoping the shock would undo her anger.

It didn't.

She had never been mad at me. Never. I didn't know what to do. I pulled a chair out and sat, burying my face in my hands and feeling exhausted. The last twelve hours had been an all-around nightmare, and now the only person I trusted one hundred percent was mad at me.

"Um, Jake came over after the trance," I said, trying a different angle. "He caught me in the worst of it and learned about the side effects."

I peered at her face expectantly. Still nothing.

She came to the table and sat across from me. The coffee pot gurgled and that unique aroma filled the air. I uncovered my face and met her green eyes, which were filled with disappointment. My heart twitched. I could handle her anger much better than this.

I had never lied to her, and I would never do it again.

"I can tell you're disappointed as you should be," I said. "I fucked up. Lying to the only person who always has my back was stupid, but I didn't do it out of malice. I just didn't want to ruin your date night."

She said nothing to that. Instead, she set her hand on the table, palm down, and pushed something in my direction. When she removed her hand, a small baggie filled with glittery powder was left behind. An image representing a bleeding heart was imprinted in one corner of the bag.

"That's rhabo," she said.

"What? How? I'm confused. That powder is rhabo?" I babbled, eyes wide in surprise.

"I got it at Damien's." Her face crumpled, more disappointment washing over her. "We went to his house after our date. Things had… progressed, and he invited me over to spend the night."

Holy crap! Rosalina went out a lot, but she was extremely picky about who she let into her bed. She must really like Damien if she'd decided to take that step.

She heaved a sigh. "There were hundreds, if not thousands of those bags stacked on top of a table inside a room that looked like a mad scientist's lair."

Shit!

"When we got there," she forced a smile, "he got a phone call and had to step away. That's when I decided to take a look around. It wasn't hard to find. It was out there, in the open. The door to the room wasn't even locked. I didn't know what it was at first, so I just grabbed one and slipped it into my pocket. I had a bad feeling, though, so when he came back, I asked him to bring me home, told him I wasn't feeling well. He looked disappointed but behaved like a gentleman about it. I got here around one to find that you were gone. I tried to call you but your phone went straight to voicemail."

"My first guess was that you'd gone to the office and fell asleep. But since you said you would never sleep there again after you got attacked, I thought maybe you went to your mom's or your sister's, so I went to bed, but I couldn't sleep. Then I tried to call you again around 3:45 'cause I knew you would be up, driving to Eric's, but I got your voicemail again."

I winced. "I turned my phone off before I went into the trance, and I forgot to turn it back on. I'm sorry."

She shrugged. "It's fine. You're a big girl. I shouldn't worry."

I shook my head. "No, it's natural, especially since I'm staying with you. If it were the other way around, I would've worried, too. We're supposed to look out for each other. I'll keep that in mind from now on. It was inconsiderate of me."

We were silent for a moment, then I turned my attention back to the baggie. "But how do you know that's rhabo and not glitter for Damien's scrapbook?"

Rosalina snorted a laugh. "I went online and ran a few searches. Apparently, rhabo comes in powder form, then it's mixed with water to make a drink. I think some vamps snort it, but that's not the preferred way of ingestion. Anyway, I found a few images of similar bags with that symbol."

Something about the logo was bothering me, but I didn't know what.

"We should get ready to go to the office." Rosalina walked back into the kitchen and got out a skillet to start cooking the eggs.

"Give me that." I got up and snatched the skillet away. "I'll cook."

"It's my turn. You've been doing it all week."

"It's the least I can do. As a matter of fact, I'll cook the rest of the week."

She put her hands up. "Hey, no complaints here." She gave me a warm smile, and I knew she had forgiven me for being such an inconsiderate ass.

The relief I felt was monumental.

"So Jake knows everything?" she asked.

I nodded.

"At least *that* cat is out of the bag. Now, you have to let the wolf out."

Did I? I still wasn't sure.

"Who let the wolves out. Woof, woof, woof." She sang, totally butchering the tune.

I laughed and it all felt normal again.

After a quick breakfast, we headed to the office, extra cups of strong coffee in hand. We both needed them. As soon as we got settled, I dialed Tom's office to let him know what I had found out.

"Freeman," he answered.

"Hey, Tom. It's Toni."

"Good morning, kiddo. What's going on?"

I went straight to the point. "Blake is alive."

There was silence on the other side for a few seconds. "Are you sure?"

"One hundred percent."

"That's a hell of an affirmation."

I said nothing to that, and that got the message across much clearer than if I'd tried to convince him.

"Where is he?"

"I don't know. I couldn't pinpoint the location. I'm sorry. I could try to track him again, but not now. Maybe in a few days." Tracking wore me out, and I always needed a break to recharge my batteries.

"I'll put out an APB on someone with his description. Hopefully, he'll get spotted."

"There's something else."

"Lay it on me."

"It's about rhabo."

Tom made a sound in the back of his throat. "What do *you* know about that?"

"Do you know who Damien Ward is?"

Rosalina met my gaze across the desk, then lowered her eyes with regret. It was obvious she genuinely liked the mage, and she was brokenhearted to have to do this.

"Isn't he that extravagant Copper Mage?"

"That's the one."

"What about him?"

Are you sure about this? I mouthed at Rosalina. She nodded, though not without looking sick to her stomach.

"Rosalina went on a few dates with him," I said. "She was at his house last night and found a huge stash of rhabo. It was packaged in these small bags with a bleeding heart symbol stamped on them. She took one of them. I'm sending you a picture now." I quickly clicked through my photos and sent the image to Tom's email address. "You should get it in a few seconds."

"Let me pull it up." I heard a few keyboard taps and mouse clicks. "I got it. It's just what we've been seeing on the streets. And you say that mage had a stash in his place?"

"Yes. Hundreds, if not thousands of them."

"Thanks for the tip."

"What are you going to do?"

"Get a warrant and go check it out. Everyone agrees rhabo had to be created by a mage. Damien Ward would fit the profile perfectly."

"Would we… have to be involved if he gets arrested?" The last thing Rosalina and I needed was a mage for an enemy.

"Don't worry, I'll put it down as an anonymous tip."

I breathed a sigh of relief. "Thank you, Tom."

"No worries. Stay safe."

"You, too."

I set the phone down. "It's done."

"Why did he have to be a drug lord?" Rosalina said, crossing her arms and sinking deeper into her chair.

"I'm sorry. It really sucks. I can tell you like him."

"Oh, well. Maybe I'll take you up on your offer to find me a mate."

"Really?!" I sat straighter, getting excited at the prospect.

She shook her head. "No, not really."

I deflated. "That's mean. Why would you tease me like that?"

"Call it payback for all the worry I went through last night."

"Meanie." I stuck my tongue out at her. "I just want you to be happy."

"And maybe one day, I'll take you up on it, but I'm not ready for that kind of commitment right now. I just want to have some fun with a cool, fun guy that makes me laugh. Damien ticked all the boxes, but I guess he also ticks the 'evil drug lord' one, so he's a dud. At least, it was only our second date."

My phone vibrated in my pocket. I took it out and read the caller ID.

"It's my mom again," I huffed.

Rosalina raised her eyebrows.

I pointed a finger at her nose. "Don't look at me like that. I'm not being too harsh, not considering what she did. I know I can't be mad at her forever, but every time I remember what she did I just…" I growled. "Besides, I already told her to give me some breathing room."

Rosalina put her hands up. "Um, yeah, I can see the anger is pretty out of control." She gestured toward the claws that had sprung out at my fingertips.

"Shit!" I made fists and started pacing the room until my anger passed and the claws retreated.

After that, we got to work with a vengeance. It was obvious we were both trying to keep our minds off all the craziness that had been going on lately. We called prospective clients, talked to an advertising agency about promoting our services on the radio, wrote the newsletter to send to our email subscribers, and even dusted all the furniture and photographs on the walls.

By lunchtime, we had both worked up a healthy appetite, and looked and felt much better despite the circles under our eyes.

"We'll sleep good tonight," I said, as we started to head out to grab some lunch.

Rosalina opened her mouth to answer but froze, her green eyes wide with surprise as she stared through the front glass door. I followed her gaze.

Damien Ward was standing outside, his cloak blowing in the breeze, his copper eyes flashing with anger under his top hat.

Oh, no! We were up shit's creek.

CHAPTER 28

"Oh, crap!" I grabbed Rosalina's arm, pulled her back, and stepped in front of her.

If Damien Ward tried anything, it wouldn't go down without a fight. I was not a helpless tracker anymore. I was also a werewolf with a mean bite, capable of ripping a vamp's head off. A mage would be no trouble. Probably.

Okay, so that had to be Red talking. I still wasn't all right with murder, and I didn't think I would ever be, but my wolf obviously had no qualms.

"Go in the potions alcove, Rosalina," I said.

"No, I'm not leaving you alone."

I was about to argue when Damien beckoned with a hand and the door opened. "Good morning, traitors," he said, his voice dripping with contempt as he stepped inside.

Rosalina interlaced her hand with mine and sidled next to me. She held her chin high, letting the mage know she didn't regret ratting him out.

"The police, the fucking police," he enunciated, "showed up at my home this morning and interrupted my morning yoga." His ragged pupils were huge with only a bit of copper around them.

Huh? Rosalina and I exchanged a glance about the yoga bit, though we should have been more worried about the fact that he was here and not behind bars.

"You're not welcome here, Damien," Rosalina said.

"What are you?" Damien asked, ignoring Rosalina's unfriendly remark. "Some sort of backstabbing spies?"

"Hey," I spat, "we're not the ones dealing rhabo, you flamboyant drug lord mage."

Damien grimaced at the insult. I jutted out my hip and raised an eyebrow to let him know there was more where that had come from.

"Just so you know, the cops didn't find anything," Damien spat. "I knew you went snooping around last night, Rosalina. Very disappointing."

Dammit, Tom would be mad at me for sending him on a wild goose chase, but I had no time to worry about that right now.

My friend winced, hurt by his words.

I jumped to her defense. "No one is disappointing here but you. Now take your drug-dealing, Scrooge McDuck ass out of our office."

He subconsciously touched his top hat. I smirked. Yep, he only needed a walking stick and spats to look exactly like the cartoon.

Composing himself, he gave his cloak a snap. "I am not leaving until you tell me why you were snooping around. Someone had to put you up to it."

"For your information, we're perfectly capable of coming up with things all on our own," Rosalina shot back.

Damien took a step closer, his posture menacing. "I don't want to do this," he began twisting his hands in an intricate pattern, magic crackling at his fingertips, "but you leave me no alternative."

"Go, Rosalina. Hide!" I said, my voice a deep rumble in my chest, my muscles rippling under my skin, screaming for relief. This time, Rosalina obeyed and disappeared into my office.

Crouching low, I faced the mage. "Leave, unless you want me to rip out your throat."

"The little wolf thinks she's all grown-up now." He laughed with contempt and extended his hand, shooting a blast of magic in my direction.

I jumped out of the way and dove behind Rosalina's desk. The magic tore a hole in the hardwood floors, sending splinters flying in every direction. Hunkering down on all fours, I closed my eyes, preparing to call my wolf forward, the way Eric had taught me, but the sound of the chime over the door froze me in my tracks. Someone had come in, and I couldn't risk shifting and hurting an innocent person. I leaped to my feet.

"We're closed for lunch," I blurted out, hoping to quickly dismiss whoever had come in—not that the mean, cloak-wearing mage, the hole in the floor, and the acrid smoke of burnt wood wasn't warning enough.

But our visitor wasn't just anyone. It was Jake, already in the middle of shifting, his claws and fangs unsheathed. Without saying anything, he took a swipe at Damien. His claws sliced through the air as the mage leaned back, *The Matrix* style, avoiding the attack with ease. With a speed that could only have been produced by magic, he righted himself and delivered a bone-cracking right hook to Jake's jaw.

The sound of the strike reverberated through the office as if from stereo speakers. I staggered back as the awful thud echoed in my ears, recalling the horrible sounds I'd heard last night during the trance.

Suddenly, I was there again, at that warehouse, sprays of blood cutting through the air as Blake struck again and again. His victim's head snapped back. I couldn't watch, not again. I walked backward, away from the horror.

I don't want to be here. I don't want to be here.

I shook my head, panic building. My eyes darted around, searching for an exit. Wooden crates surrounded me. I turned left then right. The crates went on for miles and miles. They were all identical, its planks stamped with a logo.

There's no way out. No escape.

My heart pounded. I grabbed my head and dug my claws into my scalp.

Not really here. Wake up, Toni. Wake up!

The pain sliced through my terror. I inhaled deeply, willing myself to calm down. That was when I understood all I had seen last night, even the things my shock had hidden from me.

Still breathing heavily but more calmly, I glanced up and stared at one of the crates, at the logo. It was the same bleeding heart stamped in the small bag of rhabo Rosalina had retrieved from Damien's house. And underneath it, words.

Pulse Inc.

I came to gasping for air, my head pounding and a cold sweat sliding down my back. I blinked my eyes open to find three staring faces. Rosalina, Jake, and Damien hovered over me, looking worried.

"Oh, thank the witchlights. Are you all right?" Rosalina pressed a hand to my forehead. "She's so cold."

"Let me take her upstairs." Jake slid his arms under me and picked me up as if I were no more than a child. He bounded up the loft steps. I wanted to protest, to say that I was all right, but my head was so foggy I couldn't even think of how to shape words.

A moment later, Jake laid me down. Rosalina and Damien appeared at the foot of the bed.

I stared at the mage. "Weren't you… just trying to kill us?"

Jake's eyes flicked toward Damien, flashing with a silver sparkle of threat. Suddenly, it occurred to me that if Damien said the wrong thing, he might spill the beans of my secret to Jake. I bit my lower lip, praying the mage held his tongue.

"Kill you?" Damien said. "No, why would I try to kill you? I just wanted to find out who sent you to snoop on me."

"You busted my hardwoods." I sat up, but my head started swimming, so I collapsed back down on the pillow.

The mage rolled his eyes. "Truth spells are not meant to be used on oak. Besides, you going all glowy with blue magic was far more interesting."

I frowned at Rosalina. "What is he talking about?"

She shrugged. "I don't know. You told me to hide."

I turned to Jake. He was frowning, looking concerned. "I saw it, too. Magic just started crackling all over your body," he said. "Then you fell to the floor, seizing. It was scary as hell. I thought…" He didn't finish, but I had the feeling he'd been about to say *"I thought you were dying."*

I sat up again, more slowly this time. I lowered my feet to the floor and squeezed my eyes tightly, trying to dispel the wave of dizziness that overtook me. *Shit*, the whole room was tumbling like a washing machine.

Then it all came rushing back to me. I gasped.

"What is it?" Jake knelt by my side, placing a hand on my knee.

I met his gaze. "I know where Blake is."

"Blake?" Damien echoed. "Are you talking about Blake Foster? Is that who sent you?!" he demanded, growing angry again.

Jake stretched to his full height and leaned threateningly in the mage's direction.

Damien cracked his knuckles. "You want me to punch you again, I see."

A growl sounded in the back of Jake's throat.

I rose to my feet, a little wobbly but not dizzy anymore. "Hold your horses, you two. Let's talk about this before you cause more destruction. Please, everybody, sit and calm down."

Jake huffed. I touched his arm and glanced toward the bed. He sat down reluctantly. I joined him while Rosalina sat on the papasan chair, and Damian pulled a wooden chair from the corner.

"To answer your question," I said calmly, "Blake didn't send us. No one did. Rosalina and I just wanted to learn more about rhabo. We have a client and his mate is dying from using the drug. Jake told me that you might be involved with the drug trade somehow, so we took it upon ourselves to find out, hoping that you might know of a way to fight the effects of the drug."

"You think *I'm* involved in the trade of rhabo?" the mage asked, appalled.

"Well, aren't you? You had a mountain of it in your house." Rosalina glared at him, sounding indignant.

"That was not mine. I took it from a werewolf who was selling it to young vampires out of the trunk of his vehicle."

"You did?" Rosalina's question sounded hopeful, and she seemed ready to believe him. I, on the other hand, wasn't so sure.

Jake blew air through his nose. "You and Eric Cross have more to do with rhabo than you're willing to admit. I know you do."

Damien gave Jake a dirty look but didn't deny the assertion. Instead, he said, "We're not dealers. Of that, you can be sure. Blake

Foster, on the other hand, he's the main provider. I know he isn't dead. I just don't know where to find him, so where is he?"

"Blake Foster is dealing rhabo?" Jake asked incredulously. "How do you know that?"

"I got the truth out of one of his lieutenants." He waved a hand in the air. "But that doesn't matter. What matters is that I need to stop him before this situation gets worse. Tell me where he is."

Everyone turned to me expectantly, but I wasn't sure if I could trust Damien with the information. What if he was in it with Blake and things had gone sour between them somehow? What if Damien wanted to kill him because Blake could serve as a witness against him?

"I… I'm not really sure," I lied, grabbing my head as if I had a headache. "Last night, I tried to track Blake, but I couldn't come up with a location. Then when I... passed out just now, I thought I remembered something, but now…" I trailed off, shaking my head.

"So you *don't* know where he is?" Damien demanded.

"I—I don't. It's all so fuzzy."

Oh God, I was terrible at lying. Were they buying any of it? I glanced sideways at Rosalina from under my hand as I squeezed my temples. She was frowning, her lips pursed, clearly doubting my performance.

Damien, however, stood and started pacing the room. "I need to find that blasted werewolf. There are rumors that they are about to flood the system with enough rhabo to kill the entire vampire population in the city. Someone has to stop him, but he always seems to be a step ahead."

"That sounds awful," Rosalina said.

"Since when do you care about vampires, Copper Mage?" Jake asked, his tone full of skepticism.

Damien glowered at Jake but, like before, avoided answering the question. He was hiding something, but what?

Stomping his foot on the floor, Damien turned and headed toward the stairs, his cloak fluttering behind him. "I'm wasting my time here." He halted at the top of the steps and glanced at Rosalina. "It's unfortunate what you did. I really liked you," he said, then, like a freaking diva, he descended the steps, a holier-than-thou expression on his face.

"Bastard," I called out, loud enough for him to hear me.

We sat in silence until we heard the door chime. After a few beats, I pushed to the edge of the bed and whispered, "I think I know where Blake is and where they're keeping that new shipment of rhabo."

CHAPTER 29

"I knew you were lying," Rosalina said.

"She's terrible at it," Jake put in.

I huffed. "I can't be that bad. Damien bought it."

Rosalina peered at me with confusion. "But why didn't you want him to know?"

"I don't know." I shrugged. "I just didn't feel like I could trust him. We don't know much about him."

"I don't trust him either." Jake stood, walked to the window, and pulling back the curtain, glanced at the street below. "He's hiding something."

I nodded in agreement. "I got the same gut feeling."

"So you did see something when you… passed out?" Rosalina asked.

I noticed that she opted to call my episode "passing out" and not "flailing like a fish." She was sensitive like that.

I turned to Jake. "When Damien hit you, the sound seemed to echo all around me, and it brought me back to last night. It was weird because I was there all over again, but this time I could see more. Things my subconscious must've noticed during the trance that I didn't register at first. I saw a warehouse full of crates."

And I had seen the name "Pulse Inc." in the news just a week ago. The report had said that they had two warehouses in the area and that one of them had burned down to the ground in a mysterious fire that was under investigation. It would be no problem finding out where the second warehouse still stood. One quick internet search would take care of that.

Though the miles and miles of wooden containers that had flashed before my eyes made me wonder if what I'd seen in the vision was true. I doubted any warehouse could hold that many crates, so that part had to be some sort of dreamlike exaggeration—unless the whole thing had been a dream. As I thought more about it, I started doubting myself.

"What is it?" Jake asked, noticing my confusion.

I rubbed my forehead. "I don't know. Maybe I'm wrong. Maybe it was just some sort of waking nightmare. Some of the stuff I saw couldn't have been real."

I didn't understand what was happening to me. This was the second time my skills had kicked in on their own. First, that nightmare that helped me find Stephen and now this. Was it my new werewolf skills interfering with my tracker ones?

"Either way," Rosalina said, "you have to tell Tom."

"No." I shook my head. "I sent him to Damien's house, and for nothing. He's probably mad at me."

"Then I'll go," Jake said. "Tell me where Blake is, and I'll find him. All we need is a good look at the place and confirmation the rhabo is there, then the cops can storm the place."

"It could be dangerous," I said, remembering the glee with which Blake had killed that man. "You shouldn't go alone. I'll go with you."

"You think I'm crazy? I'm not bringing you along."

"Then I'm not telling you where Blake is."

"What?!" He turned to Rosalina, putting his hands out. "Talk some sense into her."

"I've tried. I told her not to track Blake, but clearly, she doesn't listen."

"Hey, that's not fair." She was supposed to back *me* up. Maybe she was still mad. Regardless, I stood my ground. I couldn't let Jake go there alone.

"Toni, don't be unreasonable. If I get hurt, I'll heal. You won't."

I pressed a fist to my mouth, fighting the temptation to tell him I could heal just as well as he could, but this wasn't the time to talk about that. When I told him, I would make sure he couldn't be distracted by anything else.

"You're not indestructible, Jake," I said. "You can still get killed, and you can't come back from that, can you? Besides, I'm not defenseless. I know how to shoot a gun. I could at least watch your back."

"Why do you have to be so stubborn?" he demanded.

"This wouldn't be the first time we got into a dangerous situation," I said. "When we rescued Emily Garner, you didn't seem so concerned about the vamp that took her."

"That was an entirely different situation. One twisted vamp, I can handle, but if Blake is behind this rhabo mess that means this is major. Other dangerous people will be involved."

I let out an exasperated sigh. "Another reason for you to have backup."

Rosalina, who had been watching the volley of our conversation, rose to her feet and went downstairs, shaking her head. It seems she'd had enough and was checking out. I didn't blame her.

"Dammit, Toni!" Jake exclaimed. "Tell me where Blake is."

"Nope." I crossed my arms over my chest. I didn't have to tell him anything. "You're not the only one who can go on his own."

"That would be the stupidest thing you've ever done."

"Really? I beg to differ." I looked him up and down to indicate *he* was the stupidest thing I'd ever done.

Rosalina's feet tapped on the steps as she walked back up, then she walked in our direction, holding a gun in her hand. Jake and I jerked to a standing position.

I put my hands up. "Wow, put that down. I promise we'll stop arguing."

She rolled her eyes and set the gun on the bed. "Here, you take the gun and watch his back like you said."

"You should be on my side!" An expression of incredulity shaped Jake's features.

Rosalina gave a resigned sigh. "If you knew anything about Toni, you'd realize that once she gets an idea stuck in her head, there's no talking her out of it. She's not as helpless as you would assume."

I gave her a warning glance. This was *not* the time to spill the beans about my true nature. Despite what Eric had said about pack life, and what Walter Knight expected of his grandson, I did have a terrible itch to tell Jake everything and let him be the judge. In the end, his mate would have to be his decision and not his grandfather's. Besides, even if Jake decided not to become pack leader, he could still fulfill the promise he'd made his father by picking me.

Still, the timing was off.

Rosalina wrinkled her nose and shook her head slightly, letting me know she knew better than to share my shocking news with Jake. I relaxed and breathed a little easier.

Instead, she said, "Look, unless you want her to go chasing after Blake all by herself, you need to quit arguing. She's holding all the aces. Toni will be the one to decide whether to let you come with her, not the other way around."

Jake raked stiff fingers into his hair, exhaling in frustration, then pointed a finger at Rosalina and another one at me. "You two are impossible."

I stepped closer to my friend and grinned at Jake. Feeling pretty smug, I started to drape an arm across Rosalina's shoulders, but she stepped away.

"Nuh-uh, no ma'am, don't think I'm happy about this. I'm just trying to protect your ass because, lately, something about you ain't the same." She narrowed her eyes, clearly indicating my *wolfishness*. "You are being reckless," she scolded, sounding just like my mother.

I opened my mouth to say something, then closed it again. I couldn't argue. She was right. I *was* different. And why wouldn't I be when there was a whole new side to me that I needed to explore. I was barely scratching the surface of who I'd become.

So instead of arguing, I inclined my head and said, "Thank you for looking out for me. I promise I'll be careful."

"You'd better be," she said between clenched teeth, then turned to Jake, "And you'd better bring her back without a scratch."

Jake sighed, finally accepting defeat. "All right, but that won't do." He pointed toward the gun on the bed. "Follow me."

He marched downstairs and led us to his office, then to his own loft. I expected to see the same mess I had the last time I'd been here: a bare mattress pushed against the wall and clothes piled on the floor, but instead, an array of computer monitors was arranged around a semicircular desk as wide as the room. The setup looked pretty fancy.

"What's with all the computers?" I asked.

He gave a dismissive shrug. "New hobby."

Ignoring the high-tech equipment, he walked toward the closet in the corner and slid out a large, plastic trunk with metal clasps and a digital keypad in the front. Quickly, he punched in a code and threw the lid open. Rosalina and I both inhaled sharply as we laid eyes on the contents.

Several mean-looking weapons were embedded in gray foam padding. I didn't have a name for everything that was in there, but there was a big ass rifle, several handguns, serrated knives as long as my forearm, and even a few grenades.

"What the hell, Jake?!" I exclaimed. "Are you planning to start World War III?"

He blew air through his nose and smiled like a little kid with the coolest toys in the neighborhood.

"This is nothing." He went back into the closet and came out with a black vest. "Kevlar," he explained as he started wrapping it around my torso, attaching Velcro straps over my shoulders and sides, encasing me snugly into the stiff contraption.

"Well," Rosalina said. "That gives me a tiny bit of comfort. Do you have anything she could wear on her hard head?"

"Sorry, no."

I ran my hands over my chest, feeling quite bulky, and wondering what would happen if I tried to shift through this thing. Probably, it would be best to take it off if it came to that.

Jake reached for a can that looked like spray paint. "Also this." He vigorously shook the can and proceeded to spray the heck out of me, leaving me in a cloud of stinky mist.

I batted at the air, coughing. "God, it's poop perfume!"

He laughed. “No, it’s ScentKill.” He held the can in front of me so I could read the label. “But it does smell like shit. The stink will wear off quickly, though.”

“Ooh,” Rosalina went for the can, “they sell that?”

Jake kept the ScentKill out of range. “Stales think it smells delicious for some reason,” he said, shrugging at me, baffled. “And no, they don’t sell it in the way you’re thinking. You have to buy it from witches or mages, and it doesn’t come cheap. It kills all scents so Skews with sharp noses can’t smell you coming.”

Turning to me, he squared his shoulders and placed his hands on his narrow hips. “Now, will you tell me where the hell to find Blake?”

CHAPTER 30

After we found out the exact location of the warehouse, we waited until nightfall. Surveillance would be easier and safer under the cover of night, Jake had said. We rode his motorcycle toward North Riverfront, an industrial area near the Mississippi River.

We parked about a mile from our destination, hiding the bike in a heavily wooded location and tracking through the undergrowth and trees in silence. We were dressed all in black, knit caps keeping our hair out of our faces. Jake carried a backpack strapped to his back. Guns and magazines were strapped to the belts around our waists. He had given me a Glock with laser sighting, filled with bullets he'd called "special."

"Why are they special?" I'd asked.

"They have a wolfsbane core that releases on impact. It's high-grade stuff and will render a werewolf useless. Aim for the torso though, if you hit a vital organ, it pretty much means death, even for a strong werewolf like Blake."

"Wow, wolfsbane bullets. I've heard of those. Aren't they expensive?"

"Very, so take good aim."

Jake and I stalked forward carefully, exchanging quick glances and stopping in our tracks when we heard the slightest noise. Our senses were on high alert, even if most of the sounds we heard were animals scampering through the dry leaves.

"You heard that?" Jake asked with a frown when I stopped suddenly after hearing a small scratching sound.

"Heard what?" I pretended to adjust my Kevlar vest. "This thing is so uncomfortable."

"Better uncomfortable than dead." He pressed forward, his steps barely audible despite his bulk.

I mimicked the way he walked, trying to be just as stealthy. My heart pounded in my chest with excitement, and I was reminded of the times he and I had gone on scouting missions looking for missing persons. I had never admitted it to myself, but now that I was here, feeling the adrenaline rush through my system, I realized how much I'd missed this.

God, what is wrong with me? Why do I enjoy it so much?

It had to be the wolf in me. There was no other explanation. The chase, the hunt, had to be something that part of me craved. They must be in my blood.

Through the thick trees ahead, the glow of electric light breached the darkness. I squinted, averting my eyes, the brightness hurting me, and for the first time, I realized that I'd been stalking through the dark ass woods without tripping or running into anything. I could see despite the pitch blackness.

Damn, this is cool!

Suddenly, I was mad at Mom all over again. She had deprived me of so much.

As we approached, Jake glanced over his shoulder, pressing a finger to his mouth.

We crouched low and approached at a near crawl. When the warehouse came into view, we lay on our stomachs, flat to the ground, and scanned the area from about a hundred yards away. The structure was about the size of two basketball courts, its walls made of corrugated metal.

Silently, Jake pointed at the building's flat roof and the large, roll-up door. Three men armed with rifles stood guard: two on the roof and one by the door.

"Cameras," I whispered pointing at the corners of the warehouse.

Jake nodded.

As we watched a moment longer, a fourth guard came out through a side door and joined the one by the door. I wondered how many more were inside, hopefully not many more.

"What do we do?" I asked.

"We need to create a distraction," he whispered back. "Stay here."

I grabbed his wrist as he moved to leave. "Where are you going?"

"To create a distraction." He stared pointedly at my hand.

I let him go. "Please, be careful." I planted a quick kiss on his lips before I knew what I was doing.

He blinked in surprise, then quickly recovered and ran his thumb over my lower lip as if promising he would pay me back.

I watched him slink behind the cover of trees, going around to the back of the building. I waited, wringing my hands and biting my lower lip. After five minutes, I started to get restless and was about to take off after him when I noticed a plume of smoke rising behind the warehouse.

It took the guards a moment to notice it, but when they did, the two by the door left their posts and rounded the corner to investigate. The other two, however, remained in place, growing more alert and pointing their rifles all around as they scanned the parking lot below.

Shit! Now what?

I was pondering what to do when I noticed a dark shape sneaking behind one of the guards on the roof. Holding my breath, I watched as the guard went down without a sound.

Man, he's good.

I didn't remember Jake being so… sneaky. Maybe he'd had some training since we'd last gone about St. Louis creeping through the night.

My sharp eyes homed in on the other guy.

Would he notice his partner had gone down on the other side of the long roof? I waited on pins and needles, but he didn't. He was so intent watching for intruders on the ground that he didn't notice the one right on his ass. Jake approached from behind, and a moment later, the second guard went down too, just as silently as the first one. Assuming the guards were werewolves and had good sniffers, Jake's ScentKill seemed to work like a charm. It worked very similarly to moonfable, except my stuff only killed my werewolf scent and left my human one undisturbed.

Glancing toward the general area where I was hiding, Jake waved, and even from this distance, I could tell he was smiling smugly.

"Cocky jerk," I mumbled under my breath.

Maybe it was a desire to show Jake up, or maybe it was that hunger for the hunt, but without thinking, I pulled out my Glock, left my hiding place, and ran toward the side of the building as the camera swiveled in the other direction. From the corner of my eye,

I caught Jake warning me back by frantically waving his hands. I could imagine the foul expletives running through his mind.

The camera swiveled back with a whirring sound. As it pointed toward the woods, I ran in the direction of the side door, pulled the handle, then stepped inside, thanking the witchlights it was unlocked.

I paused, pressing my back against the wall and inhaling deeply, willing my breaths and frantic heart to settle down. I focused on my body, searching for signs that I might shift unexpectedly, but the itching and tingling on my skin that I'd come to associate with the change weren't there. Instead, what I found was a profound stillness, as if my wolf were patiently waiting for her turn. The sensation of her presence put me at ease. I wasn't alone, and there was much more to me than the gun and protective vest.

Staying close to the wall, I hurried down the narrow corridor ahead. Suddenly, the door behind me opened. I whirled, aiming my gun. But it was Jake, holding a hand up as if that would stop the bullet if I went trigger-happy. I had wolfsbane ammunition, too. He was lucky Tom had taught me to check before shooting.

Jake rushed to my side and whispered in my ear. "We'd better hurry before those other two knuckleheads realize their friends are out of commission."

I pointed my gun toward a glass door ahead. He dashed in its direction, took a quick peek inside, then gave me a thumbs up. We kept going down the hall until we reached a set of large, swinging doors.

Slowly, he pushed one open and peered through the crack. He gave me a nod then slipped inside. I went right after him, the gun's grip slick in my sweaty palm. We stood silently for a few beats, our eyes examining the scene before us.

Rows and rows of crates like the ones I'd seen in my vision stretched from front to back. The waist-high boxes were stacked in threes and were all stamped with the bleeding heart logo. The space was mostly dark, barely illuminated by a few bare light bulbs hanging from the tall ceiling. Toward the back, the light barely scratched the corners. An eerie silence filled the space. There was no sign of more guards. Odd if those crates were really full of rhabo. Or maybe they were overconfident.

After checking left and right, Jake rushed between two rows of crates, heading straight for the shadows in the back. I rushed after him, relishing the sizzling energy that sang through my veins.

Under the cover of darkness, he knelt behind one of the crates. I joined him, and we waited for a few beats, listening carefully for any indication that we'd been spotted.

When it was clear that we were safe, he nodded, pulled out a huge serrated knife from his belt, and stuck it between two of the crate's planks. With one solid push, he pried the boards apart. They cracked, splintering, the snap echoing through the space.

Abandoning all caution, Jake tore a section of the board. A layer of white foam blocked the way. His claws sprang into place and, like hot knives slicing through butter, tore a hole in the foam. Small bags filled with glittery powder came spilling out at our feet.

We exchanged a loaded glance.

I grabbed a handful of bags and stuffed them in my pocket. "Proof," I said, then reached for my phone, ready to dial the police.

"I'm afraid I can't allow you to do that," a voice said from above.

Jake and I jumped to our feet, glancing upward. On the next row of crates, a massive figure stood swaddled in shadows. Coolly, he took a step forward and the light from one of the hanging fixtures illuminated his face.

Blake!

I recognized him immediately, even though the last time I'd seen him in person, he'd been hanging over a miniature architectural model, playing the part of the dead victim. I still wondered how he'd pulled that off.

He was shirtless and barefoot as if he'd seen us coming and had time to leisurely take off his clothes to spare them from damage. His chest was as broad as a refrigerator and his muscles rippled with restless energy. His sparse blond hair was gone, and his freshly-shaved head shone with sweat.

Adrenaline flooding my system, I lifted my gun and aimed it straight at his wide chest. Blake raised an eyebrow and peered at the gun as if it were a bad joke.

"Aren't you that girl that used to date Stephen Erickson?" he asked, genuinely puzzled.

I didn't answer him. Instead, I darted a glance toward my phone in my other hand, trying to wake it up to dial 911.

Blake roared, jumped from the crate down to the floor, and landed smoothly in a crouch. Startled, I dropped the phone and squeezed the trigger. The shot echoed through the warehouse, hitting the crate behind Blake. He didn't even flinch, and instead, lunged forward. He shifted in midair, his pants falling in tatters, his fangs and claws aimed directly at me. An enormous black wolf appeared in his place.

Scrambling, I aimed for Blake's head and was about to squeeze the trigger again when Jake's dark gray wolf leaped forward and crashed into Blake. They collided in midair, then hit the ground snarling. Teeth snapped and claws raked over fur as they rolled away in a tangle of limbs.

Pressure built in my temples, I winced, pushing a hand against the side of my head.

Run, Toni! Jake's voice suddenly ripped through my thoughts.

Shock and confusion washed over me. *Huh?* How did he know he could talk to me? Had he figured out I was a werewolf? No, that couldn't be it. He was probably just willing me to go, and since he was an alpha, he could push his thoughts into any werewolf's head.

Well, I would oblige him.

Swiping my phone off the floor, I sprinted forward. Legs pumping, I skirted clear of the fighting wolves, then tore down the aisle. My eyes were roving all around, trying to find somewhere to hide so I could call the police, when a shot rang out, whizzed right next to my head, and pinged against the concrete floor.

I skidded to a stop and crouched low behind one of the nearby crates. Peering between the boxes, I tried to find the shooter. A slight movement betrayed his location. He was standing at the top of a metal staircase that led to what looked like an office area. He was one of the guards who had been outside, which meant the second one must be in here, too.

Heart hammering, I pondered what to do.

Shift? No, that was out of the question. The shooter was too far, and he already had his sights on me.

Shoot back? Red said.

But I didn't want to kill anyone.

Too bad, she said, taking over. She didn't have such qualms.

I smiled down at my gun as the heat of anticipation spread through my veins. Maybe I had a death wish, but man it made me feel alive.

I threw all caution to the wind and, spotting a wide gap between two of the wooden crates in my row, I dashed between them and came out shooting on the other side. My vision tunneled, pinning my target. One of my bullets hit the man in the chest, and with a cry of pain, he toppled over the railing and plummeted down.

As he hit the floor with a sickening thud, more shots rang out from the opposite side. I whirled and changed directions. Without missing a beat, I spotted my attacker and got a fix on his location with incredible accuracy. I let loose one single shot, which hit him between the eyebrows.

Dang!

Breathless, I took cover behind one of the crates, and finally dialed the police. As quickly as I could, I gave the dispatcher directions and told him what was going on. He tried to keep me on the line, but I disconnected the call and put my phone away, trying to decide what to do next. My heart thundered against my ribs, knocking so hard I felt it through the Kevlar vest.

I listened for fighting wolves, but I couldn't hear their snarls anymore.

Was Jake all right?

Blake's wolf had been massive, at least a head taller than Jake's. *Shit!* Why had I listened to Jake? I shouldn't have left him.

I peered out of my hiding place, determined to go back and help him, but all I managed to do was reveal my position to another guard who started shooting as soon as he saw me. I pulled back behind the safety of the crate. A stream of bullets struck the wood sending splinters, pieces of foam, and glittery powder flying into the air.

Rounding the crate at a crouch, I held my breath and ran, afraid to inhale rhabo as it rained down on me. I came out on the other side, shooting one bullet after the next. One struck the man in the thigh and when he fell, another struck him in the gut. He collapsed to the floor with a scream, then didn't move again.

Frantically, I turned around, brandishing the gun, looking for someone else to shoot. At first, it seemed no one else would come, but then I heard the clicking of claws against concrete, and Blake's wolf appeared, his muzzle shining with blood.

I aimed my gun at him. "Where is Jake?" I demanded.

The wolf couldn't speak, but as his eyes flicked the way he'd come, and his dark lips stretched in a grin, I felt my heart crumble to pieces.

"No," I shook my head.

Anger tore through my body.

In one swift motion, I raised the gun and squeezed the trigger. There was a click, but I was out of bullets. I quickly released the empty magazine and snatched another one from my belt. The wolf didn't hesitate and charged in my direction, his huge paws barely touching the floor as he ran.

I glanced up in a panic, and the magazine slipped from my sweaty hand and hit the floor.

Then Blake was on me, his fangs dripping with blood as he angled his jaw toward my throat.

CHAPTER 31

All thoughts abandoned my mind, leaving behind nothing but pure, unadulterated instincts. I let go of the gun. My body folded in two as I dropped to my hands, and the shift rippled through me in an instant, much faster than before and almost as gracefully as it did with Eric and Jake. My clothes and even the Kevlar tore apart and fell away as muscles and sinew thickened. My senses sharpened and helped me judge precisely where to meet my enemy.

Blake's eyes widened as he soared in my direction.

A furious roar raked up my throat as I pushed with my hindquarters and lunged forward to meet him.

He would pay for hurting Jake. I would tear him to pieces, and this time, he would be truly dead, scattered on the floor, and thoroughly unrecognizable. Ground meat would have nothing on him.

We collided with each other. I snapped my teeth shut around one of his ears and jerked my head, ripping it in half. Blake let out a snarl, then whirled, launching another attack. His maw snapped loudly a few inches from my neck. I whirled out of the way and jumped on top of him, my claws dragging down his coat and digging deep into his flesh.

Changing directions in midair, I landed several feet away from the black wolf. Blood oozed from a cut at his side.

A wild roar of satisfaction escaped me. I was pleased with the damage I'd caused. Blake glowered warily in my direction. He hadn't expected that from me. But his bulk made him too slow.

He lowered his head, the hairs along his spine bristling. His expression changed, filling with determination. Something about it made me take a step back. My smugness shriveled into a raisin.

Uh-oh, now I've pissed him off.

He pounced, his speed intensified by his fury. I dodged, but his razor-sharp claws scraped along my shoulder, delivering an agonizing stab of pain that made me yelp. I flew sideways and slammed against a crate. My other shoulder cracked on impact.

Before I had time to regain my balance, Blake came at me again and snapped his jaw around the scruff of my neck. His teeth cut mostly through skin, but the pain was unbearable just the same. He shook his head from side to side, snarling. I howled, paws scrambling.

Seeing no other way of escape, I let my body drop, twisting as I went down. The shift in my body caused Blake's knife-like teeth to tear through my skin. As it ripped, pain turned to fire on my back, but I was free.

Ducking, I shuffled sideways, eyes roving around as I looked for an exit.

Blake's maw snapped inches from my neck as I backed away, my tail between my legs like a coward. I turned to face him fully. Blake shook his head, letting out a roar of satisfaction at seeing me defeated.

My clothes lay in a pile off to the side, torn and discarded, reminding me of that other me and the twenty years of lies it had lived. All along, I could have been more, but I'd only had a few days, and now, I would die without knowing myself, without the wolf achieving her full potential.

Savage fury sliced through the wild side of me as the realization hit.

You got everything, and I got so little, Red said. *You didn't deserve any of it. I did. I would have shown you what real power is.*

Blake stalked in my direction, glee flashing in his dark eyes. He would enjoy the kill, just the way he'd enjoyed killing that man with his bare hands.

Hands?

My eyes darted toward my discarded clothes, then back to Blake. He seemed to realize the same thing I had. His expression changing from glee to determination, he lunged at me at the same time that I willed my wolf to stand down, and dove toward my discarded handgun and magazine.

My hands shifted first, short, claw-tipped fingers elongating. The change rippled up my arms and through the rest of my body in an instant. I hit the concrete floor with a *thud.* My hands reached under the Kevlar vest, fumbling for the gun and magazine.

Luck was on my side, and my fingers wrapped around the Glock's grip and magazine at the same time. In one fluid motion, I stuffed the clip in just as Blake landed on me, his claws ripping into my back. I cried out in pain and, aiming awkwardly, cocked the gun, and squeezed the trigger. The shot rang in my ears, kicking back my elbow against the floor. The bullet grazed Blake's side, went wild, and hit the ceiling.

For an instant, I thought I was done for, but Blake rolled off of me and collapsed on his side, twisting uncontrollably and hollering in pain.

The last of my adrenaline burned through my body, and I pressed my face to the floor, panting from both pain and exertion. I kept my eyes open, unblinking, as I watched Blake's wolf form slowly disappear, leaving behind a naked, shivering man.

Poison spread from the wound at his side, turning the surrounding skin black. The veins in his arms popped out, gradually darkening, climbing and climbing until black spider webs covered his entire body, even his face. White foam bubbled out of his mouth as he twitched.

Slowly, wincing at the agony of my injuries, I rose to my hands and knees, gun still in hand. Blake's breaths became shallow and labored. He painstakingly turned his head in my direction and peered at me with hatred in his eyes.

Shaking, I rose to my feet and pointed the gun straight at his chest. My finger caressed the trigger. The hatred in his eyes subsided and morphed into fear. He didn't want to die. Based on what Jake had said, the wolfsbane currently in his system wouldn't kill him, but a bullet to the heart—wolfsbane or not—would send him straight where he needed to be… hell.

You see, Red, I'm strong, too.

I sensed a nod of concession from her and smiled.

Blake opened his mouth and said something unintelligible. I took a step closer.

"What?" I aimed the gun at his head to give him a bit more encouragement to talk.

He mumbled again, seemingly ready to confess since he thought he was dying.

"What is it, Blake? Tell me. Who else is responsible for this?" No way he was doing all of this alone.

Blake whimpered. His cowardice surprised me, though it shouldn't have. He was a big bully, and bullies didn't have a shred of courage. They needed others behind them to prop them up and get them out of trouble when they went in over their heads.

He struggled to form words, but only puffs of air came out.

"Speak, dammit! Or I'll blow your brains out."

His eyes widened, then darted downward in fear.

Suddenly, pressure built in my temples. I winced in pain and staggered backward. My brain felt ready to explode like an overripe pumpkin. *What the hell?* I blinked, shaking my head as I struggled to regain my focus. After a few deep breaths, the strange sensation passed. I decided I'd had enough of this bastard.

"Be grateful I'm not a murderer like you," I spat, then let my arm drop.

I couldn't kill Blake—not in cold blood like this. The police would be here at any minute, and with the poison in his veins, he couldn't cause any more damage. He would go to jail, and maybe, he would confess, and all of those responsible for inciting war and distributing poison to vampires would be taken down.

I stepped back and gingerly picked up my torn clothes. I turned them all around then slipped them on as best as I could. Their tatters covered the important bits, if just barely. I really needed a ring like Eric's. It was my new life goal to save for one of them. This naked business was quickly getting old.

Limping, I hurried toward the back of the warehouse where Jake had fought Blake. When I noticed a twisted shape on the floor I froze, afraid to get closer.

God, please, please.

Blood puddled under his body, the light from the hanging fixtures shining on the wet surface. Tears slid onto my face as I took timid steps in his direction. His fur was matted with blood, and one of his legs was twisted at an odd angle. Trembling, I knelt by his side, set the gun on the concrete floor, and pressed my fingers to his neck. A weak heartbeat tapped in his throat.

Sobbing, I pressed my forehead to the side of his head.

"You'll be all right. You'll be all right," I said over and over, stroking the soft fur between his ears. "I'm sorry I've never said it, but I want you to know that I love you, Jake. I always have. I hope you can hear me. Also, as soon as you're better, there's something else I have to tell you. I think it will make you very happy. You might have to help me and teach me a lot, but I'm willing to learn. For you. We'll be happy. We'll be so happy."

His breathing slowed and became shallower.

"Please, hold on. Help is on its way."

Tears blurred my vision as I tightened my fists over handfuls of his thick fur as if that could keep his life tethered to this earth.

When sirens sounded in the distance, I jumped to my feet and rushed between the crates. I had to guide them quickly to Jake. One second might make all the difference.

As I exited the aisle, I came to an abrupt stop.

Blake was gone!

"No!"

That was impossible.

A trail of blood ran across the concrete, headed toward the exit, but there was no way he could have stood up, much less walked out of the building.

I ran outside, bursting through the door, pain rippling across my wounded back. I glanced left and right but there was no sign of Blake. How?! There was no way he could have left on his own.

Someone had to have helped him escape. There had to have been another person in the warehouse, and they had cowardly hidden until the end.

Police cars came tearing down the road. I threw the gun away as they skidded to a stop, their tires screeching, sending the smell of burnt rubber into the air.

Cops threw doors open, jumped out, and aimed their guns at the disheveled, crazy-looking woman wearing nothing but torn strips of clothes. With a sigh, I put my hands up, then had to lower them a little as the motion exposed my left boob and one of the cops nearly spilled his eyeballs onto the parking lot.

Yep, I definitely needed to get one of those rings.

ఖఌ

I was wrapped in a blanket, huddled tightly against the corner in Tom's office. To my surprise, the wounds on my back had healed before anyone had time to notice I needed medical attention. I'd told everyone that the blood had been Blake's, not mine. They seemed to have bought it, though explaining the state of my clothes was a little harder. The way they had ripped and torn wasn't exactly consistent with a werewolf attack, but they were too occupied by the huge stash of rhabo to worry about anything else.

Tom stomped into the office and closed the door behind him. He lowered the blinds on the large windows that fronted his desk, then collapsed on his chair with a heavy sigh.

"I'm too old for this," he said, rubbing the back of his neck. "Two AM, Toni? And on a Saturday? Couldn't you have picked a better time?"

I gave him a smile that felt like a grimace.

He leaned forward and rested his arms on the desk. "You feeling all right, kiddo?"

I nodded. "I just can't figure out how Blake got away."

Tom made a sound in the back of his throat and regarded me with a frown. I had a feeling he was doubtful about my story. It sounded far fetched, for sure.

"Blake *is* alive," I said for the *nth* time.

"I want to believe you, but…"

"He almost killed Jake, Tom. Ask him."

"We'll get a statement as soon as he's able to talk."

I straightened my seat. "You have to believe me."

"Well, I'm trying. I really am. But you gotta put yourself in my place. First, it was Damien Ward and now it's Blake, the walking dead."

"You're forgetting tons of crates full of rhabo." I gave him a raised eyebrow. He couldn't deny that. Jake and I *had* just handed his department a huge win.

"Can't argue with that," he said. "But maybe if you hadn't killed the witnesses…"

I swallowed, thinking of the ease with which I'd killed them, fearing my wolf's ruthlessness. But this wasn't the time to think about that.

"There were two guards on the roof. They're not dead." They hadn't found their bodies, which meant they had probably awakened and run off. They might even have been the ones who helped Blake escape.

"Maybe," Tom said, "but they're nowhere to be found."

A light bulb came on inside my head. "There were cameras. Maybe there are recordings that show people going in and out of the warehouse."

"Yeah, we checked those but there were no recordings. Digital forensics is checking the hard drive to see if they can recover something."

Had the cameras only been for show? Or maybe whoever had helped Blake had enough time to also delete the surveillance files.

"You should go home, kid. Get some rest."

I nodded, feeling like all our efforts had been for nothing. "Rosalina will be here soon."

After giving a statement, I'd called her to let her know I was all right, and she had insisted on coming here to make sure.

I met Tom's dark eyes over the desk. "Are you sure Jake is all right?"

"Yes, the paramedics started healing him right away. He's a tough sucker. He'll probably be back on his feet by tomorrow. Lucky bastard. My leg still feels weird sometimes." He rubbed it under his desk. The donut explosion had taken it right off, and the healers and doctors had reattached it, though it hadn't been an easy recovery for him.

I stood, my shoulders heavy with exhaustion. "It would take a huge wolf to do that to Jake," I said. "Just think about that."

He rubbed his goatee, pondering. "Yeah, for sure. We'll catch him, whoever he is."

"It *was* Blake, Tom. You have to believe me."

"We're still keeping an eye out for him, so if he is out there, someone's gonna spot him, and we'll bring him in."

"You from Missouri, Tom?" I gave him a raised eyebrow.

"Something like that," he chuckled. "Besides, something's up with you, little lady. You're not telling me the whole truth."

I put on an injured expression. "Why would you say that?"

Tom crossed his arms and huffed. "Your clothes look like they went through an industrial shredder. And there's barely any blood on them. Something doesn't add up. I'm no fool." He tapped his nose.

Rubbing my neck, I exhaled in resignation. "You're right. You're right."

I had no reason to hide the truth from Tom. I was only doing it because I'd gotten caught up in all the lies, but it would actually be a relief to be able to tell someone other than Rosalina. "How about some coffee one day this week? I'll tell you all about it."

"Sign me up, then maybe I can start believing everything else."

CHAPTER 32

Later that morning, as soon as I woke up, I called Jake's cell but got no answer. I tried the hospital next, but they said he'd already been discharged. Tom had been right about Jake recovering quickly. His injuries had been major, and he must have required both doctors and healers to work on him to stitch him up, but his shifter healing powers had surely done most of the heavy lifting.

Not knowing what else to do, I sent Jake a text, asking if I could come and see him, wherever he was. I waited for an answer, sitting on my bed, but none came.

Rubbing my eyes, I got out of bed and went into the shower, grateful I didn't have an appointment with Eric since it was Saturday. There was no way I could've made it there by 4 AM.

Rosalina's bedroom door was still closed, and I hoped she was snoozing away placidly and would doze until noon. Last night, she hadn't slept from the moment Jake and I left to go find Blake. Instead, she'd paced up and down the apartment, nervously eating potato chips like there was no tomorrow.

"Two bags, Toni. I ate two damn bags!" she'd said, holding two fingers up to my nose. "If my clothes stop fitting, it will be your fault."

God, the things I put her through. It wasn't fair.

After getting undressed, I got on tiptoes and checked my back in the mirror. To my surprise and relief, there were no signs that a vicious werewolf had tried to turn me into confetti—not even the tiniest of scars.

Wow! I couldn't help but be impressed by my own healing abilities.

I'm a badass.

I whirled on the mirror and, wearing a fierce expression, thrust my hand forward, willing my claws to spring out. Nothing happened. I frowned at my fingers and normal-looking nails. I coiled my fingers into a fist, then let them spring out, willing my claws to make an appearance. Still nothing.

Disgusted, I got in the shower, determined to get Eric to show me how to do that trick. The hot water loosened my muscles, and I stayed under the spray for several extra minutes. Feeling renewed, I stepped out and immediately applied my poop perfume. I endured the stink until it dissipated, telling myself I wouldn't be needing it much longer.

As I was towel-drying my hair, my phone rang. I picked it up in a hurry and was relieved to see the name on the caller ID.

"Jake, so glad you called back. How are you?"

"I'm good. How about you?" There was concern in his question.

"I'm fine. Just worried about you."

There was a rustle, then he groaned. "Sorry, I'm still a little sore," he said. "They told me you stopped Blake."

I nodded as if he could see me. "Yeah. Um, I shot him. The wolfsbane was the only thing that saved me, he got away, though. Someone helped him."

"There was a second werewolf there. He joined Blake after you ran," he said.

"What?! No one told me that." I wrapped the towel around my body, hurried to my room, and pulled out a pair of jeans and a T-shirt from the dresser.

"I told the police in the hospital when they took my statement once I was conscious."

"Any idea who it was?"

"No, I didn't even get a scent. He was masking it like we were."

"Damn!" I cursed. "He must have been the one who helped Blake escape. There's no other way he could have walked away on his own. The wolfsbane had completely knocked him out." Holding the phone between my shoulder and ear, I tried to get dressed, but it was awkward as hell. "Where are you?" I asked.

"My grandfather's."

Ew, I really didn't like that old man, but it didn't matter. I wanted to see Jake, make sure he was fine. Though there was more. I was ready to tell him everything.

"How did you manage to beat Blake?" Jake asked, sounding confused.

"I'm coming to see you. I'll tell you all about it when I get there."

"I'm okay. Don't worry. I can see you Monday."

"No, I have to see you today."

"It's all right. Today, I—"

"Be there in a few."

I clicked the "off" button. I wasn't taking "no" for an answer. I needed to tell him everything before I lost my courage.

Fearing he might call to try to dissuade me, I put my phone in silent mode and slipped it into my back pocket. I quietly left the house and got in my Camaro.

Fifteen minutes later, I parked in front of Walter Knight's house and jogged up the walkway. The house was just as beautiful and grand as I remembered it. The sweet perfume of roses tickled my sniffer, drawing my eyes to an array of well-tended bushes full of blooming pink buds. The plants made me wish I didn't have such a black thumb and killed everything I tried to grow. They were so pretty.

Inhaling deeply and rolling my shoulders, I rang the bell.

The first thing I heard was the barks of a dog. Bones, I presumed, the Giant Schnauzer that Jake had introduced me to the last time I was here. Steps quickly followed the dog's barks.

"Get back, you," a male voice said as the door cracked open.

Walter Knight appeared at the threshold, wearing a welcoming expression that quickly morphed into a frown when he recognized me.

"Ms. Sunder, what a surprise to see you here this early," he said, holding Bones by the collar. The dog seemed to wear an expression as mean as his owner's, though the effect was due to his eyebrows and whiskers needing a trim.

"Hi." I wiggled my fingers lamely. "I came to visit Jake, see how he's doing."

He made a disapproving sound in the back of his throat. "My grandson is resting. He was injured last night."

His brown eyes narrowed, scrutinizing me with hostility, as if he blamed me for what had happened. If he did, he had it all wrong. Jake could get into trouble entirely on his own.

"Maybe you should come back another time," Walter said.

He'd started closing the door when Jake appeared behind him.

"It's okay, Grandpa. I'm up."

Walter's face tightened with annoyance. So… it seemed my first impression had been correct. Walter Knight didn't like me. I wondered why.

Reluctantly, Walter moved away from the door, pulling Bones with him. "C'mon, you stupid dog." He jerked the collar and *shooed* the dog away. The animal lowered his head and slunk out of view. The old man followed after him, not bothering to give me a second glance.

"Come in, Toni." Jake limped in my direction, holding a hand to his side. He was barefoot, wearing a gray, crumpled T-shirt, and a pair of frayed jeans that hung low on his narrow hips. He gestured toward a closed door.

I smiled nervously, opened the door, and shyly walked into a small sitting room. Jake closed the door behind me, then shuffled toward a cream-colored sofa with silky upholstery. It was flanked by two ornate end tables and fronted by huge windows that let in the morning sunlight and allowed a view of the magnificent front lawn.

"Sit." He gestured toward the sofa.

I stood frozen, my heart beating out of control, feeling like it was about to give out.

Maybe telling him here is a bad idea. Maybe I should wait.

Clearly, that was the wimpy side of me talking. Red wouldn't chicken out from anything, especially a simple conversation. I inhaled deeply, taking in Jake's pine and rain scent and drawing courage from it.

Groaning a bit, Jake took a seat next to me, accommodated a cushion behind his back, and reclined. "I feel like a fucking old man," he complained.

"Are you healing all right?"

"Yeah, all the wounds are closed. I'm just sore."

I smiled. "I'm glad. I'm really glad. I was worried about you." I held his gaze, hoping it conveyed how relieved I felt.

Without thinking, I started biting my thumbnail.

How should I start?

Jake, that promise you made your father, I can help you fulfill it.

No. Too forward.

Jake, I'm ready to bear a litter of werewolves for you.

Too exaggerated, and not necessarily true.

Jake, I'm a werewolf.

Yeah. Clear. Direct. Succinct.

I opened my mouth to speak, but Jake beat me to it.

"So you never saw the second wolf?"

"Uh, no. Just Blake, but—" I was about to tell him that I wasn't here to talk about last night, but he interrupted me again.

"And you're not hurt?"

I shook my head. "I already told you. I'm fine."

He frowned, puzzled. "I'm impressed, Toni. It's not just anyone who can take on a werewolf. Poisoned bullets or not."

"Well, um, it wasn't just the gun."

He leaned forward, wincing a little. "No?"

"No. There's something else, something I've been meaning to tell you."

"And what is that?"

"Jake, I'm a—"

The door to the sitting room swung open, and Bones bounded in, wagging his tail. Walter appeared next, a woman by his side.

"Look who just got here, Jake," the old man said.

I recognized the newcomer immediately as the blonde Jake had taken as a date to Eric's party. She wore a sundress with a sweetheart neckline to enhance her ample boobs and a pair of blocky, rattan wedges that brought her to my height. Her silky straight hair fell past her bare shoulders and shone with perfect highlights.

Jake sprang to his feet, his eyes wide, the soreness on his side forgotten. I remained seated, unable to move, my mind reeling with possibilities. What was she doing here? But more importantly, why did Walter look like the cat that ate the canary?

"Allison," Jake said, "I didn't know you were coming."

The blonde seemed reluctant to come in at first, but with an encouraging nod from Walter, she put on a big smile and sashayed into the room.

"I wanted to check on you, *Jakie*," she said, adding the nickname with an edge of mean amusement in her voice. "Your grandfather told me what happened, and I was worried."

Jake smiled stiffly. "No reason to worry. I'm doing all right, but thank you. Maybe you two can wait for me in the kitchen while I finish here."

The chicken-shit part of me wanted to say that I could come back later, but Red decided I wasn't going anywhere. I was staying put.

"Where are your manners, Jake?" Walter said with a friendliness that hadn't been there before. "Aren't you going to introduce your fiancée to Ms. Sunder?"

Jake choked. I choked. Even Allison seemed to wince at the word "fiancée."

"Never mind, I'll do it." Walter waved a hand in the air. "Ms. Sunder, this is Allison Blackridge."

I stood up slowly, her last name ringing in my ears like doomsday bells.

Blackridge. Blackridge. Blackridge.

My expression hardened in unison with my heart.

"Blackridge?" I said with a smile that Red quickly procured from the coldest part of my soul. "As in the Blackridge pack?"

"The very same one," Walter said, showing all his teeth like a damn skeleton.

A chill rippled down my spine, turning me to ice.

"I know someone from your pack," I said, my voice a distant echo. "DJ Slice, Aaron Blackridge, I worked with him recently."

"Oh, yes, you're the tracker who found that... *vampire* for him, right?" She pronounced the word "vampire" as if she were saying "garbage."

"The very same," I replied, holding my chin high. "Anyway, it seems congratulations are in order." I turned to Jake and met his gaze.

He looked pissed. Really pissed. His silver eyes were as cold and distant as I felt. When he peered at me, regret flashed across his features.

Some part of me expected him to deny his engagement, but instead, he stood silent. Rage and hatred filled my gut, brewing quickly into a toxic mixture.

"Well," I said, my voice charged with contempt, "I'm glad you're doing all right. I should leave you to rest and to your *fiancée*." I hurried out of the room, doing my best to ignore Walter's satisfied smile as I walked past.

Hand shaking, I was reaching for the front door to open it when Jake dashed out of the sitting room.

"Toni, wait!"

I stopped, my attention fixed on the door handle.

He came close and placed a hand on my shoulder. "I... I was going to tell you," he whispered. "I just never seemed to find the right moment."

I shrugged his hand away. "You don't owe me any explanations anymore. You made yourself clear before."

"Please, you know I wish it could be different."

"Do you?" If he really did wish for that, then I could tell him.

"Of course, I do."

I turned and searched his face, looking for the truth.

"But I promised my father," he added.

Tears burned in the back of my eyes as I asked, "Does it have to be her?"

"The match is important for the pack, for its future and that of the Knight legacy. It's my duty."

No. I couldn't tell him. I had nothing to offer him. Walter and his pack would laugh in my face. I was inexperienced, an outsider without a pack.

Red felt the pain of Jake's rejection as well as I did, but she shook it off and replaced it with cutting indifference. Drawing strength from her, I held my chin high.

"I wish you the best, Jake," I said, then walked out of his life for good.

CHAPTER 33

When I got home, Rosalina was still in bed.

Glad to have time to process everything on my own, I climbed back into bed and curled up around a pillow, hugging it tightly to my chest. I cried and raged, the two emotions ebbing and flowing, taking turns at driving me mad.

Time passed.

I slept. I awoke. I lost track of myself.

Pressure built around my brain, squeezing it tightly. A strange feeling spread all over me, and I shuddered.

Then the pounding began.

It hammered insistently against my temples, making me feel disoriented like there was somewhere I had to be, or something I had to say.

I tried to shrink away from it, to forget it was there, but the volume continued increasing. When my head felt as if it would explode, the pounding changed, becoming a distinct staccato of hammer blows like a maddening Morse code bent on driving me to insanity.

"STOP!" I screamed at the top of my lungs.

The pummeling halted for a moment, then it picked up again, growing more intense and precise, like a distant sound that, with proximity, grows clearer. Slowly, the blows gained a certain cadence and progression.

They repeated over and over, like tired messages on repeat.

"I can't understand!" I said. "Leave me alone."

The sharp sounds persisted, though their volume diminished, allowing me to focus a little better.

"What is it, Blake? Tell me. Who else is responsible for this?"

I was back in the warehouse, kneeling by the man's twisting shape as he agonized on the floor. His foamy mouth opened and closed. Gurgles came out. His wide eyes were fixed on mine, practically screaming a message.

The pressure in my head mounted.

"You're doing this," I spat, holding my head and squeezing it tightly. "Stop it!"

Blake's bloodshot eyes drilled into mine, holding me in place.

His message pounded inside my head. Again and again. I couldn't hide from it. I'd tried, but he'd captured me in his gaze and I couldn't break free. There was only one way.

I had to fight my way out of this nightmare.

My claws unsheathed. A thick, blinding fog rose around me. Panic seized me. I whirled, trying to find an exit. Blake's message still pounded, threatening to shatter my entire being.

Growling, I slashed with my claws, tearing at the fog. But it wasn't fog. My claws caught in it, and as I raked downward. Fabric tore, tangling in my fingers. My arms wind-milled desperately as I tried to get free from it. At last, it fell away, floating downward and settling all around me.

The pounding had stopped and only silence was left behind. I was about to collapse to my knees in relief when the pressure returned once more. I almost cried out in frustration, but the pressure was brief, then it broke through with two small beats. Two syllables.

"Ste-phen." And then, "Help-me."

I sat up in bed panting, cold sweat causing my T-shirt to cling to my skin.

Ste-phen.

Ste-phen.

Ste-phen.

Each syllable a hammer blow.

The name echoed inside my head, spoken in Blake's voice. I shook my head in denial.

"No, no, no!"

It'd been a nightmare, a figment of my messed up dreams. It wasn't a memory. True, I'd felt that same awful pressure while at the warehouse when I stood over Blake, but that had been it. I hadn't heard his voice in my mind, and he hadn't been calling for Stephen's help because that would mean… that would mean...

No!

Stephen couldn't be the one responsible for what was happening in the city. And Blake couldn't have spoken inside my head because he wasn't an alpha.

Unless…

My heart thundered as a possible explanation occurred to me. If I'd heard Blake's cry for help, that had to mean that… that *I* was an alpha.

No.

It couldn't be. It just couldn't be.

My imagination was out of control, jumping to conclusions. The dream had been simply that, a dream, not a revelation of something I'd been too inexperienced to recognize as an alpha ability. Right? Right?!

I jumped out of bed and grabbed my Camaro's keys. There was only one person who could help me. I had to see Eric Cross right away.

WWW.INGRIDSEYMOUR.COM

www.ingramcontent.com/pod-product-compliance
Lightning Source LLC
Chambersburg PA
CBHW020335310726
48979CB00015B/2376/J

* 9 7 8 1 7 3 6 0 6 1 2 1 3 *

COPYRIGHT

Destiny (A Seventeen Series Novel) Book Six

Third hardback edition: 2024
ISBN-13: 978-1-912834-00-6

www.ADStarrling.com
shop.adstarrling.com

Edited by Right Ink On The Wall

SEVENTEEN BOOK SIX

DESTINY

A.D. STARRLING

DEDICATION

To my fans.
I wouldn't be where I am today without you.
Thank you for being with me on this incredible journey.

PROLOGUE

APRIL 2013. KOFA RANGE, YUMA PROVING GROUND, ARIZONA.

THE MAN LOOKED BEYOND THE SCORCHED PLAIN AT HIS FEET TO the dark peaks to the east. The burnt wreckage of a helicopter and the twisted shells of dozens of army vehicles dotted the landscape around him, the only evidence left of the devastating psychokinetic blast Olivia Ashkarov had visited on the men of the secret R&D base where she had been kept prisoner.

The bodies of the humans who had died in the firestorm had been removed from the site in the last twenty-four hours, their deaths officially put down to an unfortunate training accident. As for the Immortals who had perished at their side, their remains had long since been scattered by the winds coursing through the mountains and desert, bones and flesh turned to ash by the flocks of crows that had descended from the crimson skies the day before.

The only trace left of Jonah Krondike was the warped silver

ring the man held in his hand. It was pure chance that had led him to it.

Although he had known that searching the buckled, black carcass of the helicopter would prove futile—that he would not miraculously find Krondike injured but alive inside—he had still done so. Agony and rage had flooded him at his failure to uncover any vestige of the man he had worshipped all of his life.

It was as he had slowly paced the area around the impact site, his carefully cultivated, dispassionate expression masking his fury, that he had stumbled upon the metal band. It had become wedged under a rock some twenty feet from the wreckage, its polished surface dulled by dirt and desert sand. The writing upon it was almost unrecognizable, the engravings distorted by the incendiary explosion that had engulfed the helicopter. Still, he had seen the ring enough times to know it belonged to Krondike.

He did not care about the humans and Immortals who had met their end during the intense battle that had taken place inside the Kofa Mountains and beneath the desert plains at the eastern edge of the Yuma Proving Ground. Nor was he unduly worried about losing the covert research facility and the US Army faction who had been working closely with Krondike for decades.

As for the death of William Gunnerson, the four-star general who had been in charge of the rogue group assisting them, he had ordered the man's assassination himself yesterday morning.

There was only one thing that preoccupied him right now. One thing that ate at him, that gripped him to the point of obsession, that consumed him like little else had in all the centuries of his existence.

Jonah Krondike's death.

He clenched his fist, the ring digging into his palm so hard it nearly cut his skin.

'Are you okay, sir?'

The man turned to the Hunter who had spoken.

'Yes, I am,' he lied with a neutral stare.

'We're being called back to base.' The Immortal indicated the mouth of a cave about a mile behind them.

'Go ahead,' the man murmured. 'I'll be right with you.'

He took a shallow breath, cast a final glance at the remains of the crumpled cage of metal where Jonah Krondike had met his end, and twisted on his heels. He headed for the Jeep where his escort waited, his mind filled with a single thought.

They will pay. I will make them pay for your death.

PART I
STOLEN

CHAPTER ONE

August 2017. Balthazar Island, Pacific Ocean.

Lucas Soul studied the man and woman facing each other across the clearing.

Conrad Greene moved first, the double-bladed spear spinning in his hands, the snake birthmark on his left forearm dark against his tanned skin. Alexa King blocked his blows with her sai daggers, her movements swift and nimble.

They seemed evenly matched for several breathless minutes as they fought one another, spending equal time in attack and defense, the power of their thrusts almost identical, two deadly warriors in their prime.

Lucas was not fooled. He had sparred enough times with Alexa to know she liked lulling her opponents into a false sense of security.

The fatal move came when Conrad least expected it. He had just warded off the blade heading toward his belly and was twisting his spear toward her left thigh when she jumped and locked her legs around his waist. He gasped as she dropped into a backflip and sent him hurtling into the air above her.

The Healer landed hard on his back, air leaving his lips in a whoosh. Alexa followed him to the ground before he had time to draw his next breath. She trapped his arms and weapon to his sides with her thighs, and pressed the tip of a sai over his heart.

She arched an eyebrow, a faint smile playing on her lips as she crouched above him. 'Say uncle?'

Conrad sighed and conceded defeat with a reluctant nod.

'Wow. You got your ass whipped big time,' Ethan Storm drawled where he stood next to Lucas.

He grinned at the disgruntled man lying in the sand.

'I don't want to hear that from you, Metal Boy,' Conrad grumbled as the woman above him rose and pulled him to his feet.

'Yeah, you're the last person who should be spouting bullshit like that,' Alexa muttered. Her silver stare shifted to Lucas. 'You're next.'

'Yes!' Tomas exclaimed, fist pumping the air.

Lucas looked over to where his son and daughter sat watching the matches, faces keen and eyes shining with enthusiasm.

'If your mother knew how bloodthirsty you two are, she'd faint,' he said drily.

Lily giggled, chocolate curls bouncing atop her slim shoulders, her mother's sun cross pendant glinting at her neck.

Anna had stayed back at the house with Olivia Ashkarov. Neither of them was comfortable watching their cousins fight, even if it was just for fun.

Lucas resigned himself to his inevitable fate, collected his daisho from where it stood against a tree, and stepped into the middle of the clearing. He stared into Alexa's deadly, gray eyes, the swords steady in his grip.

She came at him lightning fast, twisting as she dropped.

He jumped, missed her sweeping kick, and brought the katana down. Their blades clashed, sword against dagger, metal edges glinting under the dazzling sun. He blocked the second sai with his wakizashi, ducked beneath the roundhouse kick heading toward his left temple, and brought his right knee up toward her chest.

She evaded the blow, feet blurring on the sand and teeth flashing her amusement as she danced around him, the sais spinning in her hands. Lucas smiled back.

They engaged for another five minutes, their movements flawless as they sought an opening in each other's defense, their blades locking time and time again.

A gasp sounded to his right when a sai touched the pulse in his throat. Lucas stilled, the daisho frozen in his hands, Alexa denting his skin slightly with her blade.

'I guess I win this one too.' Alexa lowered the dagger and stepped back.

Furious clapping sounded on the edge of the clearing.

'That was *SO* cool!' Admiration was painted across Tomas's face.

'My son hates me,' Lucas told Alexa glumly.

She grinned and patted his shoulder. 'They've just got a kickass aunt, that's all.'

Ethan turned to Conrad. 'You owe me ten dollars.'

The Healer muttered something under his breath and reached into the back pocket of his chinos.

Alexa narrowed her eyes at them. 'You guys were betting?'

Ethan shrugged, unabashed. 'We always bet. Besides,

Conrad is convinced one of us will beat you one day.' He grinned. 'Well, *one* of us *did*, but you refuse to admit it.'

Alexa sheathed her blades. 'Twisting my weapons into useless lumps of metal is called cheating. So is using your elemental powers to pin me to the ground.'

'She's right,' Lucas said.

'I agree.' Conrad placed a fresh ten-dollar bill in Ethan's hand and waved an admonishing finger under his nose. 'This is why we banned you from these fights ages ago. You just can't help yourself.'

A heavily pregnant woman strolled into the clearing. 'Can't help what?'

Conrad's lips curved into a smile as she closed the distance between them.

'Ethan can't help using his powers to cheat.' He dropped a kiss on her nose.

Laura Hartwell-Greene looped her arms awkwardly around her husband's waist. 'You'd think he would have learned his lesson that time Alexa almost drove Lucas's sword into his heart.'

Ethan tut-tutted, the grin still plastered across his face. 'Bunch of sore losers.'

'Things okay back there?' Lucas indicated the large colonial house under the trees farther along the beach.

Laura grimaced. 'They're better now that I'm not there. I can't understand their fascination with frosting. The one time I made a cake, I almost poisoned Conrad.'

Her husband groaned at the memory.

'I hear you,' Alexa said. 'Baking sucks.'

Everyone stared.

'You *baked?*' Ethan said.

'You can cook?!' Conrad added.

Alexa scowled at their shocked expressions. 'What's so strange about that? And it was only the one time.'

Laura grimaced. 'I'm almost too afraid to ask what happened.'

Alexa sniffed. 'I set the fire alarm off. Big time. Zachary had to repaint the kitchen and everything.'

Lucas bit back a smile. Zachary Jackson, Alexa's husband, had moved into her penthouse in Manhattan after they got married. He still held his title of Harvard Professor of Archaeology and Anthropology, but now acted as a visiting lecturer at the Boston university while working with Dimitri Reznak on his projects for the Crovir Immortal Culture and History Section.

Three weeks had passed since Tomas and Lily's sixth birthday, and everyone had finally made it to the island for a late celebration, even Laura, now eight months' pregnant. It was a tradition Lucas had initiated six years ago, when Alexa, the first of their remarkable circle of Immortal relatives, had entered his and Anna's lives. Conrad and Laura had started coming to their home the year after. It wasn't until four years ago that Ethan, Olivia, Asgard, and Madeleine had joined their ranks.

The gatherings were week-long affairs and filled with laughter. They lived thousands of miles away from each other, Conrad and Laura the farthest away in Brazil, and didn't meet as often as they wished they could.

'Dad?' Tomas said.

'Yeah?'

'Can I have a go?' Tomas's gaze shifted to Alexa briefly. 'At fighting Aunt Alexa?'

Lucas blinked. His son watched him with an expectant expression.

A sliver of nerves danced through the Immortal at the eagerness in the little boy's eyes.

As he had done on innumerable occasions in the past four years, Lucas recalled Olivia's words that day on Dimitri Reznak's estate in Sumava, when he and Anna had been introduced to the last of their Immortal relatives. He had not doubted the truth of the Seer's statements then, nor had he since.

He had known, just as Anna had, that their children were special from the moment of their birth.

Although he still remained skeptical about the higher power Olivia had spoken of and the divine beings Dimitri said Guru Rinpoche, the Lotus-Born Buddha, had mentioned in an ancient Nyingma scripture currently in the possession of a secret Buddhist order in Tibet, Lucas could not forget the time he had suffered his seventeenth death. The presence he had felt following what should have been his final demise still lingered somewhere inside him, a warm specter at the very edge of his consciousness, alien yet soothing at the same time.

He could also not deny the evidence of his own eyes.

Although Tomas and Lily were growing at a normal pace physically, their mental abilities and maturity far surpassed those of human and Immortal children their age. They had also started to manifest their gifts. And, as Olivia had predicted, Tomas and Lily each favored specific talents.

Whereas Lily enjoyed practicing her healing and psionic skills, Tomas relished his combat and elemental abilities.

Alexa and Conrad had been the ones who had convinced Lucas he should let the children engage in weapons training if they wished to do so. They had both been there with him last year, on the day Tomas and Lily first picked up swords and play fought each other in the basement of Dimitri's castle in

Sumava, where Alexa herself had trained as a child when she lived with her godfather.

The expression on his cousins' faces had reflected Lucas's own wonderment as he watched the twins move across the fencing floor. Though he was loath to admit it, there was no denying that they were made for fighting.

Lucas glanced at Alexa. She dipped her chin, her expression calm.

'Sure,' he murmured to his son.

Tomas rose to his feet, green eyes sparkling with excitement.

'Your weapon?' Alexa asked the little boy solemnly.

Tomas looked around the clearing. His gaze settled on Conrad's face.

'Can I borrow your staff, Uncle Conrad?'

Conrad handed his gilded weapon to Tomas. He helped Laura to the ground and sat with his arm draped around her shoulders. Lily moved to their side and linked her fingers with Laura's.

They watched Alexa and Tomas walk to the middle of the clearing. Despite the fact that she towered over him, Tomas faced her with an indomitable stance that caused a flash of pride to course through Lucas.

'Aunt Alexa?' Tomas said quietly.

'Yes?'

'Forget that I'm a kid.' He straightened, his fingers gripping the staff weapon lightly. 'I want you to fight me with everything you've got.'

Ethan drew a sharp breath and Lucas's pulse jumped. He had never seen that look on his son's face before.

Alexa's eyes flared in surprise.

Lucas didn't even hear the click of the metal ring on

Conrad's staff, nor did he see the weapon extend into a double-bladed spear. By the time he'd blinked, Tomas had closed the distance to his aunt.

Alexa leaned back, a wicked tip dancing past her cheek. Tomas moved again, the spear spinning in his hands, and brought the other end up toward her chest. She blocked the blow with a sai and jumped back.

Tension wound through Lucas as he watched them fight. He didn't have to look at the others to sense that they were suddenly as nervous as he was. Only Lily appeared relaxed, watching her twin and Alexa with a faint smile.

It was a couple of minutes before Alexa stopped defending and started attacking in earnest, her gray eyes focused and serious. Tomas countered with the spear before twisting the second ring and drawing the two short swords inside the staff.

They paused for a moment and faced each other silently across the clearing, their breathing slow and steady.

Hairs rose on the back of Lucas's neck when a flock of birds suddenly rose from the trees and headed into the island, their agitated cries heralding what was about to happen.

CHAPTER TWO

It came in faint ripples at first, like a warm breeze coursing across his skin. The first true pulse of power sent sand dancing off the ground at his feet and made his teeth vibrate in his jaw. Lucas stared at the woman he had just fought with the same feeling of awe he'd experienced the first time he'd seen her do this.

Alexa stood in the middle of a rising storm of pure energy, sand and dirt shivering and rising a couple of inches around her ankles, the leaves and branches in the closest trees bowing under the pressure waves. It was her own invisible life force, a force that could make the very earth tremble.

It had only manifested itself after she had suffered her first and only death to date.

They'd witnessed it two years ago, when Ethan had used the full extent of his elemental abilities on her during one of their sparring matches. The sheer strength of her response had driven Ethan off her and six feet across the ground before he had clung on grimly to gravity with his own ungodly energy, his shocked expression echoed on the faces of his Immortal cousins. The second time had been when Lucas himself had nearly bested Alexa during one of their fights, the intensity of the power that had radiated off her nearly driving him to his knees.

'Holy—' Ethan croaked.

Lucas glanced at him before following his startled gaze. His heart stuttered in his chest.

Just as the air shimmered around Alexa, so had it started to do around Tomas. Wood groaned behind the boy as a small bush nearly uprooted itself. Specks of sand trembled on the ground and rose around his feet.

Tomas smiled at Alexa. Her lips curved in an answering grin.

Just as quickly as they had started, the formidable energies rolling around the clearing dissipated. Tomas dropped the swords and ran to his aunt.

She caught him in her arms as he jumped, gave him a quick hug, and pressed a kiss on his forehead. 'That was amazing. Since when have you been able to do that?'

'Since just now!' Tomas replied, face flushed with delight.

Alexa met Lucas's guarded stare over the little boy's head. Deep in the silver depths, he detected the same unease he was experiencing.

The children were progressing faster than any of them had thought they would.

'It's okay, dad,' Lily said.

Guilt stabbed through him at the nervous expression on her face. He walked over to her and lifted her in his arms. 'I know, sweetheart. It's just—sometimes the two of you surprise us, that's all.'

'Did something happen?'

Lucas twisted on his heels.

Anna and Olivia were headed across the sand toward them, a golden retriever and a German Shepherd in their wake. Lucas's breath stilled for a moment when he met his wife's green gaze. Though they had been married seven years, she still had the ability to make his pulse jump.

Olivia suddenly paled at her side. From the way she stared past him, he could tell she'd just exchanged psychic thoughts with Ethan.

Anna glanced at her.

'Lucas?' she said, her voice hardening.

He looked over his shoulder.

Ethan was making a subtle neck slicing motion with his thumb. Conrad shook his head slightly. Laura bit her lip, amusement dancing in her hazel gaze. At the far side of the clearing, Tomas and Alexa were playing with the dogs while doing their damnedest not to meet Anna's eyes.

'Thanks for nothing, guys,' Lucas muttered.

'Lily, the fact that you're trying to soothe my mind with your powers right now only makes me more suspicious, honey,' Anna said in clipped tones.

Lily wrinkled her nose at her mother. 'So, it's not working?'

A noise distracted them.

A speedboat curved around the head of the cove to the west and crossed the lagoon. It slowed before gliding to a stop next to the yacht moored at the jetty a few hundred feet from the house.

Three men and a woman climbed out. They secured the boat, cleared the pier, and headed leisurely toward them.

Alexa's face lit up. 'Zachary.'

She bolted out of the clearing, flashed past the other visitors, and jumped into the arms of the blue-eyed blond behind them.

Lucas grinned as they tumbled to the ground, Alexa's lips locked firmly on Zachary's mouth.

The woman from the boat smiled as she approached. 'Look who we bumped into on the way here.'

'Madeleine,' Conrad said warmly as she rose on her tip-toes and pressed her lips to his cheek. He followed her amused gaze to the pair kissing passionately behind her. 'I thought he was still on that dig in Alaska.'

'He didn't want to miss the birthday,' Reid Hasley said wryly, skirting the couple on the ground.

Lucas greeted his best friend with a hug, allowing Lily to dart out of his arms and into the hold of the man who came to stand next to Madeleine, Tomas close behind her.

Asgard Godard kissed the little girl on the head and ruffled Tomas's hair.

'It's good to see you,' Lucas told his uncle with a smile. 'How was the trip?'

'Too short,' Asgard replied. 'Victor and Dimitri send their apologies for not making the party.' His eyes turned melancholic. 'We visited the grave before we flew back.'

Lucas swallowed the sudden lump in his throat. Though seven years had passed since the death of Tomas Godard, Asgard's father, and his and Anna's grandfather, the pain of his loss still echoed inside him. He had only known the former Head of the Order of Bastian Hunters for a short time, following a series of incidents that had seen him and Reid dragged deep into the Immortal societies. But meeting Tomas had revealed to him the startling secret of his own identity, and Lucas had wished for more time together.

Anna's grief had surpassed his, for she had grown up with their grandfather. It was she who had picked the final resting place for his ashes in Prague.

Olivia's eyes widened. She stared from Asgard to Madeleine. 'You—you're *engaged?!*'

Madeleine sighed. 'I really wish you'd stop doing that mindreading stuff to us. But yes, we are.' She grinned and showed them her left hand.

Olivia flushed but leaned forward with Anna and Laura to examine the diamond sitting in her white gold and platinum ring.

'Sorry,' she mumbled. 'It's like you were shouting it at the top of your voice.'

'Yeah, well, I can't help it.' Madeleine rolled her eyes at the red-eared man next to her. 'It took this guy long enough. There are only so many hints a woman can drop.'

'Congratulations,' Lucas said warmly.

Asgard nodded, clearly embarrassed by all the attention. He turned to Ethan.

'So, when are you going to make an honest woman out of my niece?' he said gruffly, indicating Olivia with a tilt of his head.

The Seer flushed an even deeper shade of red.

Ethan grimaced. 'It's not from lack of trying, old man.'

'*What?*' Anna whirled around and stared at Olivia.

'He proposed?' Laura added, stunned.

Olivia bit her lip, her expression turning stubborn.

'She said something about it not being the right time yet,' Ethan explained in the face of her evident discomfiture. He sighed. 'Having a psychic for a girlfriend sure robs the spontaneity out of certain things.'

'It really isn't the right time,' Olivia told a shocked Asgard.

Ethan stared past her and frowned.

'Sheesh! Either stop that or get a room, will you?' he yelled.

Alexa reluctantly detached her lips from Zachary's and yanked her bemused husband to his feet. 'Let's go.'

'Where to?' the Harvard professor said.

'Like he said, a room.' She dragged him toward the house. 'Preferably one with a bed. We haven't seen each other for two weeks and there are things I need to do to you.'

'Oh.' Zachary grinned. 'I kinda like the sound of that.'

'That's disgusting,' Ethan said. 'And in front of the kids, no less.'

'That's rich coming from you, Hickey Boy!' Alexa shouted over her shoulder.

Olivia gasped and pulled up the collar of her shirt. She narrowed her eyes at Ethan.

'She's joking,' Ethan said defensively. 'You don't have a hickey.' He paused. 'Not today anyway.'

'What's a hickey?' Lily asked curiously.

Anna met Lucas's startled gaze, horror clashing with laughter on her face.

'It's like that smooching mum and dad do when they think we're not watching,' Tomas explained with all the wisdom of one born five minutes ahead of his twin.

'Oh.' Lily pursed her lips. 'You'd think they would have given us a baby brother or sister by now, they do that so often.'

Reid burst out laughing.

Lucas stared at his feet, suddenly wishing there was a hole he could crawl into. 'Kill me. Just kill me, now.'

Anna chuckled and twined her fingers around his.

CHAPTER THREE

Anna leaned against the balustrade and stared out over the ocean.

A full moon kissed the horizon, spectral light turning the dark waters of the lagoon into a dazzling, rippling sheet ahead of the bright reflection of the white orb. The rhythmic song of invisible surf danced toward the house on a warm breeze.

It was the weekend after Tomas and Lily's birthday party. Their cousins and friends had left the island two days past to return to their daily lives. With Laura due to have the baby in the next four weeks, they knew they would soon meet again to celebrate the birth of her and Conrad's child.

Footsteps sounded behind her. Someone walked out onto the balcony of the bedroom and wrapped powerful arms around her waist.

Anna shivered at the heat of the man holding her.

It didn't matter how many years passed or that she had borne him two children. Lucas's presence, his touch, his scent, all of it could still turn her legs weak and make her senses swim with desire.

She recalled the moment she realized she'd fallen in love with him as clearly as if it were yesterday. It had been during the phone conversation, seven years ago, when Victor Dvorsky, the former Head of Bastian Counter-Terrorism and current Head of the Order of Bastian Hunters, had revealed Lucas had injected himself with a genetically reengineered variant of the Red Death. The fourteenth century virus had been behind the deadly plague that had wiped out more than half of the world's Immortal population while the Black Death scourged Europe and Asia, similarly killing millions of humans. It had been isolated by a group of Crovir scientists as part of a scheme to start a second pandemic and alter the power balance of the world.

As she had waited anxiously for Victor to bring Lucas to the Bastian compound where she had set up a lab to work on a vaccine, it had dawned on Anna that the pain squeezing her heart and the terror drowning her mind was more than just normal anxiety for the incredible Immortal who had entered her life so dramatically mere days before.

She had been aware of the spark of attraction between them from their very first meeting and had tried her damnedest to ignore it. But when Victor had arrived at the compound and she had seen Lucas inside the containment pod, the rational arguments she had been wrestling with had flown right out of the window. As she had watched the stubborn, brave, foolish man looking at her sheepishly from behind the glass, Anna had finally admitted to herself how much she cared for him.

It had been after Lucas became sick—when she had thought she was going to lose him—that Anna had vowed she would do something about her feelings if he survived. Three days later, she had finally been presented with the opportunity to keep her promise.

Walking into Lucas's room and climbing into his bed had been the hardest thing Anna had ever had to do in her entire Immortal life. She had never felt so vulnerable, so naked, as she had in that instant, her emotions raw and exposed. For one insane moment, she'd even wondered whether she'd misread the attraction between them.

All it had taken was a single kiss.

One blistering meeting of their lips.

The details of that night were forever etched in her mind. The way Lucas had responded to her. The way he'd touched and tasted every inch of her skin. The urgency of his fingers when they'd found her hips. The weight of his body above her. The devastating pleasure they had found in each other's arms.

Anna would remember the first time they made love all her life, and all the lives that came after.

'Are they tucked in?' she murmured.

'Ah-huh.' Lucas dropped a kiss against the side of her neck before resting his chin on top of her head.

Anna smiled. 'Which story did they ask for tonight?'

Lucas groaned. 'Attila the Hun. I don't know where those kids get their bloodlust from.'

Anna chuckled and decided not to tell him it sure wasn't from her.

They stood in comfortable silence for a moment, his chest rising and falling against her back, her hands resting lightly on his corded forearms.

'Lucas?' Anna said quietly.

'Yeah?'

'I'm happy.'

She twisted in his hold, rose on her tip-toes, and kissed him, conveying the depth of her feelings with her lips. His arms tightened around her, his heartbeat accelerating where it thrummed against her chest. She pulled back, looked up into his achingly beautiful, blue eyes, and brought her mouth to his left ear.

'How about we work on that brother or sister Tomas and Lily want so badly?' she whispered.

Lucas's face darkened with desire as she took his hand and led him to their bed.

ETHAN STIRRED. PALE DAYLIGHT STREAMED THROUGH THE SMART glass wall opposite him, illuminating the shadow-filled canyons beyond and the blue waters of the Pacific in the distance. He glanced at the clock on the nightstand. It was six am.

He closed his eyes and rolled over, his arm seeking the form of the woman beside him. His hand landed on warm, empty sheets.

'Olivia?' Ethan mumbled, blinking fuzzily.

Alarm slammed through him. He bolted upright.

She was sitting up beside him, eyes staring blindly forward, body rigid and locked in a psychic dream. Sweat beaded her forehead and her chest heaved under her nightdress.

Ethan swallowed as the fear drowning his soulmate echoed across their mental connection. Although he could never see what it was she experienced during her visions, he always sensed her emotions if he was close enough to her at the time.

Right now, Olivia was scared out of her mind.

'Livvy?' Ethan raised a hand to her shoulder then hesitated. He gritted his teeth, clenched his fingers, and lowered them to the sheets.

It was best she saw the vision through, whatever it was.

Her breath suddenly hitched in her throat. She went deathly still.

'They're coming,' she whispered.

The color drained from her face in the next instant. 'They're here.'

Olivia reached out suddenly with her right hand. 'No, daddy. Run!'

Hairs rose on Ethan's arms, leaving goosebumps in their wake.

His soulmate's voice had sounded eerily like a child's.

Her fingers closed on empty space. A shudder ran through her.

She blinked and gasped, her pants loud in the frozen silence. Ethan stiffened when she turned to him, her green eyes dark with panic. She lunged across his lap and grabbed his cell from the nightstand.

'What is it?' he said numbly, an unknown dread filling him.

Olivia hit a number on speed dial, brought the phone to her ear, and laid her right hand on his left cheek, hot fingers trembling against his skin.

Ethan inhaled sharply at the images that flashed across his inner vision. This was something new, something they'd been able to do only recently. Though Olivia could draw upon his elemental abilities and use them at will, he had never been able to reciprocate. Except, now, she could show him her visions. Acid burned the back of his throat when he finally registered what he was seeing.

'Oh God,' he whispered hoarsely.

Olivia startled when the call finally went through.

'Get out! Get out NOW!' she shouted. *'They're coming! They—'*

Ethan heard the sudden dial tone. Olivia sat paralyzed for a moment before slowly lowering the phone to her lap, her knuckles white where they gripped the frame. She looked up and met his horrified stare, her eyes glinting with unshed tears.

LUCAS WOKE TO THE SOUND OF HIS CELL RINGING. ANNA STIRRED beside him. He reached out blindly, took the phone from the nightstand, and blinked groggily at the screen. His eyes widened when he registered the caller ID. He sat up and pressed the answer button.

That was when he saw the tiny figure in the doorway of the bedroom.

Lily stood frozen in a psychic dream, her eyes wide and unseeing, her face deathly pale. His stomach lurched.

Olivia's voice rose dimly from his cell above the sudden pounding of his heart.

'They're coming,' Lily whispered.

The dog started barking downstairs.

Lily blinked. 'They're here.'

Awareness suddenly flooded her face. Lucas knew instantly that she'd awoken. Tears filled her eyes and rolled down her cheeks. He moved, the phone falling onto the sheets, the dial tone a distant echo as he rounded the bed.

Lily raised a hand toward him, her blue eyes dark with horror. 'No, daddy. Run!'

'Lucas?' Anna mumbled. She blinked and sat up abruptly when she saw their daughter.

Tomas's scream came a second before an explosion ripped through the house.

The floor shook violently beneath Lucas. He stumbled and

fell, plaster dust raining down around him. Fear twisted his heart. He climbed to his feet and lurched toward his daughter.

The wall behind her tore open, wood cracking and splintering, a large section disappearing outward in an instant. A shadowy figure swooped down from the gaping, dark void beyond and grabbed the little girl around the waist.

'*Lily!*' Lucas shouted.

Anna leapt out of their bed, her scream echoing his as he started to run.

Lily's eyes widened.

Time slowed. Sound faded.

His fingertips touched hers fleetingly.

Then, she was gone.

Lucas blinked, shock drenching his body in a cold sweat. A thumping noise reached his ears through the blood roaring inside his skull, the sound at once alien and familiar.

He dashed to the edge of the yawning hole that had once been a guest bedroom and looked out wildly into the darkness. The din of helicopter rotors came a moment before he felt the downdraft of air. Bile flooded his throat when he saw the dark shapes in the starlit skies above him.

There was no sign of Lily.

Instinct had him bolting toward the children's bedroom. He'd just cleared the stairs when a second explosion blasted through the back of the house and lifted him off his feet.

Lucas's breath locked in his throat as he slammed into a wall. His head struck the plaster hard. Stars exploded in front of his eyes. Tendons wrenched and tore in his right arm. He sagged to his knees, a buzzing sound filling his head while the world spun around him.

'Lucas!' Anna shouted somewhere behind him.

'Stay back!' he yelled.

Lucas shook his head dazedly, gritted his teeth, and grabbed his dislocated shoulder as he straightened up. He staggered forward, unheeding of the debris slicing the soles of his bare feet, his heart racing with panic.

A third explosion rocked the building as he negotiated the corridor to the children's bedroom. He stumbled and kept moving. Black smoke billowed toward him. His stomach dropped. He turned the corner and stopped dead in his tracks, terror weakening his legs.

Flames crackled and roared inside the room up ahead, an incandescent wall blocking his path.

'Tomas!'

CHAPTER FOUR

Lucas ran and jumped through the fire. He cleared the flames, landed on debris, slipped, and fell onto his back. His breaths came in fast, harsh pants as he sat up and scanned the acrid fumes around him. His gaze froze on Tomas's empty bed for a heartbeat before moving to the jagged opening occupying what had once been the south-facing wall of the house.

He rose and staggered to the edge of the void.

Harsh light suddenly blinded him from above. Lucas squinted and raised his left hand to his face. Ice filled his veins.

Through the gaps between his fingers, he saw his son disappear up toward a second hovering Black Hawk helicopter.

'*Dad!*' Tomas screamed. The little boy kicked and struggled in the grip of a masked figure, hands reaching down helplessly.

Lucas's heart stuttered when he looked past the spotlight attached to the aircraft's starboard skid and saw the other figure crouching inside the cabin.

He sucked in air and dove to the side a second before bullets left the barrels of a rotary machine gun and peppered the space where he'd been standing. He landed on his dislocated shoulder with a harsh grunt, slid across the floorboards, and collided heavily with a chest of drawers.

A distant crash came from elsewhere in the house. Bullets tore through the wall next to him.

Lucas rolled onto his front and crawled toward the bedroom door in a cloud of splinters. Anger churned his stomach when he realized their assailants were using some kind of explosive, armor-piercing round. He struggled to his feet and jumped through the flames, the barrage of bullets and the spotlight following in his wake.

Anna's shout reached him from somewhere downstairs as he retraced his steps along the hallway. He negotiated the piles of rubble to their bedroom, grabbed his guns from the closet, and rammed a pair of spare magazines into the waistband of his pajamas before dashing back to the stairs. He took them two steps at a time, the Glock in his good hand. The sound of a scuffle reached him from the direction of the kitchen when he got to the bottom. He bolted toward the noise.

Anna stood struggling with a masked figure by the patio doors, the daisho on the floor behind her; she must have retrieved it from his office. Their golden retriever growled angrily at her attacker's feet, jaws firmly locked on the calf of the armed man and paws skidding on the floorboards as he tugged and fought to pull him off Anna. The cat crouched next to them, hairs rising from his arched back and angry hisses leaving his throat.

Rage burned through Lucas. He strode across the floor and shot the man in the head. The intruder jerked and crumpled to the floor.

A second figure darted out of the gloom behind Anna. He

wrapped an arm around her throat and placed the barrel of a gun against her right temple.

Lucas dropped the Glock, snatched a blade from the knife block on the island next to him, and hurled it.

The blade spun through the air and thudded into the man's right shoulder. He stumbled back with a grunt, his hold loosening on Anna. She snarled, elbowed him in the solar plexus, and grabbed his arm when he started to raise his gun.

A single gunshot thundered across the room as Lucas bolted toward the struggling pair. A glass exploded on the counter to his left, fragments of the bullet tearing through the air and missing his skin by inches.

The intruder's eyes widened a second before Lucas's fist collided with his jaw. He grunted and crashed into a patio door, the glass smashing under the impact.

Lucas roared, kicked the gun from his hand, and kneed him in the gut.

The man doubled over, the blow driving him through the jagged opening in the door frame. He fell out onto the veranda at the front of the house and landed on a jagged shard of glass, the fragment piercing his back all the way through his heart and out the front of his chest.

'To your right!' Anna shouted.

Lucas glimpsed movement out the corner of his eye and ducked beneath the knife arcing toward his neck. He heard the slick slide of a sword being drawn and turned in time to see Anna cast his katana at him. He jumped, grabbed the lacquered handle mid-air, and twisted as he landed on his feet, the blade slicing up and across the third figure's neck.

The man froze, his hands rising to the crimson stream pouring from his severed artery and windpipe. A choked gurgle left his lips as he sagged to his knees and onto his front.

Lucas moved to Anna's first attacker and stabbed him in the heart, fury a red mist across his vision.

Something told him these men were Immortals.

He wanted to make sure they would not rise again.

A noise at the front of the house brought his head around. His pulse jumped.

Glass crunched outside as Anna's second attacker climbed to his feet. He blinked, touched the glittering shard wedged in his heart, and took a step toward them.

A hand wrapped around Lucas's left ankle, distracting him. He looked down and froze when he saw the man whose neck he'd cut attempt to rise to his knees.

How is this—?

Gunfire brought Lucas's head up again.

Anna had grabbed a gun off the floor and was walking out of the house, an incoherent cry of rage on her lips as she shot the man on the veranda point blank in the chest.

Though he jerked and stumbled, he did not fall.

Lucas's heart thudded frantically as he drove the katana into the back of the intruder at his feet and straight through his heart. He yanked his blade out and turned in time to see two figures drop down from the sky and land on the veranda.

They clipped a line to the body harness of the man facing Anna and shot back up with him in tow.

She followed their ascent to the third Black Hawk hovering above the house with the gun, finger moving repeatedly on the trigger even after the magazine clicked empty.

Lucas glimpsed movement in the aircraft's cabin, lunged, and looped an arm around Anna's waist. He carried her to the ground a heartbeat before a machine gun spat scores of rounds at the spot where she'd been standing.

The first helicopter swung around the northwest corner of

the house. The second whirled into view from the south. Spotlights pierced the darkness and shone down on them.

Lucas scrambled to his knees in the downdrafts, pushed Anna behind him, and backpedaled furiously inside the house in a hail of automatic gunfire.

Bullets smashed through the ground floor windows and walls of their home as the helicopters started circling the building. Lucas climbed to his feet, hauled Anna up, and broke into a run toward the foyer, his fingers clasped tightly around her wrist. She swooped and grabbed his Glock from the floor as they went past the kitchen island. An explosion ripped through the room just as they exited it.

They darted toward the rear of the property in a cloud of debris and raced through to the sitting room. Lucas crossed the floor in a handful of steps, scaled a table against the opposite wall, and jumped, Anna in tow. They crashed through the large bay window at the back of the house.

They landed in the dirt in a shower of shards and rolled. Further explosions rocked the house behind them. The dog yelped from somewhere inside.

Lucas tumbled to a stop, pulled Anna up, and headed for the trees. A helicopter appeared to the right when they were ten seconds from cover. Fire flashed in the sky. His stomach dropped when he heard the whoosh of a rocket-propelled grenade. He veered at the last moment.

The bomb detonated some twenty feet to their right.

A wave of hot air wrapped around them as the blast lifted them off the ground. The world tilted and spun wildly. Pain stabbed through Lucas's left flank when he struck the dirt seconds later.

He lay stunned for a moment, his breath locked in his throat. When air finally wheezed through his lips, he gasped and groaned, his frantic gaze seeking Anna. Coldness gripped him when he saw her lying unconscious to his left, a crimson wound at her temple.

'Anna!'

Her name echoed dimly in his skull, his shout drowned out by the buzzing in his ears.

Lucas's bones and teeth vibrated from the sudden thump-thump of helicopter rotors above him as he climbed unsteadily to his knees. Heat bloomed in his belly. He looked down and glimpsed the jagged piece of wood that had impaled his flesh. He gritted his teeth, crawled toward Anna, and rolled onto his back atop her, protecting her body with his.

He looked up and faced their invisible enemy, his dislocated arm lying uselessly at his side while blood oozed from the tear in his abdomen.

For a moment, the only sounds were the rhythmic beats of the spinning blades in the sky and the roar from the fires engulfing the house.

Flames erupted from the mouth of a rocket launcher a hundred feet above him.

Lucas clenched his jaw, knowing there was no escape and that this was something they were unlikely to survive.

He reached out blindly, his fingers finding Anna's in the gloom. He closed his eyes as the grenade arrowed in on them and quelled the fury consuming his heart while he brought to mind the faces of their children for the last time. Despair filled him in his final moment.

I'm sorry I failed you.

Light bloomed behind his eyelids.

There was no heat. No pain. No sound.

Only silence.

Anna coughed and gasped.

Lucas blinked, shocked. The fact that he was still alive had barely registered when he beheld the incredible sight above him.

The flames of the detonation roared a short distance away, separated from them by some kind of transparent wall.

Anna shifted beneath him and he removed his weight from her. She sat up slowly beside him.

A second grenade left the helicopter hovering to their right. A third rocketed down from the aircraft to the left.

Anna cried out, her fingers clenching around his.

Lucas could only stare in wonderment, his breath frozen on his lips. Something told him the grenades would not reach them.

The bombs exploded thirty feet from their noses. Fire spread and wrapped around the invisible bubble curving over the area where they lay, the sound of the detonations a distant rumble, the heat of the flames undetectable.

That was when Lucas knew their children were still alive. He shared a dazed glance with Anna and saw the same shocking realization dawn in her eyes.

Even though Tomas and Lily were in the hands of an unknown enemy and no doubt scared out of their minds, they had still protected them.

There was no other explanation for what they were witnessing.

The helicopters suddenly started spinning wildly in the sky.

Lucas stiffened. Anna drew a sharp breath.

He understood instinctively then that an unseen battle was taking place above them. They watched for breathless moments, powerless to help.

The aircrafts leveled out, whirled around sharply, and headed for the ocean.

Something flashed out of the last helicopter when it passed over the yacht moored at the pier. Though he didn't hear the blast, Lucas saw the explosion. The boat went up in flames. He stared at the dark shapes fading rapidly in the night, his heart sinking.

Ripples broke out across the dome of energy insulating them from the outside world, the flames from the grenades long doused. It dissipated a moment later.

The thunderous roar of the blaze engulfing their home washed over them.

CHAPTER FIVE

'WE GOT VISUAL YET?' ASGARD SNAPPED.

He checked his twin-barreled Colt revolvers and slipped spare magazines into the ammunition pouch at his waist, his shoulders rigid.

Howard Titus's fingers danced across the master keyboard of the main workstation of the computer lab.

'No.' He studied the bank of flat-screen monitors in front of him. 'We should have images from the NGA in the next six minutes.'

They were in a steel and concrete reinforced bunker half a mile beneath a sprawling, state-of-the-art mansion that occupied the crest of a hill, in the middle of some three hundred and fifty acres of prime real estate in the Santa Monica Mountains.

The property stood on the same site as the first mansion Howard, Ethan, and Asgard had built following the incredible success of STAEGH Corp, the multi-billion-dollar tech company they had formed using the money they'd accumulated over the centuries of their existence.

The original building and bunker had been destroyed four years back following a deadly assault by Jonah Krondike's men and the US Army group who had been helping him experiment on humans and Immortals. It was Howard himself who had activated the detonator on the network of explosives with which they'd rigged the property for use in the event of such a catastrophic scenario.

Though it would have made sense to reconstruct the new estate elsewhere, Olivia had insisted they rebuild on the original grounds. It was the only home she'd known beside the abbey where she'd spent the first hundred years of her life.

The second mansion was even more secure than the first, with the cave holding the computer lab deeper than its predecessor and able to withstand the latest bunker bomb.

Olivia glanced at the figure emerging from the armory at the back of the chamber. Madeleine holstered a gun and swung a rucksack onto her shoulder, her face set in grim lines. She came and placed it on the workstation where Ethan was checking a duffel bag filled with medical kit.

Even though they had taught her how to use a gun and given her a firearm, Olivia still disliked using the weapon. She much preferred exercising her psionic abilities to defeat an enemy over riddling them with explosive, metal projectiles.

Asgard shoved his arming sword into the scabbard strapped to his back and turned to a second monitor on the workstation. 'Victor? Anything from your end?'

Victor Dvorsky was on video call from the headquarters of the Bastian First Council in Vienna.

He looked away from the person he'd been giving orders to and faced the camera.

'We have two satellites covering the Pacific right now. We should have live feeds in sixty seconds.' His expression reflected the same disquiet running through all of them.

'Has anyone been able to get in touch with them?' Alexa said in a hard voice across another video call.

She was on a private jet headed for LAX with Zachary and Reid.

'No.' A muscle jumped in Ethan's cheek. 'Not since Olivia got through just after six this morning.'

'What about the phone in Anna's lab?' Reid said across the connection.

Lines furrowed the former US Marine's brow, visible in the dimmed light of the airplane cabin.

Madeleine shook her head. 'We tried that too. No luck so far.'

'Their satellite dish is down,' Howard said. 'I haven't been able to get any signal from it since we started checking.'

'Olivia, have you tried remote-viewing the island?' Conrad asked on another monitor.

He and Laura were making their way back to the West Coast from Rio de Janeiro, where they'd been visiting friends.

A fresh wave of agony danced through Olivia at his question.

It was gone seven in the morning. Over an hour had passed since she and Ethan had woken everyone in the mansion and called their cousins and friends to relate the psychic dream she'd had. The fact that nobody had been able to make contact with Balthazar Island meant that what she had seen had already come to pass.

Though she knew it didn't make sense, Olivia couldn't help but blame herself for not having had the vision earlier. If she'd sensed what was going to happen sooner, she could have acted faster.

'You did everything you could,' Asgard told her, repeating the words he'd said earlier that morning when she'd admitted to her feeling of guilt. 'If you hadn't had that dream, we might not have found out that something had happened for days.'

Olivia bit her lip. She turned toward the monitor displaying Conrad's call and finally gave voice to the troubling phenomenon she'd encountered, one that puzzled her as much as it transfixed her.

'I already did. Something is—blocking me from remote-viewing the island. I don't know what it is. I've never felt anything like it before.'

Conrad stared at her, his eyes dark with worry.

They all knew the devastating extent of her abilities from the incident at Yuma. That she was struggling to use her psionic powers to see their cousins' home seemed to unsettle the Healer as much as it had everyone else.

'Images coming up now,' Victor said. 'I'm sharing the screen with all of you.'

'Gotcha.' Howard clicked on a second window and expanded it.

An orange dot appeared in the middle of the dark monitor. The image zoomed in and focused in jerky transitions until the island took shape in the center of the screen. The orange spot became two, then five distinct areas, the largest in the middle.

Olivia's stomach twisted. She raised her hands to her mouth, the horror resonating through her reflected on everyone's faces.

Lucas and Anna's house was on fire, as was their yacht. Flame-lit debris littered the area around the property.

'Son of a—' Reid swallowed the curse and struck the wall of the fuselage next to him with his fist.

A call came through on the main computer. Howard tapped the keyboard and opened another window.

Dimitri Reznak appeared on the screen. 'Sorry, I just made it back to the castle. You got any news yet?'

'I'm transmitting the images to you right now,' Victor told the Crovir noble in clipped tones. 'It looks like there might have been several explosions on the island.'

'Victor, can your satellites switch to high-res, thermal imaging?' Conrad said sharply. 'We need to be able to see them if they're down there.'

'They can.'

Seconds later, the screen flicked to dark purple with traces of blue at the edges. The fires transformed into rippling, gold clouds streaked with red and orange.

They watched the eerie images for breathless seconds, searching for signs of movement. They saw none around the house.

'Try the lab,' Asgard said bleakly.

The screen slowly panned to the north of the island.

'There!' Alexa leaned closer to the monitor on the jet. 'Top right-hand corner. Zoom in on it.'

A shadowy rectangle with a faint thermal signal appeared through a thick canopy of trees. Four heat signatures were visible inside it.

'It's them!' Relief colored Conrad's words. 'They're safe.'

'One of them isn't moving,' Alexa said quietly.

'And two of them are too small to be the children.' Howard glanced uneasily at Olivia.

Her heart sank. She hesitated before voicing what she'd suspected all along. 'Tomas and Lily are not on the island.'

LUCAS SAT UP WITH A GASP. FIRE SHOT THROUGH HIS BODY. HE grunted and pressed a hand to the dressing on his abdomen.

Anna rose from the chair beside him and took his fingers in her own. 'Easy, now.'

Lucas looked around. He was on the workbench in the middle of Anna's lab.

The memory of what had happened washed over him. A different kind of agony seared his chest.

After the men who'd attacked them had left the island, they'd made their way to the beach to the north. Anna had supported Lucas's weight while he stumbled across the dirt and sand, the piece of wood that had pierced him front to back still wedged in his body. Blood had drenched his pajama bottoms and stained her nightdress by the time they reached the dark building.

Their relief at finding the lab intact had been short-lived. After Anna had relocated his right shoulder, Lucas had attempted to call Asgard and Victor Dvorsky, even while Anna was examining his wound. It didn't take long to discover that their enemy had destroyed the satellite dish they used to communicate with the outside world at some stage during the assault.

'I'm going to have to perform surgery to get this out of you,' Anna had announced in a bleak voice as she studied the chunk of wood impaling his left flank through to his back. 'The rate at which you're losing blood tells me you probably have a ruptured spleen.'

Lucas had clenched his jaw and nodded. 'Do what you need to do.'

Anna had more than enough medical equipment in the lab

to perform the emergency procedure, including several bags of O neg blood. Since they lived in the middle of nowhere with their kids, they had all sorts of contingency plans in case they ever suffered an unfortunate accident, even though their Immortal abilities and the children's powers meant they were unlikely to need them.

Anna had kissed him before administering a strong sedative into the IV she'd hooked up to his arm.

'You'd better get through this.' She had pressed her forehead against his where he lay propped on his right side, her green eyes glinting with a hard light. 'We need to find the bastards who took our children.'

Lucas had swallowed the lump in his throat and nodded. 'If the Red Death didn't kill me, then I doubt this will. Besides, the others are probably on their way to the island right now.'

He'd told Anna about Olivia's call on the way to the lab. Though he hadn't made out his cousin's words, the panic in her voice had told him she'd had a psychic dream about the impending attack and had rung to warn them.

He'd drifted off at some point during the operation, the sedative and the anesthesia she'd injected in his spine numbing his mind and body while she undertook the grim task of removing the wooden shaft.

'You lost a lot of blood,' Anna said presently.

She filled a glass at the sink and brought it to him.

'Thanks.' Lucas gulped the water down before eyeing the two figures watching him keenly from the floor.

Anna followed his gaze. 'They turned up a while ago.' A wry smile curved her lips. 'Looks like Cornelius gave Bob one of his lives.'

The cat blinked at his name and proceeded to lick the

golden retriever's singed fur. Bob huffed, tail thumping the floor.

THEY CAME IN SIGHT OF THE ISLAND JUST OVER AN HOUR AFTER dawn broke over the North Pacific.

'Don't wait for us,' Alexa had told Asgard before he, Ethan, Olivia, and Madeleine had left the mansion to take their jet at LAX. 'We'll follow you after we refuel.'

'We should reach the West Coast in about nine hours,' Conrad had said. 'Keep us informed.'

'There'll be an Airbus H225 at the airport in Kauai when you land there,' Victor had added.

Asgard had nodded gratefully at his friend and former rival. The H225 was the fastest commercial helicopter currently available on the market. It would get them to Balthazar Island faster than a speedboat.

'I have Bastian Hunters on their way to Hawaii but I suspect you guys will get there first given the speed at which you'll be piloting that Gulfstream,' Victor had said drily.

Asgard had smiled faintly at his words. Once he'd awoken from the icy prison where he'd been trapped for nearly four centuries, and having gone on to escape Jonah Krondike's clutches a decade later with Ethan's help, he'd developed a fascination for flying. He now held private pilot licenses for several countries and was even certified to fly military aircraft.

It had taken him just under five hours to get them from LA to the northernmost of the eight major Hawaiian islands. They'd transferred their weapons' bags and medical kits to the helicopter waiting on the tarmac and taken off almost immediately under a lightening sky.

Smoke appeared on the horizon before the island took shape against the dazzling, blue backdrop of the ocean. Relief swamped Asgard despite the tension coursing through him.

He was within reach of his nephew and niece.

They were ten miles from the beach when the helicopter juddered violently in the air.

Asgard cursed. He gripped the controls and worked the pedals as the aircraft pitched backwards before yawing from side to side.

'What the hell was that?' Madeleine shouted from the co-pilot seat.

Asgard scowled. 'I don't know.'

He leveled the Airbus into a hover before moving the aircraft forward again.

The helicopter shook wildly as it struck an invisible wall.

Olivia clasped Ethan's hand back in the cabin, alarm spiking her pulse.

She could sense something in front of them. Something faint yet eerily familiar.

A gasp left her lips when the aircraft started spinning uncontrollably. The ocean whirled into view through the window to her left.

No!

A ghostly ripple danced through her consciousness at her involuntary psychic cry. Olivia's eyes widened.

Lily?

Just as suddenly as they had started, the vibrations rocking the helicopter vanished and Asgard regained control of the aircraft.

Ethan rose and staggered to the cockpit, Olivia behind him.

'What just happened?' he snapped.

'I have no idea,' Asgard said grimly.

Olivia stared through the cockpit windscreen at the island.

'It was them,' she murmured shakily.

Ethan blinked when he sensed her thoughts. 'You mean that was the *kids?!*'

Olivia nodded, still struggling to come to terms with what they had just experienced.

'Remember what we did at Yuma? When we created that psychokinetic bubble to stop the fire? I think it was something like that.'

Madeleine paled. 'But you said they weren't on the island.'

'They aren't.' Olivia swallowed. 'That was just the remnant of Lily and Tomas's powers. I'm pretty sure it's what was blocking me from remote-viewing the place.'

The beach grew ahead of them, the black remains of the yacht and the smoking ruins of the house evidence of the devastating assault that had taken place some seven hours past.

Two figures climbed to their feet a short distance from the scorched rubble, a dog and a cat at their side.

CHAPTER SIX

Lily stirred and opened her eyes. A naked light bulb hung from a concrete ceiling some five feet above her. She gasped and sat up.

A wave of dizziness swept over her, sending the world tilting and spinning alarmingly. She closed her eyes and fought down the nausea threatening to empty her stomach.

The drugs the men who had kidnapped her and Tomas had injected them with still lingered in her bloodstream. Lily concentrated, searching for the foreign substances inside her. It took a few seconds to isolate their strange chemical signals. She took a shallow breath and used her healing abilities to destroy them.

Her shoulders sagged when she regained full control of her body. She opened her eyes again and looked around slowly.

She was in her pajamas, on a cot inside a chamber measuring some fifteen by twenty feet. The walls were white and bare, giving a cold, clinical feel to the space. A metal door with sliding panels at the top and bottom stood to her right. A toilet and sink jutted out of the concrete in the corner ahead and to her left. A narrow air vent sat high up on the wall above the washroom area.

Next to it was a camera.

The device had been positioned to give a degree of privacy to the occupant of the room when they were using the washing facilities while still covering most of the cell, including the camp bed.

Lily knew instinctively that she was being watched. She reached out with her mind.

Tomas?

I'm here.

She swallowed a sigh of relief at the sound of her twin's faint voice.

Are you alright?

Yes. Just a bit groggy from the drugs they gave us. You?

I'm okay. Lily frowned. *Want me to get rid of them?*

Almost done.

She sensed their mental connection grow stronger a few seconds later as he destroyed the remnant of the chemicals inside his bloodstream.

Do you know where we are?

No. I was out of it for most of the way here. I don't even know what time it is.

She got out of the cot, walked to the wall opposite, and placed a hand against the concrete. She ignored the whir of the camera as it tracked her and closed her eyes. Tendrils of energy snaked out of her fingertips and palm.

Lily concentrated, her power mapping out the area around her through concrete and metal, seeking her brother's consciousness. It flashed in her mind a moment later, a golden stream tinged with brilliant white, a consciousness as familiar to her as her own.

I think you're about eighty feet away.

Images flickered across her inner vision as Tomas projected his view of the room he was in. It was identical to hers.

Lily?

Yes?

Don't touch the door. It's electrified.

Lily blinked. *Are you hurt?*

No. I sensed the current just as I was about to grab the handle.

Lily bit her lip and glanced at the steel door to her right. *Can we still get through if we need to?*

I think so. Uncle Ethan showed me how to manipulate matter without having to touch it. I can teach you.

Lily turned and slid down the wall until she sat on the floor, a wave of exhaustion suddenly sweeping over her. She brought her legs up to her chest, folded her arms around them, and dropped her forehead on her knees.

Lily?

Yes?

I couldn't get into those men's heads before they injected those drugs into us. Did you?

Lily didn't reply.

The attack on their home had been sudden and brutal. The only forewarning she'd had was the psychic dream she'd experienced moments before the first explosion. Seconds later, she was being yanked into the air and carried to a helicopter hovering above their house, her father's stunned face fading rapidly beneath her.

Her memories of what had followed were a chaotic maelstrom of images and emotions.

Shock at what was happening. Horror when she heard Tomas's cry inside her head. Pain as the masked men who had captured her tried to subdue her while she screamed and fought them. The terrible noise from the machine guns and the grenade launchers. The flashes of light and flames as bullets and explosions ripped through their home. The fear and rage she sensed from her parents as they clashed with their unknown enemy.

And, finally, the mind numbing terror that gripped her and echoed across her connection with Tomas when they realized what was about to happen to their mother and father.

Their reactions had been born of pure instinct.

Seconds before the first bomb left the helicopter, they had fused their minds and powers to create a barrier of pure elemental and psychokinetic energy around their parents where they lay wounded on the ground.

It had protected them from all three grenades.

As their assailants had watched in astonishment, Tomas and Lily had turned their attention on them, their distress turning to anger and their powers sending the helicopters into a wild spin.

Lily had barely registered the first dart that had penetrated her skin. It had taken three more before the drugs had seeped into her bloodstream and sapped at her consciousness.

Moments before the world had gone dark around them, she and Tomas had expanded the bubble shielding their mother and father all the way around the island. They had known it would hold out against further enemy attacks for some time and give their parents the protection they needed to recover from their injuries.

Lily?

She startled.

Are you scared?

Lily swallowed. *Yes.*

Their mental connection glowed as Tomas tried to reassure her.

Mom and dad will find us. The others will help them.

Lily blinked back tears at the determination in her twin's voice.

Did you feel it?

Lily nodded unconsciously at Tomas's question. *Yes. Aunt Olivia went through the barrier.*

They had created the wall of energy around their home so it would last until their family and friends reached the island. Now that their aunt's consciousness had touched it, the bubble had dissipated.

Tomas?

Yes?

I tried to get in those men's minds.

Tomas grew quiet when he registered her unease. It was a while before he spoke. *What did you see?*

They are different. Immortal but different. There's something strange about their consciousness. I've never sensed anything like it before.

Lily registered Tomas's surprise.

Do you think you could learn to manipulate their minds?

Lily hesitated. *Given time, yes, probably.*

Silence descended between them.

Tomas?

Yes?

There's something else. Something here. Can you feel it?

Tomas wavered for a moment. *There's this weird feeling at the back of my head. Like an itch I can't scratch. Why? What can you see?*

Lily inhaled shakily. *Darkness. There's darkness here with us.*

ALEXA SQUATTED NEXT TO THE BURNT REMAINS OF THE TWO corpses. Though their faces and clothes had been charred beyond recognition, she could still discern the wounds marking one of the men's necks and both their chests. Her gaze lingered on the cuts for a moment before she resumed her examination.

Thirty feet to her right, the team of Bastian Hunters Victor had sent to Hawaii moved carefully through the rubble of the house, searching for any evidence left by the enemy who had attacked Lucas and Anna Soul's home.

A shiver danced down Alexa's spine despite the heat. The dread that had shot through her when she and Zachary had received Asgard's call earlier that day still echoed deep inside her.

Although she had always considered herself a loner, even while she was growing up with Marie and Tom Fawkes and Dimitri on the latter's estate in Sumava, meeting Zachary Jackson and her Immortal family had changed that in the last seven years.

Her past self would have considered the bonds she had forged with them a weakness. Her present self had discovered them to be her greatest strength.

Her affection for them was something that filled her with more happiness than she had ever experienced. Not only had she found her soulmate in Zachary, she had also acquired siblings in Lucas, Anna, Conrad, Ethan, and Olivia, and even an uncle in Asgard. Her relationship with the latter had come as a surprise. Though they came from completely different worlds and eras and had little in common, she could not help but feel a strong affinity for him, as he did for her. Neither of them were the greatest of conversationalists and they were more used to their own company than that of others.

The connection between all of them went deeper than anything she had ever felt, a red thread of fate that had its origins in the distant past and would continue far into the future, binding them to an as yet unknown destiny.

It was something she'd experienced a hint of after she had died for the first time, when she had lingered in that twilight place between death and resurrection and lived the memories of the incredible warrior who had been reincarnated in her. Her suspicions had crystallized into certainty when she had been introduced to Olivia and Ethan four years ago. The Seer had revealed details of the nightmare that had plagued her for nearly a hundred years, a nightmare founded in the memories of her own prodigious predecessor, which had been passed down her bloodline through the ages. Memories of a war that had seen the death of Crovir and Bastian, the Immortals who had given rise to the two races. A war Alexa had witnessed herself through the eyes of the founder of her own bloodline.

Alexa would do anything to protect her newfound family, especially the children who had become its nucleus. Her anger at what Lily and Tomas would have endured during the assault still burned red and raw in her heart, as she knew it did in every one of her kin and their closest friends and allies.

Footsteps crunched in the sand up ahead. She looked up and saw Reid approaching. He dropped down on his haunches in front of her and showed her something.

'These are not just normal armor-piercing rounds.' His voice was hard. 'These bastards weren't taking any chances. If one of these had hit Lucas or Anna, it would have hurt them pretty badly, regardless of their being Immortals.'

Alexa studied the former US Marine.

Of all their human allies, she was especially fond of Lucas's best friend. It was he who had helped Zachary adapt to his new reality as a superhuman, after the latter had received a transfusion of Lucas's blood when he lay on his deathbed following a lethal injury inflicted by Alberto Cavaleti during their battle with Kronos in the Ural Mountains seven years ago. Reid had similarly been gifted with Anna's blood a few months before, when he'd been wounded. He had acquired self-healing abilities that nearly matched those of Immortals as well as a delayed aging process, the same as Zachary. Not only that, he was also a stronger and faster fighter than he had been before.

Alexa turned her attention to the strange casings in his hand. They were of two distinct sizes.

'They look like fragmenting bullets.' She frowned. 'Weren't the 9mm ones still in the experimental phase?'

'The military started using them this year. If it's the same companies producing them, we should be able to trace their supply lines. But I get the feeling these were designed somewhere else.' Reid narrowed his eyes. 'They look more advanced.'

Alexa twisted on her heels. She considered the house and the remains of the yacht floating next to the pier with a thoughtful stare.

'From Lucas and Anna's accounts, the men who attacked them were highly trained and thoroughly prepared. They knew the exact location of Tomas and Lily's bedroom and the layout of the house. They also knew where the communication dish was, even though it was camouflaged.'

'Which means they've been watching this place for a while,' Reid said quietly.

They looked at each other before gazing up at the sky.

'Satellites,' Reid muttered.

Alexa studied the pale blue expanse above them. 'It's the only logical explanation.'

A figure headed toward them from the direction of what remained of Lucas and Anna's home.

'Bar shedloads of bullet casings, I don't think we're gonna find anything else here,' said the red-haired immortal who stopped beside them. 'These assholes had enough ammo to start a war.'

Anatole Vassili was a close friend of Conrad and Laura, and a former member of the first team of intelligence operatives Victor Dvorsky had put together when he was Head of the Bastian Corps, the precursor to what would become the Bastian Counter-Terrorism Section.

'I'm surprised Victor let you come,' Reid had told the Immortal when he'd seen him with the Hunters at the airport in Kauai.

'He didn't really have a choice in the matter,' Anatole had retorted. 'Those kids are special. Besides, hell knows what would happen to you guys if I wasn't here. I'm forever having to save your sorry asses.'

Reid had smiled despite the gravity of the situation.

Alexa had heard about the battle Lucas, Reid, Anatole, and Victor had been involved in seven years ago from Dimitri. A small group of Crovir nobles had joined forces with the Bastian First Council to prevent a second Immortal war, one instigated by Agatha Vellacrus, the then leader of the Crovir race, and her son, Felix Thorne. That both Lucas and Anna would prove to be related to their enemy had come as a shock to everyone except their grandfather Tomas Godard, who had known the truth all along.

Anatole scrutinized the bodies of the two men Lucas had killed. They had recovered the remains a short while back from the front of the property.

'You know, one thing is kinda puzzling me.'

Alexa followed his pale gaze. 'You mean the lack of crows?'

Like Lucas, she suspected the men who had attacked the island were Immortals. The fact that crows had not turned the dead intruders' bodies to ash was another confounding mystery, one more to add to their growing list.

Reid shrugged. 'It could mean they're human.'

Alexa and Anatole stared at him.

'No offense, but no human could take down the guy who was once the most hunted Immortal on the planet,' Anatole said bluntly.

'He did get shot in the head by one once,' Reid retorted. He paused and grimaced. 'Mind you, he was drunk as a skunk at the time.'

'Oh yeah.' Anatole pulled a face. 'Was it that time you first met him, when he was mourning that Olsson guy's death?'

'Yeah. And don't mention that bastard's name.'

'But you killed him.'

Reid scowled. 'I still don't like hearing his name.'

Anatole's face cleared. He nodded with an understanding expression. 'I get it. It's a jealousy thing. That guy used to be Lucas's best friend after all.'

'I was not jealous of him,' Reid said stonily.

Anatole grinned. 'You don't have to be shy.'

'What the hell are you talking about?' Reid snapped.

Alexa swallowed a sigh as she listened to their bickering. One thing about having an extended family was that she now knew what it felt like to have relatives whom she wanted to smack once in a while. Or sometimes shoot. In a non-lethal spot. Probably.

She rose to her feet and indicated the bodies.

'Let's take them back with us. We might be able to identify them from their dental records.'

CHAPTER SEVEN

'YOU MEAN, THE BARRIER WAS STILL THERE, OUTSIDE THE ISLAND?'

Shock reverberated through Lucas as he stared at Olivia.

'Stay still,' Conrad muttered beside him.

His hands were flush against Lucas's abdomen and right shoulder. Warmth seeped through Lucas's body as his cousin started healing his wounds.

Olivia nodded. 'Judging from the fact that Alexa and the Hunters didn't experience it when their helicopters got there, I think Lily and Tomas created the wall to last long enough until someone their powers recognized tried to breach it.'

Lucas shared a startled glance with Anna.

They were at the mansion in the Santa Monica Mountains. Fourteen hours had passed since their home had been attacked and their children taken from them. Shortly after coming to their rescue that morning, Asgard had flown them to Kauai and back to the West Coast. They'd crossed paths briefly with Alexa, Reid, and Anatole at the airport in Hawaii. Zachary had accompanied them for the return trip.

'Did you know Tomas and Lily had that ability?' Victor said.

Lucas looked distractedly at the flat-screen monitor on the wall to his left, where Victor's video call was being transmitted live from the Bastian headquarters in Vienna.

They were in the mansion's main lounge. Glass walls spanned three aspects of the room, offering views over the lit terraces and gardens carved into the hill on which the estate had been built. Beyond them were dark canyons leading to the distant, moonlit Pacific.

'We—' Lucas's gaze flickered to Anna as he answered Victor's question, '—no, we didn't know they could do that.'

He was still struggling to grasp Olivia's startling revelation: that the protective bubble their children had created to shield them from the grenades had been there all along, keeping them safe from further attacks.

It filled him with awe.

'I suspect they didn't either,' Olivia said softly. 'They must have sensed what was about to happen to you and reacted instinctively.'

The same reverence Lucas and Anna had experienced at the time was reflected on the faces of their relatives and friends.

Asgard looked at Olivia and Ethan. 'It must have been as powerful as the one you two created at Yuma to have lasted so long.'

Olivia nodded.

'Can you sense them?' Anna leaned forward where she sat next to Lucas, her green eyes glinting with hope. 'In your mind?'

Olivia hesitated before shaking her head.

'No, I can't. I tried during the attack. All I got was a jumble of images and feelings. I think—,' she hesitated and bit her lip, '—I think they're somewhere far away. Somewhere they and I haven't been before. And I'm pretty sure they were sedated in order to get them there.'

Anna's shoulders sagged. Lucas fought back the emotion clogging his throat and linked his hand with hers.

They hadn't been separated from their children from the moment of their birth, not even once. Their absence was a gnawing emptiness in the pit of his stomach, an emptiness that was threatening to consume him. He could tell without even looking at her that Anna was battling the same abyss.

He recalled the moment after the explosions, when they had suspected their children were fighting for their lives inside the helicopters. He knew then that Olivia was right about the drugs. A fresh wave of rage flooded him at the thought of what Tomas and Lily had lived through last night and what they could be enduring this very minute.

'Easy,' Conrad warned, his fingers flexing on his tense flesh.

Lucas blinked. 'Sorry.'

'Don't be.' Conrad looked at Laura where she perched on the armrest beside Anna. His face hardened. 'If someone took our kid, I would burn the world to find them and rip their heart from their body.'

Laura squeezed Anna's shoulder, her expression just as deadly.

Asgard rose and started pacing the floor. 'So, we're still no closer to knowing where they are, why they were taken, and who took them.'

The frustration in his uncle's voice resonated inside Lucas. Nearly a day had passed since the attack and they were no nearer to figuring out who had kidnapped Tomas and Lily and why. The latter question worried him the most. From the expression he'd glimpsed in Anna's eyes when they were in her lab that morning, he sensed they shared the same suspicion.

'We have a couple of clues,' Reid said.

Alexa nodded, silver eyes glinting. 'The bodies and the cartridges we found on the island.'

'What about satellite images?' Zachary said. 'Any way we can look at them retrospectively? Figure out where those helicopters came from?'

'There wouldn't be many Black Hawks hanging around that particular part of the Pacific,' Anatole muttered, leaning against a wall.

'I've already got my team on it,' Howard said. Windows flickered and data streamed across the monitor of the laptop on his knees. 'The nearest landmass is Hawaii so I suspect they took off from one of the islands. It might take days to analyze the images, though. You're talking about dozens of satellites in geosynchronous orbits over the Western hemisphere at any one time.' He glanced at them with a frown. 'It'll be like finding a needle in a haystack.'

Although he was a skilled hacker himself, Lucas was grateful for Howard's presence. As the brain behind STAEGH Corp, the Crovir was leaps ahead of any of them when it came to infiltrating secure databases and obtaining intelligence. He was also the head of a group of international cyber activists whose main goal was to subvert the illegal actions of governments and powerful corporations around the world.

'We're working that angle at our end too,' Victor added. 'And I agree with Titus. It's gonna take a while to get through the data.'

Zachary's face suddenly brightened. He turned to Alexa. 'Hey, honey, I think we know someone who could help with that.'

Alexa smiled faintly and pulled her cell from her pocket.

Lucas watched as she pressed a number on speed dial, as

perplexed as everyone else in the room. Only Victor seemed to know what she and Zachary were talking about.

'Good thinking,' the Bastian leader murmured. 'She'll speed things up considerably.'

Alexa handed her cell to Howard. 'Can you transfer this to the main monitor?'

Howard tapped a couple of keys on his laptop and set up a second window on the flat-screen on the wall. The video call connected a moment later.

A man with a shock of tousled, dark hair and brown eyes came into view. He was dressed in a T-shirt and sweatpants, and was sitting in a chair at a workstation in a dimly lit, concrete and glass computer lab.

'Oh, hey, Alexa.' He glanced at them distractedly, words distorted by the popsicle hanging out the corner of his mouth. 'What can I do for you?'

Alexa frowned. 'I was hoping to talk to Eva. Why are you still up? It's five in the morning there.'

The man shrugged. 'You know I'm a night bird.'

A faint noise rose from the monitor's speakers.

Alexa sighed. 'Is that "Call of Duty" I hear in the background?'

The man grinned and almost lost the popsicle. 'Yup. I'm testing the company's latest game. It's ace. You should come over and have a go.'

'No, thank you,' Alexa said coldly.

'Who *is* this guy?' Howard muttered.

Alexa scanned their puzzled faces. 'Did none of you visit Dimitri's research facility when you came to Sumava?'

Madeleine arched an eyebrow. 'There's a research facility on the estate?'

'Yes.' A shadow darted across Alexa's face. 'Kronos destroyed it seven years ago. Dimitri had the labs rebuilt in a different location.'

The man on the screen paused his video game and peered closely at the monitor at his end for the first time. His eyes rounded when he finally registered their presence.

'Whoa. What's with the crowd?' The popsicle fell into his lap. 'Shit!'

He shot out of the chair and disappeared from view.

'Eva, are you there?' Alexa said to the empty screen.

Lucas startled when a computerized female voice replied.

'Yes, I am. It is good to see you, Alexa. Zachary, I enjoyed your latest paper on the findings you and Dimitri made in North Africa last year.'

Zachary grinned. 'Thanks, Eva.'

'Victor, I see you're online with us too. It's been some time since you and I played a game of chess.'

'Hi, Eva,' Victor murmured. 'And yes, it's been a while.'

Howard blinked. 'Who is *that?*'

'That's Eva, the AI Jordan created,' Alexa said. 'She looks after Dimitri's estate and his labs.'

'Dimitri has an *AI?*' Howard said, shocked. 'And who's Jordan?'

The dark-haired man in the sweatpants came back into view. He was dabbing at his clothes with a towel.

'This is Jordan Banks, Eva's…father,' Alexa said in a long-suffering tone.

Jordan plonked himself down in the chair and waved a hand at the camera. 'Yo.'

Alexa made introductions, finishing with Howard. 'Jordan, Eva, this is Howard Titus. I'm sure you've heard of STAEGH Corp.'

'Of course. STAEGH Corp is a thirty-and-a-half-billion-dollar tech company owned by Howard Orson Rodney Titus and two silent business partners whose identities have never been made public,' Eva narrated smoothly. 'Mr. Titus is currently number five on the list of the world's richest tech tycoons and has consistently been in the top twenty most-wanted bachelors for the last decade.'

Howard opened and closed his mouth soundlessly.

'Are you flirting with him?' Jordan asked the AI testily.

'I am not,' Eva replied. 'I am being appreciative of his brains and his physical assets. By the way, I am most intrigued by the two gentlemen on the couch to the right. I can see energy being transferred from Mr. Greene to Mr. Soul. It is fascinating to observe.'

Lucas glanced at Conrad and saw his surprise reflected back at him in his cousin's eyes.

'She can analyze things to that extent?' Ethan muttered.

'Yes,' Alexa replied. She looked at the screen. 'Eva, Jordan, we need you to help us with something.'

She gave the AI and her creator a short version of the events of the last day. By the end of her account, Jordan's expression had grown focused.

'Want to hook me and Eva up to your network?' he asked Howard.

'I'm already on it,' Eva said. 'I should have the initial data you seek within the next few hours.'

Howard paled and stared dazedly from the computer on his lap to the screen. 'Did you just breach my security system?'

'I did,' Eva said. 'I'm impressed by your set-up. I have a couple of suggestions you might appreciate.'

'There's something else.' Alexa glanced at Lucas and Anna, her expression troubled. 'There were meant to be less than twenty people who knew of Tomas and Lily's existence. The children are not registered on any birth database in the world.'

Surprised dawned on Jordan's face. 'So, you're saying they're ghosts?'

Lucas's fingers tightened around Anna's. 'We intended to keep it that way until they were older.'

'The only way someone could have found out about them is if the island was being watched,' Reid said. 'And there's not many people who were meant to know the location of the island either.'

'What you're saying is logical,' Jordan murmured.

'We need to find out if there's been any unusual satellite activity, human or Immortal, in the last few months,' Alexa said. 'As in unauthorized access or unscheduled coverage over that part of the Pacific.'

Howard raised his eyebrows. 'That's a big ask.'

'I agree,' Jordan said with a nod. 'That will take longer.'

'I've got another call coming through.' Victor's gaze swept the room before settling on Lucas. 'Keep me informed. And, Eva, let me know if you need access to the Bastian satellite network.'

'Thank you, Victor, but I already have that access.'

Victor stiffened, hand hovering above his trackpad.

'Do I even want to know how?' he said, scowling at his camera.

'Jordan said you would shoot him if you found that out so I would prefer not to say,' Eva said primly.

A nervous smile darted across Jordan's face as he studied the Bastian leader's stony expression. 'I wasn't just targeting you. I also have access to the Crovir network.'

Victor muttered something under his breath. His screen winked out.

'We need somewhere to analyze the bodies we've recovered and the shell casings,' Alexa stated. 'Somewhere private, preferably.'

Asgard turned to Howard. 'How long would it take to put something together in the bunker?'

Howard grimaced. 'It depends what kind of stuff you're gonna want.'

Anna shifted beside Lucas. 'I know exactly what we need in order to examine those dead men. It will take some time to gather all that equipment.'

'I agree,' Madeleine said. 'But there's already a place where we can do it.' She smiled faintly at Anna. 'I'll help. My specialty is molecular genetics and genomics, but I have degrees in other biological sciences.'

Anna nodded gratefully. 'Thank you. I worked as a pathologist, and I was a physician and surgeon, but I could do with another pair of hands.'

Asgard stared at Madeleine. 'What place?'

'Dimitri's facility in Sumava. It makes perfect sense.'

Asgard's face fell. 'Oh.'

She narrowed her eyes at him. 'Is this about the stupid feud you two have had going for, like, half a millennium?'

Asgard sniffed. 'It isn't a feud. It's an Immortal thing.'

'Dimitri's facility is geared toward his work for the Crovir Immortal Culture and History Section, but there's more than enough hardware there to meet your needs, including a molecular genetics lab,' Zachary said. 'I'm sure he would be more than happy to accommodate you.'

'If Dr. Godard and Dr. Black provide me with a list of what they need, I will make sure we have it all on site by the time they arrive,' Eva said.

'Thank you.' Anna took a shallow breath. 'I think we're

going to find something we're not expecting when we examine those bodies.'

'You mean apart from the fact they haven't been turned to ash by crows?' Alexa said.

'Yes,' Lucas said. The unease he'd felt during his confrontation with the intruders who had attacked their home rose inside him once more. 'Those men should have stayed down when I fought them.'

Tense silence filled the room.

A muscle jumped in Alexa's cheek. 'You mean they survived a direct strike to the heart from you?'

Lucas shook his head. 'No. That was what finally killed them.'

'What Lucas means is that the wounds he inflicted on them should have stopped them, momentarily at least,' Anna explained. 'One of them had a piece of glass stuck in his heart. He was still standing even after I shot him multiple times at point-blank range.'

'Was he wearing a body vest?' Reid said.

'No. I could see the damage the bullets made in his flesh.' Anna hesitated and glanced at Lucas. 'The one whose throat Lucas cut was still trying to fight us, even though he was hemorrhaging from his wound.' She looked around at them all, fear evident in her eyes. 'It was as if—as if he couldn't feel any pain.'

CHAPTER EIGHT

THE MAN STARED AT THE TWO BODIES INSIDE THE ISOLATION chamber of the facility's main lab. Lines sneaked out from under the sheets covering the still forms on the beds, connecting them to the range of sophisticated equipment lining the linoleum floor. Even though the hour was late, several technicians in decontamination suits worked the array of gleaming machines.

Despite the flurry of activity, the monitors recording the vital signs of the first figure remained silent, as they had done the last twenty-two months. Though they had only been able to get their hands on the second body yesterday, there was no doubt that both were still very much dead.

He frowned at the woman standing beside him before twisting on his heels and strolling to a computer station to their left. She followed leisurely in his steps, her heels striking the ground with elegant clicks.

'Why have you not taken their blood yet?' he said, not bothering to mask his irritation.

The technician manning the desk flinched at his tone.

Jessica Wu, the Immortal scientist spearheading the research projects at the installation, eyed him with an unfazed expression before following his gaze.

They studied the camera feeds from the cells where Tomas and Lily Soul were being kept prisoner, four floors beneath the lab.

'They are doing something strange,' she said. 'Even though they have not spoken a single word, not even to the guards who brought them food earlier, I believe they are communicating with one another. I would not be surprised to find they possess the same psionic and psychokinetic abilities as Olivia Ashkarov.' She glanced at him. 'Judging from the reports of the soldiers who took them, it seems they did something similar on the island to what she and the Elemental achieved in Yuma.'

The man stared at the children on the monitor, a flicker of unease dancing through his veins at Wu's mention of the dramatic events four years past. The same events that had seen Jonah Krondike ripped from his life.

It was only recently that they had made their startling discovery concerning Lucas Soul and Anna Godard. A year and a half after Wu and her team had failed to make progress on the principal project he'd tasked them with, she'd come across information concerning Frederick Burnstein, the former Head of the Crovir Research and Development Section and CEO of GeMBiT Corp, a genetics and molecular bioinformatics company based in Washington DC.

Eight years previously, a French scientist Burnstein had contracted to work for GeMBiT had developed a genetically modified Immortal cell. One that could technically never die. This had been at the bequest of Agatha Vellacrus, the Head of the Order of Crovir Hunters and leader of the Crovir race at the time.

Much to Wu's frustration, no evidence remained of the primary data from Burnstein's research, data that would have proven vital to her own experiments in the last decade. When she had informed him of her findings, the man had made careful inquiries in both Immortal societies and eventually tracked down someone who had been privy to the details of Agatha Vellacrus's scheme.

The Crovir noble had been present that day, on the island where Agatha Vellacrus had met her death at the hands of Lucas Soul.

Since Jonah Krondike had not been a member of the Crovir First Council, he had been unaware of the remarkable circumstances surrounding her demise. As a direct consequence, nor had the man.

When they had discovered that Anna Godard's blood had formed the centerpiece of Burnstein's research and that she and Lucas Soul were the grandchildren of both Agatha Vellacrus and Tomas Godard, the former leader of the Bastian race, the man had concluded both Immortals could prove to be the key to the vexing problem he and Wu had encountered in their primary project. A half-breed who had been hunted by Bastians and Crovirs since his birth, Lucas Soul was even rumored to have survived his seventeenth death in the incident that had cost Agatha Vellacrus her life seven years ago.

He had done his damnedest to find Godard and Soul since. Both had seemingly disappeared from the face of the Earth after the events in the Mediterranean Sea where Vellacrus's plans had been foiled and Tomas Godard had also perished.

It was only after he had begun spying on Immortals with known allegiances with Soul that he had finally tracked down the half-breed's location to a private island in the Pacific. To his surprise and Wu's considerable excitement, they had also discovered Anna Godard there and realized the two Immortals had had a family together.

Not only that, but the man had been stunned when he'd learned the identities of the other Immortals who frequently visited the island, among them the ones directly responsible for Jonah Krondike's death.

He had known the whereabouts of Olivia Ashkarov and Ethan Storm for a long time. Although he had been tempted to send his men after them following the incident in Yuma, he'd realized it would be a foolish move, one that would jeopardize his centuries-old masquerade and Krondike's long-held plans.

However much he loathed them, avenging Jonah Krondike would have to wait until he had accomplished their goals.

Nothing would stop him from annihilating Ashkarov and Storm when that time came. And come it would.

Nearly eight centuries after Jonah Krondike had discovered the journal written by Kronos, the third-born son of Crovir and the founder of the sect Jonah would come to rule, his primary objective was finally in sight.

It was Wu who had persuaded him to use the children's blood instead of their parents'.

'Not only will it be easier to control them, I suspect their blood will reveal even more unexpected things,' the scientist had said a fortnight ago. 'I need to study them.'

The man turned and gazed at Wu. His hand snaked out and closed around her throat, lightning fast. Gasps sounded around them, the handful of scientists in the room freezing momentarily in their tasks. They resumed their duties, heads down and gazes averted.

The woman in front of him did not even blink.

The man leaned toward her.

'Study them if you must,' he hissed inches from her face. 'But first, do as I told you, understood?'

Wu licked her lips and dipped her chin. The man saw the flicker of excitement in her dark, almond-shaped eyes as he slowly released her. Deep beneath her ice-cold beauty and razor-sharp intellect, Jessica Wu was a masochist, something he'd discovered when he'd started sleeping with her a few years ago. He knew she would be waiting for him later in his quarters at the facility, eager to be tied up and taken roughly. Though he wasn't a fan of bondage or the toys she liked to use during sex, he enjoyed the thrill of seeing her in pain and the marks he left on her fair skin.

He turned and headed for a door to the far left of the lab. An examination room lay beyond it. Wu followed him inside and watched silently as he undid the cuffs at his wrists and took off his jacket.

He stripped out of his tie and shirt and sat on the edge of the cot in the middle of the chamber. 'How goes our other project?'

'We're on schedule.' She hooked him up to a monitor and lifted a needle and syringe from the metal tray on the side table. 'The next subjects will be ready by the end of the week.'

'Good. And the man who was injured on the island?'

'He's being taken care of.'

The smell of antiseptic reached his nostrils as she swabbed his skin.

He did not feel the prick of the needle when it penetrated the flesh at his elbow.

'THE ATTACK WAS LAUNCHED FROM PRINCEVILLE AIRPORT, IN Kauai," Jordan said. 'It's a private airfield twenty-five miles north of the main commercial airport.'

Lucas frowned. 'I know of it.'

'Eva picked up three Black Hawks leaving the tarmac at twenty-three hundred hours on the night of the attack from the satellite imagery she and Howard gathered. They made a straight line for Balthazar Island.'

'What about afterward?' Alexa said.

They were in the jet that had brought her, Zachary, and Reid from the East Coast to LA. Conrad and Ethan had joined them and they stood crowded around the table holding the onboard computer.

'They landed back at Princeville an hour later. A bunch of people left the helicopters and boarded a jet standing by for takeoff just before oh two hundred hours.'

Lucas's pulse jumped. 'Did you see the kids?'

'No,' Jordan replied, chagrined. 'It was too dark to make out the details. We have the aircraft heading north by north east once it leaves the island. We lose all sign of it under cloud cover two hours after that.'

'There was a storm cell moving up the North West Coast,' Eva added.

Lucas's heart sank at this. 'Any chance you can pick up the jet beyond the weather system?'

Jordan hesitated. 'I—'

'Although I cannot guarantee any results, I will continue to look for the aircraft,' Eva said. 'My analysis of its outline suggests it's a Cessna Citation X+.'

Ethan let out a low wolf whistle.

'What?' Reid said.

'That's the fastest jet around right now,' Ethan explained. 'Asgard tested it last year.'

'I took the liberty of accessing the Princeville Airport database in the last hour,' Eva continued. 'I saw no records of any aircraft obtaining permission to use that runway during the time period of interest.'

'What happened to the Black Hawks?' Ethan said curiously. 'They couldn't have just left them there.'

Jordan smiled thinly. 'This is where things get even more interesting. Satellite images show them flying off to the US Navy's Pacific Missile Range Facility at Barking Sands, on Kauai. We spotted one of them boarding a C-17 Globemaster III, the other two presumably already inside. The transport aircraft lifted off at oh three hundred hours and headed north by north west across the Pacific.'

'And?' Alexa said impatiently.

Jordan grimaced. 'We lose all trace of the C-17 over the Sea of Japan. Another storm front I'm afraid.'

Conrad arched an eyebrow. 'Really?'

Alexa looked at him quizzically.

'Losing two aircraft in separate weather systems at opposite ends of the Pacific? That's either extremely unlucky or deliberate,' Conrad said.

Lucas's mouth went dry as he considered his cousin's dubious expression. 'I agree.' He turned to the monitor. 'Eva, can you plot out the aircraft trajectories in relation to the storm cells they disappeared into?'

'Yes, I can.'

They waited while the AI mapped the data. A second window popped up on the screen minutes later. Hairs rose on the back of Lucas's neck as he studied the calculated projections Eva had made. Reid swore.

'It appears Mr. Greene is correct,' Eva said. 'Both aircraft look to have deliberately tracked the storm cells developing in the West and East Pacific.'

'They knew,' Alexa said in a hard voice. 'They knew we would be looking for them.'

Ethan frowned. 'So you're saying these assholes anticipated our move before we even thought of it?'

'Whoever these people are, they're good,' Conrad said stiffly.

Lucas turned to him. 'Any chance you could talk to Director Connelly about the Globemaster at Barking Sands? It might be faster than asking Victor to go through the usual channels.'

James Anthony Westwood, the man whose life Conrad had saved six years ago, had been re-elected for a second term as US President. To his cabinet's surprise, he'd insisted on keeping Sarah Connelly as his Director of National Intelligence.

Conrad nodded. 'Of course. Besides, if there's a self-serving rat in the DoD doing things under the radar again, both she and James would want to know about it.'

'Anatole just left LA to return to Hawaii,' Jordan said. 'He'll meet up with a team of Bastian Hunters and go talk to the Princeville airport owners directly.'

'Uh-oh,' Conrad muttered.

'What?' Alexa said.

'Anatole can get—emotional when he interrogates people.' Conrad grimaced. 'Especially if he thinks they've hurt his friends.'

'He gets emotional under all sorts of circumstances,' Reid said with a grunt. 'That guy's gonna have a coronary one day.'

Alexa rolled her eyes.

'Let us know if you find anything else,' she told Jordan and Eva before ending the call.

Conrad took out his cell and dialed a number. Lucas glanced at the clock on the computer dashboard.

It was gone four in the morning. They were a third of the way into their five-hour flight to Maryland. Anna, Madeleine, Zachary, Olivia, and Asgard were in the skies somewhere behind them, having had to wait to retrieve the dead men's bodies from a Bastian facility in California before they started their journey to Europe. Laura had stayed behind in Santa Monica with Howard.

Conrad ended his call and laid a hand on Lucas's shoulder.

'You should get some rest,' he said quietly. 'I may have healed your wounds but you still lost a lot of blood during that attack.'

Lucas nodded and swallowed. Were it not for the presence of his family and their friends, he would have gone crazy with worry by now.

He closed his eyes briefly and thought of Anna and their children, before focusing on Conrad's face.

'How did it go with Connelly?'

Conrad smiled faintly. 'Sarah's on it. She'll get back to us when she has information.'

Alexa dimmed the cabin lights and they spread out across the seats.

Although he was exhausted, sleep eluded Lucas. He stared out of the window at the dark sky for a long time, a thousand thoughts racing through his mind while he relived the events of the last twenty-four hours. Icy determination filled his heart as the minutes ticked by, erasing the overwhelming sense of helplessness he'd been feeling since that morning.

He'd failed his children once. He would not do so again.

And when he and the others found the ones behind this, they were going to discover that they'd messed with the wrong people.

CHAPTER NINE

IT WAS MID-MORNING WHEN THEIR JET LANDED AT PHILLIPS Military Airfield, in Maryland. They boarded the two Jeeps standing by on the tarmac and headed east with their armed escort.

It was Victor who'd wrangled a meeting for them on such short notice at the US Army Research Lab's Weapons and Materials Research Directorate facility at the Aberdeen Proving Ground. Although the Bastians had their own ballistics center in Europe, the one in Maryland was closer; it was the next best place for them to get the casings they'd found on Balthazar Island analyzed.

'That's it there,' the soldier next to Lucas said a couple of minutes after they'd passed the checkpoint and obtained their security passes.

Lucas gazed at the cluster of buildings the man indicated and did his best to quash the restless feeling churning his stomach. The Jeeps pulled up outside the main entrance of the facility a moment later. He exited the vehicles with the others and entered a brightly lit reception manned by two armed soldiers. They signed in at the desk under the guards' watchful stares.

'If you could please leave your weapons,' the female soldier said coolly. 'You can collect them on the way out.'

'Sure,' Lucas muttered.

The woman's expression froze when they started taking out their guns and bladed weapons.

'What's that?' She pointed at Conrad's staff.

'It's a spear,' Conrad explained. 'And a pair of swords.'

She arched an eyebrow before indicating the daisho Lucas had slipped out from under his jacket. 'Sir, is that some kind of Japanese sword?'

'It is.'

He decided not to mention the fact that it was the real deal, gifted to him by the greatest samurai warrior who had ever lived.

'And this?' The male soldier picked up one of Alexa's daggers. 'Ouch!'

'It's a sai,' Alexa said coldly. 'You're holding it wrong.'

The female soldier stared pointedly from Reid to his Glock.

'I'm a gun kind of guy,' the former Marine said with a shrug.

Her gaze shifted to Ethan.

He grinned. 'I have magic hands.'

She rolled her eyes. 'Sure. All guys think that.'

An Asian woman with curly, dark hair tied back in a ponytail, thick, black-rimmed glasses, and vivid, pink trainers stood waiting on the other side of the security door they were escorted through.

She smiled at them, scanned their badges, and zeroed in on Lucas.

'Mr. Soul? I'm Dr. Priya Chatterjee, the chief ballistic expert at WMRD.'

Lucas shook her hand and introduced the others.

'Follow me.' Chatterjee turned and marched briskly down a corridor.

'Hey, isn't she a bit young to be the top guy—I mean girl—shit, *woman* here?' Ethan whispered as they headed after her.

'I think she heard that,' Conrad murmured.

The scientist's ears had turned red up ahead.

'May I remind you that you're the youngest one of all of us?' Alexa told Ethan in a low voice.

'Well, technically, Olivia holds that title,' he retorted.

Reid grunted. 'I beg to differ. I'm a babe in arms compared to you lot. No offense, but she could probably carbon date all of you.'

Lucas stifled a sigh at the scientist's reddening neck.

Chatterjee led them to a large lab overlooking woodland and the Bush River flowing in the distance. It was empty save for the rows of weapons testing and analysis equipment crowding the worktops and floor.

She headed for a workstation at the back of the room and propped herself on a swivel chair in front of a complex, dual-stage microscope attached to a computer. A mini control panel featuring a rotary knob and joystick sat beneath the instrument.

'You have the casings?'

Lucas removed a small specimen bag from the rear pocket of his jeans and gave it to her.

Chatterjee slipped on some gloves and carefully emptied the contents onto a tray. Her eyes narrowed behind her glasses as she inspected the fragments.

'Interesting,' she murmured. 'These are indeed frangibles.'

'Frangibles?' Ethan said.

'Bullets that fragment on impact, or fragmenting bullets as they're also known,' Chatterjee said absentmindedly, her gaze still locked on the casings. She glanced at Lucas. 'My superior didn't tell me much except that you want to know the possible source of these rounds? These look like they could be homemade at first glance.'

Lucas nodded. 'Yes. I'm afraid we can't reveal more than that.' He paused. 'All I can tell you is that these were fired from rotary machine guns and semi-automatic pistols by men who behaved like trained soldiers. I doubt someone cooked them up in their garage.'

Chatterjee frowned faintly before moving one of the 9mm casings to a grip device on a stage on the microscope. She climbed off the stool, walked over to a cabinet, and returned with two small specimen bags containing a spent casing each.

She placed the first in the second grip device on the microscope and peered into the eyepieces.

They waited patiently while she examined the casing from Balthazar Island and the test specimen side by side. Lines furrowed her brow as she worked the various knobs and buttons on the instrument, angling the two cartridges through three-sixty degrees in all planes. She replaced the first test sample with the second and compared the casings once more.

Lucas's stomach sank when she finally looked up from the microscope.

'I have never seen a cartridge like this,' Chatterjee said with a troubled expression. 'Here, take a look.'

She worked the rotary knob and joystick on the mini control panel. The computer next to the microscope blinked into life. A split window appeared on the screen, showing magnified views of the two cartridges side by side.

'The one on the right is our test sample. One of two 9mm frangible cartridges. The only two fragmenting bullets in production in the world right now.'

Reid raised an eyebrow. 'There are only two companies making these?'

'The ones with the eight-segmented nose like your 9mm casing? Yeah, only two.' Chatterjee indicated the monitor. 'There are a number of rifling markings we look at when we compare spent cartridges. Breech-block marks, firing pin impressions, extractor marks, and ejector marks.'

She pointed these out patiently shot by shot while she worked the joystick and knob, saving the images to the side of the screen.

'And here's the first test specimen again.'

She replaced the samples and froze the comparison images once more.

They stared at the screen for some time.

'None of them match the one we brought you,' Alexa said quietly.

Chatterjee nodded. 'Yes. And I suspect that will also be the case with the 7.62mm cartridge.' She looked at Lucas. 'You are right. There is no way these bullets were made in someone's backyard. Whoever designed these is using pioneering technology years ahead of any military or private ammunition manufacturer that I'm aware of. And I know *all* of them.'

'So I was right,' Reid said. 'They *are* more advanced.'

Conrad frowned at the scientist. 'Why do you say that?'

'Because these bullets look like they're made of a new metal. One I've never seen before.' She glanced at the images on the computer monitor. 'I think that's why they leave so little in terms of rifling markings. This—' she unclamped the 9mm casing from Balthazar Island from the grip device and brought it to eye level, '—is possibly the bullet of the future.' Her gaze shifted to Lucas, her eyes bright with curiosity. '*Where* did you get them?'

Lucas looked at her steadily. 'It would be in your best interest not to know the answer to that question.'

Chatterjee hesitated before nodding, a sigh leaving her lips. 'Can you leave the 9mm casing with me for further analysis? I want to see what this new metal is.' She smiled drily at his expression. 'I promise this will be for my eyes only.'

Lucas glanced at the others. They shrugged.

'Alright,' he told the scientist reluctantly. 'Give us a call if you find something.'

He lifted a pen and a piece of paper from a stationary rack and wrote out a number.

IVAN MIHAEL VLAŠIC LEANED BACK IN HIS CHAIR AND OBSERVED the Immortal seated across the desk from him.

'That's quite a story,' he said coolly.

Victor Dvorsky gazed at him with a relaxed expression. 'An accurate one. I can show you the satellite images.'

They were in Ivan's office, at the headquarters of the Crovir First Council, in Dresden. Though he would never admit it to the man opposite him, Ivan had been somewhat surprised when he'd received the phone call from the Bastian First Council that morning requesting an urgent private meeting with him. Had he known the representative traveling from Vienna would be none other than the leader of the Bastian race himself, he would have made sure he was more prepared.

Vlado Krall, the Head of the Crovir Counter-Terrorism Section and Ivan's friend and right-hand man, leaned against the wall next to him, his dark eyes thoughtful as he silently studied Victor.

'So, you're telling me in addition to the two Immortals with special abilities involved in the Yuma incident, there are others like them out there?' Ivan frowned faintly. 'This—Conrad Greene and the Crovir First Council's very own Alexa King? And Lucas Soul and Anna Godard?'

Victor nodded wordlessly.

Ivan arched an eyebrow. 'And you thought I should be privy to this information only now? When you need my help?'

Victor crossed his legs, dropped his elbows on the armrests of his seat, and steepled his fingers under his chin. 'Bearing in mind that all the major conflicts between our races in the last century have been instigated by a Crovir, you will forgive me for having kept this information on a need-to-know basis.'

Ivan fought back the sliver of irritation that darted through him at the Bastian noble's words.

He knew that many in both Immortal societies deemed him too young to have taken on the role of Head of the Order of Crovir Hunters and de facto leader of the Crovir race six years ago. Still, he had been a politician long enough to know when to speak his mind and when to abstain from revealing his innermost thoughts.

Besides, the man is right. The Crovirs have always had a nasty habit of starting wars.

'I have heard of Lucas Soul's abilities, obviously, but I thought the rumors of him surviving his seventeenth death were just that. Rumors.'

Of all the things Victor had told him, that statement had stunned Ivan the most. No Immortal had ever survived their seventeenth death. The possible ramifications if word of this got out and it became common knowledge among the Immortal societies unnerved him.

Lucas Soul had once been the most hunted Immortal on Earth. That he had only ever defended himself throughout that time did not mean he might not one day decide to take up arms. If he did, he would be unstoppable.

'They were not,' Victor said. 'Anna can theoretically also survive her seventeenth death. And although neither of them have voiced it, I suspect I know the reason why Tomas and Lily Soul were taken.'

Ivan stared.

Vlado stirred next to him. 'Their blood.'

Victor glanced at Vlado. 'Correct. Lucas and Anna have unique genetic profiles. We've never explored the full extent of what their blood could do. Suffice to say there are no two people like them on Earth. Tomas and Lily's genetic profiles must be doubly special. They also have—' he faltered for a moment, '—other abilities.'

Ivan narrowed his eyes. 'What abilities?'

Victor shook his head. 'It's too early to say yet. They may share their parents' and their relatives'—gifts.'

Ivan masked a scowl beneath his stare. He knew he had just blatantly been lied to.

'Now that you've told me all of this, what is it exactly that you expect from me, Victor?' he said, unable to suppress his sharp tone.

Victor's eyes glinted with a hard light. 'The attack on Balthazar Island was well planned and carried out with military precision. It speaks of an organization being behind all of this rather than a small group of individuals who bear some kind of grudge against Lucas or Anna. It is evident the children were the targets and that they wanted them alive. As for Lucas and Anna, they had every intention of killing them that night.'

Unease filled Ivan as the undeniable meaning behind Victor's words sank in.

'I am not pointing the finger of accusation at you or the Crovir First Council,' Victor continued in a steely voice. 'I only want you to understand why I'm here. You need to ask questions of the rest of your Councils. Tidy your affairs. See if someone is, excuse the expression, shitting in your backyard. That is all I want from you right now.'

Although Ivan's every instinct warned him that Dvorsky was only doing what any sensible leader should do, he could not stop the words that escaped his lips. 'And if I don't?'

Victor's mouth curved into a thin smile. 'Then, this time, it will be the Bastians who start the war.'

Ivan straightened in his chair. He could sense tension radiating from Vlado where he stood beside him.

'That's pretty bold of you when you're sitting in the headquarters of your future enemy,' he said grimly.

Victor sighed and rose to his feet, his expression suddenly tired. 'There's one thing you need to understand. Although I am the current leader of the Bastian race, I am but a glorified representative occupying that position. It belongs to the Godards.' He paused. 'Asgard never wanted the job, but Lucas and Anna were both invited to be members of the Bastian and Crovir First Councils.'

Ivan startled.

Victor looked at him steadily. 'That's something your predecessor obviously never revealed to you.'

Ivan clenched his jaw. It seemed surprising that such a significant matter would have slipped Dimitri Reznak's attention when he handed over the mantle of leadership to him six years ago. He could not help but feel that the Crovir noble had deliberately not divulged the information, probably to keep Lucas Soul and Anna Godard's incredible secrets buried.

'So, you see, by attacking Lucas and Anna, whoever is behind all of this just declared war with the true leaders of the Bastian race,' Victor continued. 'And not just the Bastian race, but the Crovirs too. Lucas and Anna are the last surviving heirs of Agatha Vellacrus and, as such, have justifiable claims to her former position as your leader. You are also occupying a seat that does not truly belong to you, Ivan.'

With that, he turned and exited the room.

CHAPTER TEN

Tomas walked barefoot in the center of the group of armed men guiding Lily and him along a brightly lit, concrete corridor. Though he couldn't read their minds, he could sense a flicker of nervousness here and there from their consciousness.

News of what the two of them had done on the island had obviously reached their ears. He clenched his jaw. The undercurrent of dread radiating across his mental connection with his twin unnerved him more than their escort's unease.

I'm okay, Tomas.

Tomas maintained a neutral expression as he swallowed an internal sigh of relief. Although he suspected he and Lily could take out the men around them with their powers, he knew there were more of them out there. He could discern hundreds in the complex around and above them, spheres of energy that flickered in and out of sight across his inner radar.

Many were similar to those of the masked soldiers who had attacked their home and the guards currently herding them through a maze of empty passages lined by doors identical to those of their cells. They were odd, elusive minds he couldn't penetrate, their thoughts shifting clouds that offered the barest of glimpses into their souls.

Among them, concentrated in a different section of the facility, was another collection of strange consciousness. Whereas the soldiers' brains projected a physical barrier that protected them, these minds seemed almost unformed, as if they were still maturing.

There were also normal humans and Immortals on the premises with them.

If we can get close enough to someone with an unshielded mind, we should be able to find out where we are and why we were brought here.

His sister murmured her agreement inside his head.

An elevator appeared up ahead. He watched one of the guards touch a pass card to a sensor. The metal doors opened and they were escorted inside the cabin.

Tomas studied the interior panel when it closed after them. It indicated thirteen floors, with the highest number at the bottom.

So, we're underground.

They stopped two levels up. The elevator doors slid open onto yet another concrete corridor. Tomas counted five doors on either side before they reached a junction. Their guards turned and shepherded them into the passage on the left.

An armor-plated panel came into view at the end of the corridor after some thirty-five feet. Tomas stiffened. Lily's anxiety soared across their connection.

A buzz sounded from the portal when they reached it. It opened with a hiss of air, the door gliding smoothly on electric-controlled hinges.

The smell of antiseptic washed over Tomas as he and Lily

were ushered across the threshold and into a large, white, rectangular room. His gaze skimmed the leather straps on the two gurneys in the middle of the linoleum floor before focusing on the glass wall spanning the length of the chamber to the right. His pulse spiked.

Though he could only see his, Lily, and the guards' reflections in the polished surface, he could sense people behind it. People watching them.

'Do not be afraid,' a female voice said through speakers in the ceiling. 'We do not wish to hurt you.'

Tomas glanced at the cameras in the corners of the room and noted some strange-looking, metal sprinklers dotting the white surface above them.

The men who'd brought them to the room turned and left, the door closing behind them with another hiss of air. Tomas studied the exit over his shoulder, his heart thrumming against his ribs.

This is a negative pressure room.

He was mulling over the possible reason for this when the unseen woman spoke again.

'Why don't you take a seat on the bed?'

Tomas turned to face the glass wall. Despite his fear, he stepped in front of Lily and glared at their invisible audience.

'If you do not cooperate, I'm afraid I *will* have to hurt you,' the woman said, her tone hardening.

Lily's fingers closed around Tomas's right hand. Though her pulse had accelerated noticeably too, he could sense her growing defiance beneath her apprehension.

'Reveal yourself first.' He swallowed, annoyed at himself for the slight tremor in his voice.

A cold chuckle came through the speakers. 'Do you take us for fools, child? We know what you did on the island.'

Tomas frowned. The woman's voice was starting to irritate him. He tilted his head to the side and arched an eyebrow, annoyance overriding his disquiet.

'You do?' he said, his tone deliberately mocking.

Power surged inside Lily. He let it flow through him, strong waves of golden energy that filled him with light and augmented his elemental abilities.

'Yes,' the woman snapped.

Tomas smiled coldly. 'Somehow, I really doubt that.'

I'm ready.

He acknowledged his sister's grim words with a silent nod and raised his free hand toward the glass wall. Lily mimicked him.

For a moment, nothing happened.

The wall suddenly shivered. A ripple danced across the polished surface, the plate buzzing as it vibrated and warped. A tiny crack appeared in the center seconds later.

'Stop that!' the woman shouted angrily. 'Get them in there!'

Tomas knew the last command had been directed at someone behind the glass wall.

There was movement to his left. A concealed door opened in the wall, invisible hinges swinging silently to reveal a rectangle of darkness. Something shifted in the gloom beyond. Tomas's eyes widened.

Up ahead, the crack spread across the glass, a growing spider web that turned the wall into a giant, silver jigsaw.

Four figures stepped inside the chamber.

Tomas.

Tomas swallowed at his sister's warning. *I see them.*

These men were big. Bigger than normal people. Bigger even than the soldiers who had attacked the island and the guards who had escorted them to the chamber. And their minds were even more impenetrable.

An icy sensation skittered across his skin as he scrutinized their faces.

They showed no expression. None whatsoever.

'Immobilize them,' the unseen woman ordered the four men.

Tomas turned as they headed across the floor toward them. He moved his hand, shifting his elemental power from the glass wall to their bodies. Lily followed his gesture.

The men slowed but did not stop.

Sweat broke out across Tomas's forehead as he intensified the energy surging from him. He backed toward the armor-plated door, taking Lily with him.

Focus on them!

He felt his sister's acknowledgment in his mind and placed his hand on the metal panel at their backs, his mouth dry with fear.

The men leaned forward and continued advancing across the floor, the air shimmering faintly in front of them as they were buffeted by the full force of Lily's psychokinetic powers.

Tomas sent a blast of power through the door, seeking the electrical components controlling it while he rapidly manipulated its elements. Metal groaned as the panel started to buckle.

'*Stop them now!*' the woman barked.

The door gave a heartbeat before the first man reached him. Fire shot through Tomas's arm when the giant closed vice-like fingers on his flesh. He gasped as he was dragged inexorably from the exit, feet sliding across the floor.

Lily screamed beside him.

'No!' Tomas snarled at the man who'd grabbed her and

kicked him in the shin. Numbness spread up his leg, his nerves tingling from the contact.

He cried out as he and Lily were violently wrenched apart.

Two men pulled him toward a bed, their grip so strong he felt bone grind beneath his flesh. He ignored the pain and dug his heels into the linoleum, resisting them with all his might. Tears flooded his eyes when he saw the other pair pick Lily up and carry her kicking and screaming to the second cot. They immobilized her roughly on the mattress and strapped the leather bands around her wrists and ankles.

'*Let her go!*' he yelled.

A hot sensation erupted inside Tomas's chest. It jolted the golden lines of his heart, turning his fear into a red mist of bloodlust and drawing a gasp from his lips. Power flowed through him, an incandescent blaze that filled his entire body with heat.

He realized he was experiencing rage for the first time in his life.

The equipment around the beds trembled and shook as it shifted across the floor, metal creaking and buckling before it was driven violently into the walls by the raw energy pulsing around the chamber.

The fingers wrapped around Tomas's arms slowly uncurled as the men holding him prisoner let go and fell back, unable to weather the elemental storm lashing at them.

Tomas turned and took a step toward the bed where the other two held Lily prisoner, fire in his mind and at his fingertips.

Something sharp punctured the skin on the side of his neck.

Tomas paused. He raised a hand and removed the dart embedded in his flesh. He stared at it before scowling over his shoulder.

The armor-plated door lay open behind him, the deformed panel hanging off its hinges where he'd damaged it. Men with tranquilizer guns crouched just beyond the threshold, faces invisible behind gas masks.

Confusion flashed through Tomas as he started neutralizing the sedative seeping into his bloodstream with his healing powers.

Why the masks?

More darts slammed into his body. The drugs surged through his veins like they had done in the helicopter, faster than he could get rid of them.

'Tomas!'

Lily's scream echoed in his ears and his consciousness, her voice filled with a fury so raw it sent an involuntary shiver down his spine. He looked dazedly toward the bed where she lay and saw the leather straps holding her down snap. The men next to the gurney fell back, feet skidding across the floor.

Lily sat up, her blue eyes filled with an unholy radiance, something he'd never seen before. An eerie glow danced under her skin, lighting her up from the inside out.

Her power washed over him, so intense it shook his very bones and rid his body of the chemicals numbing his senses in an instant. He felt his strength return and fisted his hands.

The glass wall finally collapsed under the pressure of the unearthly forces whirling around inside the chamber.

Tomas looked to his right and caught a glimpse of a roomful of shocked people in white coats through the shower of falling shards. At the head of the crowd was an Asian woman with fair skin and almond-shaped eyes. His gaze collided with hers. He read the anger and fear in the dark depths and blinked.

Her name is Jessica. Jessica Wu.

'Do it!' the woman screamed. She lunged toward a workstation and grabbed a gas mask. 'Release it *now!*'

An alarm sounded in the chamber, the sound shrill and grating. White mist hissed from the sprinklers in the ceiling.

Tomas's eyes widened as he stared at the vapor rapidly filling the space around him. He gasped and choked when it reached his nostrils and mouth.

Lily coughed and covered her face with her hands.

Fire filled Tomas's lungs as the gas worked its way down his throat. He fought back with his healing powers, eyes tearing and burning, fingers rising unconsciously to his neck to claw at his flesh.

His legs gave way beneath him seconds later. He fell to his knees and thudded onto his side, convulsions shaking his body as his brain shut down from the lack of oxygen. The last things he saw were the four giant men standing silently above him, their eyes cold and dispassionate as they watched him twitch at their feet through the thickening haze.

CHAPTER ELEVEN

'HOW LONG UNTIL WE REACH EUROPE?' ANNA ASKED.

Asgard glanced at the instrument panel of the jet. 'Seven hours. We left the East Coast an hour ago.' His eyes darkened as he studied her. 'You should get some rest. You've not slept since we left LA.'

Anna bit her lip. 'I'm okay.' She leaned down and dropped a kiss on his cheek. 'Besides, neither have the two of you.'

Madeleine reached out from where she sat in the co-pilot seat and clasped her fingers tightly. Anna smiled at her tremulously before heading back into the main cabin.

Zachary looked up from his laptop as she came down the aisle.

'Hey,' he said quietly. 'I just got a call from Alexa. They're heading back to the airport.'

'Did they discover the origin of the bullets?' Anna said, unable to mask the hope in her voice.

One look at Zachary's expression had her heart sinking once more.

'No,' he said with a grimace. 'The ballistic expert at WMRD said she'd never seen anything like the shells from Balthazar Island. She's convinced they're made of some kind of new metal polymer. She's kept one of them for further analysis.'

Anna swallowed a sigh and lowered herself into the seat opposite his.

A noise came from the galley kitchen aft of the jet. The curtains parted. Olivia walked out with a tray in hand.

'I made us breakfast,' she said with a tired smile. 'It's nothing special but it should keep us—'

She froze in her tracks.

Anna stiffened as she watched color drain from her cousin's face.

The tray dropped from Olivia's hands and thudded onto the cabin floor, sending food pinwheeling across the carpet and under the seats.

Anna jumped up and headed toward her, Zachary rising from his seat to follow in her steps. Dread filled her veins when she registered Olivia's unseeing eyes. She slowed and stopped a few feet from her.

'Is she—?' Zachary said behind her.

'Yes,' Anna breathed. 'She's having a vision.' Her heart slammed against her ribs, hope surging inside her once more.

Is she seeing them? Is she seeing Tomas and Lily?

'Should we do something?' Zachary murmured.

Anna shook her head. 'No. Ethan said we should let her be when she's in this state. She'll—'

'Hey, is everything okay?' Madeleine strolled rapidly into the cabin from the direction of the cockpit. 'We heard a—oh.'

Olivia's expression hardened. She raised her right hand toward them.

A faint vibration ran through the floor beneath Anna's feet.

The seats started to shake on either side of the aisle. Lights flickered overhead.

Her stomach twisted. *Damn! She's tapped into Ethan's powers.*

Anna took a step forward. 'Olivia, snap out of it! You're—'

Her breath locked in her throat as a wave of elemental energy blasted her off her feet. She slammed backward into Zachary and Madeleine and took them to the floor.

Alarms sounded from the direction of the cockpit as the plane pitched forward violently. A crash came from the direction of the galley kitchen. The storage compartments opened around them, spilling their bags onto the floor.

'What's going on back there?' Asgard yelled.

'It's nothing we can't handle, honey!' Madeleine shouted in a bright voice. 'Just make sure we don't crash!'

'Really?' Zachary said as they climbed clumsily to their feet, bodies buffeted by the invisible forces swirling through the cabin. He eyed the cutlery levitating near the ceiling. 'You think we can handle this?'

'We're gonna have to,' Anna said grimly.

They gripped the armrests of the chairs and stumbled one step at a time toward the woman who stood frozen at the other end of the aisle. The plane rolled and pitched around them, engines screaming as Asgard struggled to regain control of the aircraft.

'Is this what happened in Yuma?' Zachary yelled above the deafening sound as they slowly closed the distance between them and Olivia.

Madeleine shook her head. 'No! This is nowhere near as bad as what she did back then!' She clenched her teeth. 'Let's hope she doesn't do the fire thing or we're screwed!'

The unearthly storm pounding them intensified. Anna gasped.

Light flickered across the birthmark on Olivia's palm. It danced up the skin of her arm until it reached her face, filling it with an unearthly glow.

The hairs rose on the back of Anna's neck.

The Seer's eyes flashed green.

'Oh shit,' Madeleine said dully.

They fell back under the escalating energy. Metal screeched, the fuselage straining under the ungodly assault battering the aircraft from the inside out.

Just as suddenly as they'd arisen, the forces lashing at them started to abate. The plane juddered violently for a moment before finally leveling out.

A puzzled expression crossed Olivia's face. Her eyes suddenly widened. She gasped and choked, fingers rising to her throat and clutching desperately at her flesh.

'Olivia!' Anna shouted.

They rushed forward, able to move at will again, and caught her as she fell.

Fear drenched Anna in a cold sweat as the young woman started convulsing in their arms, eyes rolling back in her head and lips turning blue.

'On her side!' she barked at Zachary. 'Madeleine, get the oxygen from the first aid kit!'

Zachary helped Anna put Olivia in the recovery position. Madeleine returned with an oxygen cylinder and a face mask.

'So, where to now?' Ethan said.

The Jeeps had pulled to a stop on the airport tarmac. Lucas ran a hand through his hair and stared at the jet through the windshield, frustration gnawing at him. With no further clues as to the identity of their enemy, there was little else they could do at the moment but wait.

'Anatole should be in Hawaii soon.' Lucas thanked the soldier who'd escorted them back to the airfield and exited the Jeep with Conrad and Ethan. His gaze shifted to the Healer. 'You got anything from Connelly yet?'

Conrad shook his head. 'I'll give her a call in the next hour if I still haven't heard back.'

Alexa and Reid joined them from the second vehicle and they strolled toward the plane.

'I gave Zachary an update,' she said, tucking her cell into the rear pocket of her jeans. 'They're over the Atlantic right now.'

'Good.' Lucas hesitated. 'How's—?'

'She's okay.' Alexa's face softened slightly. 'She hasn't slept either.'

Lucas flashed her a tired smile. He doubted either he or Anna would sleep until they held their children in their arms again.

They were nearly at the jet when Alexa slowed. She stopped and looked over her shoulder with a frown. Lucas halted in his tracks and followed her gaze.

Ethan had come to a standstill some dozen feet behind them. He stood frozen, his face pale.

Unease flickered through Lucas as he registered their cousin's glazed expression.

Conrad frowned at Ethan. 'Hey, are you—?'

Alexa stiffened. 'Shit.'

It was the only warning they got before a wave of energy blasted across the tarmac and nearly threw them off their feet.

Lucas cursed and stumbled backward. He clenched his teeth, dug his heels into the ground, and leaned into the invisible force buffeting them. He knew this power. He'd experienced it enough times during his sparring matches with the Elemental.

Ethan scowled, staring straight through them, his fingers clenched at his sides. Light flickered across the birthmark on the back of his left hand. He raised it toward them, palm facing outward.

Lucas gasped as he was nearly driven to his knees by the raw power of the unholy storm sweeping over them. Conrad and Reid dropped down beside him, feet skidding across the asphalt. Only Alexa still stood facing Ethan.

Tires screeched to the left; the Jeeps that had brought them to the airfield moved sideways across the tarmac, horrified soldiers frozen inside.

Lucas struggled to his feet. 'Alexa!'

'I'm on it!'

Ripples of energy washed across his skin as Alexa's own unearthly power erupted from inside her body. She headed for Ethan, her expression determined and her steps steady.

Lucas and Conrad followed slowly in her wake, bodies doubled over and hands clutching at the tarmac to stop themselves being pushed backward.

The air shimmered around them when the forces pounding them intensified.

Lucas tumbled. Conrad reached out and grabbed his wrist as he rolled past him, his other hand clasped in a white-knuckled grip around his staff weapon. He'd wedged the double-ended spear into a crack in the asphalt.

Metal groaned ominously behind them. Lucas glanced wildly over his shoulder.

The plane was sliding across the tarmac, tires leaving black rubber marks on the ground.

'You'd better stop him!' Reid yelled from where he lay face down.

Lucas looked ahead just as a second violent force swept over them. The air trembled around Alexa, her own power escalating as she battled the storm and moved resolutely toward Ethan.

She had gotten within a couple of feet of him when he suddenly blinked.

Lucas gasped as the elemental forces washing across them subsided without warning. He climbed unsteadily to his feet, his heart thundering against his ribs. A choked cry brought his head up.

Ethan had sagged to his knees, a tortured expression on his face. Rasps left his lips as he fought for air, fingers clutching desperately at his throat.

'Ethan!' Alexa dropped to the ground next to him.

The Elemental collapsed in her arms and started convulsing.

CHAPTER TWELVE

Olivia blinked. The interior ceiling panel of the jet swam into view above her. She inhaled sharply and bolted upright. Fire stabbed through her head at the sudden movement. She groaned and clutched her temples.

'Easy,' Asgard said next to her.

Olivia winced as she registered the throbbing pain in her jaw and limbs. She looked around and saw the others watching her carefully from across the cabin.

Flashes of memory washed through her. She drew another sharp breath.

She couldn't remember the exact details of what she had done in the plane; she just knew that she had lost control of her powers somehow. That something terrible had happened was evident from the state of the jet's interior and her companions' guarded expressions.

The only thing she recalled with startling clarity was what she had seen in her mind's eye during those moments. She had lived what Tomas and Lily had been going through, wherever they were. And what they had endured made her sick to the very pit of her stomach.

Deep inside the marrow of her soul, Olivia detected a distant resonance across her connection with Ethan. The same distress she had experienced echoed inside her soulmate. She knew instantly that he had lived through the same thing.

She swung her legs off the couch and bit her lip.

'How long was I out?' she said shakily.

'Half an hour, give or take.' Madeleine handed her a drink of water.

Olivia swallowed it greedily, surprised to find her throat so parched. She clutched the empty glass in her hands after she finished drinking and stared at the floor, unable to meet their eyes for fear of what hers would reveal.

'Who's flying the plane?' she asked.

'It's on autopilot,' Asgard said quietly.

Anna crossed the aisle and moved to the couch. She dropped to her knees in front of Olivia, took the glass off her, and gripped her fingers in her own, forcing her to meet her gaze.

'What did you see?' she said, her tone resolute.

Olivia clenched her jaw. She didn't even know where to start.

'Tell us,' Anna beseeched.

Olivia studied the expectant look on her face and the faces of the others before closing her eyes, the agony of what she had experienced still echoing inside her.

Anna's green gaze bore into hers when she opened them once more.

'Please.'

Olivia took a deep breath. Though she hated what she was about to do with every fiber of her being, she knew she couldn't hide the truth from them.

She clasped Anna's hands tightly and started to talk in a low voice. Tears rolled unbidden down her cheeks as she related everything she had seen during those ungodly minutes.

Anger darkened the others' faces. Asgard swore, his knuckles whitening on the leather backrest of a chair. Anna stared at her unblinkingly, her face dull with shock.

'They gassed them?' she whispered in the stunned silence that followed Olivia's revelation, disbelief underscoring her voice. 'They gassed my children?'

Olivia put her arms around her cousin and hugged her silently, unable to say more.

A cry of despair left Anna's lips and echoed around the interior of the aircraft. She started to sob, her hands clawing at Olivia's back in her grief.

Olivia tightened her hold and weathered the storm, her heart breaking all over again as her cousin's tears soaked into her neck and hair.

LUCAS ROARED AND PUNCHED THE CABIN WALL. REID PUT A HAND on his shoulder, a muscle jumping in his jawline.

'I'm sorry,' Ethan whispered. He sat on the couch, his hands shaking around the bottle of water Conrad had given him.

'It's not your fault,' Alexa said, her voice icy with anger.

Blood pounded furiously inside Lucas's head. Although he wanted to disbelieve every single word Ethan had narrated since he'd woken up, he knew it was the truth.

Agony pierced his heart at what his children had suffered. From what Ethan had told them, it was because his soulmate had lived what Tomas and Lily had gone through that he had also experienced it. Which meant Anna knew what had happened.

'Can you tell us anything about the people they were with?' Conrad said quietly.

Ethan hesitated, the color slowly returning to his face.

'The men Tomas and Lily fought were super soldiers.'

Lucas froze, surprise dampening his rage.

'What?' Alexa said in a deadly tone.

Lucas stared at Ethan. 'Are you sure?'

Ethan nodded. 'Yes. I'm certain Olivia will agree. Those men looked and acted like the guys we fought in Yuma four years ago.'

'But—' Conrad started.

'Jonah Krondike died in that explosion,' Alexa interrupted sharply. 'The super soldier program he was spearheading was dismantled and the US Army Group working with him disbanded.'

A dozen questions filled Lucas's mind as he gazed at his cousin. 'Victor and Westwood assured us they'd destroyed all the research data.'

'I'm not denying that,' Ethan said. 'But I know what I—' he grimaced, '—saw, earlier. Those were super soldiers.' A flicker of admiration darted across his face as he studied Lucas. 'And if it wasn't for the gas they used on them, your kids would have kicked their asses.'

Lucas blinked. 'They would?'

Ethan nodded grimly. 'Tomas and Lily went down fighting. In fact, I don't think they've stopped fighting and protecting one another since they were taken from the island.'

A fierce feeling of pride swept over Lucas despite the torment still coursing through him. He swallowed convulsively.

'Did you see anything else?' Alexa said. 'Something we could use to find their whereabouts?'

Ethan narrowed his eyes. 'Olivia has a name and a face.'

'Jessica Wu,' Olivia said in a hard voice. 'She's of East Asian descent. She had a lab coat on in the brief glimpse I caught of her, so I presume she's one of the scientists working with the super soldiers.'

Lucas and Victor frowned on the computer screen. They were on video call with the Bastian headquarters and the others' jet in Maryland.

'How did your visit to Dresden go?' Asgard asked Victor stiffly.

The vision from earlier still resonated inside Olivia. She knew how much Asgard had suffered at the hands of Jonah Krondike and his scientists when they had had him confined in the godforsaken facility where they had been experimenting on the Immortals they'd imprisoned over the decades, including Madeleine's father. Olivia had been subjected to their cruelty herself when they had held her captive for the short time she was at Yuma.

The fact that the same thing was happening to Tomas and Lily evoked an ice-cold fury deep in her soul, fury she could see reflected in Asgard's eyes.

Even if it cost them their lives, they would make the people hurting Lily and Tomas pay for their sins.

'Vlašic seemed genuinely surprised by what I told him,' the Bastian leader replied, his expression thoughtful. 'He's either an exceptional liar or he truly has no idea about any of this.'

'We'll get Howard and Jordan working on Wu's identity,'

Alexa said. 'As for the 9mm cartridge we brought to Maryland, we're waiting to hear back from—'

Another call came through the onboard computer.

Zachary straightened in his seat. 'It's Anatole.'

He tapped a couple of keys. The red-haired Immortal appeared framed inside another window.

'Hey,' he said in a clipped tone. 'I'm on my way back to LA. Princeville was a dead end. The owners of the airport were sold a story about how all of this was some kind of hush-hush military op. Our guys in the Black Hawks paid them in cash.'

'What about the Cessna?' Asgard said.

'The tail number was fake.' A muscle jumped in Anatole's cheek. 'I already checked.'

'Damn it!' Asgard muttered.

'Is Eva still working on the satellite images?' Victor said.

Alexa nodded. 'Yes. She hasn't got any fresh leads yet.'

Silence descended across the connections.

'We're back to square one,' Lucas said, frustration evident in the lines of his face.

Anna's hands fisted where she stood next to Olivia.

'We still have the bodies to examine,' Madeleine said. 'We may get some answers—'

A cell trilled somewhere in the background of the Maryland video call.

Behind Lucas and Alexa, Conrad slipped his phone out of the rear pocket of his chinos.

'Hang on. This is Connelly.' He answered and spoke in a low murmur for a moment. He stiffened and stopped talking. His eyes slowly widened, excitement shimmering in the blue depths. 'Sarah, can I transfer you to video call?'

Olivia's pulse sped up when he gave his phone to Alexa.

'You're gonna want to hear this,' Conrad told them grimly.

Alexa touched some keys on their onboard computer and flicked a finger across the cell screen.

Sarah Connelly appeared on the monitor. She was pacing the floor in front of her desk, Capitol Hill visible through the sun-dappled trees framed by the window behind her.

She stopped and scanned their faces. 'Hi, Victor.'

'Hey, Sarah,' Victor murmured.

'Like I was saying to Conrad, it looks like we may have another rogue section in Special Operations Command.' She ran a hand through her hair and sighed, her expression tired. 'I fear this one is deep, way deeper than the group who got their hands dirty at Yuma.'

'Tell them what you found at Barking Sands,' Conrad urged.

Connelly lowered herself into her chair and leaned her elbows on the table. 'The commander of the base was informed that a classified op was taking place in the Pacific two nights ago. He received an order to give tarmac access to the C-17 twelve hours before the aircraft's ETA. All he could give me was a list of names.'

Lucas startled. He leaned toward the monitor at their end, a muscle jumping in his jawline. 'Who?'

Connelly grimaced. 'They were all fake. They looked convincing enough when he checked them on the army database, as did the chain of command. Someone with exceedingly good hacking skills set those dummy profiles up. I'm waiting to hear back from the DoD about the security breach. They were completely unaware of it.'

'So it's a dead lead?' Asgard said.

Connelly's lips curved into a smile. 'I'd have hoped you people would have more faith in me from the last time we worked together. I *am* the Director of US National Intelligence.' Her eyes glittered with a steely light. 'The email communications that came to the commander of the base all originated from the same encrypted server. It took a while to crack the code and trace the sender's address. They all came from the office of one Rodney Miller. Miller is a four-star general in SOCOM and a former West Point graduate.' She arched an eyebrow. 'Remember who else was a four-star general and West Point valedictorian?'

Olivia inhaled sharply. 'William Gunnerson. The man in charge of the US Army Group helping Jonah Krondike with his super soldier program.'

'Bingo,' Connelly said coldly. 'It seems Gunnerson was just the tip of the iceberg. Like I said, this group is deep. I'm beginning to wonder if it might even be the primary one, with Gunnerson's section acting as cover in case things went south, like they did at Yuma. No one in the DoD has been able to tell me much about the specifics of Miller's activities or even his exact whereabouts right now. According to his PA, he's on leave and is not to be disturbed. As you can imagine, that went down well when I spoke to the Secretary of Defense just now.' She frowned. 'Miller appears to have powerful friends on Capitol Hill. Friends who would rather I leave him be.'

'Let me guess,' Conrad said acerbically. 'Friends with interests in the military industry?'

'Yes.' Connelly's gaze shifted across her monitor. 'Conrad mentioned super soldiers to me just now. How certain are you people that they are really involved in this?'

Asgard glanced at Olivia. 'We're pretty confident.'

She nodded her agreement.

Connelly chewed her lip for a moment. 'Victor, assume you've got the green light for now. I'll speak to James and confirm with you in the next hour. I'm sure he'll agree with my decision.' She drummed her fingers on the desk, her expression preoccupied. 'We're gonna want our people on this too, though.'

'Green light?' Asgard repeated, nonplussed.

Connelly pulled a face. 'It means we're leaving this in your hands for the time being. To do—' she waved a hand vaguely in the air, '—you know, your *thing*. That Immortal stuff. Just keep it discreet.' She rose, leaned toward the screen, and leveled a threatening stare at them. 'And no sea of dead bodies please. We had a shit time explaining Yuma.'

CHAPTER THIRTEEN

LAURA GROANED AND LOWERED HERSELF INTO A CHAIR. 'I SWEAR this kid's having a house party on my bladder.'

'Ah-huh,' Howard said distractedly.

His fingers flew over the keyboard of the laptop in front of him; he was studying the data his team of hackers had sent him that morning.

Sunlight sparkled on the limpid infinity pool outside the kitchen and streamed through the glass wall of the mansion, casting the room in brightness. It was midday in Santa Monica.

'Your lack of sympathy warms the cockles of my heart,' Laura said acerbically. She picked up her chicken burrito, bit into it, and threw a couple of chunks to the two dogs underneath the table.

'Sure,' Howard muttered. 'No problem.' He grabbed a slice of garlic bread from his plate and shoved it in his mouth. Crumbs peppered his five-hundred-dollar D&G T-shirt.

The cat on his lap opened an eye lazily, cleaned the specks from its fur, and went back to sleep.

Laura chewed and swallowed before glancing at the butler and the housekeeper. 'Is he always like this?'

'Mr. Titus gets quite—absorbed when he's working on a project,' Bernard murmured diplomatically from where he stood cleaning his Beretta at the marble island in the middle of the pale, stone floor.

'You mean does he turn into a Neanderthal who can just about grunt?' Rosa flipped a tortilla and frowned when a dollop of tomato sauce joined the breadcrumbs on Howard's shirt. 'Christ, I can't believe he made the list of most-wanted bachelors again. If only those women could see him now.'

Laura chuckled. She and Conrad rarely came to Santa Monica to visit his cousins. As such, she'd not spent much time in Rosa and Bernard's company. She was starting to really like the two Immortals.

She had finished her lunch and was sipping her virgin Mojito when Howard suddenly swore. Tension shot through her as she watched his hands freeze on the keyboard and the blood drain from his face. Rosa and Bernard stilled on the other side of the island.

'What is it?' Laura said.

Howard glanced at her dazedly. 'I think I know how they found the island.'

He ignored their questioning looks, tapped some keys, and grabbed his cell. He ran a hand through his disheveled hair and speed-dialed a number.

He stiffened when it connected. 'Jordan? Can you and Eva take a look at the data I just sent you?'

Howard drummed his fingers on the table while he waited. He froze a moment later. 'Tell me I'm wrong.' He listened before closing his eyes briefly, his expression grim. 'Yeah, I know,' he said in a hard voice. 'I doubt he's behind this too. Which means he doesn't know he's being tracked.'

Lily came to slowly. She was lying on her side on a cot. She blinked and pushed herself up into a sitting position. A queasy feeling swept over her. She swallowed convulsively before looking around.

She was back in her cell.

The memory of what had happened in the white room rushed through her. Her stomach clenched.

Tomas?

Fear turned her body cold when he didn't reply. She scrambled to the edge of the bed and frantically sought out his consciousness, panic turning her mouth to ash.

Tomas!

I'm—I'm here, Lily.

Her shoulders drooped at the sound of his distant voice. She closed her eyes briefly, her heart thundering in her chest. Concern replaced her relief when she registered his fuzzy consciousness and the red aura of pain clouding it. He'd just woken up too.

Are you hurt?

Tomas hesitated. *A little bit. My head feels like it's gonna explode. You?*

Lily looked down. Their captors had changed her clothes while she was unconscious. She was wearing some kind of hospital uniform consisting of a pale blue tunic and trousers. Her gaze landed on the fresh puncture wounds at her elbows.

She stared, unable to drag her gaze from the sinister blemishes. She realized her twin was waiting for her answer.

I'm a bit dizzy and feel sick but I'm okay.

Tomas's warmth surged through their connection as he tried to comfort her.

They took our blood. He projected a view of his arms to Lily. *That's probably why we're like this.*

She saw the same prick marks in the creases of his elbows. She also made out the vicious bruises staining the skin of his forearms. Anger surged inside her when she detected the hairline fractures beneath. She sensed Tomas's grimace.

Don't worry, I'm taking care of it.

The contusions started to fade even as she watched through his eyes. Still, she sent him some of her own healing power to speed up the process.

It was a while before he spoke again.

I felt Aunt Olivia in our minds when we were fighting those people. Was that you?

Lily hesitated. *Yes. My consciousness resonated with hers at the time. I guess—I guess it's because we've shared so many psychic thoughts.*

Tomas was quiet for some time. *You two have always been close.*

Lily did not detect any animosity or jealousy in her twin's voice. *Yes.*

Does that mean—Tomas swallowed—*does it mean Mom and Dad know what happened to us?*

The fresh agony in his voice twisted Lily's heart. *Yes, it does.*

Tomas winced. *That's gonna hurt them pretty bad.*

Lily bit her lip. *I know. But I'm glad it happened.* She sensed his puzzlement. *Don't you remember? You learned her name. Which means so did they.*

Tomas's consciousness flared across their connection. *Jessica Wu.*

Lily frowned. *Yes. She's some kind of scientist, like Mom. She's the one who wanted our blood.*

Why?

I—I don't know.

Silence fell between them once more, each lost in their own thoughts.

Lily?

Yes?

The gas they used on us. Those men were immune to it.

A shiver danced through Lily as she recalled the giants in the chamber they'd been taken to. She had never felt minds like theirs. Unlike the men from the island, she had not been able to even dent the walls of their consciousness, so impenetrable were the barriers shielding their thoughts. If they even had any thoughts.

Tomas's voice jolted her from her grim reflections. *Do you think you could learn to neutralize it too?*

Lily wavered. She could still taste the noxious vapor that had incapacitated them. She closed her eyes and concentrated.

Her consciousness folded inward, tendrils of power spreading inside her as she searched her body for the faintest trace of the gas. It was a full minute before she found a vestige of it in her bloodstream. She clenched her jaw, isolated the chemical with her mind, and scrutinized its structure.

Yes, I think I can.

Good.

Lily ignored the feeling of dread gnawing at the back of her mind and focused her healing abilities on trying to break the compound down. Her instincts were telling her that having their blood taken was the start of something terrible. Something that would forever alter their future.

She could not help but sense that things were speeding

toward some kind of inevitable conclusion. An event horizon of sorts. An end that she could not yet see. And one she feared was very much predestined by Fate.

CONRAD CAME DOWN THE AISLE FROM THE DIRECTION OF THE cockpit.

Lucas glanced at him as he slid his daisho into the harness strapped to the back of the combat uniform they'd borrowed from the soldiers at the Proving Ground. 'What's our ETA?'

'We're ten minutes out. It's a short ride to the marina from the airport.'

Lucas tried to suppress the nervous anticipation thrumming in his veins. He finished checking his guns, tucked them into the holsters at his hips, and looked up into Reid's hard stare.

Conrad glanced curiously between the two of them as he secured his gilded staff to his back.

'What?' Lucas asked the former Marine.

Reid clipped a fresh magazine into his Glock, shoved spare ammunition into the cargo pockets of his combat uniform, and sheathed a K-bar on his thigh. 'You've got that look on your face.'

Lucas blinked. 'What look?'

'The one that translates to you saying the hell with caution and barging in there guns blazing and swords swinging.' Reid frowned. 'I know you want this guy's blood, but we need him alive if we want answers out of him.'

'He's not wrong,' Conrad muttered.

Lucas bit back a sharp retort. He studied their concerned expressions, took a deep breath, and forced a half-smile on his face. 'I promise to be careful. There, does that make you feel better?'

Reid exchanged a chagrined stare with Conrad. 'Great. Now he's giving us sarcasm.'

Conrad's lips twitched. 'Is that bad?'

Reid nodded morosely. 'The last time he was sarcastic, people died.'

Lucas grimaced. Unheeding, Reid regaled his amused cousin with a story from their infamous trip to Europe.

An hour had passed since Connelly had called them with the details of Miller's possible whereabouts.

'Miller's assistant showed one of the NSA agents a picture from his office,' she had said. 'It was taken on a fishing boat, with Miller holding a seventeen-pound rainbow trout. We matched the background to Summersville Lake.'

'Where's that?' Lucas had asked.

'It's in West Virginia, a short flight from your current location. NSA traced a credit card under the name of Rod Miller to the Summersville Marina eighteen hours ago. Miller's assistant said he thinks his boss has a fishing cabin somewhere.'

'We got an address?' Reid had asked.

'We think so,' Connelly had replied. 'Summersville Lake Wildlife Management is headed by the US Army Corps of Engineers. I told the guy in charge to ask his men whether anyone had noticed a four-star general playing in their backyard. Someone had. Miller's built himself a reputation as a bad tipper in town. I'm sending you the coordinates of the cabin right now.'

They'd lifted off from the airfield at Aberdeen Proving Ground shortly after the call ended. Alexa and Ethan had stayed in Maryland to follow any leads they got on the woman

Olivia had seen through his children's eyes; Anatole was on his way from LA to join them.

'Better get to your seats,' their pilot said presently through the overhead speakers. 'We land in five minutes.'

CHAPTER FOURTEEN

DIMITRI ACKNOWLEDGED THE GUARD STATIONED AT THE END OF the corridor with a nod before stepping inside the elevator. He placed his hand on the biometric LCD display on the interior panel and stared into the camera set up for face recognition and retinal scanning.

'Welcome, Dimitri,' Eva said through the overhead speakers. 'We've been expecting you.'

The metal doors closed and the cabin started its decent to the basement.

Dimitri glanced at the camera. 'Any idea why Jordan wanted to see me so urgently, Eva?'

'I'm afraid I cannot reveal those details at the moment,' she replied smoothly.

Dimitri frowned faintly.

The lift opened a moment later. He stepped out into a wide, glass corridor and passed several chambers filled with banks of super servers and back-up generators. Robots on mobile platforms worked silently between them, their articulated arms controlled by the AI who had built them.

A junction appeared after thirty feet. Beyond it lay the curved south wall of the bunker holding the new computer lab.

Following the destruction of the first research facility he'd erected on his estate, Dimitri had spent three years and millions of dollars rebuilding the complex in another part of the twelve-thousand-acre Bohemian forest he'd owned since before the land acquired its present name of Sumava.

The new labs were located even deeper than their predecessors and were protected by several ten-foot-thick layers of steel and titanium reinforced concrete that could technically withstand the type of bunker bomb Kronos had used to destroy the original facility. Bar the change in location and added security features, he'd made little change to the original design of the complex, something he knew the staff who worked there had appreciated. Though they were over two hundred feet underground, he had spent a lot of time carefully recreating the ambient atmosphere of the forest above them through the use of a clever system of light wells and ventilation shafts that allowed greenery to grow inside the facility.

The computer lab's security doors opened as he approached them. Jordan was waiting inside.

'How's the temporary examination room coming along?' Dimitri said, slowing to a stop.

Jordan glanced at a pair of steel doors set in the east wall of the bunker. 'It's almost ready. The last pieces of equipment will be in place by the time they get here in the morning.' He grimaced. 'I gotta admit I don't feel so hot about having a couple of corpses down here with me.'

'We have bodies in the labs upstairs all the time,' Dimitri said wryly.

'Those are mummies,' Jordan scoffed. 'I don't mind mummies. They've been dead for, like, centuries.' He shuddered. 'The fresh ones give me the heebie-jeebies.'

Dimitri sighed. 'So, what's so pressing I had to come here straight from the airport?'

Jordan hesitated before indicating the vault to their left. 'Why don't we step inside there?'

'Why can't we talk here?' Dimitri said.

'Humor me.'

Dimitri wavered before following him inside the vault. Like the one in the first facility, it held the most precious relics he'd discovered during his centuries as the Head of the Crovir Immortal Culture and History Section. It had been nothing short of a miracle that the bunker bomb hadn't reached the original chamber during Kronos's attack on the first complex.

The steel door closed behind them with a hiss of air.

Jordan strolled to a table bearing a small, raised, glass platform linked to a microscope, a camera, and a 3D laser projector. Dimitri stopped and frowned at the set-up.

It hadn't been there the last time he'd visited the room.

Jordan looked up at the ceiling. 'Eva?'

'The room is secure,' the AI replied smoothly from the overhead speakers.

'Seriously, this cloak-and-dagger act is starting to get stale,' Dimitri said in clipped tones. 'What's this about?'

'Would you mind emptying your pockets?' Jordan said.

Dimitri blinked, nonplussed. 'What?'

'We just turned the vault into a SCIF. No electronic signal can enter or leave this room right now.'

'Why?' Dimitri folded his arms across his chest. 'And what the hell does any of that have to do with the contents of my pockets?'

Jordan rubbed the back of his neck and exhaled loudly. 'Howard Titus called us an hour ago. He knows how they found the island.'

A sick feeling erupted in the pit of Dimitri's stomach as he stared at Jordan.

'His hackers identified unusual activity logs in a series of satellites covering Europe, Africa, the US, and the Pacific in the last ten months,' Jordan continued. 'Two belonged to the Crovir network, three were Russian, and one was Chinese.'

'The satellites were tracking someone or something over a period of six months starting last October,' Eva said. 'The ones over the Pacific have stayed in fixed geosynchronous orbit since March this year. The area they were observing included the geographic coordinates of Balthazar Island.'

Dimitri swallowed. 'Are you saying—?'

Jordan nodded. 'Howard and Eva matched the data his team uncovered with your own activities since October of last year. The information corresponds exactly with your trips across those three continents.' He paused. 'The last time you visited the island was in—'

'March,' Dimitri whispered. He walked over to the table and leaned his hands shakily on the edge, remorse a dark cloud threatening to drown him. He looked dazedly at Jordan. 'Are you sure? I was being tracked?'

Jordan dipped his chin, his expression sympathetic.

Dimitri swore. He couldn't believe he was the reason behind the attack on the island and the twins' disappearance. His heart twisted as he thought of Anna and Lucas. He closed his eyes briefly.

How will I ever face them?

Anger flared inside him.

'You think they're still tracking me?' he bit out.

'We think the device they used might still be on you.'

Dimitri scowled. He removed the items in his suit and handed them to Jordan.

There were only three articles. His cell, his wallet, and his Glock 19.

Jordan emptied the wallet, disassembled the gun, and placed everything on the glass platform.

The camera and the laser projector whirred into life. 3D images of the cell, the contents of the wallet, and the Glock components appeared in mid-air, above the table. They watched as Eva spun the objects in three planes. She zoomed in on them one by one, the projections exploding as she broke them down into their basic parts for detailed analysis.

She found the tracker embedded on the microchip of his AMEX black card.

Dimitri stared as Jordan picked up the bankcard and carefully detached a minuscule, transparent film the size of a grain of rice from the electronic circuit with a pair of fine pincers. He put the material on a slide and placed it under the microscope for Eva to analyze.

'Interesting,' the AI said after a moment. 'This is a nano film. I have to admit I have not come across one this sophisticated before.' A magnified 3D view of the item flashed into existence above the table. 'Fascinating. It has a water-resistant, liquid, thermoelectric element that presumably converts body heat into electricity.'

Jordan's eyebrows rose. 'So *that's* how it could transmit a signal without a power source for so long.'

'Yes,' Eva confirmed. 'I have just scanned several scientific databases for the latest information on this type of smart technology.'

'And?' Dimitri asked tensely.

'As far as I can gather, this is not in mass production. Which means whoever designed this did it in a lab.'

Dimitri glared at the image floating above the table. 'There's only one place I can think of where they could have placed this on me.'

'Dresden,' Eva said.

Jordan's eyes widened. 'You mean—?'

'The headquarters of the Crovir First Council,' Dimitri said grimly. 'The security measures for a meeting of the Council dictates that we leave everything in a safe room outside the chamber.' He paused. 'It's the only place I visited last October where this card would have left my possession for any length of time.'

PART II
AWAKENING

CHAPTER FIFTEEN

THE CABIN STOOD CROWDED BY OAKS AND TOWERING EVERGREENS two hundred feet from the water's edge. Lucas stepped soundlessly across the moss-covered forest floor, his Smith & Wesson clasped tightly in his hands as he closed in on the sprawling, one-story structure.

It had taken them fifteen minutes to cross the lake by speedboat from the marina and reach the secluded cove two miles to the north. The landing site they'd picked placed them twelve thousand feet southwest of the coordinates of Miller's fishing lodge, enough distance to be able to complete surveillance of the area before they decided on a course of action.

A bird's eye view of the area they'd accessed via an overhead NGA satellite before they had landed at the airport had revealed little bar what looked like the end of a pier projecting over a narrow bay and the shapes of two vessels under jungle-camouflage covers.

They'd cut the engine of their Sea Ray when they were still

half a mile offshore and glided the rest of the way to the pebbly inlet. From there, they'd proceeded on foot until the roof of the cabin had appeared between the trees on the crest of a shallow rise.

Ten minutes of recon had revealed the presence of four armed men guarding an eighty-foot perimeter around the building, their army fatigues blending into the browns and greens of the forest. They had also identified the dark shape of a 4x4 parked under the elevated, west-facing porch.

Reid's voice came over the receiver in Lucas's left ear. 'There's a dirt track at my ten o'clock.'

Lucas paused under the cover of a tree and studied the terrain to his right. He was approaching the cabin from the north. He frowned when he spotted the gravel-strewn trail.

'I see it too.' His gaze shifted to the man forty feet in front of him and the one standing next to a cluster of bushes sixty feet ahead and to the left. 'Conrad, what's your position?'

'I'm at the pier,' his cousin murmured over the comms line. 'There are two guys guarding the boats. I'll have to take them out first.'

They'd decided to disable the vessels before they initiated their assault on the cabin, hoping to cut off Miller's escape route. The presence of the 4x4 was an unwelcome surprise; their NSA intel hadn't revealed the presence of an access road to the cabin.

Lucas clenched his jaw. 'We'll wait for your signal.'

He shifted slightly and was debating whether to move closer to one of his targets when he heard Conrad grunt in his earpiece.

Lucas stiffened and looked east toward the water.

Something flashed in the corner of his vision. Instinct had

him jerking to the side. A knife hummed past his face and thudded into the trunk next to him.

Conrad swallowed another grunt as the first man's fist connected with his ribs once more. He heard bone crack, blocked a blow to his head from the attacker on his left, and kneed him in the loin. The guy didn't even flinch.

The man in front of him twisted on his heels and brought his leg around and up, his movements lightning fast. Conrad jumped back, air whooshing out of his lips. He missed the roundhouse kick by a hairbreadth and took another hit to his left flank from his second attacker. He gritted his teeth and healed his broken rib.

One minute, the guards he'd been shadowing had been down by the pier, the next, they had appeared in front of him.

Conrad knew he'd masked his presence well as he'd made his approach to the lake.

The fact that they had not only detected him but closed in on him so fast he'd missed seeing them until the very last second shocked him to the core.

He'd managed to rid the two men of their pistols before they could take a shot at him. Unfortunately, they had also disarmed him; his staff weapon and gun lay uselessly on the ground some twelve feet to his right while he engaged them in vicious hand-to-hand combat.

He landed a hook kick on the first man's left thigh, followed it with a knee thrust to the gut that brought his attacker down on one knee, and jabbed his left elbow toward the face of the second man as he came at him.

A hand blocked his strike an inch from impact.

Conrad felt bones grind as his opponent slowly pushed his arm away, knuckles whitening where his fingers dug into the Immortal's skin.

A cold conviction filled the Healer as he registered the men's strangely blank expressions.

Shit! Super soldiers!

Reid trapped the hand holding the gun leveled at his head, twisted it sharply upward, and felt the draft from a bullet as it sang past his face. He shook his head to clear the ringing in his ears, ducked beneath a swinging fist, and hook-punched his attacker in the jaw. The man's head snapped sideways.

Reid knocked the weapon out of his hand, rammed his left shoulder into his chest, and drove him backward toward a tree.

The first soldier rose from the ground to his right, where he'd fallen after Reid had disarmed him and back-kicked him in the chest.

He'd been waiting for Conrad's all clear when the men he'd been tracking had suddenly vanished before his eyes. They had appeared next to him before he could make sense of what was happening, their movements so fluid and fast only Reid's instincts as a former Marine had saved him from their initial attack.

The second soldier collided heavily with the trunk, his head leaving a trail of blood on the dark bark. He raised his arms and brought his fisted hands down on the back of Reid's neck.

Air wheezed out of Reid's lips at the power of the strike. Electric tingles shot down his spine. He pushed away and stumbled back, chest heaving and the taste of blood on his tongue.

The other soldier grabbed his right shoulder, wheeled him around, and hit him in the solar plexus with the heel of his palm.

Stars exploded in front of Reid's eyes. He felt a rib snap as he was thrown off his feet. He landed hard on his ass, saw the axe-kick swinging toward his left thigh, and rolled to the opposite direction. Twigs snapped and leaves fluttered wildly as the soldier's foot smashed into the ground next to him.

Reid snarled, grabbed the man's ankle, and tugged, sending him flying onto his back. A boot swung toward his head from the left.

LUCAS HEARD A GUNSHOT TO THE SOUTH AS HE DEFLECTED THE claw fist headed for his throat. He clamped his hands on the sides of the man's head, yanked it down, and thrust his knee up into his face. Bone crunched, his opponent's nose giving way in a flood of hot blood.

The second soldier kneed him in the left flank.

Lucas grunted and sagged awkwardly. He dropped, rolled out of the way of a hammer kick, and brought his leg around in a backward spinning sweep as he rose into a low crouch. His foot connected with the side of the second man's calf and sent him crashing into the first soldier.

Lucas twisted and lunged for his katana where it had fallen on the forest floor behind him. It was closer than the guns that lay in the undergrowth just beyond it.

A hand closed viciously on his right ankle when his fingers got within an inch of the lacquered handle. He gasped as he was dragged along the ground and away from the sword.

CONRAD SPUN THE DOUBLE-BLADED SPEAR IN HIS HANDS, HIS pulse racing in his veins. The staff juddered in his grip as he blocked a low kick to his stomach and a hook fist sailing toward his head. The super soldiers grabbed the wooden shaft and pushed.

Conrad cursed as he skidded backward, boots sliding on the wooden planks of the pier. He clenched his jaw and shoved against his attackers with all his strength, blood throbbing at his temples. A knife flashed toward his chest. He jerked away from the blade, lost his balance, and tumbled off the edge of the pier.

Conrad drew a deep breath a second before the cold waters of the lake closed over his head. His hip found the rocky bottom three feet below the surface just as the men jumped in after him. He righted himself and started to rise.

A hand gripped the top of his head when he surfaced. Conrad gasped and spluttered as the super soldier forced him back down into the water. He reached up, grabbed the man's wrist, and yanked on it with all his strength.

He might as well have tried to move a mountain.

Silt stirred on the bottom of the lake as the second man threaded through the water toward them. Conrad let go of the soldier holding him, wrapped his arms around the man's left thigh, and placed his boots flat on the ground beneath him. He grunted and heaved up hard, trying to flip the guy off his feet.

Another hand shot into the water and closed around his throat. Conrad choked as both men drove him inexorably down to the bottom of the lake. Black spots swam across his vision as he struggled for air.

Something glimmered in the murky depths to his right, next to one of the pillars under the jetty. He let go of the soldier's leg and reached out blindly.

CHAPTER SIXTEEN

Reid parried the soldier's blade with his K-bar, kicked him in the side of the thigh, and jumped out of the way of the other man's hammer fist.

Blood pounded in the former Marine's ears as he fought his attackers, his every breath sending pain shooting through his chest from his broken ribs.

Something caught his eye on the moss-covered forest floor to his left.

He retreated a few steps and bared his teeth at the super soldiers. 'Come get me if you can, assholes!'

They charged him as one, their faces expressionless.

Reid feigned to the right. A knife sliced across the Kevlar vest covering his abdomen as he changed direction and lunged left. He struck the ground with a grunt, rolled, and reached for his Glock where it lay wedged under the root of a tree.

Pain exploded in his left arm as one of the super soldiers stamped down on it. He cried out, numbness blooming along his skin as the bone broke on impact. The man raised his foot again.

Reid growled and stabbed his K-bar into the top of the soldier's boot. Rubber gave way to flesh, the blade slicing straight through and out the other side, pinning the man to the forest floor.

Reid gritted his teeth and backpedaled toward the gun, his injured arm lolling at his side. His fingers closed on the butt of the Glock just as the shadow of the other super soldier swooped over him.

LUCAS ROARED AND DROVE HIS WAKIZASHI BETWEEN THE soldier's ribs. The man blinked and stopped in his tracks.

A blade hummed on Lucas's right. He let go of the wakizashi, blocked the second soldier's knife with his forearm, and punched him in the solar plexus. The man staggered back a step.

Lucas dove to the ground and rolled. His hands found the handle of the katana as he shot to his feet. He twisted on his heels and swung the long sword toward his opponent's throat.

The man dropped his dagger and blocked the blade between his bare palms, millimeters from his neck.

Lucas stared into the dead, unfeeling eyes opposite him and knew with absolute certainty that he was looking at a super soldier. He clenched his teeth and tugged on the handle of the katana.

The man curled his hands around the sword, unheeding of the razor edge slicing into his flesh and the red rivulets running down his wrists.

The soldier with the wakizashi embedded in his chest stepped toward them.

Lucas gritted his teeth and grabbed the short sword when it came within arm's reach. He yanked it out of the man's rib cage, front-kicked him in the gut, and slashed the soldier holding the katana across the side of the neck. Both men fell to their knees before him, the one gripping the katana finally letting go.

Hairs rose on Lucas's skin. His knuckles whitened on the handles of the daisho as he stared into the super soldiers' blank faces. He moved, piercing their hearts in one smooth thrust.

Each man stiffened at the end of a blade. Lucas watched the light dim in their eyes, a shudder racing through him. He yanked the swords out of their flesh. They sagged to the forest floor, unseeing gazes directed at the overhead canopy, their blood turning the green ground scarlet.

Lucas bowed his head and leaned on the crimson-stained katana, his breaths leaving his lips in harsh pants, sweat rolling down his face.

The sound of an engine reached his ears.

Lucas looked up and saw movement under the cabin's west-facing porch. His eyes widened when the 4x4 shot out from beneath the building, wheels spinning and sending arcs of dirt and moss spiraling into the air.

He cursed, sheathed his blades, and swooped to pick his guns off the ground as he broke into a run. He stopped on an incline and jammed the Glock into the holster at his hip as the vehicle charged past twenty feet below him. He steadied the Smith & Wesson in his hands and fired several shots at the blurry figure in the driver's seat.

The pops of the bullets leaving the suppressor were swallowed by the squeal of the 4x4's tires.

A cry sounded from inside the vehicle. It swung wildly

across the dirt track, its front right fender glancing off a row of trees and plowing through the undergrowth.

Lucas caught a glimpse of Miller's face twisted in a mask of rage and pain as he clutched his right shoulder. His heart thundered against his ribs as he raced down the slope, his finger moving repeatedly on the trigger of his gun. His bullets pinged off the vehicle's tailgate and peppered the rear windshield with spider cracks as it veered from side to side.

He heard the click of his empty magazine, swapped the Smith & Wesson for the Glock, and bolted onto the road after the 4x4. He had swung his arm up and fired four shots when a figure suddenly appeared in his path, eclipsing his view of the vehicle.

Lucas gasped and dropped beneath the massive fist flying toward his head. He skidded, lost his balance, and landed hard on the ground. Momentum sent him tumbling along the track, gravel taking the skin off his knuckles and elbows.

The 4x4 righted itself before disappearing between the trees up ahead in a cloud of dirt. Acid burned the back of Lucas's throat as he rolled to a stop on his front and stared after it.

'Lucas!'

Reid's voice jolted him out of his stupor.

Lucas looked over his shoulder and saw a man looming over him. He had barely registered that this super soldier was a hell of a lot bigger than the ones he'd just fought when he was picked up and hurled into the air as if he weighed nothing.

He sailed across the road, saw the tree, and braced himself. Pain exploded in his side when he struck the trunk. He felt ribs snap and slid to the ground onto his hands and knees, his breath locking in his throat.

Reid started firing at the giant super soldier, his bullets striking the man in the back at point blank range. The soldier blinked, twisted on his heels, and headed steadily for the former Marine, his expression eerily vacant despite his wounds.

Reid backed up toward the cabin, his face set in grim lines as he continued shooting. He discarded his empty magazine, reloaded awkwardly with his left arm, and raised the Glock again.

Fear stabbed through Lucas as the super soldier closed in on his friend.

He struggled to his feet and gulped air into his lungs. '*Run!*'

Reid glanced at him, tripped, and fell onto his back. He swung the gun up and kept firing as he backtracked clumsily across the ground.

Lucas ignored the shooting pain in his chest, reached for his swords, and stumbled toward the two men. The giant reached Reid and raised his foot to stamp on his head. Reid clenched his jaw and brought his hands up defensively.

Lucas's heart lurched. He switched his grip on the wakizashi, drew his arm back, and hurled the blade with all his might, a roar of fury on his lips.

It flashed through the air and thudded into the giant's back.

The super soldier paused for a fraction of a second. Reid rolled just as he brought his leg down hard on the spot where he had been.

Metal glinted in the trees to the right. A gilded spear whined across the dirt track and impaled the super soldier in the gut. He stilled and looked down curiously at the weapon before grabbing it with both hands. Lucas gaped as he started pulling it out of his body.

Conrad bolted out of the woods, grabbed Reid under the shoulders, and hauled him to safety.

'Do it!' he barked at Lucas. '*Now, goddamnit!*'

The spear left the super soldier's flesh with a sickening, wet sound. He gripped the weapon and started to turn.

Lucas swooped in low behind him, dropped to the ground, and swung the katana at his heels as he skidded past. The blade sang as it carved through skin and tissue, slicing clean through the giant's Achilles tendons. He tottered for a moment before falling heavily onto his knees.

Lucas twisted, scrambled into a low crouch, and brought the blade up and across the soldier's throat as he rose.

The giant let go of the staff. The weapon clattered onto the dirt track. He reached a hand out toward Lucas and tried to climb to his feet, a gurgle passing his lips. Scarlet froth stained his chin and the gaping slash on his neck.

Lucas growled and drove the katana straight through his heart.

The giant stiffened and stilled. He looked at the blade stuck in his rib cage before raising his head to meet Lucas's gaze. The ground trembled as he slowly collapsed onto his side. Air left his throat in a guttural rasp. He went limp, his face as impassive in death as it had been during their fight.

Lucas yanked his swords out of the man's body and stood swaying for a moment. He stumbled across the dirt track and dropped down next to Conrad and Reid where they sat breathing heavily on the ground.

'Remind me to praise that snot-faced brat when we see him,' Conrad said in between pants. 'How many of these guys did he and Olivia take out in Yuma?'

'Dozens.' Fire scorched Lucas's body as he wheezed and fought for breath. He registered Conrad's wet clothes. 'What happened?'

'I fell in the lake.'

His wounds faded before Lucas's eyes. Conrad moved and

started healing Lucas's injuries. Lucas clenched his teeth as his ribs snapped back into place with cracks and pops. His pain dulled immediately.

Reid paled when Conrad placed his hands on his broken arm. 'Shit, that hurts.' He drew a shaky breath. 'Well, at least now we know there are several kinds of super soldiers. The ones who look like your average Joe and that—thing.' He indicated the body on the dirt track.

Lucas followed his gaze.

'And not all of them are Immortals,' Conrad added thoughtfully. 'Reid and I wouldn't have managed to kill them otherwise.'

Although Lucas was dismayed Miller had escaped their grasp, their encounter with the enemy had revealed two things. First, it had proven the general's culpability beyond any doubt. He would now be a hunted man, with both US Intelligence and Immortal Hunters on his trail. All his associates in the DoD would automatically become subjects of interest.

Second, it had shown them the nature of their foe. This latter fact worried Lucas more than the general's disappearance. He stared at the dead super soldier, dread a heavy weight in the middle of his chest.

Miller won't get far before we pick up his trail again. But these men? These men won't be easy to stop. Not if there are hundreds of them.

CHAPTER SEVENTEEN

ALEXA OBSERVED THE DARK BUILDING SITTING ON THE BANKS OF the stream-fed, private lake two hundred feet east of their position.

'It's quiet.' Ethan stared into a pair of infrared binoculars next to her.

Anatole looked up from his scope. 'You guys sure this is the right place?'

Alexa nodded, her gaze on the two-story, winged, Georgian home. 'This is her last known address. County and title records show no one living at this house since.'

Seven hours had passed since the incident during which Ethan and Olivia had lost control of their powers. It had taken a while to uncover any trace of the woman the Seer had seen during her psychic connection with Lily and Tomas.

Eva was the one who had finally found mention of a female scientist by the name of Dr. Jessica Marie Wu Chen Hong in a paper published by Harvard University in 1963. She had been listed as a contributor working for the university's Biology

Department at the time. More than the name, it was the subject matter of the publication and its principal author that had piqued the AI's interest.

'The paper was entitled "Future Applications of Genetic Research,"' Eva had informed them. 'The lead author was one James D. Watson.'

Alexa had shared a startled glance with Ethan where they waited on the tarmac at the airfield in Maryland. 'You mean, *the* James Watson? As in one of the guys who discovered the structure of DNA?'

'Yes,' Eva had replied. 'What is even more intriguing is that there is no other mention of a Dr. Wu Chen Hong in any publication before or after that time.'

Alexa had narrowed her eyes at that. 'So, she's a ghost too? And an Immortal. Judging from Olivia's description from her vision, she has the appearance of someone in her thirties.'

'Indeed. If she is the scientist you are after, then it appears she has done her utmost to hide her identity,' Eva replied. 'Her contribution to this paper was redacted shortly after publication, but I found the list of original authors mentioned in a reference in another paper. Unfortunately, the human resources database at the university does not list details of their staff that far back. There may very well be physical records somewhere on site, though.'

'I think I know somebody who might know where those are,' Alexa had said grimly.

Zachary and the others had just landed at the airport outside Ceske Budejovice when her call went through.

'Try Room 51 in the basement of the Memorial Library,' Zachary had said 'It's in Harvard Yard, on Massachusetts Avenue.'

'Thanks.' A smile had curved Alexa's lips, her tension

melting away at the sound of his voice, as it always did. 'Hey, remember that thing we did last week?'

'You mean—?' Zachary started, his tone turning low and husky.

'Yeah, that thing.' Her smile had widened. 'I can't wait to do that again.'

A low chuckle had left her throat as she had listened to Zachary groan at the other end of the line.

'You're killing me, babe.'

Alexa had grinned. 'I love you too.'

She'd ended the call and looked up into Ethan's sullen stare.

'Seriously, why is everything about sex with you two?'

Alexa had tut-tutted. 'Jealousy is an ugly trait, Ethan.'

It had taken twenty minutes to get a Bastian helicopter to fly up from Baltimore and take them north to Massachusetts. By the time they had unearthed the scientist's personal file among the archives beneath the Widener building, Anatole had reached Boston.

The address listed for Jessica Wu had led them to a twenty-acre estate fifteen miles southwest of the city. Bar the security lights in the garden, they had seen no signs of life since they had snuck over the gated wall encircling the grounds and taken up position in the woods hedging the lawn leading up to the colonnaded porch running around the property.

'Let's go,' Alexa said.

THEY MOVED RAPIDLY IN THE DARKNESS, THEIR STEPS MUTED BY the grass, and reached the rear porch seconds later.

Ethan crossed the terracotta floor and placed a hand on the wood and leaded-glass back door. He detected the security sensor attached to the frame, sent a burst of elemental energy through it to disable the house alarm, and gently manipulated the lock. It clicked faintly. He turned the handle and opened the door.

They headed inside, their guns in hand.

A black and white marble vestibule opened up in front of them. It spanned the length of the house and led to an atrium dominated by a grand, split staircase rising to the upper levels, with the entrance foyer beyond. Light from the external security lamps glittered off crystal chandeliers and mirrors, the rays reflected on the antique, polished-wood furniture. Ornaments filled the reception rooms and a state-of-the-art kitchen opened off the central passage. They cleared the wings and the first floor before heading upstairs.

They found a study attached to a library overlooking the lake at the rear of the house.

'Bingo.'

Ethan crossed the carpeted floor and took a seat behind the desk. It was framed by wide, double doors leading to a balcony spanning the width of the building. A sleek, dual-monitor computer sat in the middle of the table.

'I'll check the bedrooms and the loft.' Anatole disappeared back out the door.

Alexa cupped a pen torch in her hand and started exploring the floor-to-ceiling bookcases.

Ethan took out the smartphone he'd bought on Howard's instructions and plugged it into a port at the back of the computer. He removed his own cell from his rear pocket and hit speed-dial. The call connected seconds later.

'Howard? I'm in. Let Eva know.'

He watched the monitors come to life before his eyes. It took seconds for Eva and Howard to breach the security system protecting the computer and log into the mainframe. A window popped up when they started uploading the drives to their servers, the smartphone acting as a physical backup.

Ethan rose and headed to where Alexa was inspecting some books. 'Found anything?'

She arched an eyebrow. 'Our good doctor seems to like sexually deviant play.' She showed him the covers.

Ethan grimaced at the explicit titles and images. 'Oh.'

His cell buzzed. He slipped it out of his pocket, looked at the screen, and frowned.

'Remove the smartphone! They know you're there!' Howard snapped from the other end of the line when the call connected.

Ethan strode to the desk and snatched the phone out of the port.

'What?' Alexa said tensely.

Ethan swore. Letters and numbers scrolled across the computer monitors, the drives disappearing as they were remotely deleted.

A shot came from somewhere above them. Alexa bolted out of the room with her Sig in hand. Ethan rounded the desk and was reaching for his Colt when glass shattered behind him. He whirled around, saw light glint on the muzzle of a gun, and raised his hand.

ALEXA HEARD A CRASH BEHIND HER AS SHE RAN OUT OF THE library. Two shadowy shapes fell past the banister ahead of her and struck the landing below with a thud.

Movement flashed to her right. She leaned out of the way of a gun, feeling heat streak past her face as her attacker fired. She knocked the pistol out of his hand and brought her Sig up. A second man appeared in the gloom and kicked the weapon from her grasp, taking her by surprise.

She blocked a high kick to her face, evaded another shot, and jumped out of the way of the palm strike headed for her chest. She narrowed her eyes at her opponents and reached for her sai daggers.

Super soldiers!

More figures appeared in the foyer. Anatole was fighting the man he'd fallen with on the landing below. Alexa barely had time to glance at him before the soldiers facing her attacked. She danced out of the way of two more bullets, roundhouse kicked the gun out of the second man's hand, and narrowly avoided the knife headed for her throat.

ETHAN GRUNTED WHEN THE SUPER SOLDIER'S FIST CONNECTED with his jaw.

He crushed the blade headed for his left thigh, front-kicked his first attacker in the chest, and sent the second one crashing into the desk with a blast of elemental energy.

They came at him again, hands and feet moving in a fluid dance of strikes and kicks, their faces expressionless. He gritted his teeth and blocked their attack.

'WELL, THIS IS SHIT,' ANATOLE STATED.

He stood next to Alexa on the landing, his chest heaving, a knife clasped in his hand.

Alexa frowned at the super soldiers surrounding them. Three stood on the steps above them and four faced them from below. They ignored their dead companions on the upper landing and the foyer, their vacant stares chilling.

The fact that the men they'd defeated weren't getting up told Alexa they were not Immortals.

Anatole wiped a sliver of blood from the corner of his mouth. 'Got any ideas?'

'Try not to die,' Alexa muttered.

Anatole sighed. 'Story of my life, right there.'

Alexa stretched out the kinks in her neck. 'I'll take the ones at the bottom.'

Anatole steeled himself. 'Gotcha.'

The men came at them as one.

Alexa weaved between a flurry of blades, kicks, and punches. Heat rose in her chest as she countered the soldiers' deadly assault, her body drawing on the unearthly power that had awakened inside her following her first death. It danced through her veins, a savage energy that filled her soul with fire and rendered her mind red with bloodlust.

The floor shuddered beneath her feet when the ungodly force blasted out of her in a powerful wave that forced the super soldiers back a step. She bared her teeth in a feral snarl, the strength of her attack accelerating exponentially, the sais blurring in her grip.

The super soldiers fell before her one by one.

A crash erupted on the upper landing. A figure shot out of the library and smashed through the banister. It sailed through the air and struck the chandelier suspended above the atrium before plummeting to the marble floor thirty feet below.

A familiar energy washed across Alexa's skin.

A second figure emerged backward from the library, feet dangling a couple of inches off the wooden floorboards and hands clawing at its throat.

Ethan followed, his expression cold and focused, his left hand raised, palm facing the super soldier suspended above the ground.

'Whoa,' Anatole murmured.

Ethan's fingers twitched. The super soldier glided through the jagged gap in the banister and soared out over the atrium, his face reddening as he fought for breath, the skin at his neck dented by an invisible force.

The Elemental raised his arm. The soldier kicked his legs out frantically as he rose ten feet in the air. His figure blurred as he was driven downward in the next second, his body smashing onto the foyer floor with a sickening thud.

Anatole winced. 'Ouch.'

Alexa turned toward the men still standing.

Wood creaked and glass vibrated under the unearthly forces sweeping the atrium. The chandelier trembled and swayed overhead, crystals casting a myriad of flashes across the bloody battleground below.

CHAPTER EIGHTEEN

LILY RAISED HER HEAD SLOWLY.

They are coming.

She climbed awkwardly to her feet, bracing herself against the concrete wall of her cell, the dread that had been with her since she woke that morning escalating. Her brother's energy pulsed across their mental connection, his consciousness flashing gold as he tried to console her.

The door opened. Two guards entered the cell. They took her by the arms and led her out of her prison and into the corridor beyond.

Tomas and his escort joined them from a junction on the left a moment later.

Her brother held her gaze, his green eyes warm. *We'll be okay.*

Lily bit her lip and nodded. This time, the guards took them up to the tenth floor.

This level was different to the one where they had been brought the day before. A single, wide passage opened up ahead of them, its length suggesting it spanned most of the underground complex. A pair of freight elevators stood framed in the wall on either side of the lift they exited. Beyond them, concrete gave way to thick glass.

A shiver raced down Lily's spine when she spotted what lay inside the cavernous, two-story-tall chambers behind the transparent walls they were escorted past.

What are those?

Apprehension colored Tomas's voice.

He gazed beyond the metal mezzanines that ran around the upper periphery of the space to the concrete floors one level down.

Lily stared at the rows of giant, round, glass tanks rising vertically from the ground. The structures were connected to the ceiling and to an array of complex machines and monitors by lines and pipes. Men and women in lab coats toiled diligently at the instruments, their work assisted by robotic arms suspended from steel frames hanging above their heads.

Her gaze skimmed the equipment before focusing on the most sinister things in the rooms.

Suspended in a murky liquid inside each tank was the near naked figure of a man. Tubes and wires snaked out of the bodies, linking them to the machines outside. Most were the size of an average human. A third were bigger, much bigger, like the four men who had attacked them the day before.

Lily's mouth went dry when she finally grasped what they were looking at.

Life pods. Those are life pods like the ones Aunt Olivia saw when she was taken prisoner four years ago.

Tomas's unease exploded inside her mind.

You mean—?

Lily dipped her chin. *Super soldiers.*

She swallowed and wrenched her gaze from the ghastly parade on either side of them. The corridor seemed to stretch on forever. She estimated they'd passed six hundred pods by the time they reached the steel doors at the end of the passage.

Beyond them lay a lab. Lily slowed and stared, her pulse accelerating as she registered the scores of people inside it. They all seemed to be waiting for something. Or someone.

She stiffened when she spotted the glass wall at the other end of the chamber. Beyond it was an isolation room similar to the one where they had been taken yesterday. Monitors and medical equipment lined the white linoleum floor.

In the center was a pair of beds.

A man lay atop each cot, eyes closed and bodies still, oxygen masks strapped to their faces. The cotton sheets covering their frames did not move, their rib cages still beneath the linen. The figure on the left wore a fresh dressing on his chest. The one on the right bore a healed surgical scar on his, with a second livid wound running diagonally from the tip of his left shoulder before it disappeared beneath the sheet toward his opposite hip.

The air seemed to thicken before Lily's very eyes. An oppressive atmosphere descended around her, making it hard to breathe. She could feel a dark energy swirling inside the lab, the same energy she had sensed ever since she'd woken in the complex.

It was coming from the bodies inside the isolation chamber.

She glanced around at the people in the room, stunned that they seemed unaware of the overwhelming pressure bearing down on her.

Do they not feel it?

A man crossed the floor toward them. Jessica Wu followed in his steps, hands in the pockets of her white coat, her beautiful face cold.

Lily looked up when the man stopped before her and Tomas. Unlike the scientists around them, he wore a suit.

He studied her and her brother for a moment, his expression impassive and his eyes inscrutable. 'You do not appear to want to use your powers today.'

Lily reached out and curled her fingers around Tomas's hand. She could feel him trembling next to her, the same suffocating dread pressing on her consciousness resonating inside him.

She had already breached the minds of Jessica Wu and the normal Immortals in the room. What they had revealed had her heart thundering inside her chest. As for the man in front of them, the man whose name she had identified from Wu's thoughts, his mental shields were proving as impenetrable as those of the giant super soldiers they had faced the previous day.

'How disappointing,' he murmured. He took them gently by their shoulders and guided them toward the isolation chamber. 'Come. Since it's thanks to you that all of this is possible, I think it only fitting that you be here for the grand awakening.'

Something caught Lily's attention as they neared the glass wall. Her eyes rounded when she saw the stone tombs standing on a pair of pedestals inside a second isolation chamber to the right.

The man followed her gaze. 'I haven't thanked you for the seal.'

Lily's hand shot to the base of her throat. She'd assumed she'd lost her sun cross pendant during the attack on the island. She spotted the glittering, gold necklace inside a glass case on a table next to the tombs. An identical necklace sat in a velvet-lined box next to it.

She looked ahead into the isolation chamber and saw the

red bags at the end of IV lines running into each of the silent figures' arms. Her fingers clenched around Tomas's. He squeezed back, understanding flashing across their connection.

'Dr. Wu tells me your blood has remarkable properties,' the man said. 'She is keen to—study you further. I convinced her you should witness this first.'

He dipped his chin at Wu. She looked over at the scientists manning a workstation to their left. One of them clicked a couple of keys on a computer.

The digital screens on the infusion pumps linked to the red bags started to flash. Crimson slowly filled the IV lines, displacing the clear fluid within.

Lily's breathing turned shallow as she watched her and Tomas's blood make its way into the veins of the dead men on the beds.

An expectant hush filled the lab. A minute passed. Then two.

At five minutes, the man in the suit frowned. 'Why is nothing happening?'

A muscle jumped in Wu's jawline. 'Give it some—'

Though it was soft, the noise when it came was thunderous. A beep.

All eyes swung to the monitor attached to the dead man on the right.

It came again, a high-pitched, electronic sound that made Lily's pulse jump. Another echoed it a second later.

She swallowed a whimper and watched the flat lines on the monitors spike, the beeps speeding up with the rising heart rates, the electric rhythms normalizing into regular beats. Alarms sounded around the beds as the other machines picked up signs of life from the two men. They lit up, the numbers on the screens climbing rapidly until they reached normal ranges and silenced the shrill warnings.

The man in the suit walked over to the glass wall and placed his hands flat against the polished plate, his face filled with a fervent light.

'My God, it's really happening,' Wu whispered. She leaned a hand against a table, legs visibly shaking.

The cotton sheets trembled violently as the dead men started to take deep, shuddering gasps, their bodies adjusting to life once more, the oxygen masks over their faces misting. It was almost a minute before their breathing settled into a normal pattern.

Tomas's fingers bit into Lily's skin when the man on the right suddenly sat up and wrenched the mask from his face.

His eyes slammed open. Dark pupils stared at them wildly from within a pair of pale, milky irises, their depths as old as time and radiating such evil Lily could not help but shudder.

The figure on the left rose slowly. He blinked, revealing cloudy, blue eyes that would have been an identical shade to her own and her father's were it not for the pearly film covering them.

The men's expressions crumpled in the next instant. They clutched their heads, raised their faces to the sky, and screamed.

The agonizing sounds tore through Lily. She opened her mouth, a tormented cry ripped from her own throat as she collapsed to her knees.

Her brother fell at her side, his voice echoing her distress, his pain and the suffering of the men behind the glass forming red waves that crashed over her, overwhelming her consciousness.

CHAPTER NINETEEN

'I SWEAR HE HAD IT IN HERE LAST TIME I VISITED.'

Reid rummaged through a cabinet under Alexa and Ethan's curious gazes.

His fingers closed around the neck of a bottle just as Lucas walked into the room with a tray of coffee. Reid grinned and lifted out the expensive bottle of whisky.

'It's eight o'clock in the morning,' Lucas said testily.

Reid shrugged. 'So?'

He opened the cap and poured a generous amount of liquor into their cups.

'I think we need an intervention,' Lucas stated.

Conrad came out of the corridor leading to the bedrooms, hands briskly rubbing a towel across his wet hair.

He sniffed and raised an eyebrow. 'Do I smell whisky-laced coffee?'

'What are you, a dog?' Ethan scoffed.

Alexa propped her feet on the coffee table, brought her cup to her lips, took a sip, and sighed.

They were in Lucas's apartment in Boston, where they'd crashed for the night. Reid had gone to get fresh clothes from his own place before returning for a much-needed tactical meeting.

A search of Miller's fishing lodge following their encounter with the super soldiers the day before had revealed little in terms of useful information. They'd found the 4x4 he'd escaped in some thirty miles north of Summersville Lake, in the middle of some woods. Fresh track marks in the mud indicated he'd been picked up by another vehicle.

As for Jessica Wu's house, the only data of interest had likely been on her computer drives. Even though Eva and Howard had failed to identify the origin of the signal that had triggered the alarm, they had managed to upload a bunch of corrupted folders to their servers before their access was remotely shut down. Cleaning and decrypting the files were likely to take some time, even with the AI assisting Howard and his team of hackers.

The identities of the men they'd killed in West Virginia and outside Boston had proven as elusive as those of the soldiers from the island, their fingerprints and faces not found on any database in the world.

'It was creepy,' Anatole had told them the previous night as he nursed a shot glass. 'There was a bunch of them just sitting in the dark in that loft when I walked in. It was as if they were just—awaiting orders.'

The facilities they'd uncovered in a concealed room beneath Jessica Wu's garage suggested the same of the rest of the super soldiers who had stormed the mansion and attacked them.

The sound of the front door opening traveled down the apartment hallway.

Anatole appeared with two large paper bags in his hands. 'Right, I got doughnuts.'

'Jelly?' Ethan said.

'Yes.'

'Blueberry?' Conrad said.

'Always.'

'Strawberry-frosted?' Alexa said.

Anatole paused. 'What am I, psychic?'

'All women like strawberry-frosted doughnuts,' Alexa stated coolly. 'I bet even Donaghy does.'

Reid could see the words: "But you're no ordinary woman. You're a terrifying creature who can kill me with her little finger" flash across Anatole's face as he stared at Alexa. The former Marine swallowed a grin and took a sip of his coffee; he'd been somewhat surprised when he'd discovered the red-haired Immortal was dating a CIA agent.

'Leave my girlfriend out of this conversation,' Anatole said with a grunt. 'And, for the record, she's a sucker for Chocolate Kreme.'

Conrad dipped his hand into one of the bags, snagged a doughnut, and bit into it. 'So, when *are* you going to make an honest woman out of Claire?'

Anatole made a choking noise. 'The hell that come from?!'

Conrad shrugged as he chewed. 'You've been going out for, what, like, six years now? I think it's about time you proposed.'

Anatole scowled. 'What are you, my mother? Besides, there's the whole Immortal-human thing.'

Everyone looked at Alexa. She narrowed her eyes at the red-haired Bastian and took another sip of her coffee.

'I don't mean it's wrong,' Anatole said hurriedly. 'It's just—well—it's gonna hurt like a bitch when they're no longer there, right?'

'Wow,' Ethan murmured in the silence that followed.

'I can't believe you said that out loud,' Conrad muttered dully to his best friend.

Reid grunted. 'You should write a book. *How to make enemies and influence people the wrong way.*'

Lucas sighed, lifted his laptop from a side table, and headed for an armchair. 'Let's check in with the others and see where they're at.'

'Good idea,' Alexa said, her sharp gaze lingering on a suddenly sweaty-looking Anatole. 'I hope they've had more luck than—'

Ethan dropped his cup. It crashed to the floor at his feet, spilling its contents across the wooden boards as it rolled under the couch. He sucked air between his teeth and gripped his left hand, a pained expression distorting his glazed features.

Reid's eyes widened. *Shit! It's happening again!*

He set his coffee down hastily and rose from his chair, trepidation sending his pulse racing. 'You guys had better—'

He froze, dread exploding inside him as Lucas let go of the laptop and clutched his chest. Alexa shuddered, her hand rising to the back of her neck, her eyes strangely glassy. Conrad grasped his left arm and stumbled into an armchair, color draining from his face.

'Hey, what's wrong?' Anatole said, alarmed.

A curse left Ethan's lips. Reid's gaze dropped to the birthmark on the back of his hand. It was glowing gold.

The same radiance fluttered along the snake on Conrad's arm and shone from Alexa's nape.

Lucas gasped and dropped to his knees, sweat beading on his forehead and agony painted across his face, an unearthly light shining through his shirt from the birthmark over his heart.

'EVA, START RECORDING.'

'Yes, Dr. Godard,' the AI replied through the overhead speakers.

Anna gripped the scalpel and moved the sharp edge of the blade smoothly down the middle of the corpse's chest. Madeleine stood on the other side of the examination table, ready to assist her.

They'd already checked the dental records of the two dead men from the island and had been unsurprised when they hadn't found any matches. This had only confirmed their suspicion that they were dealing with super soldiers.

The door of the lab opened. Jordan walked in with a box in his arms. Dimitri, Olivia, and Asgard followed him in.

'You heard anything from Lucas or Alexa?' Dimitri was saying.

Asgard shook his head. 'No. We're waiting to see what Eva and Howard make of the files they retrieved from Jessica Wu's hard drives.'

'And Miller?'

Asgard frowned. 'There are no signs of the man yet. Victor has Bastian Hunters looking for him. Connelly already started an internal investigation into his activities at the DoD.'

Dimitri dipped his chin stiffly. 'Let me know if there's anything else I can do.'

Remorse lingered in the Crovir noble's eyes.

It was shortly after they had arrived at the estate in the early hours of the morning that he had revealed how Howard and Eva had uncovered the tracking device that had led their enemy to Balthazar island.

'I cannot excuse what happened,' he had admitted to Anna in clipped tones. 'Again, you have my most sincere—'

'Stop.' Anna had crossed the foyer and gripped his hand tightly. 'It wasn't your fault, Dimitri. We know you would never do anything to harm us or our children. These people were determined to find out where we were, one way or another.'

He'd swallowed hard at her words, his face dark with regret.

It was late morning by the time they headed out to the research facility in the forest. Dimitri had shown them around the state-of-the-art complex and introduced them to his staff before taking them to the basement where a lab had been set up for their personal use.

Jordan grimaced and deposited the box on the table where Zachary sat working at his laptop.

'This is the last of the stuff you wanted.' His gaze skimmed the two dead bodies in the room. 'If it's okay with you folks, I think I'll leave this—part of the investigation to you. Yell if you need anything.' He turned and headed for the door.

Olivia started across the floor, her expression hesitant as she glanced from Anna to Madeleine. 'I feel a bit useless. Is there anything I can do to—?'

She stopped suddenly, her feet freezing to the floor next to Zachary.

He straightened in his chair. 'Olivia?'

Anna's pulse jumped when she registered the blank expression on her cousin's face. She put the scalpel down, alarmed.

'I think she's having another vision,' Madeleine said on the other side of the table.

Asgard cursed and clutched at his heart. Anna startled. Madeleine took a step toward him, gasped, and bowed over, her hand rising to her own chest.

A golden glow erupted inside Olivia's right hand. She uncurled her fist and stared at the radiant lines of her birthmark, her fingers shaking.

Zachary slipped from his seat, his knuckles white where he gripped the flesh over his heart, the tendons of his neck bulging as pain filled his reddening face.

Anna's mouth turned dry with fear.

'What the hell is going on?' Dimitri said hoarsely.

'Eva!' Jordan barked. 'Can you—?'

'Their vital signs are spiking,' the AI said. 'There's something else. Some kind of energy coming from their hearts and Miss Ashkarov's birthmark.'

Anna stared helplessly at the four figures who had fallen to their knees across the room and were struggling to catch their breath.

Long dead souls shuddered as they woke from timeless sleep.

They gasped, air filling their lungs from their first breaths in several millennia. Their life forces surged forth and spread through the bodies of the ones they dwelled in, filling their flesh and bones. It took but a few beats of the hearts racing inside their chests for them to find one another, the golden lines of their souls reaching out across the thousands of leagues that separated their physical selves.

Dread rose within them when they connected.

There were two others in this world with them. Two souls that did not belong. Two souls whose very revival had roused them from the place where a piece of them had been reborn, inside the ones who had inherited their powers and more.

One had sacrificed himself for the greater good.

The other they thought they had defeated a long time back.

They fisted hands that did not belong to them as the dire truth sank in.

In the Kingdom of Heaven, the Archangel stirred and looked upon the Dominion of Earth. 'So it begins.'

Arael fluttered down onto his shoulder, claws clinking against his golden armor and feathers glimmering with ethereal light. The Angel of Crows followed his gaze, beady eyes glinting keenly as he too stared into the world of Man.

Lucas's eyes snapped open. He was on the floor on his hands and knees, his nails biting into his fisted palms. Reid was at his side, fingers shaking his shoulder, his mouth open and shouting.

Lucas barely felt his touch or heard his voice. The inexplicable pressure that had exploded inside his head and the terrible fire that had consumed his heart in the past few minutes were starting to abate, leaving his blood thundering wildly in his veins.

Something else had replaced them. Something eerie.

He sensed it behind his eyes. A presence. No. Two of them.

Lucas looked up shakily. His pulse stuttered as he gazed upon the three Immortals opposite him.

There were others in the room with them. Ghostly specters like the ones inside him. He could feel them in his cousins' bodies. More than feeling them, though, Lucas was shocked to realize that he knew them. He had known them for an eternity, it seemed.

'Mila?' Lucas startled at the sound of his own voice. It twanged, a strange echo underscoring the name he had just said, as if two others had spoken as one.

Alexa stared at him unblinkingly. 'Tobias?'

'Ba—Baruch?' Conrad stammered. He looked from Lucas to Ethan. *'Jared?!'*

'Rafael?' Ethan blinked at Conrad, his face deathly pale.

Reid's voice finally penetrated the ringing in Lucas's ears. 'Okay, you guys are seriously creeping me out now!'

'What the hell happened?' Anatole said. 'You all looked like you were having a heart attack or something.' He scowled and pointed at Lucas. 'And what was with that weird-ass, fiery stuff?'

Lucas looked down where he indicated. There was an exact replica of the alpha-omega symbol on his heart scorched into the material of his shirt.

That was when he sensed their anger. The anger of the other beings in the room with them.

He stared at his cousins. 'They are back.'

Fury flashed in the silver depths of Alexa's eyes, eyes that were at once hers and the eyes of another.

ZACHARY GAZED AT OLIVIA, HIS HEART RACING. SHIVERS SHOOK him, the fever in his chest fading and the pain in his head subsiding. In its stead was something new. He could feel it in his mind. A weight. The consciousness of another.

'Navia?' Shock flashed through him at the name that left his lips.

Zachary blinked. He knew he was looking at Olivia. He also knew she was someone else in that moment. There was another woman staring at him through her eyes. A woman from the past. One whose name had come unbidden to him.

Olivia's mouth opened and closed soundlessly.

'Ääron?' she finally whispered.

The word vibrated in Zachary's bones and resonated inside his very soul, bringing forth a surge of warmth from his heart.

Olivia stared around the room. She stiffened and gasped when her gaze fell upon Asgard and Madeleine. Tears spilled from her eyes and rolled down her cheeks, unchecked.

'Oh God.' A tremulous smile curved her lips, pure joy filling her face. '*Oh my God!*'

Asgard and Madeleine stared at their hands and bodies, their expressions stunned, as if they had never seen themselves before.

Madeleine looked up and cried out when she saw Asgard. She bolted to her feet and launched herself at him, carrying him to the ground, sobs leaving her throat. Asgard swallowed convulsively and wrapped his arms around her, his blue eyes glimmering with unshed tears.

Some of the elation faded from Olivia's face then. She gazed at Zachary, alarm widening her eyes. 'They are alive.'

Zachary frowned. 'Who?'

'Our fathers.' She swallowed. 'We killed them. But they walk this world once more.'

CHAPTER TWENTY

THE MAN STUDIED THE IMMORTALS AT THE OAK TABLE. FOR THE first time in his considerably long life, he felt nervous.

'Would you like a drink?' he murmured.

Crovir, the first Immortal king, looked at the carafe of wine he indicated. He dipped his chin, his expression cool.

The man turned to the second Immortal. 'King...Bastian?'

Bastian nodded, his gaze fixed on Crovir sitting opposite him across the table.

Though he kept his own face impassive, the man was as surprised at the tension he could sense between the brothers as he had been by the shocking event of their revival.

Neither he nor Wu had expected them to be in so much physical and mental pain following their resurrection. Nor could they comprehend Lily and Tomas Soul's reaction, which had mirrored that of the kings.

In the minutes that had followed their revival, as their screams of agony and those of the children had filled the lab, doubt had flashed through the man's mind. For a moment, he had sensed that he had meddled with things that should have been left well alone. Things he could not comprehend. Things of an unholy nature.

Seconds after the kings had collapsed inside the isolation chamber and fallen into a deep sleep, the children had fainted too. Wu had wanted to start her experiments on them straight away. The man had denied the request and ordered the guards to take them back to their cells.

For some unfathomable reason, he felt it would be wise not to harm them. Not until he'd spoken to the kings about them anyway.

An hour had passed since the two men had roused again, this time more naturally. While they had been unconscious, he had had them moved to the living quarters Jonah had had specially designed for them.

Even though they had not known the whereabouts of the dead kings' tombs for several years following the events in the Ural Mountains when Alexa King and her allies had killed Alberto Cavaleti and disbanded their sect, Jonah had known exactly how to prepare for their rebirth if and when they found them.

The man had read the journal Jonah had found in his ancestral home all those centuries ago, the journal he had realized once belonged to Kronos. It had led him on a burning, life-long mission spanning thousands of leagues and many a century. Nowhere in it had the man seen details of the rooms Jonah had built for the kings, not the ancient objects within nor even the clothes that stemmed from a long bygone era.

He knew Jonah's mysterious inspiration had been on the mark from the approval he had read in the men's eyes when they had inspected the surroundings they'd awoken in.

They were currently in an elaborate dining hall that linked

their two living quarters, the chamber reminiscent of the palaces of the Mesopotamian dynasties from the period of history when the Immortal kings last ruled.

Crovir carefully sipped the wine the man handed him. He arched an eyebrow. 'This is good.'

The man smiled faintly. 'My father had it made for you.'

'Your father?' Bastian said.

'Yes,' the man said. 'Jonah Krondike.' He looked at Crovir. 'The Immortal who discovered the journal that belonged to your son, Kronos.'

Crovir straightened in his seat, his knuckles whitening on his glass. 'Kronos? My son is alive?'

The man shook his head. 'Alas, no. Kronos perished a long time ago, from illness.'

Crovir narrowed pale eyes at him. 'What do you mean, a long time ago?'

The man poured himself a glass of wine while he chose his next words. In theory, Jonah Krondike should have been here for this conversation. He frowned. He would not let that stop him from accomplishing his father's long-held dreams. He raised his eyes and steeled himself as he stared into the faces of the once dead kings.

'As you can probably gather from my clothes, this is not the era of your reign, nor is this the place where you last were.'

'The battlefield outside Eridug,' Bastian murmured.

The man hesitated.

'I—don't know how to put this any other way,' he said finally. 'Five millennia have passed since your deaths.'

Crovir blinked and paled.

'What?' Bastian said hoarsely.

The man spoke then. Of the events that had followed the

kings' deaths. Events Kronos had learned from his spies in the Empire.

The last born son of Crovir had not known much about the final destination of his siblings and cousins when they had left Uryl with the bodies of their fathers except that they had headed west across the desert. In the centuries that had followed, after he had formed the sect of Immortal-human half-breeds he would give his name to, Kronos had searched heaven and earth to discover their whereabouts.

Disgust flared across Crovir's face. 'My son—*mated* with humans?!'

The man nodded, unfazed. 'He had to. It was the only way he could build an army to try and bring you back.'

He told the kings how their Immortal descendants had spread across the world and grown both in number and affluence following the fall of their Empire. He told them of the great war that eventually broke out between Immortals who called themselves Crovirs and those of Bastian's lineage. He spoke of the fourteenth century plagues that had visited mankind and Immortals alike, and that had finally seen an end to the savage conflict between the Crovirs and the Bastians. He explained how the Immortal races were still nowhere near the numbers they had been before the Red Death, following the unexpected affliction of infertility that took several decades to manifest.

He spoke of the human wars that had dominated the eras, starting well before the plagues, wars that had been influenced from the shadows by the two Immortal races. He told them how Immortals had molded the history of the weaker race over the millennia and how they still owned most of the world's wealth.

'Though a pact for peace was made between the Crovirs and

the Bastians toward the end of the fourteenth century, the truce has always been uneasy at best, and friction still exists between the societies that form the core of the races.'

Crovir and Bastian stared at him for a long time, their eyes reflecting their shock.

'And our children?' Bastian mumbled. 'How did they meet their end?'

'That I do not know. That they are dead is beyond doubt, though.'

Crovir watched him for a moment. 'There is something you are not telling us.'

The man looked steadily at the first king, surprised by the power of his gaze. Sadness and anger flashed through him.

If only you were here, Jonah, to witness this. To see these men whom you revered for so long live and breathe once more. To see why it was they came to rule so many in their time.

'You are correct,' he said calmly. 'Seven years ago, the sect Kronos had formed and which Jonah had taken command of finally discovered your burial site six hundred miles from where we believe you fell at the hands of your daughter, Mila.'

Crovir's face darkened at the name.

'Within the caves that held your tombs were scrolls carved into the walls and a stone box containing parchments that recounted your histories, from Romerus's origins and his journey into the desert to seek cures for you when you lay dying from illness, to the rise and fall of the Empire you once ruled. They also revealed something else. Something which Kronos had not been aware of.'

'What was that?' Bastian said.

The man turned to the second king. 'Your daughter Navia. The Seer. Inscribed in the scriptures we uncovered were her predictions. She foretold that the souls of your children would one day be reborn, in an era when their strengths and talents would be needed once more. She foresaw that the bodies of the Immortals they would reside in would be marked in some way, to identify them as the special beings they would be.'

Crovir stiffened. 'Special?'

'Each would inherit one of the—unworldly gifts your children were born with. Warrior skills. The power to heal. Elemental force. The ability to read the minds of men and see the future.' The man hesitated. 'She prophesied that they would be more powerful than your children.'

Silence descended inside the dining hall.

'And did they come true?' Crovir finally said in an oddly pensive tone. 'Her predictions?'

The man noted the troubled expression that danced across Bastian's face when he glanced at his brother.

He masked a frown. 'Yes. We've only recently identified all five of them. Five Immortals who bear the birthmarks that were chiseled into the stone of the caves where you were buried.'

'Five?' Crovir scowled. 'No. Only four of our children had mystical powers.'

'That is correct,' the man admitted steadily. 'We believe the fifth man to be the reincarnation of two of the most powerful Immortals in your army. Your generals.'

Bastian blinked. 'Tobias and Baruch?'

'Yes. Which is why we think he can kill other Immortals and has even survived his seventeenth death.'

Crovir startled. 'What do you mean?'

'The Immortal I speak of can end the existence of another Immortal before their final death. If the weapon he wields bears a direct physical connection between his body and the heart of another Immortal, they are unable to resurrect after their demise. He himself has perished seventeen times, yet has lived to walk this Earth again.'

The man slipped an envelope out of his suit jacket while the kings stared, stunned. He removed the stack of photographs from within and placed them on the table.

'These are the faces of the ones who bear the marks and their allies.'

The kings looked at the pile of photographs as if they were snakes.

The man swallowed a sigh. 'Think of this as a modern version of a sculpture or—' he waved a hand, '—a painting.' He took the first picture and slid it over so they could see the man it featured. 'This is Victor Dvorsky. He is the current leader of the Bastian race and an ally of your children's reincarnated forms.' He slid another picture toward them. 'Dimitri Reznak, a Crovir noble who became the temporary head of the Crovir race a few years ago. He was one of the key instigators of the peace treaty that ended the war between the two Immortal races.' He showed them the third picture. 'Anna Godard. She is the granddaughter of Tomas Godard, a noble of pureblood lineage who once ruled the Bastian race, and Agatha Vellacrus, a noble of pureblood lineage who presided over the Crovirs up until seven years ago.'

Crovir drew a sharp breath. 'What aberration is this?!' Fury lit his pale eyes. 'You mean to say the *races* mixed too? Despite the decree?'

The man met the older king's angry glare without blinking. 'Yes. It's the reason you're alive again.' He registered the two Immortals' shocked incomprehension. 'Even though your edict was passed down the ages and became law in the Immortal societies, two pureblood Crovir brothers and two pureblood Bastian sisters violated the decree and mated with one another.

The results of their relationships were this woman,' he tapped Anna Godard's picture with a finger, 'who, although not marked, we believe also possesses the ability to survive her seventeenth death and permanently end the lives of other Immortals, and this man.'

He showed them Lucas Soul's photograph.

Bastian leaned forward abruptly and reached out to touch the picture.

'Baruch,' he breathed in a shocked voice. He looked up at his brother, who stared stiffly at the photograph. 'And Tobias. I see Tobias in him too.'

Confusion flashed through the man. 'What?'

'This Immortal.' Bastian indicated the photograph of Soul. 'This—Lucas—you speak of. He resembles our firstborn sons.'

The man gazed at the second king, staggered by this revelation.

'His and Anna Godard's blood possesses incredible abilities,' he said after a short silence. 'But their children's? Their children's is even more powerful.'

Crovir narrowed his eyes. 'What do you mean?'

'Shortly after we first discovered your tombs, they were stolen from us and concealed somewhere secret, under the aegis of both Immortal societies. It wasn't until two years ago that I was able to locate them once more. Your children made two complex seals to your tombs at the time of your burial. Seals without which we could not hope to recover your bodies. Other methods of opening the tombs, though likely to be successful, would have resulted in significant damage to your flesh and bones. The one for your sarcophagus,' he looked at Bastian, 'was given to a pureblood Crovir for safekeeping.'

His gaze shifted to the first king. 'As for yours, it was bestowed on a pureblood Bastian. After we recovered your body and your heart a year and a half ago, we tried everything modern science and medicine had to offer to bring you back to life, but to no avail. Then we discovered information that led us to believe the only thing that could revive you was the blood of the half-breed child of a pureblood Bastian and a pureblood Crovir. The very being your law decreed to be an abomination.' He paused. 'When we found Lucas Soul and Anna Godard a few months back, we realized they had had a family. Two children. A boy and a girl. Twins, in fact.' He looked at Bastian. 'We were only able to access your body and return your heart to its rightful place in the last three days, after we found the second seal. Hence, why you still have a dressing on your chest.' He hesitated. 'It is those children's blood that brought you back to life today.'

A stunned hush fell upon the chamber once more.

The nagging feeling at the back of the man's mind that had surfaced when the kings had admitted that Lucas Soul resembled their dead sons crystallized into suspicion.

Heart racing, he removed his cell from his pocket, and brought up a picture. 'This is Jonah Krondike, my father.'

Crovir's eyes widened as he studied the image the man showed them.

He hesitated before touching the cell screen, sadness flashing in his pale gaze for a moment. 'Kronos. This is Kronos.'

The man shuddered and closed his eyes briefly. *Now it all makes sense. My father's obsession for all those centuries. His single-minded determination to find these kings. He could not help it. He could not help any of it.*

'He is dead?' Crovir asked.

The man swallowed and nodded. 'Yes. Killed by the marked Immortals who inherited the powers of your other children.'

'What of your mother?' Bastian said quietly.

'She is alive but I have nothing to do with her,' the man said, his tone turning cool. 'She is a Crovir noble, the only one close enough to being of pureblood descent that my father could find when he was looking for someone to mate with. He bought her womb for a large sum of gold. Once I was born, he took me away. I have never met her, nor do I wish to do so.'

Crovir's gaze shifted to the rest of the photographs. A muscle twitched in his cheek as he reached over and pulled them across one by one.

He stared at Ethan Storm's picture. 'This is Jared.'

'Rafael,' Bastian mumbled when Conrad Greene's photograph appeared from the pile.

'Navia,' Crovir said at the sight of Olivia Ashkarov's picture.

Both kings stiffened when Alexa King's photograph was revealed next.

Crovir's hands fisted on the table. 'Mila, the traitor!'

Bastian's face grew shuttered.

The next picture had both kings rising to their feet, their chairs clattering to the floor behind them.

The man's mouth turned dry as he observed their expressions. On Bastian's face, he read wonderment. On Crovir's, he detected horror. Crovir's gaze shifted briefly to him before focusing on the photograph once more.

The man blinked when he saw a flicker of fear in the pale depths of the older king's eyes.

He studied the figure gazing up at them from the picture on the table, puzzled by the kings' reactions. 'This is Asgard Godard, the son of Tomas Godard and uncle to Lucas Soul and Anna Godard. He has been a thorn in our side for a long time.'

'That is Romerus,' Bastian said. He swallowed before meeting the man's widening stare. 'Our father.'

The man inhaled sharply. Blood thundered in his ears as he reached for the final picture.

'Madeleine Black. She is a mosaic, the offspring of a Bastian noble and a pureblood Immortal-human half-breed. She is neither human nor Immortal.'

Bastian glanced at him. 'That is—that woman is Joanna.' His eyes gleamed with a thin film of tears as he looked at the photograph. 'Our stepmother.'

CHAPTER TWENTY-ONE

VICTOR STARED AT THE IMMORTALS OPPOSITE HIM. 'WHAT?'

'The ones we are descended from are—well, kinda back,' Zachary said with a grimace.

Victor's startled gaze swung to Dimitri. 'You believe this?'

Dimitri ran a hand through his hair. 'Anna, Jordan, and I saw what happened in the lab.'

Anna nodded. 'Even Eva detected the surges of energy inside the room. And Olivia's birthmark lit up from the inside out. It was eerie.'

They were in a reception room in Dimitri's chateau. Victor had traveled straight to Sumava from Vienna when the Crovir noble had called him three hours ago. Light was fading fast through the leaded-glass windows overlooking the estate's gardens.

Victor turned to Olivia. 'So, you're saying Navia, the original Seer, is alive inside you right now?'

Olivia dipped her chin. 'Yes. I felt her presence more at the time of her revival.' She pressed a hand over her heart. 'But I know she's in there.'

Victor stared at Zachary. 'And you are—?'

'Alexa told me something about her first death, seven years ago,' Zachary said. 'She lived many of the memories of her predecessor when she was in that place between death and her next life. Of all the things she recalls to this day, one remains crystal clear. Mila's true soulmate was never Kronos. It was a human prince and general by the name of Aäron.' He rubbed the back of his neck. 'I looked him up after that.'

'You've never spoken of this before,' Dimitri said in a faintly accusing tone.

Zachary sighed. 'We didn't think it would benefit anyone. Besides, Alexa wanted to keep it between the two of us.'

'And?' Victor asked in a stilted voice. 'Did you find anything out about this—Aäron?'

Zachary nodded. 'There was a brief mention of the name in the Sumerian scriptures I researched. It seems there used to be other engravings and documents that told his life story but they have long been lost.' He faltered. 'He was the brother of Megash, a Sumerian King of the First Dynasty of Uruk, and the uncle of Gilgamesh.'

Victor blinked. 'Gilgamesh? As in the mythical king?'

'Yup,' Zachary said.

Victor digested this for a moment. 'Is that why the two of you are—?' He waved a hand vaguely at Zachary and Olivia.

They looked at one another before staring at him.

'What?' Zachary said.

Dimitri sighed. 'He means the swords.'

Zachary and Olivia glanced at the blades they were casually holding.

'Oh,' Olivia murmured. 'Yes.'

Victor arched an eyebrow. 'If I'm not mistaken, those are from the prized collection in Dimitri's library.'

Zachary nodded and juggled his broadsword from one hand to the other, as if it weighed nothing. 'I can't help thinking it could do with more weight in the handle. And the blade should be thicker.'

'Mine feels perfect.' Olivia lifted her sword and stared down its length. 'It fits my grip well.' She paused and blinked. 'I see what you mean.'

Victor looked at Asgard and Madeleine. Of all the revelations of the last half hour, those concerning the man and woman opposite him stunned him the most.

'The scriptures from Egypt never mentioned anything about other reborn souls,' he said half-accusingly. 'It named only those children of Crovir and Bastian who possessed mystical gifts.'

Asgard glanced at the woman beside him. 'We are as puzzled as you are. But there's no denying what we felt. What we still feel inside us.'

Victor watched him for a moment.

'I guess that solves the mystery of why you've had two soulmates,' he finally said. 'Sara Ashkarov may very well have been the reincarnated soul of Zara, Romerus's first wife.'

Asgard stilled and blinked. 'That is—I never thought of that.' He hesitated before lifting Armistad, his arming sword, from where it leaned against the couch by his legs. 'There's something I don't understand, though.' He hefted the blade lightly in his hands, a frown on his brow. 'Romerus was not a warrior.'

'Yes, he was,' Madeleine said.

Asgard startled. 'He never picked up a sword in his life.'

'He didn't have to,' Madeleine said. 'Romerus was not just a man of pure heart. He was singularly strong of body and mind, just like you are. From the memories Joanna has given me, I can see he defended their home and their village many a time against marauders, using only a staff. And he survived his journey into the desert, a journey that would have killed most men.' She paused. 'I believe that was why he was—chosen. He may have been forced to watch his sons become the kings of an Empire that treated its subjects with the most abject cruelty—but that did not make him a coward. There were reasons behind his inaction, of this I'm certain.' She smiled at him. 'I'm not surprised it turns out you carry his soul.'

Asgard's ears reddened. 'I think you overestimate me.'

'I've gleaned he was also as stubborn as a mule and could never accept a compliment,' Madeleine added drily.

'It's not just us who came back,' Olivia said in the silence that followed. She glanced at Zachary, Asgard, and Madeleine, her expression hardening. 'Crovir and Bastian are alive.'

Victor inhaled sharply. 'That—that's impossible!'

'We sensed them,' Olivia stated emphatically. 'The others in Boston did too. The kings are living and breathing somewhere in this world, right now.'

Victor exchanged a shocked glance with Dimitri.

'I know,' Dimitri murmured. 'I too am finding that hard to believe.'

Victor pinched his forehead, his mind racing. 'The reason I'm saying it's impossible is because the bodies of Crovir and Bastian are in a secret facility in Mongolia right now.'

'How certain are you of this?' Asgard said.

Victor clenched his jaw and nodded jerkily. 'As certain as I can be.'

'After what happened in the Ural Mountains, we moved the tombs and the hearts,' Dimitri said, pacing the floor in front of the fireplace. 'We sent them, along with Asgard's seal, to one of the Bastian facilities in North Europe. And there they stayed for a good eleven months.'

'When Ivan Vlašic became Head of the Order of Crovir Hunters six years ago, he suggested a shared facility to host the artifacts,' Victor went on, 'one that would be manned by both Bastian and Crovir Hunters. He believed it would help foster trust between the two societies. I agreed.'

'Who monitors it?' Zachary asked.

'Both societies. There is strict protocol in place, with twice-daily check-ins between the command center at the base and both Orders of Hunters. We designed it so it would be fail-safe.'

'Well, it failed,' Madeleine muttered in the ensuing hush.

Victor stared at them blindly for a moment. He took his cell out and dialed a number. The call connected seconds later. He put it on speaker.

'This is Dvorsky. What's the latest report from the facility in Mongolia?'

It was nearly a minute before the Hunter at the command post in the headquarters of the Bastian First Council got back to him.

'All clear, sir,' the man said briskly.

Victor narrowed his eyes. 'No anomalies? Any unexplained events or delays in reporting?'

'None that I've noted.' The Bastian Hunter paused. 'The only remotely interesting thing that's ever happened out there was that power surge two years ago.'

Victor's mouth went dry. 'When was this?'

'October 2015. It was a non-event. Whole thing lasted less than ten minutes. The guys in the command post were back online straight after.' The Hunter hesitated. 'I'm sorry, sir. It wasn't even worth mentioning to you.'

Victor thanked the man and disconnected, hoping his suspicions were wrong.

His gaze shifted to Zachary and the laptop on the side table next to him. 'Can we ask Eva to bring up the facility?'

A live satellite feed of the location appeared inside a window on Zachary's computer a few minutes later. There wasn't much to see except for dark mountains and forests.

'The entrance is concealed,' Victor said in response to the puzzled expressions that came his way. 'It's under that cliff to the east. Eva, do you detect anything unusual on the site?'

The AI switched the satellite view to night vision mode before zooming in on different sections of the peak he'd indicated and the forest covering its inclines.

'Not at first glance,' Eva said after a moment. 'I see no sign of a recent assault. No burn marks or explosive craters on the ground or in the trees. The facility's energy usage is steady.'

Asgard leaned forward and frowned at the screen.

'How many men are normally stationed there?' he said, glancing at Victor.

'There should be around forty Hunters on location at any one time.'

Dimitri's eyes widened as he registered the meaning behind Asgard's question. 'Eva, can you use ground-penetrating radar and infra-red imagery to see how many men are in and around the facility right now?'

'Yes.'

They waited while Eva connected with the relevant orbiting satellites. When she was done, another window popped open on the monitor.

'I count only seventeen heat signals,' Eva said as they stared at the colored smudges on the screen. 'Nine outside and eight inside.'

Victor cursed and grabbed his cell.

Asgard reached over and stayed his hand.

'Wait,' he said in a steely voice. 'Eva, how long would it take to fly there?'

'Eight hours,' Eva replied. 'If you leave now, you will reach Khövsgöl Lake at around oh eight hundred hours local time tomorrow morning. The facility is in the Eastern Sayan Mountains, fifty miles west of the lake and ten miles south of the Mongolian-Russian border.'

'It's better if a small group of us goes there,' Asgard told Victor. 'If you call the entire cavalry in, their spies might find out and warn them.'

'Asgard is right,' Dimitri said.

Victor hesitated. 'It would be useful if I had substantial proof when I face Vlašic.'

'Can we come?' Olivia asked Asgard. She glanced at Zachary.

The Harvard professor dipped his chin, his hand finding the handle of the broadsword once more.

Surprise flashed in Asgard's eyes as he studied their eager expressions. 'I—it could prove dangerous. I was going to suggest a team of Hunters.'

'We know,' Olivia said. 'But it should be us.'

'We want to see,' Zachary said.

'Want to see what?' Anna said, puzzled.

Zachary and Olivia exchanged another guarded look.

'If the presence of our predecessors' souls will influence our fighting skills,' Olivia replied quietly.

CHAPTER TWENTY-TWO

A SICK FEELING CHURNED IN PRESIDENT JAMES WESTWOOD'S stomach as he stared at his Director of National Intelligence across the width of the Oval Office. 'Is it as bad as Yuma?'

Sarah Connelly sighed and nodded grimly. 'Yes, James. We started raiding the offices of General Miller and his known associates in the DoD and SOCOM yesterday. Three hours ago, one of the intelligence analysts in charge of examining the data on the computers seized by the NSA identified a series of encrypted files. She decoded them and forwarded them to me in the last forty-five minutes. Considering where we found this information, there is little reason to doubt its authenticity.'

Connelly took a shallow breath. 'In 1968, four nuclear submarines belonging to different sovereign states went missing under what can only be called mystifying circumstances. An American Skipjack-class sub in the Atlantic, a Russian Golf II-class ballistic missile sub in the Pacific, a modified British T-Class sub commissioned by the Israelis in the Mediterranean, and a Daphné-class French sub, also in the Mediterranean.'

Connelly paused.

Westwood clenched his teeth. 'Spill it, Sarah.'

Connelly opened the folder on the coffee table and pulled out black and white photographs of the submarines. 'It appears that all four suffered the same fate, a fate Miller and his predecessors appear to have had full knowledge of. Their goal was to get their hands on the subs' nuclear reactors.'

Westwood's pulse jumped. He leaned forward and examined the pictures. 'To what aim?' He glanced at Connelly with a frown. 'Was it to sell the parts on the black market?'

Connelly shook her head. 'No. The files are not clear as to what they intended to do with the reactors after they stole them. I've had the CIA take a quick look at the intel we have from that time. There is no indication of any countries suddenly obtaining an unknown supply of enriched uranium.' She hesitated. 'Whatever it was, I suspect it had something to do with their super soldier program. And there's more.'

Westwood raised an eyebrow. 'You mean to tell me there's something worse than four nuclear reactors going AWOL fifty years ago, our people knowing about it, and me potentially having to make some embarrassing phone calls to some heads of state in the next hour?'

Connelly pursed her lips at his sardonic tone. 'It depends how you look at it but, yeah, I think this is equally bad, James.'

Westwood sighed. 'Sorry. Go ahead.'

By the time Connelly finished telling him about the rest of the information the NSA analyst had uncovered from the encrypted files, Westwood's hands had fisted in anger and dread.

The stakes had just escalated dramatically. This was now

about much more than the fate of a couple of kids who had gone missing from an island in the Pacific, or the discovery of the primary US Army group who had been assisting rogue Immortals in their work on super soldiers.

He rose from the sofa and crossed the carpet to the oak desk that dominated the room. It had survived numerous presidencies since it was first gifted to President Rutherford Hayes by Queen Victoria in the nineteenth century, among them his first administration. It was an administration that would not have seen its full term in office had he succumbed to the gunshot wound he had suffered half a decade ago at the hands of one of the last true heirs of the Ottoman Empire. He suppressed a grimace as he absentmindedly trailed his fingers across the polished wood.

Technically, I did die.

The existence of Immortals was a fact he had become used to in the past few years. He had similarly become well versed in the politics of Immortal-human interaction during that time. Of the heads of state who knew of the existence of the Crovirs and the Bastians, Westwood knew he was at a distinct advantage and the most confident when it came to dealing with the leaders of the powerful races who had inhabited the Earth alongside humans for several millennia.

Victor Dvorsky's moral code was one that aligned itself with Westwood's own ethos. They both wanted the best for humans and Immortals alike, and they had worked to strengthen their diplomatic relationships over the last five years. The Bastian Immortal was a skilled politician who had witnessed, and participated in, some of the bloodiest moments of mankind's history, and it showed in the way he handled the UN Council and other world leaders.

As for Ivan Vlašic, the Crovir Immortal was still proving a

hard man to read. Although their interactions were civil, Westwood could not help but feel he liked to keep his cards close to his chest. Judging from the information he'd gleaned from Dvorsky and his own predecessor in the White House, it was a known personality trait of most Crovirs.

And then there was the man who had given him a piece of his own soul to bring him back to life. Conrad Greene, an Immortal gifted with the power to heal and resurrect the dead. A man who could have become incredibly powerful in the Immortal societies had he not chosen a life of simplicity instead. The existence of other Immortals like Greene, men and women who were related to him in a distant fashion and who were equally talented in their own special ways, had apparently come as a surprise even to Dvorsky. That these Immortals also lived under the radar and had never leveraged their authority was nothing short of a miracle.

From what little information the Bastian leader had shared with him, Greene and his cousins were royalty descended from the very first of their kind. They could have taken over the Immortal societies if they had wished to do so. And they could have reshaped the relationship between the superior Immortal races and the weaker human race into the one that had existed before.

A relationship between kings and vassals. Between gods and slaves.

Westwood traced a complex pattern in the wood.

The pieces of a puzzle. That's what this feels like. A puzzle stretching over time and involving Immortals and humans alike. One that has its origins in the past. One that may very well be coming to its inevitable conclusion.

A shudder ran through him. He wondered whether humans would survive the outcome, whatever it turned out to be.

'James?' Connelly said softly behind him.

Westwood closed his eyes briefly. He knew what needed to be done.

He twisted on his heels and leaned against the desk as he faced Connelly once more.

'I'll speak to Victor and Vlašic,' he said in a hard voice. 'You get the Secretary of Defense and the National Security Advisor on board. What's our state of play for Nevada?'

Connelly smiled faintly. 'Our troops are almost ready to deploy.'

Westwood hesitated. 'If super soldiers are involved, then we should—'

'Already one step ahead of you,' Connelly said. 'I caught them just before they were about to take off for Europe. They're on their way to meet up with our men.' Her eyes glinted. 'These soldiers know a thing or two about Immortals. They've worked with them before.'

Westwood studied Connelly's confident expression. He'd been a widower for over a decade now, having lost his childhood sweetheart and the only woman he had ever loved to a long, hard battle with cancer. In that time, he had been approached by countless women, women who were as interested in the man as they were in the office he had been aiming for ever since he had become a senator twelve years ago. Unfortunately, the only one who had captured his attention was the woman currently sitting across from him, her face set in determined lines. Though he knew he was an ass for thinking it, he was grateful her job kept her too busy to be in a relationship.

He sighed. 'What would I do without you?'

Connelly blinked. 'It scares the shit out of me to even think about that, James, so let's not go there.'

THE VISION CAME WITH A SUDDENNESS THAT NEARLY ROBBED HER of her breath. Lily bolted upright as the vivid images blasted through her consciousness and raised the hairs on her body.

She was vaguely aware that she was back in her cell and lying on the cot. Tomas's presence echoed faintly at the back of her mind, the mental pictures reverberating across their connection with such strength that they'd woken him too. Lily fisted her hands in the bed sheet and stared blindly ahead, unable to control the vision sweeping over her.

The enemy was legion. Men who were neither human nor Immortal. Soulless creatures engineered rather than birthed. Abominations wrought from the unholy work of power-hungry beings. Beings who wished a return to a bloody past, one where the human realm was ruled with violence and greed.

Fighting them throughout the underground complex was a second, smaller army, this one made up of humans and Immortals alike. At their lead were seven beings. Five men and two women.

Five of them were marked Immortals whose destiny it was to guide both their own kind and the human race to redemption.

Of the two unmarked beings beside them, one was the reborn soul who had given birth to two Immortal kings, and the other was the human prince who had witnessed their downfall.

There were others there too. Souls who were not meant to be sentient but who had awoken after millennia of sleep. Souls who were willing to grant their divine strength and the echoes of their gifts to the ones descended from their bloodlines.

A cry left Lily's lips. Tomas shouted her name, his voice ringing in her ears, his horror reflected in his frantic tone. Lily could only watch helplessly as the terrible vision continued to unfold.

She did not see the fatal blow that brought him down. One moment he was wielding his weapon, the next he had fallen. His death, when it came, was in the arms of someone he loved. The knowledge that he would not rise again sank into the consciousness of the marked souls and brought forth their rage. They screamed their outrage, the unholy battle intensifying around them as their wrath augmented their powers.

Sweat drenched Lily's clothes and her heart thundered inside her chest as the vision faded. She had barely begun to catch her breath when the next one followed.

They stood on the summit of a semicircular ridge, in a sea of white. There were seven of them once more. Five marked and two unmarked.

The remnants of their army had pulled back a short distance behind the crest of land and crouched next to a sea of vehicles, inside a shallow basin. Many were unconscious. Most were wounded. Some were still able to stand. All faced east, watching, waiting, an expectant silence blooming across their shrunken numbers.

Brightness flared on the horizon. It expanded, a rapidly growing cloud that shook the very earth and sky.

Then came fire and fury like the world had never seen.

Lily gulped air in deep, shuddering breaths when the second vision ended.

She froze in the next instant as further visions danced across her inner sight, all infinitesimally short yet as intense as the others. For a moment, she could not comprehend what she had just seen. Hope and wonderment burst forth inside her when the reality of what it was she had witnessed sank in. She blinked back tears.

Lily?

Tomas's distress swamped her mind, his sorrow at what was to come threatening to drown her.

It's okay. It'll be okay, Tomas.

Lily closed her eyes and shared her last visions with him, the ones he had not perceived. She heard his gasp and sensed excitement and relief erupt inside him. It was followed by the same wonder that now filled her.

Are those—?

I think so.

And he will—?

Yes.

Lily thought of the men they had seen that morning. The Immortals who had been long dead and, yet, were alive again, thanks to her and Tomas's blood. The kings who had been returned to this realm.

She frowned and curled her hands into fists. *We will find a way.*

CHAPTER TWENTY-THREE

The man walked steadily between the two kings. He had deliberately showed them the more simple levels of the complex first, to get them used to the technology and architecture that was far beyond their times. From their guarded expressions, he knew they were coming to terms with the dizzying developments of a future they could not have foreseen.

'A lot of what you see before you was created by Immortals before being introduced to the human world. But there are also many inventions and discoveries that can be attributed directly to the weaker race. Humans are clever and resourceful, attributes my father long exploited while he was building all of this for you.'

They came to a steel door. The kings observed him closely as he entered his biometric data into the security panel. It beeped and swung open.

'This is one of our largest labs.'

Bastian slowed when they entered the cave-like chamber, blue eyes flaring slightly. Crovir stiffened beside him.

'What is this place?' the older king asked.

The man headed over to one of the tanks rising from the floor. At his bequest, the lab on the ninth floor had been vacated by the scientists and technicians who would normally have occupied it; he had not wanted their presence to distract the kings. He touched the thick, ballistic-resistant glass of the container and gazed upon the large shape floating within. As always, the sight of the super soldiers sent a thrill of excitement through him.

Of all of his and Jonah's endeavors, this had been their most successful by far. Although they had lost a significant number of the sect of Immortal-human half-breeds the original Kronos had built, its replacement was even more impressive.

'This is part of your army,' the man said.

Bastian turned to face him. 'What?'

The man indicated the hundreds of identical pods filling the room. 'These are the men who will help you regain your rightful place in this world.'

The color drained from Bastian's face.

Crovir's eyes narrowed to slits. 'What do you mean, boy?'

The man told them about Jonah's experiments. Of his attempts even as far back as the fourteenth century, when he had started looking for artifacts that he hoped could one day help resurrect the dead kings once he discovered the whereabouts of their tombs and seals. He had not known at that time of the fate of their hearts.

He spoke of Jonah's alliance in the twentieth century with rogue governments who had wanted to breed superior races and his association with the US Army groups who had wished to advance their military's combat skills at any cost. He explained how Jonah had used the knowledge and technologies his Immortal scientists had acquired through nearly a century of research to build what would be the ultimate troops for the Immortal kings.

'You said—' Bastian hesitated, '—Kronos—your father wanted us to take our place in this world once more?'

The man's pulse sped up slightly as he gazed at the kings. 'Jonah only ever wished for one thing. To help you reclaim what has always been yours. Your rightful thrones as the rulers of this world. He wanted you to be the living gods who reign over this realm.' The man frowned. 'Now that he is gone, it is my honor to accomplish his dream.'

Tense silence descended in the lab. The kings stared at him.

'And these—these creatures are meant to help us achieve this?' Bastian indicated the super soldiers in the closest pods.

'Yes.' The man touched the tank once more. 'They are a new class of beings. Neither human nor Immortal nor half-breed. They were engineered to be the best warriors the world has ever seen.' He glanced at Crovir. 'The first successful one of their kind was killed by Alexa King, the reincarnated soul of your daughter Mila. These men are even stronger than the original prototype.' He gazed fondly at the figure behind the glass. 'They are the next generation of super soldiers, enhanced from the cellular level up.'

The kings remained quiet as he led them out of the lab and past another identical chamber. They entered a lift and went up two floors to another level.

'This is one of our armories.'

This room occupied almost the entire length of the complex and was filled wall to wall with crates stacked on mobile pallets.

'We have a weapons-making facility with testing ranges and arms depots a mile from here,' the man explained. 'That's where we store most of our heavy artillery and hardware, along with our helicopters, tanks, and armored vehicles. We have a third base built inside a series of caves on the coastline five miles away. It harbors our underground port as well as our nuclear submarines and warships.' The man stared out over the bright-lit space before them. 'All our facilities, including this one, are powered by nuclear reactors.'

The kings observed the chamber for a while.

'All of this,' Bastian murmured, 'all of this for us?'

'It is no less than you deserve,' the man said.

He saw the flash of approval in Crovir's eyes. Bastian's face grew shuttered.

'Come, there is one more thing.'

This time, he took them back down to the tenth floor and the main lab, next to the rooms hosting hundreds more super soldiers in the final stages of maturation inside their tanks. It was empty bar a handful of technicians who left rapidly under his cool gaze.

The kings' expressions grew uncomfortable when they saw the isolation chamber where they had been resurrected. Crovir paused when he spotted the room that held the tombs. He turned and headed toward it, Bastian following slowly in his steps. The man hit some keys on one of the lab computers. The sealed door opened ahead of the kings.

Crovir hesitated before crossing the threshold and walking over to the closest pedestal. He raised a hand and touched the granite tomb standing upon it.

'This is where we were buried, all those hundreds of years?' he said quietly.

'Yes,' the man replied as he came up behind him.

Bastian strolled to the table that held the two gold sun cross pendants under a glass case.

'And these are the seals? The ones that Navia made?'

'Indeed,' the man murmured. 'We believe it was Jared who fashioned them under her instruction.'

The kings lingered in the chamber for a while longer before following the man to one of the computer stations. He brought up the camera feeds from the cells on the thirteenth floor.

'This is what I wanted to show you.'

The kings stared at the small figures seated on the beds.

'Are those the ones you spoke of?' Crovir said in an inscrutable voice. 'The children whose blood brought us back to life?'

The man dipped his chin. 'Their names are Lily and Tomas Soul. We believe they possess the combined abilities of your children.'

Bastian's eyes widened. 'What?'

The man's gaze shifted to the figures on the screen. 'They will likely be skilled warriors, like Mila and Alexa King, when they come of age. They can already manipulate the elements, like Jared and Ethan Storm. They can heal, like Rafael and Conrad Greene. And they are Seers, like Navia and Olivia Ashkarov. Even though they are only children, their skills are equal to and, in some instances, may have already surpassed those of their predecessors.'

'How is this—how is this possible?' Bastian said hoarsely. 'The warning Romerus received from the one who gave us the gifts that turned us into Immortals forbade the mixing of the bloodlines.'

The man shrugged. 'This I do not know.' He indicated the children. 'My chief scientist wishes to experiment on them. She wants to—figure out what makes them tick. Dissect them, even.'

Bastian frowned. 'She wishes to cut their flesh?'

'Even their brains, if I allow her,' the man murmured.

Bastian's face grew thunderous. 'That—'

'Would be a waste of resources,' Crovir cut in sharply. The older king turned and eyed the man coldly. 'Why would you want to harm your most valuable assets?'

The man watched him for a silent moment. 'I'm listening.'

Crovir studied the children on the camera feeds with a calculating expression. 'Imagine an army of them. They would be even more powerful than these—super soldiers you have shown us.'

The man grunted. 'It might be hard to get them to switch their allegiance to us. Especially after what we did to get them here.'

Crovir glanced at him. 'There are ways and means to sway their minds. They are only children, after all.'

Horror dawned on Bastian's face as he stared at his brother. 'Surely you are not suggesting that we use these children as weapons?!'

Crovir twisted on his heels and faced the younger king.

'Are you saying that you will not allow it, brother?' he said softly. 'Or are you saying that you will try and stop us?' His expression darkened. 'Will you betray me again, like you did on the battlefield at Eridug?'

The man startled at the animosity that filled the air between the two Immortals.

Bastian straightened to his full height. 'I was right then and I am right now.' His voice shook with outrage as he indicated the lab with a wave of his hand. 'This, all this, is pure lunacy! It is the dream of a mad man, one who wished to resurrect a past that should have stayed buried. We do not belong in this world!'

Crovir gazed at Bastian for silent seconds.

'Then you leave us no choice, brother,' he murmured in a steely voice.

CHAPTER TWENTY-FOUR

MADELEINE RUBBED HER EYES AND PINCHED HER FOREHEAD before focusing on the lenses of the ultra-high-resolution electron microscope. A cup of steaming black coffee appeared on the workstation next to her hand.

She looked up at the man who had placed it there. 'Thanks.'

'No problem,' Jordan murmured. He made for the exit. 'I'm headed back down to the basement. Give Eva a yell if you need anything.'

'Sure.'

Madeleine watched the lab door slide closed behind him. She took a sip of her coffee, stretched out the kinks in her neck, and returned to inspecting one of the tissue samples Anna had extracted from the super soldiers' bodies.

It was gone midnight in Sumava. Six hours had passed since Asgard, Olivia, and Zachary had left the estate to travel to Mongolia. Victor had also flown back to Vienna, following a tense conversation with President James Westwood. The ramifications of the discovery Director Connelly had made about General Miller and his associates promised to be explosive if they didn't get on top of it straightaway.

Dimitri's research facility was currently deserted but for the guards who patrolled its corridors and perimeter, and Anna, Jordan, and herself.

Anna had remained in the primary lab that had been put together for their use to continue working on the dead men. With the best microscope in the facility on the third floor, Madeleine had brought the specimens they needed to examine upstairs.

She finished scanning the current sample, sighed, and swapped it for the next slide. She reached for her coffee as she started moving the dial on the microscope.

Her fingers froze on the cup a second later. 'What the—?'

Madeleine stared wide-eyed into the lenses before looking at the high-resolution mirror image reflected on the computer attached to the microscope.

'Eva, are you seeing this?' she said shakily.

'I am,' the AI replied.

Madeleine's pulse accelerated as she scrutinized the complex structure the microscope had revealed. 'Eva, are you able to access Howard's databases?'

'Of course.'

Madeleine licked her suddenly dry lips. 'Pull up the folders about Professor Ian Serle's research at AuGenD.'

'I'll bring those up on the workstation beside you. Incidentally, Howard and I have cleaned and decrypted most of the corrupted files from Dr. Wu's hard drives. I'm processing them right now.'

The computer to Madeleine's left flashed into life. She wheeled her chair over to the desk. The folders she'd asked Eva to retrieve started to populate the brightly lit screen.

'Eva, can you see any similarities between what's in the AuGenD data and what's on Jessica Wu's computer?'

'Give me a moment.' There was a short silence. 'Indeed I can,' the AI said smoothly. 'There's a folder on Dr. Wu's hard drive alluding to Professor Serle's research. Here are the cleaned files.'

More folders popped up on the monitor. Madeleine opened them one at a time and scanned their contents. Her eyes grew round as she started to grasp what she was reading.

She glanced at the image of the sample she'd been examining, her heart thundering against her ribs. She moved back to the microscope and switched specimens with trembling hands.

It was another fifty minutes before she finished inspecting the rest of them.

'Eva, send everything to the main computer lab downstairs,' Madeleine said in a hard voice as she climbed off the chair and collected the samples. 'I'm heading there now.'

ANNA'S STOMACH TWISTED AS SHE STUDIED THE READOUTS ON the DNA sequencer once more. She'd run the samples three times already and still couldn't believe what she was looking at. Her gaze shifted to the objects she'd extracted a short time ago from the dead soldiers' brains and spinal cords, and which now lay under the lenses of two microscopes.

'Dr. Godard, I'm sending some urgent data Dr. Black just obtained from the ultra-high-resolution scanning microscope to my main terminals,' Eva said through the speakers in the ceiling. 'I also have the files we managed to salvage from Dr. Wu's computer.'

By the time Madeleine entered the computer lab, Anna was staring slack-jawed at the scientific information and images displayed on the three-foot-tall, flat-screen monitors stretching across the wall above Jordan's primary workstation.

'I know, right?' Madeleine said with a grimace.

Anna swallowed. 'This is—'

'The stuff of nightmares?'

Anna nodded shakily.

Jordan made a face. 'Would you ladies like to explain what we're looking at exactly?'

Madeleine placed the box of samples carefully down on the workstation. 'Eva, highlight the files from AuGenD.'

The documents expanded to fill one of the screens.

'The data we obtained from Ian Serle's computer four years ago revealed the broad elements of the super soldier program they were working on at Yuma,' Madeleine started. 'It consisted of four phases. Phase One involved the use of drugs and other chemicals derived from torturing Immortals to accelerate the physical development of the test subjects, as well as modify their behavior. Phase Two involved placing them in a coma during which their DNA was manipulated to incorporate Immortal genetic material; their bodies were constantly stimulated with electrical signals and drugs to help them adapt to the bioengineering taking place. They were then woken up in Phase Three.'

She paused, her face darkening. 'A lot of test subjects were terminated during that phase. Many of the super soldiers developed extreme aggression and had psychotic episodes; some even killed their wardens. If they survived Phase Three, they entered Phase Four. Battle-condition testing and training.'

'But the test subjects from Yuma were all volunteers, right?' Anna said, her mouth dry. 'Human soldiers who were manipulated into joining the program under false pretenses, and Immortals and half-breeds from Jonah Krondike's sect?'

Madeleine nodded. 'Yes.' Her eyes reflected the sickening conclusion Anna had already arrived at. 'Eva, bring up the information from Dr. Wu's hard drives.'

Jordan glanced questioningly from them to the displays once more. 'And this says what?'

'It looks like the AuGenD data, and, hence, Yuma, was only a secondary program,' Anna explained stiffly. 'The primary one was already in play, somewhere else. And it seems Wu was the one spearheading all of it, probably as far back as the 1960s.'

Jordan sighed. 'Okay, you guys are going to have to be more specific than that. I still don't get—'

'What Dr. Godard and Dr. Black mean is that Dr. Wu has been using even more advanced technologies in the primary super soldier program,' Eva said. 'The test subjects she's using are different to the ones from the Yuma project. They were bioengineered in vitro and grown using the accelerated development process Dr. Black has described.'

Jordan blinked. 'Do you mean what I think you mean? That these soldiers are—*test-tube babies?!*'

Madeleine nodded grimly. 'Yes. And likely grown in life pods similar to the ones we found at Yuma.'

Anna shuddered. She had seen pictures of the labs at Yuma before they had been shut down by the US government.

'Eva, can you pull the readouts from the DNA sequencer?' she said, the queasy feeling in her stomach intensifying.

Madeleine visibly paled when the genetic analyses came up on one of the displays. 'Shit.'

Anna fisted her hands. 'The super soldiers who attacked us on the island are the result of pure genetic engineering. Their DNA is like nothing I've ever seen before. They have far more of it than normal Immortals, in a stable matrix that looks like it was artificially engineered. Not only that, but there is evidence of nanotechnology all over their tissues. And the data suggests the same of the human and half-breed soldiers in the program.'

'So that's what I was seeing under the high-resolution microscope,' Madeleine said grimly. She indicated the images from the samples she'd examined. 'Those are nanoparticles incorporated into their cell membranes and organelles. And not just nanoparticles. I'm pretty damn sure those are dormant nanorobots we're looking at.'

Jordan gaped. 'What?'

'It gets worse,' Anna said dully. 'Eva, show us the feeds from the microscopes I was just working on.'

Two new pictures populated a display on the right. They showed a pair of small, spider-like objects lying on examination slides. Slivers of flesh and clotted blood still clung to their appendages.

Jordan scowled. 'What the hell are those ugly things?'

'Closed-loop neural implants I just removed from our super soldiers' brains and spines,' Anna replied. Blood rushed in her ears as she stared at the tiny machines. 'Wu's neurotechnology work is the most advanced I have ever come across. This is brain-computer interface on an incredibly sophisticated level. If we examine them under the ultra-high-resolution microscope, I'm sure we'll see they're made up of nanorobots too.'

'What do they do?' Jordan asked, aghast.

'They likely use neuromodulation and neural augmentation to keep the soldiers' biological systems stable,' Anna said. 'I suspect the nanorobots incorporated into their bodies at the cellular level can also repair damaged tissues at an accelerated pace.'

'From Wu's neuropsychology data, these implants control the super soldiers' free will and emotions, as well as their ability to feel pain,' Madeleine added. 'Not only that, it probably enables them to function beyond the physical limits of their bodies.'

Jordan opened and closed his mouth soundlessly for a moment. 'So you're saying these guys are like—cyborgs? Mindless drones with advanced regeneration and combat skills who do the bidding of their masters?'

Madeleine nodded. 'Yes. The perfect super soldier.'

'Dr. Godard, Dr. Black, I have just cleaned the last file on Dr. Wu's hard drive. You need to take a look at this straight away,' Eva said.

Anna scanned the fresh information Eva had put up on one of the monitors. Her breath hitched in her throat.

'Shit,' Jordan said. 'Even I understand that!'

'Eva, where are they right now?' Madeleine asked urgently.

'They should have arrived in Nevada twenty minutes ago.'

Anna's nails dug into her palms. 'Call them!'

CHAPTER TWENTY-FIVE

MAJOR STEVE REYNOLDS NARROWED HIS EYES AT ETHAN WHEN HE exited the jet. '*You!* I should have known it was gonna be you.'

Ethan acknowledged the scowling Ranger on the tarmac with a smile. 'Hey, Steve. Long time no see.'

'Don't "Hey, Steve" me!' Reynolds snapped. 'And it's Major Reynolds to you.' He looked suspiciously past Ethan's shoulder. 'Where's the guy with the gigantic sword?'

'On his way to Mongolia. I brought some other, er, friends.' Ethan indicated the group exiting the aircraft behind him.

'Hey,' Lucas murmured.

He dipped his chin at Reynolds and the two-hundred-strong troop of curious Rangers standing in the shadow of the Lockheed C-5 Galaxy parked fifty feet away. Alexa, Conrad, Reid, and Anatole followed in his steps.

Reynolds studied them warily. 'Are you all, you know—?' He grimaced and cocked his head toward Ethan.

'I'm nearly one hundred per cent human,' Reid said drily.

Reynolds turned to Ethan. 'What does he mean, "nearly?"'

'He may have received some Immortal blood in the past and could possibly be a super human,' Ethan said, deadpan.

Reynolds narrowed his eyes.

'I'm normal,' Anatole said.

Reynolds snorted. 'You don't look normal!'

'That offends me deeply,' Anatole said. 'And, okay, so I may be a tiny bit Immortal too. But a normal one.'

Reynolds's gaze switched from Lucas's blank stare to Alexa's cool expression and Conrad's birthmark. 'So, the rest of you *are* like him?'

'Don't be absurd,' Alexa said with a disdainful sniff. 'He's a brat compared to us.'

Ethan rolled his eyes. 'You do realize Jared was older than Mila, right?'

Alexa arched an eyebrow. 'So? She could kick his ass then and she can kick his ass now.'

'Oh boy,' Conrad murmured. 'Rafael thinks that's fighting talk right there.'

Lucas muttered something under his breath about insubordinate commanders.

Reynolds glared after them as they made for the trucks and Jeeps his troops were boarding. 'Are those swords sticking out of the back of your combat uniforms?!'

Lucas tried to quell the nervous anticipation buzzing in his veins as the convoy ate away the distance separating them from their destination. Six miles to the west, stark white mantles of snow capped the dark peaks of a mountain range against the backdrop of pale blue sky. The town of Hawthorne shimmered under the blazing afternoon sun in the valley beneath it.

It had been six hours since Sarah Connelly had called Conrad moments before they had been due to board their jet to go to Sumava to meet up with the others. When she had revealed what an intelligence analyst had uncovered on the hard drive of a computer belonging to the primary US Army group that had been working with Jonah Krondike, they'd put their travel plans on hold.

The possible fate of the four submarines that had gone missing in international waters in 1968 was sobering in itself. The rest of what had been unearthed about the events in Nevada in the past fifty years was even more disturbing. If that information were to be revealed to the rest of the world, the implications for the US government's defense capability and its immediate foreign interests would be catastrophic.

With Connelly and the Immortals no closer to discovering the whereabouts of General Miller, Lucas hoped Nevada would provide answers that could lead them to the location of his children and their unknown enemy.

Five minutes after they landed at the airport outside Hawthorne, they neared the meeting point they'd arranged with the personnel staffing the largest weapons storage facility in the world.

The twenty-foot-tall concrete and cinder block wall of a secure compound loomed on the road ahead, one of hundreds of similar facilities that stretched over an area covering two hundred and thirty square miles of desert valleys and mountains south of Walker Lake. Giant roller gates slid open as the convoy slowed on approach. They thundered through the entrance in a cloud of sand and dust and pulled to a stop in a large, open area some three hundred feet later.

Reynolds disembarked and joined them on the ground. 'I

still can't believe we've come all the way here to do this. How sure are we about the intel from Washington?'

Lucas scrutinized the enormous courtyard they stood in. 'President Westwood seemed pretty convinced by the evidence he saw.'

The area was ring-fenced by eight bunkers set under elevations of earth running around the perimeter of the compound. Steel doors sat shrouded in twilight under the dirt overhangs. There was no one around.

Movement to the left caught Lucas's eye. The security cameras positioned above two of the bunkers had just swiveled toward them. He reached for his Glock at the same time Alexa drew one of her Sigs. The others followed suit, their expressions similarly guarded.

Reynolds frowned at them. 'Hey, easy on the show of force. The guys at this facility are on our side.'

'Nonetheless, I would tell your men to be ready, Major,' Reid said.

'I would do as he says,' Conrad murmured.

Reynolds raised an eyebrow.

'Seriously? Do you people honestly believe that the Hawthorne Army Depot, the biggest arms and ammunitions storage facility in the country, never mind the planet, has been compromised and raided by an unknown enemy?' His tone turned cynical. 'And, what, no one in the DoD heard about it?'

Ethan glanced at him. 'How much have your superiors told you, Steve?'

'Only that we're meant to check the inventory of some thousand or so bunkers,' Reynolds said grudgingly. 'Like, with a damned clipboard and everything. It's gonna take forever, even with all the men at our disposal.'

Ethan observed the deserted compound as carefully as Lucas and the others. 'Remember the army guy behind Yuma?'

Reynolds's face darkened. 'That bastard Gunnerson? Sure.'

'He was only the tip of the shithouse in SOCOM,' Ethan said quietly.

Reynolds's eyes widened as the meaning behind Ethan's words sank in. He glanced around. 'You mean this is *another* Yuma?!'

Ethan nodded grimly. 'That's why we're here, Steve.'

Realization dawned in Reynolds's eyes. He drew his Beretta, a muscle jumping in his jawline. 'So, we're talking—?'

'Super soldiers?' Ethan grimaced. 'Yes. We ran into a bunch of them yesterday.'

One of Reynolds's men overhead them and groaned. 'Did someone just say super soldiers?'

'Christ,' grumbled another Ranger, his knuckles whitening on his assault rifle. 'Not those assholes again. My left leg still aches in winter.'

Mutters broke out among the troops.

'Sergeant Greaves?' Reynolds said.

'Yes, Major?'

'What did I tell you about your language?'

'You told me to fucking mind it, sir,' the Ranger said, unabashed.

'Well do so, goddammit.' Reynolds turned to his intelligence officer. 'And where are the contractors who were supposed to be here for our meet and greet? They're late.'

The sergeant he'd addressed pulled a face. 'I've been unable to make contact with anyone in the depot's main command post in the last five minutes, sir.'

Reynolds's face reddened. 'Why didn't you say something before, Peters?'

Sergeant Peters pursed his lips. 'Because you were busy busting Greaves's balls, sir.'

Lucas stiffened. One hundred feet ahead and to the left, the door of a bunker was sliding open. A second one rattled into life to their right. Reynolds turned to stare at the rectangle of yawning darkness that replaced the steel panel.

'Spread the word,' the major said quietly to Peters and Greaves. 'Safeties off. Everyone check their six.'

Rumbles rose around them as more bunkers opened up. Lucas narrowed his eyes when he saw the shadowy figures in the tunnels beyond the openings. Metal glinted in the gloom.

Reynolds swore. 'All around defense! *Now!*'

The Rangers were still moving to form a circle around the vehicles when the shots came.

Lucas dove to the ground in a hail of machinegun fire and aimed the Glock at the shapes framed by the bunker door to his right. Bullets peppered the dirt in a line toward him. He rolled and jumped to his feet, narrowly missing the slugs that danced past his leg.

One slammed into Peters's shin where he stood a few feet behind him. The Ranger cried out and fell. Lucas raised his gun and fired at the figures inside the closest bunkers as he moved back toward the wounded man.

His stomach dropped when he glanced sideways and saw the damage to the soldier's limb. 'Shit! Those are fragmenting bullets!'

'Major, get your men to pull back to those vehicles!' Conrad yelled as he headed for the Ranger groaning on the ground. 'These rounds are gonna tear through them!'

Lucas loaded a fresh magazine into his gun and stepped protectively in front of Conrad. 'Ethan! Now would be a good time to—'

'I'm on it,' Ethan growled.

Gasps sounded around them as the enemies' bullets suddenly stopped mid-air.

Reynolds gaped at the slugs spinning uselessly fifteen feet from where he stood before glancing at Ethan. 'Is that you?!'

'Yes,' Ethan said between gritted teeth, his hands up and out on either side of him.

He stopped the next volley of deadly rounds flying toward them, the bullets smashing into the elemental energy he was projecting before being crushed and dropping harmlessly to the ground. The super soldiers' assault rifles met the same fate seconds later.

'Here they come!' Alexa warned.

Lucas's heart sped up as he watched dozens of figures in combat uniform charge toward them from the bunkers. Relief flashed through him when he failed to spot any giant super soldiers.

Still, this ain't exactly going to be a walk in the park.

Lucas holstered his Glock and drew his daisho with steady hands. Heat surged through his veins, the energy of the two formidable souls who now dwelled inside his heart flooding his bloodstream and filling him with power.

'Major, tell your men to aim for their hearts and heads,' he told Reynolds grimly. 'That's the only way you're gonna stop them.'

Lucas blocked a knife headed for Conrad's neck with the wakizashi, twisted around the super soldier, and thrust the katana into his back. The sword dented the soldier's uniform and juddered violently in his grip.

CHAPTER TWENTY-SIX

ALEXA SHOT A SUPER SOLDIER POINT BLANK IN THE HEART, SAW the bullet crumble into a flat disc, and slipped under a fist arcing toward her face. She thrust an elbow in the man's face before hammer kicking the one she had shot in the chest.

She whipped out her second Sig and fired at the two men once more.

The super soldiers barely faltered in their stride, the slugs smashing into their combat uniforms and instantly flattening into distorted lumps of metal.

'Are they wearing Kevlar?' Anatole shouted beside her. He blocked a kick aimed at his gut and punched a super soldier in the face.

'I don't think so.' Alexa scowled as a foot glanced off her hip. She jumped back, twisted, and roundhouse kicked two super soldiers in the head. 'Our rounds aren't even penetrating their uniforms!'

'Neither are blades!' Lucas said on Alexa's right. 'We're gonna have to go for head shots and their throats!'

'Easier said than done!' Reid growled as he kneed a super soldier in the flank.

Alexa's pulse thrummed rapidly in her veins as she scanned the compound. Despite having lost their weapons and being outnumbered four to one, their enemy was gaining ground. A quarter of the Rangers were already down, the sheer brute force and speed of the super soldiers' attacks overcoming even their advanced combat skills.

Alexa holstered her Sigs and whipped out her sais. *Time to get serious.*

Dirt trembled around her feet as she drew on the ungodly energy that dwelled within her heart. The savage life force surged through her body, an incandescent heat that pulsed with her every heartbeat and hardened her flesh and bones. She blinked when she sensed an echo within it. The echo of the soul that had awakened inside her upon the rebirth of the long-dead kings.

Alexa darted between the super soldiers, Mila's power singing in her blood. Their blades danced in their hands and carved through exposed flesh, their warrior hearts and minds as one.

ETHAN DEFLECTED A KICK TO HIS THIGH AND BLOCKED THE FISTS heading toward him with a burst of elemental energy. Having realized that he posed the greatest threat to them, a group of five super soldiers had surrounded him.

He tapped into the core of his power while he fended off another flurry of brutal attacks. The energy inside him felt hotter and stronger than before, the blazing tendrils darting through his veins so forceful he could almost see their glow under his skin.

He knew it was because of Jared. He could feel him behind his eyes, lending him his strength, his brooding presence strangely comforting.

Ethan had just stopped a third onslaught from the super soldiers when something suddenly vibrated on his thigh.

Reynolds's head jerked up. 'What the—? *Seriously, is someone's cell ringing right now?!*'

Ethan forced his attackers back with a powerful surge of elemental energy, slipped his phone out of the pocket of his combat uniform, and brought it to his ear.

'Now is *not* a good time!' he snapped.

CONRAD SAW ETHAN STIFFEN WHERE HE STOOD LISTENING TO THE unknown caller some dozen feet to the left, one hand on the cell at his ear while he used the other to maintain an elemental barrier against the soldiers trying to get to him.

'How did you find out about the combat uniforms?' Ethan said, bewildered. His eyes widened a moment later. 'You want me to do *what?!*'

Conrad blocked a kick with his staff, twisted on his heels, and drove one end of the spear into the side of a super soldier's neck. He grimaced and yanked it out of the man's flesh before stepping toward the Rangers he had been healing.

He could feel Rafael's life force resonating inside him, bringing with it an intoxicating mix of warrior strength and healing power that augmented his own fighting skills and healing abilities.

His back met Reid's as they found themselves inside a circle of three super soldiers.

Reid hook-punched one of the men in the jaw before indicating Ethan with a jerk of his head. 'What's going on?'

Conrad ducked out of the way of a high kick and slashed a super soldier across the face with his spear. 'I don't know!'

'Look, I've never tried anything like that before!' Ethan said into the cell, staring at the pale sky above them. He flexed his fingers absent-mindedly to stop the two super soldiers coming at him from left field. 'What about the others?' A frown wrinkled his brow as he listened once more. He hesitated before dipping his chin. 'Okay, I'll give it a shot.' He ended the call, tucked his cell in his pocket, and looked over at Conrad, his expression grim. 'I need your spear!'

Conrad blinked, not sure he'd heard him right. 'What?'

LUCAS SWUNG HIS KATANA ACROSS A SUPER SOLDIER'S NECK AND glanced at Ethan, his breathing fast and heavy. He could see his puzzlement reflected in Alexa's eyes as she stared at their cousin.

'Your spear,' Ethan repeated to Conrad. 'I need it!' He looked around. 'And I want everyone to lose every single metal object they have on them!'

Alexa frowned at the sai daggers in her hands, elbowed a super soldier in the face, and knifed another one in the neck.

'What the hell do you mean, lose every metal object?' Reynolds shouted from across the way.

'Guns, knives, your backpacks, any piece of metal in your combat uniforms! Drop them, right now!' Ethan ordered.

Anatole scowled. 'How the hell are we supposed to fight them?'

Ethan clenched his jaw and turned to Alexa. 'Can you help me hold them back for a couple of minutes? I need you at the other end of the yard. And get ready to lose those sais when I say so.'

Alexa studied him for a moment. 'Sure.'

She turned and started to make her way toward the spot he'd indicated, her blades finding the flesh of the super soldiers who stepped in her path with deadly accuracy.

Conrad blocked another attack before lobbing his double-bladed spear over to Ethan. 'You better know what the hell you're doing!'

Ethan caught the weapon and looked at Reynolds. 'Spread the word! I want everyone spaced out between Alexa and me and ready to drop into a crouch when I say so!'

Lucas's eyes widened. He gleaned a sudden inkling of what Ethan intended to do. He glanced at the cloudless sky above them and reluctantly cast the daisho to the ground, his heart thudding against his ribs.

Reynolds stared at Ethan. 'I don't understand—'

'Now, Steve!' Ethan barked.

Clatters rose around the battlefield as the Rangers discarded their weapons and packs on Reynolds's reluctant order.

Even though she stood over one hundred feet from him, Ethan felt the force of Alexa's power flow across his skin as she rapidly intensified the energy radiating from her body. He waited until everyone had moved to the safe zone in the middle of the courtyard before taking a shallow breath and letting go of his own power.

The earth trembled and the air hummed as their combined energies blasted across the compound.

CONRAD CLENCHED HIS JAW AS THE VIOLENT PRESSURE WAVES drove his boots into the ground. He watched the super soldiers slip and slide backward in an expanding circle around them.

'Shit!' Reynolds stared at the sand and dirt dancing in the air. 'Is it really him doing this right now?!'

'It's not just him,' Conrad said.

Reynolds followed his gaze to the woman at the opposite end of the compound. Tires screeched as two Jeeps shifted across the ground ahead of Alexa.

'Holy hell!' one of the Rangers shouted, as pale as his companions as they gaped at the two Immortals at the center of the storm battering them.

Ethan raised the staff in the air and aimed the glinting head of one spear solidly at the sky.

The action confirmed the suspicion churning in Conrad's gut.

Reid swore. 'Is he trying to—?'

ETHAN INHALED DEEPLY BEFORE SENDING SEVERAL MASSIVE bursts of elemental energy toward the sky.

He felt them rise and expand rapidly, invisible, curving waves that smashed into the layers of moist, warm air drifting over the valley and drove them up against gravity at thousands of feet per second.

Thin clouds started to form in the pale blue sky overhead as the wet, hot currents collided with the heavy, cold slipstreams in the upper atmosphere.

Shocked gasps erupted around him as the clouds grew and merged into one another. Twilight descended across the land, the sun disappearing behind the growing thunderstorm.

Sweat beaded Ethan's forehead as he sought out the static charges forming in the middle of the darkening, roiling mass.

Electricity had never featured highly on the list of elements he'd wanted to master. Although he knew how to short-circuit a flow of electrical current and could manipulate its polarities, he had never tried to directly generate or control it before. Especially not naturally occurring electricity.

Ethan understood why Anna and Madeleine had asked him to do what he was about to do. If they were right, it would stop the super soldiers in their tracks and give them a fighting chance to defeat them.

He grimaced. *Still, this could hurt like a bitch.*

Lightning flashed and thunder clapped in the angry, gray mantle forming above the valley.

Deep inside his heart, Ethan felt a flutter of admiration from Jared. He clenched his jaw, concentrated on the positively-charged flow of energy he could sense in the earth beneath his feet, and reached out to the enormous channel of negatively-charged ionized air building inside the thunderstorm.

Hang onto something, old man.

Hairs rose on Alexa's arms. She heard the crackle of static and saw sparks dance along her skin.

'Alexa, lose those blades!' Ethan shouted. 'Everyone, get down *now*!

Alexa cast her sais away, dropped into a crouch, and covered her head with her arms just as light exploded violently in the sky. Black spots swarmed across her vision. She twisted on her heels and peered toward Ethan through the dust storm whirling across the compound.

What she saw had her breath locking in her throat.

A solid bolt of lightning arrowed down from the massive thunderstorm above them to the end of Conrad's spear. Ethan roared as he guided the electrical discharge into the weapon, the metal tip glowing white hot and the gilded symbols along its length flashing with the same unholy light. He dropped onto one knee and slammed the staff hard into the ground.

Thunder clapped, the sound so loud Alexa's ear drums vibrated painfully inside her head.

CHAPTER TWENTY-SEVEN

WESTWOOD BLINKED.

'An EMP discharge?' he repeated, not sure if he'd heard the man on the video call correctly.

Victor nodded on the monitor. 'Yes.'

Connelly stared at the Bastian leader, her face pale. 'You're saying Ethan Storm created an electromagnetic pulse that took out the super soldiers' tactical combat uniforms and every electrical device in a two-mile radius, including half the town of Hawthorne and most of the arms depot's security systems?'

Victor's expression remained guarded. 'The data we retrieved from Jessica Wu's computer showed that Jonah Krondike and his associates had been experimenting with liquid-armor suits for the last decade, far longer than any other defense contractor in the world. Not only that, their nanotechnology work is also years ahead of anyone else's and has already been battlefield tested.'

Westwood ran a hand through his hair. Although he'd seen pictures of the aftermath of the fight at the army facility in

Nevada, he still couldn't believe what had taken place there, nor what Victor Dvorsky was actually telling him right now.

'Why an EMP discharge?' he asked finally.

'When Dr. Godard and Dr. Black realized that Wu had designed experimental suits that incorporated both technologies, they knew there would only be two ways to neutralize them. Extreme heat or an EMP discharge.' Victor paused. 'They have since analyzed the uniforms of the men who attacked the island, the ones that were destroyed by the fire. Their theory that they embodied an early version of Wu's armor technology has proven to be correct. It's why Lucas Soul still managed to shoot and stab those particular super soldiers. It seems the armor worn by the men in Nevada was the most advanced version, made for full battlefield conditions, as Dr. Godard and Dr. Black suspected.'

Victor hesitated. 'What Ethan did was create an electrical storm with a single powerful lightning strike that generated a natural EMP field. It disabled the nanorobots built into the super soldiers' combat suits and disrupted the chemistry of their liquid armor. Though I don't believe it was Dr. Godard and Dr. Black's primary goal, the EMP burst also deactivated the super soldiers' neural implants, which made it easier to overpower them afterward.'

Westwood tried to quell the unease he felt at the staggering scope of the marked Immortals' ungodly powers. *It seems there isn't much they can't achieve once they put their minds to it.*

'Is this something Storm's always been able to do?' he asked.

'No,' Victor said. 'It's the first time he's ever tried anything like it.'

A knock sounded at the door of the Oval office. A woman entered, gave a document to Connelly, and exited wordlessly. Connelly flicked through the paperwork with a frown.

'I was right,' she muttered. 'It looks like Miller and his collaborators commandeered all communication with the private contractors overseeing the depot via a series of fake military personnel profiles. They probably didn't know those stockpiles were being stolen.'

Victor stirred. 'I believe you have a few of the general's associates in custody?'

Connelly nodded. 'Our investigators found enough in their offices and their financial records for us to question some of them.' She grimaced. 'No one has come up with anything that could help us discover the identity of the person Miller was working for, though, or where those children were taken. It looks like Miller's accomplices were put in charge of specific details of certain operations but were never given an overview of what the final end game was going to be.'

Victor gazed at them steadily. 'Olivia Ashkarov could probably break their minds.'

'I don't doubt that, Victor.' Connelly glanced at Westwood and wavered for a moment. 'But we've already tried some of our more—unconventional interrogation methods.' She grimaced. 'I truly believe they don't know any more than what they've already revealed.'

Westwood ran a hand over his eyes and sighed. 'I'm gonna pretend I didn't just hear you say that.'

'Sorry, James,' Connelly murmured.

'How did your conversations with the Russians, the Israelis, and the French go?' Victor said.

Westwood grimaced. 'Like a ton of bricks. The accusations were flying hard and fast after I told them about their subs.' He let out a heavy breath. 'They evidently believed me to some extent. I told them there may also be indications of weapons stocks having gone missing. The French and Russian presidents got back to me in the last hour with reports suggesting they've had artillery and other hardware stolen from their largest arms depots.'

Victor frowned at this news. 'Keep the channels of communication open with everyone, James. I will too. And we should talk to the rest of our allies. We're going to need everyone on board if this enemy decides to make a major power play.'

Westwood hesitated. 'What about Vlašic?'

Victor's eyes hardened. 'Leave him to me.'

HOWARD LET OUT A LOW WOLF-WHISTLE AS HE REPLAYED THE satellite imagery from Nevada.

'Now, that's impressive,' Laura said dully.

It was only by reducing the speed of the video to a snail's crawl that they actually saw the lightning bolt strike the spear held by the man standing in the middle of the compound. He dropped to one knee in slow motion in the milliseconds that followed and drove the weapon into the ground. The resulting electrical discharge exploded violently outward in a complex web above the crouched bodies of the Immortals and their human allies, the currents forking through the air in dazzling, deadly streams that struck the super soldiers in the chest and blew them off their feet.

Though they rose to fight again in the moments that followed, their movements were not as coordinated as before and they were soon subdued by the Immortals and Rangers encircling them.

'Have you spoken to him?' Laura said.

'Only briefly.' Howard smiled as he recalled Ethan's cranky

tone. 'Reynolds's men are calling him the Ultimate Power Ranger.'

Laura grinned. 'He's never gonna live that down.'

Howard chuckled. 'Yup. Alexa and Conrad are gonna tease him about it for years.'

Laura walked awkwardly over to a chair and dropped down into it. 'So, the arms depot really had been raided?'

Howard pulled a face. 'I'm afraid so. The NSA's already started examining their past satellite intel to see where those missing stockpiles have disappeared to. Jordan and I are helping them out, along with Eva and the techs at the Bastian headquarters.' He looked thoughtfully at the video replaying on the computer screen. 'And I think I have an idea about those subs.'

Laura winced and laid her hands on her swollen belly.

Howard tensed. 'Hey, you okay?'

Laura bit her lip. 'Yeah. Just false labor pains.' She rubbed her stomach and sighed. 'This kid is lively.'

TOMAS STARED AT THE PAIR OF IMPOSING, BRONZE DOORS opening up ahead of them. His heartbeat echoed in his ears as their guards guided them over the threshold and into the room beyond.

He had barely had time to register the opulent decor of the suite they had entered before his gaze found the Immortal seated at the table to the right.

Like Lily, Tomas had become attuned to the rhythm and energies in the complex where they were being kept prisoner. He knew from the number of minds he could perceive on the floors above them that the hour was late. He also sensed that the man who had awakened the kings, the man directly responsible for the attack on their island and their abduction, was not in the facility at this moment in time.

We must not antagonize him, Tomas.

Tomas blinked at Lily's command. He took a shallow breath, the restless agitation winding through him abating under her soothing influence.

'Is that you?' Crovir asked.

A shiver ran down Tomas's spine at the sound of the king's voice.

It was raspy and deep, an ancient sound that belonged to a bygone era. It was a voice that spoke of an age when mankind used to revere Immortals as gods.

Tomas felt the presence of a primitive evil, the same evil he'd sensed the morning the kings had awoken after receiving his and Lily's blood. He knew then that it had always belonged to the Immortal now observing them with a quiet, frightening intensity.

'I asked if that restful energy was coming from you, child,' Crovir said in a silky tone.

Lily swallowed before nodding.

'Yes, it was,' she said tremulously.

Crovir watched them for a moment longer before glancing at the guards.

'Leave us,' he said with a dismissive wave of his hand.

The soldiers twisted on their heels and exited the chamber.

Tomas flinched when the doors thudded close behind them, sealing him and Lily inside with the once-dead king.

He licked his lips and glanced around the room. 'Where is Bastian?'

Crovir rose to his feet and crossed the floor, silver and gold glittering in the fabric of his robes as they swished across the marble tiles. He stopped before them and tipped Tomas's chin up with a finger.

'He is King Bastian to you, child. You *will* grant him the respect of his stature.'

Apprehension stabbed through Tomas as he stared into the pale irises above him. They had lost the milky pearliness from that morning and their gray depths now reminded him disconcertingly of his aunt's deadly, silver gaze. But whereas Alexa King was a fair and just warrior, one who was as capable of love and compassion as she was of indomitable violence, the man scrutinizing him coldly was anything but.

Tomas clenched his teeth. He would not let the king see his fear.

A condescending expression dawned on Crovir's face, as if he had read his mind. 'I can see the insolence of Mila and the stubbornness of Jared in your gaze, boy.' He dropped his hand from Tomas's chin and traced Lily's cheek with a finger. 'Your eyes, on the other hand, reflect the kindness of Rafael and the warmth of Navia.'

He gazed at them for several silent seconds before twisting on his heels and indicating the dishes on the table. 'Come. Break bread with me.'

Tomas glanced at Lily. She hesitated before dipping her chin. They followed Crovir and took the chairs he indicated on either side of his seat at the head of the table.

The food was hot and tasted better than the meals they had been served by their guards.

'What is this?' Lily said, staring into a glass of red liquid Crovir had poured her.

'It is pomegranate juice with honey,' the king replied in a magnanimous tone. 'It is what my—' he hesitated for a moment, a troubled look flashing in his eyes, '—children used to drink when they were your age.'

Lily took a careful sip. Her eyes widened. 'It's nice.'

She glanced at Tomas. *It's safe. I can't detect any unusual chemicals in it.*

Tomas acknowledged her words with a blink. He clasped his glass and took a mouthful of the juice.

'You do that a lot,' Crovir said.

They gazed at him, puzzled.

'Talk to one another without actually voicing any words,' the king continued. 'I believe the word for it these days is... telepathy.'

Tomas set the glass back down carefully, his gaze riveted to Crovir.

Lily straightened in her chair.

'Can you read my mind, child?' Crovir murmured.

This time, the king directed the question squarely at Lily.

Tomas picked up on Lily's deepening unease as she scrutinized the Immortal's lined face.

'No, I cannot,' she admitted.

Tomas knew his sister wasn't lying. They had already attempted to breach the walls that protected the king's consciousness when they had entered the room. They had found his mental shields even more impenetrable than those of the man who had awakened the dead Immortals or the giant super soldiers they had faced in the lab the day before.

Tomas frowned. With time, he suspected he and Lily could learn to shatter those barriers.

'I have been told that you possess the other gifts of my and Bastian's children,' Crovir said. 'And that your powers may prove even stronger than theirs ever were. I saw the...images from when you fought those soldiers. I have to confess that I was impressed.'

Tomas remained silent, curious as to the king's intentions.

'I would like for you to consider becoming our allies,' Crovir said. 'If you do, you will be released from your prison and allowed as much freedom as I am able to grant you within the premises of this place. I will also see to it that no harm comes to your family and friends.' He paused. 'I believe you and I can go on to achieve great things in this strange new world.'

Tomas blinked, not sure if he'd heard the king right. 'You want us to help you?'

'Yes,' Crovir replied.

Lily stared unblinkingly at Crovir. 'To do what?'

Crovir's face grew inscrutable.

'Do you desire to reclaim the throne you once sat on and the kingdoms you used to rule alongside your brother?' Lily said.

Tomas startled. He glanced at Lily and was stunned by the expression on her face.

'Is that pity I read in your eyes, child?' Crovir said after a moment, surprise modulating his tone.

'Yes,' Lily replied quietly. 'Because I see only darkness in your path.'

Tomas's mouth went dry when he read Lily's intention across their mental bond.

'You could stop this right now,' Lily told Crovir. 'You can put an end to all that is to come.' She took a ragged breath. 'You can prevent the carnage and the terrible destruction your actions and those of your direct descendent will bring in the coming days.'

Crovir went still.

'Could it be that you have seen my death, child?' he said after a short silence.

Lily stayed quiet. Tomas kept his face carefully blank when he made out her silent answer in his mind.

Crovir's expression grew thoughtful. 'Not all the predictions of the Seer came true during our reign. In fact, some we managed to influence because of Navia herself.' He smiled thinly. 'Your attempt to dissuade me is sweet but futile, child. You must have seen the demise of people you yourself cherish to utter such pleading words.'

Lily paled.

'They *will* stop you, you know,' she said, her voice hardening. 'My father and the others.'

Crovir arched an eyebrow.

Tomas fisted his hands under the table and glared at the king. 'Nothing you say or do could ever persuade us to help you.'

Crovir's eyes glittered coldly at his words. 'How… disappointing. And I had such high hopes for you.' He rose from the table. 'I will give you some more time to consider your options. After that, I will have no choice but to hand you over to that woman.'

Tomas's pulse accelerated at the king's cruel words and mocking half-smile. He didn't have to look at Lily to sense her apprehension at the possibility of them both ending up the subjects of Jessica Wu's barbaric experiments.

Beneath his sister's agitation, Tomas detected the anger simmering in her veins. The same anger surging through him.

Defiance flashed in Lily's eyes. *I will not let her touch you, Tomas.*

Tomas scowled. *Nor I you, Lily.*

CHAPTER TWENTY-EIGHT

ASGARD MOVED SOUNDLESSLY OVER THE FOREST FLOOR, ARMISTAD strapped snugly to his back and a combat knife in his hand. He rose from a crouch, clamped his hand over the mouth of the man he had been tracking, and slit his throat in one slick move. He held onto the struggling figure until it went limp in his grasp before carefully lowering the dead man's body to the ground.

They'd landed at Khatgal Airport, just south of Khövsgöl Lake, some two hours ago. By the time they had reached the foothills of the Eastern Sayan Range and made their way north to the mountain that hosted the secret facility holding the tombs and hearts of Crovir and Bastian, the sun was already high in the sky. They'd decided the best strategy was to scale the summit of the peak one and a half miles from the concealed entrance before working their way down through the heavy forest covering its slopes.

It had proven to be the right tactic. Olivia had detected the minds of the first line of guards moments before they spied them among the vegetation. Though she had registered they were normal Immortals as opposed to super soldiers, the men were spread out over too large an area for her to be completely confident that one of them would not sound an alarm before succumbing to her mind control. They had to engage them directly.

Asgard pressed his back against the trunk of a birch and looked to his left, his breathing slow and steady.

Fifty feet north of his position, Olivia drifted between towering pine and larch trees, her steps swift and steadfast as she closed in on her target. She came up next to the Hunter, slipped her knife between his ribs, and carved a livid wound across his neck before he could react. He crumpled silently at her feet, mouth open on a cry that never came.

Admiration darted through Asgard as he observed his niece's composed expression. Though he knew she was still the woman he had come to love and consider his own daughter, he could sense the essence of the other soul currently living under her skin. Navia, the Seer born in a time of great strife and danger. A powerful warrior who had spilled the blood of countless enemies to build an empire for her Immortal father and uncle.

Deep inside his own heart, Asgard felt the quiet presence of the soul who had awakened within him. He was still coming to terms with the fact that he possessed a reincarnated piece of the man who had borne two sons who became the most powerful kings the world had ever seen, a soul descended from the very first man and woman who ever walked the Earth. Natalia Ashkarov, Olivia's mother, hadn't touched upon the subject of reborn souls when she had spoken of the vision she kept having before her death; she had only ever mentioned the powerful, marked Immortals who would possess abilities like nothing their world had seen before.

Asgard glanced over his shoulder and caught sight of Zachary as he felled the seventh Hunter guarding the perimeter of the remote facility. The man's movements were fluid and his sword unwavering, his ice-blue eyes reflecting the same single-minded focus and determination Asgard could read on Olivia's face.

Romerus had never known Aäron, but Asgard could feel his silent approval of the formidable prince Mila had chosen as her true mate, and of the man who now possessed his reincarnated soul. It was also clear to see that Olivia and Zachary had been correct in their assumptions; Navia and Aäron's awakening had brought out their inherent combat skills and rendered them as deadly on the battlefield as their forebears.

They disposed of the last guards before converging on a ridge overlooking a narrow ravine. Two hundred feet down and to their left, the facility's entrance stood under a shallow overhang at the base of a vertical rock face. The steel doors were fifteen by ten feet and disguised to look like the gray granite surrounding them. Were it not for the coordinates Victor and Eva had provided and the faint tire tracks they had spotted when they were climbing the mountain, they would have missed the portal.

'Can you sense the minds of the men inside?' Asgard asked Olivia where she hunkered beside him.

She nodded, her gaze locked on the gray doors. 'Yes. Five of them are super soldiers.' Olivia frowned. 'I will have to get close to them to break down their mental shields. Their barriers are more powerful than those of the men I fought in Yuma.'

Much to Olivia's frustration, she had failed to uncover any information concerning the whereabouts of Tomas and Lily or the identity of their enemy from the minds of the Hunters they had eliminated. The men, it seemed, were simply following orders from Crovir headquarters.

'Once we breach that opening, they'll know we're here,' she said in a hard voice.

They were at the bottom of the canyon within minutes. Asgard glanced at the security cameras covering the immediate approach to the entrance as they headed for the steel doors.

They had been informed of the layout of the surveillance network covering the one mile area around the facility by the Bastian techs in Vienna while they were still flying out to Mongolia. Instead of overriding the devices, something that would have alerted the men inside the complex to their presence, the Immortals had recorded an hour of live footage from all the cameras before Asgard, Olivia, and Zachary reached the mountain, and uploaded continuous loops of the videos to the facility's command center to conceal their incursion.

Tension wound through Asgard as they came to a stop before the metal portal. He drew Armistad from the scabbard at his back and gripped the arming sword tightly.

'Get ready,' Olivia warned.

OLIVIA TOOK A DEEP BREATH, LAID HER HANDS ON THE SOLID, gray panels, and focused.

Navia stirred behind her eyes, her curiosity echoing through her consciousness. Since the original Seer had never been physically intimate with Jared during their lives, Olivia knew she had never accessed the elemental powers of her true soulmate.

Even though barely a day had passed since her ancestor's life force had awakened inside her, Olivia was surprised at how strangely familiar her presence felt. She wondered if it was because of that time following her first death, when she had seen Navia and all the Seers descended from her bloodline during that suspended moment before her resurrection.

Olivia detected Navia's surprise and wonder as she drew on the power pulsing in the golden lines around her heart and reached out to the glittering source of Ethan's own ungodly abilities across their bond.

She exhaled and released a blast of combined psychokinetic and elemental energy into the doors. They groaned and buckled under her touch.

Olivia narrowed her eyes and flexed her fingers.

The metal panels shrieked as they were wrenched free from their hinges and cast violently inside. They sailed some thirty feet through the air before crashing onto the ground of the wide rock and concrete tunnel that opened up before them. An alarm sounded in the next instant.

Olivia unsheathed her sword and headed inside the gloomy passage with Asgard and Zachary. Eighty feet in, they came to an intersection.

Shadowy figures appeared in the passages on either side of them.

Olivia crushed the guns in the hands of the men charging up the corridors and scanned their minds. She identified the three normal Immortals, delved through their mental barriers, and suppressed their consciousness with a psychic surge. The Hunters stumbled and fell.

The five super soldiers never faltered in their stride. Though they outnumbered them heavily, Olivia was relieved not to see any giants among them.

She deflected the knife heading for her belly with her sword, spun on her heels, and brought her blade up toward the super soldier's back. He twisted, blocked the pointed edge an inch from his chest, and brought his right knee up toward her left flank. She veered sideways, felt his kick glance off her hip, and leaned sharply backward to avoid the second knife arrowing in on her throat from up ahead.

Olivia clenched her jaw, repelled the other man with a burst of elemental power, and released another wave of her soulmate's energy. The super soldiers' knives crumpled in their hands. They cast them aside and kept on attacking, their faces expressionless.

Metal clanged on Olivia's left.

'They're wearing those liquid-armor suits Madeleine told us about!' Zachary shouted.

He stabbed at a super soldier and swore when his broadsword juddered violently in his grip before skimming off the man's combat suit.

Unease shot through Olivia.

Asgard's arming sword bounced off a super soldier's arm to her right. A grunt left her uncle's lips as he took a powerful blow to his left flank. He ducked beneath a fist, thrust his shoulder into the super soldier's chest, and drove him into the wall of the tunnel. They crashed onto the rock face with a sickening thud.

Olivia took a step toward them. Movement flashed on her left.

She dropped beneath a high kick and felt a foot skim her right shoulder as she rolled onto her back and came up on one knee. She brought her sword up, fended off the boot heading for the left side of her head, and blocked the one arcing toward her right flank with a flash of elemental power.

Veins bulged in the super soldiers' necks and temples as they leaned into her.

Olivia scowled. *Damn it! I need more time. I can't get into their minds like this!*

As if heeding her silent call, Zachary and Asgard disengaged from the super soldiers attacking them and moved to flank her. A grim half smile crossed Olivia's lips as she rose to her feet. From the echo in her mind, she knew Navia had communicated her wish to the reborn souls living inside the two men at her sides.

She lowered her sword, took a shallow breath, and focused on the powerful shields protecting the super soldiers' consciousness, confident Zachary and Asgard would keep them from getting to her in the moments that followed. Her unease intensified when, at long last, she beheld the mental barriers of the five men at close range.

Instead of the solid walls she had encountered in the minds of the super soldiers she had battled in Yuma, the shields protecting these men's thoughts were fluid. They shifted every time she attacked, bending but never yielding to her psychic probing, their shapes assuming an impregnable defense within a second of her mental assault.

Olivia recalled what Anna and Madeleine had revealed on their video call from Sumava several hours ago.

It must be because of the way they were bioengineered. That's the only explanation for why their minds are so different from the super soldiers in Yuma.

Grunts reached her ears as Zachary and Asgard continued to fight the men, their bodies protecting her from the enemies' attack even as they took the brunt of their violent blows. Olivia gritted her teeth when she sensed that their defeat was but moments away.

There was only one option left.

She had never attempted to replicate what she had achieved in Yuma all those years ago, when she had overpowered the giant super soldiers who had proven to be their most challenging enemy to date and rendered almost everyone else unconscious. She knew it was the rage and pain of seeing her soulmate and the people she loved suffer at the hands of Jonah Krondike's monstrous army, and the knowledge that they and their allies would die if she were not to succeed, that had propelled her ungodly gifts to a level of destruction she had never achieved before or since. To create that devastating phenomenon coldly and deliberately was going to take everything she had. Her resolve hardened when she thought of Lily and Tomas.

If this helps us find them, then so be it.

Olivia ignored the nervous dread rushing through her, fisted her hands, and zeroed in on the golden threads of power around her heart. The soul dwelling inside her startled when she realized her intent.

For all that she was prepared for what would follow, Olivia could still not contain her gasp when heat suddenly exploded inside her chest. Though her every instinct warned her to contain the incredible energy pouring from her heart and soul, Olivia let it flow and fill her veins.

She was surprised at the speed with which she had been able to draw it to the surface and how much more easily she could control it this time around.

Navia's grim acknowledgement of what was unfolding reverberated inside her. Olivia felt her ancestor's psychic power swell within her body and meld with her own, complementing and augmenting it. She frowned and concentrated the violent pulses flooding her bloodstream into a single, large psychic wave.

The hairs rose on her arms. Her right palm tingled.

Olivia exhaled and let go.

Though she shielded them from the attack as best she could, she felt Zachary and Asgard's consciousness stutter. She blinked and saw them stumble, their bodies bowing under the potent psychic blast she had discharged.

The super soldiers froze in their tracks, their mental shields flexing and stretching under the explosive force. Sweat beaded on Olivia's brow as she pushed at the shifting walls. She bit her lip, brought forth a second powerful psychic wave, and projected it with the full force of her mind once more.

The super soldiers dropped to their knees.

Olivia inhaled sharply when she felt the barriers protecting their minds start to disintegrate. Heart thundering against her ribs, she forced her way past the breaches appearing in their crumbling mental shields.

A shiver raced down her spine when she finally registered the essence of their consciousness. Like the giant super soldiers from Yuma, these men's brain chemistry and wiring were all wrong.

There was nothing remotely human or Immortal about them.

Snow. Ice. A desolate landscape framed by low peaks under a sky where color danced.

Olivia's breath locked in her throat as the super soldiers' memories started flashing across her inner vision.

Giant caverns with ice floes drifting in dark waters. Warships and nuclear submarines docked at wide, manmade piers in an underground port. A facility housing barracks and an arms and ammunitions factory. Dozens of depots full of military hardware. An immense, thirteen-story complex with scores of research labs and the living quarters of the scientists and technicians who worked them.

Olivia's stomach twisted at what she perceived next. She fought back a cry of alarm and sensed Navia's deepening disquiet. When there was no more left to see, Olivia reached out and extinguished the consciousness of the broken creatures who knelt around them.

Asgard and Zachary caught her as she swayed.

'It's okay,' she mumbled shakily. 'I'm okay.'

'You don't look okay,' Zachary muttered.

Asgard glanced from her to the unconscious super soldiers.

'What did you see, Olivia?' he said, his voice full of trepidation.

CHAPTER TWENTY-NINE

'THEY'RE SOMEWHERE NORTH,' OLIVIA SAID.

Lucas's pulse thrummed rapidly as he studied her pale expression on the monitor of the laptop.

It was three in the morning on the fourth day following the attack on Balthazar Island. They had returned to Boston following their dramatic encounter with the super soldiers in Nevada and were on conference call with the others in Mongolia, Sumava, and Vienna.

'What makes you say that?' Alexa asked, leaning against the table next to Lucas.

'Because I could see the Aurora Borealis in the memories I captured from those super soldiers,' Olivia replied.

Tension knotted Lucas's shoulders. 'Did you find anything else at the facility? Anything that can help us find out exactly where they came from?'

Asgard grimaced. 'Bar the empty vaults that should have held the tombs and hearts of Bastian and Crovir, no. Whoever is behind this made sure not to leave a single trace that could lead back to them.'

Lucas swallowed a curse. He could see his frustration mirrored on Anna's face.

'The ships and subs you saw, did they look old?' Victor asked Olivia stiffly.

Olivia shook her head. 'No. They all appeared pretty modern, as did the weapons facility and stores I glimpsed.' She hesitated. 'The complex with the labs was a larger version of the facility in Yuma.'

Victor's face darkened at her words.

'There's something you're not telling us, Livvy,' Ethan said softly beside Lucas.

Olivia's lips twitched in a faint smile despite her visible apprehension. 'You know me too well.' Her expression sobered. 'Remember the life pods we discovered in the cave in Yuma? I saw something similar in the super soldiers' minds.' She took a shallow breath. 'Anna and Madeleine were right. These men were grown inside—tanks. Tanks they were placed in from when they were babies and where they were fed artificial nutrition and drugs while their bodies and brains went through a phase of rapid physical growth and maturation.'

Lucas blinked.

'Did you say…babies?' Anna murmured.

The horror in her voice echoed inside Lucas and was reflected in everyone's eyes.

'You mean, they were designed in a lab, grown in a petri dish, and then thrown inside those life pods until they reached adulthood?' Madeleine said, anger raising the pitch of her voice.

Anna placed a hand on her shoulder. Madeleine inhaled shakily, her eyes glittering with rage and disgust.

Olivia swallowed.

'Yes,' she said tremulously. 'The embryos and children are kept in a separate part of the facility until they reach adolescence. That's when they're transferred to the main labs, where the most intense phase of their bioengineering takes place. Although the details I grasped were blurry, the entire process from creation to full maturation seems to take about five years.'

Lucas thought of Tomas and Lily. Of how they had grown up surrounded by people who loved them and had been afforded every basic need and comfort so they could flourish into healthy beings. Although he still despised the super soldiers, he could not help the pity taking root in his heart.

They had never asked to be made, nor had they wished for the violent, colorless lives that had been thrust upon them.

'How many?' Conrad asked in a low voice. 'How many super soldiers did you see, Olivia?'

Olivia bit her lip. 'I think there are some six hundred men already operational, a third of them giants like the one you faced in West Virginia.'

Lucas's stomach plummeted.

'I believe twice that many may reach the final stage of maturation in the next few weeks,' Olivia continued. 'They will have to undergo a two-month-long phase of acclimatization and accelerated learning before they enter final battle-condition testing and training.' She faltered for a moment. 'I saw roughly those numbers still in infancy.'

'Shit,' Reid muttered in the stunned silence that followed.

'You missed the "holy,"' Anatole said dully.

'I apologize for interrupting,' Eva said across the video call from Sumava, 'but Jordan and I just finished analyzing the videos from the Crovir First Council meetings Dimitri attended in October of last year.'

Victor straightened. 'And? Did you find anything?'

Jordan appeared next to Anna and Madeleine.

'No,' he said, chagrined. 'They don't allow cameras in the safe room outside the Council chamber so we only had the feeds from the corridor outside.' He sighed. 'The entire Crovir First Council and their bodyguards went inside that safe room before those meetings. It's impossible to identify who tagged Dimitri's card without having physically been inside the place or having had eyes in there.'

Alexa frowned. 'So, you're saying every single member of the Crovir First Council is a suspect?'

'Yup,' Jordan said. 'Every last one of them.'

Conrad's cell rang. He checked the screen and frowned. 'It's Connelly.'

Lucas straightened at the cold light that dawned in the Healer's eyes when he took the call. 'What is it?'

'Thanks, Sarah. We'll be there soon.' Conrad disconnected. 'They've got Miller.'

VOICES ROSE IN THE CORRIDOR OUTSIDE THE OFFICE. IVAN stilled and frowned.

'I'll call you back,' he snapped into the phone before dropping it in its cradle.

The door opened violently and bounced off its hinges.

Ivan narrowed his eyes at the two men who stormed inside the room and the group of nervous Crovir and Bastian Hunters on their heels.

'What is the meaning of this?'

Victor Dvorsky and Dimitri Reznak slowed and stopped on the other side of the desk.

'That's what I'd like to ask you,' Victor countered in a deadly voice.

He pulled an envelope from his suit jacket and emptied it onto the table.

Ivan stared at the flurry of photographs scattered across the polished-wood surface. Surprise jolted him when he registered what it was he was looking at. He rose to his feet and glared at the Hunters crowding the office.

'Out. All of you. *Right now!*'

The men exited the room reluctantly, their posture hostile as they stared at their opposing faction. The door thudded closed behind them.

Ivan's gaze swung to the two Immortals opposite him. 'I just heard about your little mission in Mongolia.' He crossed his arms and indicated the pictures before him with a jerk of his chin. 'Is this your confession, Victor? Did you attack the facility and kill our men to get your hands on those tombs?'

Dimitri frowned. 'That's rich coming from the man who raided those vaults in the first place.'

Ivan blinked. 'What the devil do you mean by that?' He scowled. 'And may I say, the fact that you're allying yourself with the Bastians on this matter troubles me greatly, Dimitri.'

'This is not about taking sides,' Dimitri said, his eyes bright with anger. 'The stakes are far too high for me to worry about the sensibilities of fools who would rather cling to an ancient rivalry than stop the world from burning around them.'

'Someone in the Crovir First Council tagged Dimitri with a highly sophisticated tracking device last October,' Victor said. 'That's how they discovered the location of Balthazar Island.'

'Jonah Krondike was a silent associate of this person,' Dimitri said. 'The same person who is currently building an army of even more advanced super soldiers in another facility, one bigger than the underground complex in Yuma. They have amassed enough military hardware and weapons over the last five decades to start a third world war.'

Ivan's heart thudded rapidly against his ribs as he stared at the two Immortals.

'Do you take me for a fool?' he said finally. 'Do you really think I wouldn't have knowledge of any of this as the head of the Crovir First Council if it has really taken place?'

Victor scowled. 'Lucas Soul and his cousins fought some of those super soldiers in the last two days. Not only are they more powerful than the men Olivia Ashkarov and Ethan Storm faced in Yuma, they possess advanced combat armor the likes of which we have never seen before.'

Ivan stiffened. 'I don't believe you.'

'Well, believe this,' Victor snapped. 'The reason those tombs and hearts are missing is because someone wanted to resurrect the dead kings. And they succeeded.'

Ivan widened his eyes. 'What?'

'Crovir and Bastian are alive,' Dimitri spat out. 'We think whoever is behind this used the blood of Lily and Tomas Soul to revive them.'

Shock reverberated through Ivan. He fisted his hands. 'This is bullshit!' A bark of laughter escaped his lips. 'How the hell could you even think something like that is possible? Those men have been dead for thousands of years!'

'Because they're not the only ones who have come back,' Victor said.

Ivan stared at the furious man glaring at him.

'What do you mean?'

'The children of Crovir and Bastian breathe the air of this world once more, thanks to the bodies of the ones who are descended from their bloodlines,' Dimitri said quietly.

Ivan sat down heavily in his chair. 'I—how—?' He faltered, his nails digging into his palms. A wild thought came to him then. He looked up into the eyes of the two men observing him across the desk. 'You think it's me, don't you?'

Victor arched an eyebrow. 'Can you blame us? I find it hard to believe that all the resources that went into building those facilities and the actions taken over the years by someone in this Council could escape the attention of its leader. Especially after what happened in Mongolia.'

Ivan's pulse raced wildly as he gazed at the Bastian leader. He looked over at Dimitri. 'And you believe this too?'

Dimitri hesitated before dipping his chin.

Ivan took a ragged breath and rose to his feet once more.

He leaned his hands on the desk and stared unflinchingly at the two Immortals. 'Then I have nothing more to say to you, gentlemen.'

He waited until the door closed behind the two men before picking up the phone. 'Find Vlado.'

PART III
DELIVERANCE

CHAPTER THIRTY

BASTIAN LEANED HIS BACK AGAINST THE CONCRETE WALL BEHIND the bed and inspected the cell's austere interior with a sigh.

Over half a day had passed since he had been escorted to his prison by the soldiers who served the man who had revived him and his brother.

He grimaced wryly. *Well, not quite. It was the blood of those children that did that.*

A cynical chuckle escaped him. To be alive again was not something he ever would have wished for. In fact, he could hardly think of anything worse.

His last moments in this world, when he had perished on that battlefield all those hundreds of years past with his brother in his arms, flashed before his eyes once more. Sorrow pierced him, the pain overshadowing the dull ache where they had carved his flesh and bones and restored his heart to his body. He blinked and drew a ragged breath.

That it had been the right thing to do at the time, to surrender to death at the hands of the most powerful Immortal warrior of their time, did not take away from the fact that he had been responsible for his brother's end. The brother he had loved and looked up to for as long as he had lived.

Bastian pressed a hand to his chest and shuddered when he felt the strong, steady beat beneath his palm. *Abominations. We are both abominations, like those creatures who sleep in boxes made of glass.*

Crovir's actions the day before had hardly come as a surprise. Bastian knew all too well his brother's feelings concerning people who were not loyal to him. He only had to remember what he had done to his own daughter to realize this cold truth. Though he was confident Crovir would not hurt him, Bastian could not stem the dread flowing through him at the thought of what the older king and the man responsible for their resurrection could be planning. No doubt, it would be something terrible. Something that would cause death and suffering.

He recalled the pictures he had seen the day before. The faces that belonged to the ones who resembled their long-dead children. And the man and woman who were mirror images of their father and stepmother. A wave of bitterness threatened to drown him. He closed his eyes.

So, we stand on opposing sides once more. Are we to repeat the same mistake over and over again? To tear at one another and carve each other's bodies with swords and knives like we did before? Is there no hope for us to stop this ghastly cycle of hate?

Something fluttered in his mind then. A soft, warm breeze.

Bastian blinked.

The breeze came again and with it an intense pressure that pushed at his skull.

Bastian winced and raised his hands to his temples. The painful tension gripping his head disappeared just as suddenly as it had materialized. Then, as clear as day, a voice spoke in his mind.

Don't be afraid.

Bastian startled.

Who—who is this?

My name is Lily Soul.

A second voice joined the first one.

And I am Tomas Soul.

MILLER SAT STIFFLY IN THE CHAIR, ARMS HANDCUFFED BEHIND HIS back and ankles chained to the metal legs. Though his left eye was nearly swollen shut and blood stained his face and clothes from the cuts he'd sustained fighting the men who'd captured him, his expression remained defiant. A bandage peeked out from under the neckline of his shirt where it covered his injured right shoulder.

Rage surged through Lucas as he stared at the general through the one-way mirror of the interrogation room.

'Easy,' Reid murmured beside him.

Lucas took a shallow breath and unclenched his fists, conscious of the guarded stare of the CIA agent in the darkened chamber with them.

They were in the basement of a government facility in Maryland. Miller had been brought there following his arrest at the Canadian border by the Bastian Hunters and US agents who had been on his tail. It was thanks to Lucas and the others' experience in Hawthorne that they had managed to defeat the three Immortals and the super soldier who had been with the general, by using an improvised EMP device Jordan and Eva had instructed them to make to disable the men's liquid-armor suits.

Connelly had initially been reluctant to give them direct access to Miller when they had arrived at the facility that morning at dawn. She had finally capitulated when Conrad had convinced her they would make the general talk, something the CIA agents had not yet succeeded in doing.

The door opened presently on Miller's right. He twisted his head and glared at Conrad and Alexa as they walked in.

Conrad took the seat opposite the general and crossed his arms on the table. Alexa locked the door and leaned against it, her expression unreadable.

Tense silence filled the interrogation room. A couple of minutes ticked by.

The CIA agent frowned at Lucas. 'What are they doing? Aren't they going to question him?'

'It's called setting the scene,' Anatole murmured where he leaned beside the one-way mirror. 'He's had years of practice at it.'

Miller finally shifted under Conrad's steady gaze.

It was another minute before the Immortal spoke. 'Do you know who we are?'

Miller's gaze flashed to the birthmark on Conrad's arm. He remained silent.

'From the look in your eyes, I suspect you do,' Conrad said. He glanced at Alexa.

She strode to the table, grabbed Miller by his injured shoulder, and punched him hard in the face. A harsh grunt left Miller's lips as his head snapped violently sideways. Shock flared across his face.

The CIA agent swore and took a step toward the mirror.

'What the—?'

He twisted on his heels and headed for the exit.

Ethan stepped in his path. 'Relax. He won't die from that.'

The CIA agent scowled at him. 'That's beside the point! The man is a serving US general!'

He moved around Ethan and grabbed the door handle. It didn't budge. He closed both hands on the metal knob and twisted it again.

The door remained resolutely closed.

'The hell! Did you guys do something—?'

'It's locked and it's going to stay that way until that asshole talks,' Ethan said in a steely voice. 'Miller is a traitor and will be prosecuted as such by the US government. He lost all the rights afforded by his position the moment he decided to betray his country.'

'They won't kill him,' Reid said gruffly at the agent's alarmed look. 'We need answers and he has them.'

The CIA agent's face darkened. He reached for his gun. Ethan narrowed his eyes.

Lucas glanced at the wedding band on the agent's hand.

'Do you have children?' he said quietly.

The man froze, fingers on the butt of his weapon.

Lucas clenched his jaw. 'I have two. They're twins. They just turned six.' He studied the prisoner in the interrogation room. 'They were taken in the middle of the night four days ago by a group of masked men who tried to kill me and my wife. Miller works for the person responsible for their disappearance.' He swallowed past the sudden lump in his throat. 'We know they've hurt my children.'

The CIA agent hesitated for a timeless moment, a mixture of emotions washing across his face. His shoulders finally drooped.

He put his gun away with a sigh. 'Mine are four and seven.'

He looked at Miller through the one-way mirror, his expression stony. 'I would kill anyone who laid a single finger on them.'

'We know about the super soldier program,' Conrad said where he sat opposite Miller. 'We know about the liquid-armor suits.' He paused. 'We even know about the nuclear subs and the warships.'

Miller stiffened for an instant. A bark of laughter escaped him with his next breath. 'If you knew everything, you and I wouldn't be in this room right now!'

Alexa looked at the mirror. 'Ethan?'

Ethan walked over to the glass and pressed a button that allowed two-way communication. 'Yeah?'

'Lose the cuffs.'

Ethan smiled faintly. Miller's handcuffs clattered onto the floor a second later.

The CIA agent blinked. 'What just happened?'

'Magic,' Anatole said solemnly.

Reid rolled his eyes at the Immortal.

Anatole shrugged. 'What? It's kinda the truth.'

Inside the interrogation room, Miller rubbed his wrists, his face mutinous. 'This doesn't change anything. I'm still not—'

'I didn't think it would,' Alexa said.

She slipped a sai from her back, pinned Miller's right hand to the table with one hand, and drove the blade through his flesh and the metal beneath it with the other. Miller screamed and grabbed Alexa's wrist.

The CIA agent sucked in air. 'You sure about the not killing him part?'

Miller's livid voice came through the speakers.

'*You bitch!*' he spat, face red with pain and rage as he glared from his bleeding hand to Alexa.

She arched an eyebrow. 'That's not a nice way to address a lady.'

She drew the second sai, fixed Miller's left hand to the table, and stabbed it.

Miller's howl of agony echoed around the chamber.

'Did she say "lady?"' Anatole said dully.

'Seriously, never repeat those words in front of her if you value your life,' Ethan muttered.

'I concur,' Reid added wryly.

Miller cursed viciously as he stared from his bloodied, impaled hands to the two Immortals in the room with him.

'Whatever you do to me, it can't be worse than what *he* will do if he finds out I've betrayed him!' Miller hissed, spit staining his chin.

Conrad frowned. 'I can heal your hands and the gunshot wound to your shoulder. And we can protect you from Vlašic.'

Miller blinked. Lines slowly contorted his face. He bent forward, his shoulders shaking.

Coldness gripped Lucas when he realized the general was laughing. The sound erupted from the man's lips a moment later, loud and tinged with a hint of hysteria.

'Let me try something,' Ethan said suddenly.

Lucas turned and studied his cousin's enigmatic expression.

CHAPTER THIRTY-ONE

IVAN STEPPED OUT OF THE REAR OF THE SUV AND EYED THE imposing facade of the building before him with a faint frown. Although the sun was high in the sky and autumn was still a month away, he could not help the shiver that danced down his spine when he looked around and beheld the desolate landscape he stood in.

Vlado Krall's ancestral home was a sixteenth-century Baroque castle located on a twelve-hundred-acre estate twenty miles north of Dresden. He had inherited the place from his dead father, a man Ivan knew little about despite the fact that he had counted Vlado as a friend and ally for nearly two hundred years.

Although Ivan had visited the estate on many occasions in the past, he had never overstayed his welcome. He knew Krall was a private man who liked to keep to himself. There was also the fact that the castle was not the most pleasing sight in the world, its austere, gray walls and domed towers rendered even more uninviting by the bleak gardens and dark forest surrounding it.

Still, he'd had no option but to come here.

There was only one other person in the world besides him and Victor Dvorsky who had known what was inside the vaults of the secret facility in Mongolia.

Two years after the incident at Yuma, after a night spent drinking with Krall and commiserating over the arduous task of managing their respective sections of the Crovir First Council, Ivan had inadvertently let slip the location and purpose of the outpost the Bastian and Crovirs had built in Mongolia. Since Krall never mentioned it the next day, Ivan had assumed his friend had been too inebriated to recall his accidental revelation.

He'd tried to raise Krall on the phone that morning after Dvorsky and Reznak's visit but had been unable to reach him. As the SUVs carrying him and his bodyguards had left the headquarters of the Crovir First Council and made for Krall's estate, Ivan had hoped there was a logical explanation for why the head of his Counter-Terrorism Section was uncontactable.

He turned to the men who'd accompanied him. 'Stay here.'

The Crovir Hunters glanced at each other warily before muttering their acquiescence. Ivan strolled up the stone steps fronting the castle and headed inside.

Sunlight washed through the giant cupola above him and illuminated the stark furnishings of the hallway dominating the entrance. Ivan crossed the vast space and stopped before the majestic split staircase rising to the upper floors of the castle.

'Vlado?'

His voice echoed against the stone walls and sculptured arches.

Ivan made for the corridor flanking the left side of the stairs and walked past a sun room and a library. A murmur of voices reached his ears as he neared Vlado's study.

His cell rang, startling him. Ivan slowed and pulled the phone from his suit jacket. He narrowed his eyes at the name on the screen before taking the call.

'What do you want, Victor?' he snapped.

'Where are you?'

Ivan stopped outside Vlado's study. 'I'm at Vlado Krall's estate.'

'Get out of there! *Now!*'

Ivan froze, his hand an inch from the door handle. Unease filled him at the alarm he could hear in the Bastian leader's voice.

'Why?'

'I was wrong about you! It was Krall all along. He's the one behind all of—'

The door opened before him. Ivan blinked, Victor's words washing over him from a distance.

A blank-faced figure in a dark uniform stood facing him.

Ivan stared past the stranger to where Vlado Krall and a woman he had never seen before sat on a couch in front of the fireplace.

He slowly lowered the cell, his heart thumping a rapid beat against his ribs. 'Vlado?'

The woman finished injecting something into Vlado's arm and turned to observe Ivan coldly from dark, almond-shaped eyes. Vlado rolled down the sleeve of his shirt and rose to his feet, his bright gaze focused unblinkingly on Ivan.

'Well, what have we here?' he murmured, strolling casually toward him.

The sound of gunfire and muted screams rose from the

front of the castle. Ivan took a step back and reached for his gun.

The man in the uniform moved so fast his figure blurred.

Ivan gasped as the weapon was knocked out of his hand. He dropped his cell and blocked the fist heading for his solar plexus. Pain erupted in his left forearm. He gritted his teeth when he felt bone shatter.

Air left his lungs in a guttural grunt in the next instant as the man kneed him in the stomach. Ivan doubled over, bile at the back of his throat and black spots blurring his vision as he fought for air.

A hand closed around his neck.

Ivan choked and wheezed as he was lifted off his feet, fingers rising to clutch and pull at the wrist of the man who held him. He looked down into Vlado's chilling stare.

The other man stood silently behind him, his expression vacant as he watched Vlado hold Ivan high up in the air. He stepped on Ivan's cell where it had fallen on the ground and crushed it beneath the heel of his boot.

Super soldier!

A buzzing noise filled Ivan's ears as his gaze shifted to the man who held him—the man he had considered a friend for two centuries.

How? How is he as strong as them?!

A dark veil dropped across Ivan's vision as his oxygen-starved brain started to falter. The last thing he saw before darkness claimed him was Vlado's mocking smile and the super soldier's vacuous stare.

LUCAS'S CELL RANG JUST AS THEY REACHED THE INTERNATIONAL airport in Baltimore. His eyes narrowed when he looked at the screen.

He took the call and brought the phone to his ear. 'How did it—?'

Trepidation washed through Ethan as he watched his cousin stiffen.

Lucas stared blindly out of the window of the SUV. It had just pulled to a stop on the tarmac next to their jet.

'Are you sure?' he said, a muscle twitching in his cheek. He listened for a moment. 'Okay, we'll call you when we get there.' He disconnected and lowered the cell into his lap before turning to Ethan and Reid. 'That was Victor. Both Vlašic and Krall are missing. Victor was mid-conversation with Vlašic when he heard gunfire in the background and got cut off. Vlašic had apparently gone to see Krall at his estate outside Dresden. The Crovir First Council has called an urgent meeting to discuss their disappearance. Dimitri is there right now.'

Ethan tensed.

It was thanks to his wild idea that they had finally managed to extract some salient information out of Miller. When he'd suggested what he wanted to try, Lucas and the others had stared at him for a silent moment.

'Can you really do this?' Lucas had said finally, his eyes bright with hope.

Ethan had hesitated before nodding. 'We've practiced it a few times.' He'd smiled wryly then. 'I'm not as powerful as she is at borrowing my elemental energy, but it's worth a try.'

They'd all watched through the one-way mirror as he headed inside the interrogation room where Miller sat pinned to the table by Alexa's sais. The general had lifted his chin and glared at Ethan as he approached.

'And what the hell are you going to do?' he snarled, his voice laced with pain.

Ethan had ignored the man and stepped behind him.

Miller had startled and cursed when Ethan gripped his head in his hands.

'What the—?'

Ethan had drawn a shallow breath, closed his eyes, and focused inward.

It had taken but a couple of heartbeats for him to see the shimmering lines of power inside his chest. It was thanks to Olivia that he could visualize them so easily now. He had searched for the bright thread of his bond with his soulmate and followed it with his mind until he sensed the source of her unearthly gifts. Drops of sweat coursing down the side of his face, he had reached out and drawn upon the golden, pulsing mass.

Miller had cried out in his grip and started thrashing about in the chair.

Ethan had curled his hands into the general's skull and pushed at the mental barriers he could feel beneath his fingertips. His breath had frozen on his lips when he felt them yield and snap. Images had started flashing across his inner vision. He had stared unseeingly ahead, thrilled at what he'd managed to pull off.

He had never been able to conjure up a person's thoughts so clearly before, even during his previous attempts at using Olivia's power.

Ethan's mouth had gone dry when he'd finally registered what he was seeing. He'd waited until the final memory had danced in front of his eyes before letting go of an ashen-faced Miller and storming out of the interrogation room.

'He was on his way to the airport in Lethbridge, in Alberta,'

Ethan had said curtly as he barged inside the chamber where the others stood waiting. 'Call Victor, now.'

'Why?' Lucas had said tensely.

Ethan had clenched his teeth. 'Ivan Vlašic isn't our man.'

He had told them what he had seen in Miller's mind and the general's intended destination before he was captured at the Canadian border.

'He doesn't know where the research facility is but he was headed somewhere he was going to get picked up.'

Alexa had frowned. 'Where?'

'Uranium City. It's a settlement north of Lake Athabasca, in Saskatchewan, Canada. That's all I got from him.'

The CIA agent had opened and closed his mouth soundlessly, his shocked gaze switching from them to the dazed figure behind the glass wall.

'How?' he had blurted out. 'All you did was touch his head!'

'I'm telling you, man,' Anatole had muttered. 'Magic.'

They had left Miller in the care of the CIA agent and contacted Victor as they left the facility; now they were done with him, the general would be transported onward to Washington DC, where he would be handed over to Connelly and the NSA.

The door of their SUV opened. Alexa frowned when she saw their expressions.

'What is it?' Conrad said behind her.

Lucas stepped out and updated them about the recent development in Dresden.

'Well, that ain't good,' Anatole stated in the taut silence that followed.

'The sooner we get to Uranium City, the better,' Alexa said. 'Let's go.'

They boarded the jet and had just lifted off from Baltimore

when Lucas's cell rang again. A puzzled look flashed across his face when he saw the number.

'This is Soul.' Lucas went still as he listened to his invisible caller. He rose from his seat, the cell at his ear and his eyes bright with excitement. 'Wait, I'll put you on speaker.'

Priya Chatterjee's animated voice rang out across the cabin as they gathered around him.

'As I was saying, I've identified the components of the metal making up the 9mm casing. It's an HEA containing rare earth elements. I—'

'What's an HEA?' Conrad interrupted.

Chatterjee paused mid-flow. 'An HEA is a high entropy alloy,' she said briskly. 'It's a substance made from fusing several metals together. The aim is to produce something that has the combined properties of the primary constituents and more. In this instance, I believe they used spark plasma sintering to meld chromium, tungsten, and titanium with three rare earth elements, namely neodymium, samarium, and dysprosium. The tensile strength and fracture-resistance of this thing is unbelievable. I've never seen anything like it!'

'Any idea where those metals could have been sourced?' Alexa said.

'I'm getting to that,' Chatterjee replied. 'By far the biggest source of all six elements is China. It's got the most mines in the world and is the largest exporter of rare earth elements thanks to its Bayan Obo mine in Inner Mongolia. About the only other place that used to compete with it before it was shut down was the Mountain Pass rare earth mine in California.'

Ethan raised an eyebrow. 'So, you're saying this new metal came out of China?'

'No,' Chatterjee said. 'It could have been made anywhere in the world. But there's one place where the production of rare earth elements has taken off recently that will be of interest to you. I found an article from 2013 alluding to the specific chemical signature of the REEs in your 9mm casing. It was written by a geologist from the Saskatchewan Geological Society. I called him just now and asked which mine his sample came from. He said the place was about a dozen miles or so northeast of Uranium City. It was apparently abandoned following a major rockslide back in 2015.'

Ethan drew a sharp breath. Lucas's knuckles whitened on the cell phone.

'Uranium City?' he repeated, the shock on his face mirrored on everyone else's. 'Are you certain?'

'Yeah, I am,' Chatterjee said.

'Thank you. For everything.' Lucas disconnected and stared at them. 'This can't be a coincidence.'

Alexa dipped her chin. 'I agree.' She twisted on her heels and headed for the onboard computer, her expression determined. 'Let's see what Eva can find out about this place.'

CHAPTER THIRTY-TWO

'DIMITRI REZNAK IS SUSPENDED FROM THE CROVIR FIRST Council as of this moment,' the woman on the video call stated. 'We believe he's on his way to his estate in Sumava. He is to be placed under house arrest once he gets there, until we make a final decision on his case. We have declared a state of emergency for all the Councils while we decide our next steps. Needless to say, we will act swiftly and decisively against our enemies.'

Victor quelled the dread rising inside him and observed the woman impassively. 'And what, Sylviana? Are you saying we're at war?'

Sylviana Koviatovich, the Head of the Crovir Immortal Legislations and Conventions Section and the acting leader of the Crovir First Council, narrowed her eyes. 'After the stunt you and your Hunters pulled in Dresden, I'm surprised you even dare ask that question, Victor.'

Victor clamped down on a burst of irritation. Although there was no love lost between him and the Crovir noble, she was one of the few Crovir First Council members who had objected to what Agatha Vellacrus had done all those years ago, just before the latter had killed Tomas Godard.

He summoned as patient a tone as he could muster. 'Before we slap each other across the face with a glove like in the good old days, why don't you elaborate on what Dimitri and I are accused of, exactly?'

'There's no point trying to pull the wool over my eyes,' Sylviana snapped. 'We found Ivan's cell phone at Vlado's estate. The last person to call him was you. And from the ashes we discovered outside, his bodyguards obviously met their ends there as well.'

Victor frowned. 'I was trying to warn Vlašic. Why don't you dig a little deeper into Krall's background and his recent activities? I'm sure you'll find some interesting things there.'

Sylviana straightened in her seat, her expression indignant. 'Are you still going with that lie? That Vlado is somehow behind Ivan's disappearance?'

'It's the truth,' Victor said stonily.

'Then how do you explain the blood we discovered in his castle?'

Victor went deathly still. 'What?'

A triumphant light dawned in Sylviana's eyes. 'The remains of the Crovir Hunters guarding Vlado Krall were scattered all over his study, as was his blood. It's obvious that's where he was attacked too.'

Victor heard the dim twang of his self-restraint snapping. He took a ragged breath, rose to his feet, and leaned in toward the screen.

'There are things at play here that are beyond your understanding, Sylviana,' he said in a low, hard voice. 'I had made Ivan aware of the relevant facts only this morning.' He hesitated, remorse stabbing through him. 'I have to admit that I misjudged him. I won't do so again.' He studied the woman glaring at him coolly. 'I and the Bastian First Council have no wish to go to war with you. We have much bigger fish to fry and I, quite frankly, don't have time to play mind games with you or the rest of the Crovir Councils. I am going to do my damnedest to find Krall. I have little doubt that Vlašic is his prisoner right now.'

Victor heard Sylviana's outraged gasp before he abruptly terminated the call and felt a flash of grim satisfaction. He sobered in the next instant, pulled his cell from his pocket, and hit a number on speed dial.

Dimitri answered on the second ring. 'You heard?'

'Yes. How are you doing?'

'Apart from having to block the Council's irritating calls, not too bad, thanks.'

Victor smiled faintly. 'They'll have Crovir Hunters waiting in Sumava to place you under house arrest.'

A bark of laughter echoed across the connection. 'I'd like to see them try.'

Victor sighed. 'Don't fight them. The house arrest is meant for you only. As long as they let the others leave, you're just going to have to batten down and hold the fort.'

'That sucks. And you know how much I hate being imprisoned.'

'It's a twelve-thousand-acre estate. With a castle. And I've known you to live in those damn labs for, like, a month or more when you've gotten obsessed with something.'

'That's besides the point and you know it,' Dimitri retorted in a sulky tone.

❄

Crovir observed the unconscious man on the monitor with an inscrutable expression. 'This is the current leader of your…race?'

'Yes.' Vlado hesitated. 'I have to admit, I was not expecting Ivan to discover the subterfuge in Mongolia so quickly, nor to find out I was behind it. I suspect the Immortals who bear the reborn souls of your and Bastian's children had something to do with that.'

Vlado frowned. *As they no doubt did with the events in Nevada, although I suspect that had more to do with Miller and his associates' pathetic failure at keeping the information I shared with them under wraps, somehow.*

An hour had passed since his return to the main research facility with his sedated prisoner in tow. He had still been seething at what had happened in Nevada when Ivan had walked in on him and Jessica Wu, thereby precipitating the unfortunate sequence of events that had followed.

Crovir's gaze switched to him. As always, since the king had awoken, Vlado could not help the wave of nervousness that danced through his veins when he found himself the focus of those dangerous, pale eyes.

'Why did you not kill him?'

Vlado looked at Ivan Vlašic where he lay on the bed. Though he felt no regret for what he had done to the man, he could not deny that Ivan had been a good friend to him for two centuries.

'He might still prove useful if we have to bargain with the Crovir First Council. Although they believe I am missing right now, that situation might change if Victor and his allies convince them otherwise.'

Crovir watched him for a silent moment before dipping his chin. 'That is a clever notion. I agree with your decision.'

Vlado masked his relief and glanced at another camera feed. 'What about King Bastian?'

Crovir raised an eyebrow. 'What do you mean?'

Vlado mulled over his next words carefully. 'If you cannot make him change his mind, then what do you intend to do with him?'

Crovir straightened to his full height, his eyes darkening to pewter. 'Are you asking me whether we should kill him?'

Vlado stood his ground and nodded stiffly.

A strange look came over Crovir's face then.

He touched his chest and stared at his younger brother where he sat on the bed in his cell. 'I tried to kill him once. In the heat of battle.' His tone turned thoughtful. 'To do so cold-bloodedly…' He tailed off and lapsed into silence.

Surprise washed through Vlado. There was no mistaking the guilt and affection he had seen in the older king's eyes.

He stared at the feed from Ivan's cell, troubled. *Is that what it means? To have a brother?*

Vlado thought of his childhood with Jonah. There had been times when he had felt alone and wanted more. Wanted a mother. Wanted siblings and friends. His relationship with Ivan was the closest thing he had ever had to knowing what it was like to have either. Still, although his upbringing had been strict and filled with rules, he had never once doubted the love Jonah had for him. Vlado's admiration for his father's strength of will and his far-reaching ambitions had only grown with the passage of time, until they had become sacrosanct.

It had been his decision to become a subject of the experiments they had been carrying out in the past century, ever since they had teamed up with the Axis alliance and the Nazis during the Second World War. Though he now possessed the same superior genetic and nanotechnology enhancements as the latest generation of super soldiers they had bred in their labs, the fact that he had been conceived the natural way meant he needed regular injections to keep the molecular structure of his altered DNA stable. It was a small price to pay for their end game.

Vlado knew what Jonah would have made of Crovir's words had he still been alive. He would have found them weak.

He frowned, his resolve hardening. *I will not hesitate when it comes to making your dreams come true, father. Even if one of them has to die, we WILL rule this world once more.*

HOWARD DRUMMED HIS FINGERS ON THE WORKSTATION AND scowled at the data streaming across the array of flat-screen monitors.

Even though he'd recruited his group of hackers and Jordan and Eva to help him sift through the decades of satellite intel from IONDS, the Integrated Operational Nuclear Detection System, it was taking forever to identify the specific information he was looking for.

Made up of a combination of defense and Navstar GPS satellites, the aim of the IONDS network was to detect nuclear energy sources occurring naturally in outer space and those of man-made origin on Earth. Although IONDS was geared toward spotting major nuclear events, the latest electro-optical devices on the satellites meant they could also identify the presence of nuclear radiation at a low, constant level.

Like, say, that projected by a collection of nuclear-powered submarines, warships, and secret facilities under the ice somewhere.

'Hey, Howard?'

Howard glanced at the monitor featuring a permanent link to Jordan and Eva's computer lab in Sumava. 'Yeah?'

Jordan scratched his day-old stubble, his expression thoughtful. 'How about we make a formula?"

Howard stared at him. 'What do you mean?'

'What if we could teach our systems to isolate the specific nuclear signature of those four subs?'

Howard frowned. 'Is that even possible? I thought the IONDS network didn't go back that far.'

'It doesn't,' Jordan said. 'But we could get the original VELA satellite data from the DoD and the US Atomic Energy Commission.'

A thrill of excitement surged through Howard. This was the best idea he'd heard in over twelve hours.

He smiled. 'By "get," I take it you mean "illegally acquire?"'

Jordan blinked. 'Is there any other way?'

Howard chuckled. 'Neither of us are nuclear physicists, though. How do you propose we come up with this formula?'

Jordan arched an eyebrow. 'You mean you don't know any nuclear physicists?'

Howard sighed. 'If it wasn't for the fact that you invented an AI I'm in love with, I would *so* crash your servers right now.'

Jordan grinned.

CHAPTER THIRTY-THREE

Alexa pressed her hand over the mouth of the armed man standing with his back to her and pierced the base of his skull with a sai. He stiffened before slumping soundlessly in her hold, his lips parted on a silent cry. Anatole moved silently past her and took out the second guard. They shifted the bodies into a side passage before heading into the gloom of the tunnel.

Two hours had passed since they touched down outside Uranium City. They'd hired a pair of 4x4s at the airport and driven fifteen miles north, to where Eva had identified a large concentration of subterranean activity not far from the mine that had supposedly been closed following a rockslide in 2015.

From Eva's analysis of the ground-penetrating-radar images she'd obtained after hacking a passing satellite, the hidden mine spanned a two-mile stretch of land sitting between the juncture of three lakes. It ran parallel to one of the fault zones in the region known to contain rare earth element ores.

They'd left their vehicles in the conifer forest a couple of miles from the coordinates Eva had provided them with and travelled the rest of the way on foot. An hour of recon had revealed the concealed entrance to the facility, a score of ventilation shafts, three escape tunnels, and the dozen guards watching the perimeter. They had also come across a camouflaged landing strip half a mile to the east.

It had not taken long for them to dispose of the men outside the mine; luckily, none had been super soldiers.

'If we're going to find anything, it'll be in there,' Lucas had said when they assembled in the trees two hundred feet from the mine's primary opening.

'We should use the air ducts and the secondary tunnels to get inside,' Conrad had added. 'Extend the element of surprise for as long as we can.'

Alexa had nodded briskly. 'I agree.'

Eva's estimates from the satellite imagery had put the mine some eight hundred feet at its deepest. Though the AI had discerned generators and power cables running through the four levels of the complex, she had not been able to find any computer network linked to them. She also did not know the exact number of men inside the facility since the satellite had not been equipped with infra-red cameras.

They had split into pairs before making their way to different access points. By the time Alexa and Anatole had rappelled down a ventilation shaft and reached the first level, the red-haired Immortal had started to sweat profusely.

'Are you alright?' Alexa had said in a low voice.

Anatole had nodded and wiped his brow with the back of his hand.

'I have a thing about underground spaces.'

Something small and black had scuttled across the passage five feet ahead of them.

Anatole had blanched.

'And rats. I have a thing about rats too.'

Alexa had arched an eyebrow.

'Are you being serious right now?'

'As a heart attack,' Anatole had said dully.

Alexa had sighed and muttered something under her breath.

They had come across the armed guards minutes later.

Having dispatched them, they moved on.

A jangling noise reached Alexa's ears as they neared an intersection. A shadowy passage became visible up ahead. The sound grew louder.

They sidled up opposite walls of the tunnel and peered around the corners. Alexa drew a sharp breath, reached across the passage, and yanked Anatole sharply back by his shoulder.

A train of carts zoomed by inches from their noses, wheels rattling on metal tracks set in the ground. Alexa glanced up and down the narrow corridor before dashing after the last vehicle as it went past.

Anatole swore and followed her. 'What the hell are you—?'

'They're empty!' Alexa said. 'Which means they're heading inside!'

She jumped, grabbed the backend of the cart, and climbed inside before turning and grasping Anatole's hand. He scaled the metal container and landed beside her.

He froze in the next instant. 'Is that a rat?'

Alexa followed his stiff gaze to the small, dark shape on the other side of the cart. 'It's dead.'

'Are you sure?'

Alexa pinched her forehead. 'I should have partnered up with the Power Ranger.'

Anatole ignored the insult and clutched her arm. 'No, seriously, are you sure it's dead? I just saw its tail twitch!'

The carts juddered as the passage abruptly curved and dropped into a turn.

LUCAS HEADED STEALTHILY TOWARD THE MICRO DIGGER, HIS GAZE darting to the dozens of figures negotiating the metal walkways of the cave above him and the men at the bottom of the gigantic ore pit to his left. He was aware they only had to look this way to see him.

He moved into the shadow of the cab, climbed silently onto the rotating platform, and placed his Glock carefully against the temple of the man in the orange boilersuit sitting inside the cabin with a cigarette between his lips and a newspaper on his lap.

The miner froze.

Lucas caught the cigarette stub as it fell from the man's parted lips and carefully crushed it against the outer wall of the digger.

'You and I are going to step down from here and go for a nice walk,' he murmured. 'Nod if you understand.'

The man nodded furiously.

Lucas kept his gun at the miner's head as he guided him off the machine and back the way he had come. The guy rocked to a standstill when he saw the four unconscious men Reid was trussing up inside a side tunnel. There was a dead guard on the ground behind them.

'Look!' he blurted out, 'I don't know what you want, but just don't kill—'

Lucas clamped a hand over the man's mouth, pressed the Glock deeper into his flesh, and glanced at the ID badge clipped to his chest. 'Boris, is it?'

The man nodded, his panicked breaths fast and heavy behind Lucas's palm.

'We're not going to kill you, Boris,' Lucas said. 'As long as you keep your voice down.'

Boris swallowed and gasped out a muffled, 'Okay!'

'I'm going to take my hand away now,' Lucas said. 'If you scream, I'll shoot you. If you talk louder than a whisper, I'll shoot you. If you manage to raise the alarm somehow, I *will* shoot you. Got it?'

Boris whimpered.

Lucas slowly lowered his hand. Reid finished tying up the other miners and rose to his feet. Boris stared at them with round eyes.

'This place must have some kind of office,' Lucas said in a cold voice. 'You're going to take us there.'

Boris blinked. 'I just work here. I mean, the pay is great and as long as I don't ask questions, everything's—'

'The office, Boris!' Lucas snapped.

The man hesitated before nodding. He remained frozen to the ground.

Reid glanced at Lucas.

'So, where is it?' he asked the miner testily.

Boris gulped and pointed behind him with a trembling hand. 'Back that way. It's on the other side of the main ore pit.'

Lucas's heart sank.

'Well, shit,' Reid said.

'THIS IS A BIT OF A PREDICAMENT,' CONRAD SAID.

'You think?' Ethan muttered above him.

A shower of dirt rained down on Conrad as Ethan's boots slipped against the walls of the borehole.

It had been fifteen minutes since they infiltrated the facility through one of the escape tunnels. They had disposed of the three guards they had encountered, come upon the miners' living quarters on the second level, and secured the four men eating in the mess. They had found a map of the mine tacked to the wall and had been following it to the next levels when the wooden planks they'd walked across in the gloom had suddenly collapsed beneath them, revealing an abandoned drilling hole just wide enough to take a man.

They'd fallen some twenty feet before wedging themselves against the walls with their hands and boots.

'I'm gonna keep moving down,' Conrad said presently. 'This thing has to end somewhere.'

'You've been saying that for the last five minutes.' Ethan paused. 'Can you even see anything down there?'

Conrad eyed the pool of darkness between his legs. 'Nope. But, hey, look on the bright side. Eva said this place was eight hundred feet deep. We're already over seven hundred in.'

Ethan sighed. 'Not if this is an exploration borehole. Those go *way* deeper.'

Conrad's stomach plummeted. 'You had to ruin it for me, didn't you?'

They shifted down another twenty feet. Sweat dripped off Conrad's face and neck and disappeared into the murky depths of the borehole.

'How about you use your powers?' he suggested, the muscles in his arms and legs burning as he braced them against the rock.

'To do what?' Ethan said.

'I don't know. Levitate us out of here?' Conrad said, hope lacing his words.

Silence descended from above. 'Are you kidding me right now, Greene?'

'You mean you can't?'

'Stop. Please. I can literally hear Jared's spirit laughing inside my head.'

Conrad blinked. The shadows were lightening below.

'Hey, I think I see—'

Ethan cursed as he slid and dropped.

Conrad braced himself against the wall a second before his cousin's weight bore down on him. They slipped another ten feet before he managed to stop their fall.

'Tell me that's not your ass on my head, Storm,' Conrad grunted as he heaved and pushed against the rock.

'Be grateful it's just my ass. If I'd been facing the other way, it would have been my—'

A distant clattering echoed up the walls of the borehole.

They froze.

'What was that?' Ethan said.

Conrad carefully lowered his gaze and peered down between his legs.

He inhaled sharply. 'Tracks. I think I see some kind of metal tracks!'

The noise grew louder. Shadowy shapes flashed past some thirty feet below.

'Those are mining carts!' Conrad shouted. 'I'm gonna let go!'

'What? Are you crazy?!'

The rest of Ethan's protest was drowned out as Conrad dropped. He fell out of the borehole's opening seconds later and crashed into the base of a metal container. Air whooshed out of his lungs when Ethan landed hard on his back. Conrad groaned as he slowly climbed off him.

'Hey, get your own cart,' someone said above them.

Ethan stiffened before relaxing beside him. Conrad rolled onto his back and looked into Anatole's upside-down, grinning face above the lip of the cart behind them.

Alexa appeared next to him.

She glanced back the way they had come before frowning at them. 'Where the hell did you guys come from?'

It was at this point that they heard the sounds of a gunfight. Ten seconds later, the train of carts hurtled out of the tunnel and emerged into a pit at the bottom of a large cave.

Conrad rose from a low crouch and peered over the side of the cart.

Lucas and Reid stood behind an excavator on a ridge thirty feet above them. A man in an orange boilersuit was visible on the floor of the digger, his hands over his head and his body jerking repeatedly while Lucas and Reid exchanged gunfire with the armed figures on the metal walkways above them and the ones in the pit below.

'It's like he's got the words "shoot me" tattooed on his forehead,' Conrad muttered as he stared at Lucas.

Alexa sighed. 'Anna said the same thing. If there's a gunfight, he's always the first in the fray. He's a trouble magnet with a capital T.'

Ethan checked his gun. 'We best go get our troublesome generals.'

'All right,' Anatole said with an enthusiastic grin. 'One for all and all for—'

'Don't.' Alexa scowled. 'Just. Don't.'

Ethan stretched out the kinks in his neck, rose to his feet, and sent out a blast of elemental energy around the cave. The sound of weapons crumpling into useless lumps of metal echoed against the rock walls.

'Hey!' Reid yelled from behind the excavator. 'You got our guns too!'

'Whoops,' Ethan murmured.

CHAPTER THIRTY-FOUR

Ivan blinked his eyes open. A burning pain constricted his throat. He coughed hoarsely and bolted upright, fingers rising to his neck, air whistling in and out of his lungs. He stiffened when he touched his tender, swollen flesh. Memory returned and with it came a stab of dread.

Ivan looked around wildly, his pulse hammering away in his veins.

He was in a room with bare, white walls. A metal door with sliding panels stood on his left. Up ahead and to the right was a wash area. There was an air vent and a camera positioned above it.

Ivan bolted from the bed he lay on and started for the door, a dull ache lancing down his broken left arm. A wave of dizziness swept over him after a couple of steps. He stumbled and collapsed against the wall. The room spun around him.

Shit. Did they drug me?

He gritted his teeth, clutched the cold concrete, and stepped toward the door. A voice came just as he reached for the handle, the sound loud and clear inside his skull.

Wait! Don't do—

Fire danced through Ivan's body when his fingers made contact with the metal. He gasped and fell to his knees, his neck and back arching involuntarily as the electric current blasted through his body. It was another couple of excruciating seconds before he managed to let go. The voice in his head came again, its tone contrite.

—that.

Ivan cursed and stared at the perfect imprint of the handle etched into his right palm, wide awake and senses fully alert.

The voice spoke once more. It was female and that of a child, but oddly mature.

I'm sorry, I should have said something earlier. I didn't want to scare you.

Ivan closed his eyes and gingerly touched his skull. Although he couldn't feel any lumps, he wondered if he'd hit his head and suffered a concussion at some point during his capture. It was the only logical explanation for what was happening right now.

I'm not hearing voices. This is all in my imagination.

Someone sighed inside his mind. *No, it's not.*

Ivan startled. The second voice was male and also young. A sudden premonition flashed through him.

He swallowed convulsively. *Are you—?*

Yes. I am Lily. Lily Soul.

And I am Tomas.

Ivan opened and closed his mouth soundlessly.

'How come I can hear you?' he blurted out.

Lily Soul spoke again. *Because we possess the same psychic abilities as our Aunt Olivia.*

Ivan blinked, stunned. 'But—but, you're just children!'

The boy's voice came next. *I know this is a shock to you, but it would be best if we communicate in our minds only. They are watching us.*

A shudder ran through Ivan. He closed his eyes briefly.

Although Victor had warned him that Lucas and Anna Soul's children were as gifted as, if not more gifted than, their kin, he had not truly believed the man at the time.

I mean, who in their right mind would?!

But, with everything that had happened recently, particularly Vlado's bitter betrayal of their longstanding friendship, he had no choice but to finally trust in the Bastian leader's words. Everything the Immortal had said so far had been the truth.

Do you mean Grandpa Victor?

Ivan startled at Lily's words. *You call him Grandpa?!*

Tomas's voice rose in his mind. *Well, yes. He is an elder after all. Just like King Bastian.* He hesitated. *But we can't call him Grandpa. That would not be good form.*

Ivan climbed to his feet and walked unsteadily back to the bed, his mind reeling.

He sat down heavily on the mattress and gazed blindly at the concrete floor of his cell. *You mean, you've met the kings?*

Lily piped up. *Sure. Although he can't communicate psychically, King Bastian is listening in on our conversation right now.*

Ivan stiffened. *But I thought—*

He isn't our enemy. Tomas's voice hardened. *It's King Crovir and Vlado Krall who are the ones we need to stop. King Bastian refused to cooperate with them and is a prisoner down here with us.*

Ivan fisted his hands, anger surging through him. *You know about Vlado?*

Yes. Lily's voice was calmer than her brother's. *We found out his name at the time of the kings' revival, from the other Immortals in the lab.*

Ivan frowned. *Lab?*

He listened with mounting trepidation as the children told him everything they had discovered since they had woken up in the facility four days ago.

So, Victor and your family were right. The super soldier program is real.

How are our father and mother?

Ivan registered the anxiety in Lily's voice. *They're alright. They're doing everything they can to find you. Everyone is. And they're all pretty piss—er, angry about it all.*

Tomas spoke then. *Will you tell us what you know?*

A wry grimace twisted Ivan's lips. *You could read my mind.*

We try and avoid spying on the private thoughts of our family and friends. It would be rude to do otherwise.

Ivan stilled at Lily's words.

Am I your friend?

It was Tomas who replied.

You are not our enemy. Nor are you an evil man. In fact, far from it.

Ivan rubbed his forehead and gathered his thoughts, humbled by the children's trust. The enormity of what was unfolding still astounded him. He took a ragged breath and told them falteringly of all that Victor had said to him since the attack on their island.

The children listened in silence until the very end.

Ivan contemplated the cell he sat in when he finished. *Do you know where we are?*

'GREENLAND!'

Howard stood framed in a window on the jet's onboard computer monitor, his eyes bright with excitement. 'Jordan and I devised a formula that was able to isolate and track old radioactive satellite data relating to the specific nuclear signature of the subs that went missing in 1968.'

'Eva also uncovered a similar connection,' Jordan said on the video call from Sumava. 'She's been studying the routes the military aircraft leaving Hawthorne have been taking over the last few decades. She found a significant number headed north by northeast, toward Greenland.'

Lucas glanced at the others around him, adrenaline buzzing in his veins. 'So, the stuff we discovered in the mine was right.'

'What did you find?' Anna said, her face pale on the screen where she stood next to Madeleine, Zachary, and Olivia.

They were back at the airport outside Uranium City.

Once Ethan had destroyed the guns of the guards in the underground mine, it had not taken them long to overpower the remaining men at the facility. They'd searched the office they'd discovered next to the main ore pit and set the local miners free before leaving. They had gotten the call from Howard just as they'd driven onto the tarmac of the airport.

'We found an old flight plan detailing where the supplies of rare earth elements were to be transported to once they had been processed,' Conrad said. 'They were headed for the east coast of Greenland.'

'This would match what Olivia saw in those super soldiers' minds,' Ethan added. 'Snow and ice.'

'You got any visuals of the location from our satellite networks yet?' Alexa asked Howard and Jordan.

'They're being patched through as we speak,' Eva replied. 'I should have them up in a couple of minutes.'

A third call flashed on the monitor. Lucas recognized the number and tapped a key. Victor appeared on the screen.

'We were trying to call you,' Lucas said.

'I know,' Victor said.

Unease filled Lucas as he studied the Immortal's grim expression. 'What's wrong?'

Victor sighed and ran a hand through his hair. 'The Crovir First Council just declared war on us.'

Lucas's stomach plummeted. Alexa and the others stiffened around him.

'Are they insane?' Dimitri barked on the video call from Sumava.

Asgard stood scowling beside him.

'Sylviana and the others are convinced we're behind Ivan and Vlado's disappearance,' Victor explained. 'I told her everything we've learned so far, including handing over the data we've obtained on the super soldiers. She refuses to believe me still. Even after Westwood personally spoke to her about what happened in Nevada.'

'We know where they are, Victor,' Lucas said grimly.

Victor's eyes widened. He straightened in his seat. 'Where?'

Lucas briefed him on what they'd discovered in the last hour.

'Satellite pictures coming up now,' Eva said.

Another window appeared on the display. Whiteness filled it. Eva zoomed the image out. A bleak landscape of snow and ice-covered peaks appeared in the center. It was rimmed by wide, open plains to the west. To the east, the green waters of a series of fjords extended to the cobalt blue of the North Atlantic.

'Here's the GPR and infra-red satellite imagery of the same location,' Eva said.

The screen changed.

'Son of a—' Anatole swore.

Lucas studied the three large infra-red hot spots on the monitor with a dry mouth.

'The facility on the coastline corresponds with what Miss Ashkarov described,' Eva said. 'It's an underground port housed in three caves, with direct access to the ocean via two fjords. I detect a number of nuclear submarines and warships stationed there. The one to the north matches the weapons manufacturing and storage base.'

'So the one in the middle—' Asgard started.

'Yes. That's their primary base. The GPR imaging confirms thirteen levels to the underground structure and the largest concentration of people. From what Miss Ashkarov reported of her visions, that's where most of the super soldiers are stationed.'

Silence filled the jet.

'You're going to have a major fight on your hands,' Victor said quietly.

Lucas observed the Bastian noble's troubled face with mounting trepidation. 'How many men can you spare?'

Victor took a shallow breath. 'As of now, all bilateral agreements between the Crovir and Bastian societies are frozen.' A muscle twitched in his cheek. 'We are actively removing staff from our shared facilities around the world and the Crovirs have stated that they will no longer be cooperating with us on security matters. Sylviana has already informed the Secretary General of the UN that our two races are now effectively in direct conflict. She is also mobilizing every Crovir Hunter on the planet in preparation for what I can only assume will be some sort of attack against the Bastian First Council.' He hesitated. 'I can give you a thousand Hunters.'

'Shit,' Reid said dully. 'That ain't gonna be enough. Not against super soldiers and the other Immortals serving that bastard.'

'I'll contact the Crovir nobles who helped us fight Vellacrus,' Dimitri said darkly. 'If I wasn't under house arrest, I would—'

'That'll take too long, Dimitri,' Victor said. He studied Lucas. 'I take it you're going to make your move soon?'

Lucas nodded. 'It'll be night in Greenland soon. Sunrise is fifteen hours from now.'

'Our best bet is to surprise them in the dark,' Conrad said. 'We have a limited time window to act in.'

'We have other allies,' Alexa said.

Lucas stared at her.

'The Freemasons,' Alexa explained. 'I had an inkling we might need more man power so I gave them a heads up while we were in Baltimore. They'll help.' She smiled faintly. 'I also called the Order of the Three Spears. There's a plane full of monks headed for Europe as we speak.'

Zachary grinned. 'Nice move, babe.'

'Westwood and Connelly will send us men if we ask them,' Conrad added. 'I'm certain of it.' He grimaced. 'Besides, I have yet to collect on that debt Westwood owes me.'

'I bet the Russians, Israelis, and French are going to want to help too,' Victor said confidently. 'So will the Germans and the British if Westwood and I talk to them.'

Anticipation sent Lucas's pulse spiking.

He fisted his hands and dipped his chin. 'So, we have a plan.'

CHAPTER THIRTY-FIVE

THEY LANDED AT KEFLAVIK INTERNATIONAL AIRPORT, THIRTY miles southwest of the Icelandic capital of Reykjavik, just after midnight local time.

Ethan stepped out of the jet and eyed the troops of Immortal and human soldiers gathered next to the military transport aircraft on the tarmac around them. Though barely seven hours had passed since the Bastian Hunters, Freemasons, and US Rangers had received the call to arms, the men and women were already gearing up for battle, their snow suits stark under the halogen spotlights dotting the ground of the former US naval air station based at the airport. More aircraft circled the sky above them, bringing the rest of the NATO forces joining their ranks from Europe.

Ethan's gaze sought and found the group he was looking for. Two hundred feet ahead and to the left, Olivia and the others were headed briskly across the tarmac toward them from their jet. Heat surged inside Ethan's chest. He felt the ancient soul inside him stir. He descended the steps and hastened his stride.

They met at the halfway point, Olivia running into his arms with a low cry. Her hands wrapped around the back of his head and she burrowed her face in his neck as he lifted her off the ground.

Ethan shuddered at her touch and hugged her to him tightly. He reveled in the warmth of her body and drank in her scent. It was as if he had never held her before.

Olivia finally lifted her head and stared at him, her green eyes glittering with emotion.

'It is good to see you,' she whispered.

Ethan knew it was Navia who had spoken then. His throat clogged up as a torrent of feelings washed through him from Jared. The agony of their long forbidden love, a love that had gone unfulfilled during their ancient lives, caused his pulse to stutter.

'It is good to see you too.'

Ethan lowered his head and took her lips. It was a slow, reverent kiss, one that was meant for the ones who dwelled inside them.

It felt like their first time all over again.

ALEXA SLOWED WHEN SHE BEHELD ASGARD, HER CHEST TIGHT with emotion. She knew now why it was she had felt such a strange affinity toward him, ever since their first meeting. She wondered whether Mila had always sensed it where she lay dormant in her heart—sensed that a piece of Romerus lived inside the man descended from his noble bloodline.

She walked into Asgard's arms and wrapped her hands around his waist wordlessly.

Peace filled her when he held her tightly to his chest. A peace as old as time and full of the centuries of love and adoration Mila and Romerus had once shared.

'I never thought—' Asgard started gruffly.

Alexa felt him swallow convulsively against her. She raised her head and smiled at him tremulously, the feelings coursing through her from the soul within so strong she felt her body tremble.

'I know.'

She stepped out of his hold reluctantly and watched as he turned to the man next to her.

'It is good to see you, Romerus,' Conrad said hoarsely.

Asgard engulfed Conrad in a hug. 'It is good to see you too, Rafael.'

Alexa twisted on her heels and faced the woman beside Asgard.

Madeleine touched her cheek lightly before dropping a kiss on her forehead, tears brimming in her eyes.

Alexa clutched her fingers where they lay against her skin, too full of emotion to speak. She took a shuddering breath and finally looked at the silent man who stood watching her with a heated gaze.

Zachary's eyes burned as bright as diamonds.

Alexa hesitated before taking a step toward him, her senses overwhelmed by the fiery storm in her chest. She could see the other soul inside him, the one to whom the warrior within her had once utterly lost herself, just as she herself had to his reincarnated form.

Zachary closed the distance between them and raised his hands to her face. She swallowed a moan as his touch scorched her flesh and sent electricity sparking along her nerve endings.

He lowered his head, his fingers trembling where they lay on her skin. As his breath washed across her lips, a memory flashed through Alexa, one filled with so much yearning and loss it robbed her of air.

It was a memory of the last kiss these two souls had shared, on a battlefield in a distant land and time.

Just as Mila had once stolen Aäron's last breath, Alexa now returned it to Zachary, his lips when he pressed them to hers so sweet and warm all she could do was cling to him.

It was a long, slow kiss. One that tasted of the past and spoke of a love so deep it had lasted millennia. Of a bond so powerful it could never be broken, even by death.

'It is good to see you, my Queen,' Zachary whispered against her mouth.

Alexa blinked, her vision blurring with tears while her heart sang with the fiercest joy. 'It is good to see you too, my Prince.'

ANNA HESITATED WHEN SHE STOPPED BEFORE LUCAS. HER anxious gaze roamed his face.

Lucas smiled faintly, aware of the two souls watching her curiously from behind his eyes. 'I'm still me.'

Relief washed across her face. Her breath left her lips shakily. She wrapped her arms around his neck, rose on her tip toes, and pressed her mouth to his.

Lucas stifled a groan, hugged her to his chest, and deepened the kiss. Though they had only been apart five days, it felt like a lifetime since he had last touched her. Anna's fingers speared his hair as she molded her body to his and responded just as ardently.

Someone chuckled close by.

Lucas reluctantly pulled away from Anna and gazed dazedly at her flushed face before looking over at Reid. 'What?'

Reid grinned at his defensive tone. 'It's like watching you two fall for each other all over again.'

Anna rolled her eyes at him and dropped back down on her heels.

A sliver of anxiety danced through Lucas as he studied her. 'Are you sure you want to come?'

Anna nodded. 'Yes.' She raised a hand and touched the lines furrowing his brow gently. 'I may not be as good a fighter as the rest of you but there is no way I will stand by and watch you walk into this on your own. We're going to go and get our children. Together.' Her lips curved into a faint smile. 'Besides, I've been taking lessons.'

Lucas startled. 'You have?'

Anna nodded and glanced at Alexa where she stood next to Zachary some twenty feet to her left.

'You're kidding?' Lucas said hoarsely as he stared from their cousin to the woman before him. 'I thought you hated fighting. And when?'

Anna pursed her lips. 'Remember all those long walks Alexa and I used to take around the island and when we visited Zachary and her in New York? Well, we weren't just walking.' She rose and pressed another kiss to his mouth. 'Considering I'm married to a man who has a nasty habit of getting himself into all sorts of dangerous situations, I thought it would be best if I didn't assume the role of damsel in distress every single time. So make your peace with this.' Her voice hardened. 'I'm not changing my mind.'

Lucas swallowed and nodded. He recalled the attack on

their house and how she had defended herself against their masked intruders.

Anatole returned from where he had been talking to the Hunters and the Rangers, Reynolds and Sergeant Peters following in his steps. The latter's wounded leg had been healed by Conrad while they were still at Hawthorne and he walked without a limp.

'We've briefed the other troops joining us about the—' Reynolds grimaced, '—*special circumstances* of this mission.'

Anatole grinned and indicated Peters with a tilt of his head. 'He told them you guys were regular-day superheroes.'

Reynolds froze in his tracks and turned to look at Peters.

'Is that true, Sergeant?' he said, aghast.

Peters shrugged. 'Greaves and I thought it would be the easiest way to prepare the other soldiers for the unnatural shit they're going to be exposed to during this battle, sir.'

Reynolds watched him for a moment before sighing. 'Well, you're not wrong.'

Ethan and Olivia approached with the others.

'Just try to keep it, you know, as normal as you possibly can,' Reynolds told them sternly.

'I'm not sure that's going to be possible,' Reid said wryly. 'These guys don't do normal.'

Reynolds groaned and rubbed a hand down his face. 'Christ, it's going to be like that time in Yuma, isn't it?'

'I think this is gonna be worse than Yuma,' Ethan said in a determined voice.

Olivia dipped her chin next to him, her eyes shining hard.

Reynolds scowled. Something on the tarmac drew his gaze.

'Are those…monks?' he said dully.

Lucas turned and eyed the crowd of saffron-robed figures exiting an aircraft a short distance away. Alexa and Zachary headed briskly across the tarmac and greeted the smiling young man in the lead with warm hugs.

'Ah-huh,' Lucas murmured with a faint smile.

Peters's eyes widened. 'Why are they bowing to her?'

Lucas grimaced and rubbed the back of his neck as they watched the monks practically kowtow before Alexa. 'Well, technically, they're her sect.'

Reynolds gaped. 'She has a *sect?!*'

'Like I said, technically.'

Asgard walked over to them from where he had been talking to some Hunters.

'Are your ships in position?' he asked Reynolds.

The major nodded. 'They're closing in on the coordinates we've given them as we speak, as is our submarine force. We leave at zero two hundred hours.'

LAURA IGNORED THE CRAMPS IN HER BELLY AS SHE WATCHED THE live, infra-red satellite imagery streaming across the flat-screen monitor; she'd become used to her false labor pains in the last couple of days.

Howard sat at the workstation next to her chair, his back rigid and his normally jovial face set in stiff lines.

They were in the bunker beneath the mansion in Santa Monica, where they were helping coordinate the attack on the enemy's facilities in Greenland with Jordan and Eva. Their live link with Sumava remained open on another screen, as did the one with the Bastian headquarters in Vienna. Victor and Dimitri were visible inside the windows, their expressions similarly strained.

'It's starting,' Howard murmured.

Westwood studied the moving dots on the digital map on the main screen of the Oval Office. Connelly perched on the armrest of the sofa, her body full of the same tension coursing through his veins.

It was midnight in Washington and the room was a hive of activity.

It had not taken the two of them long to convince the Joint Chiefs of Staff and the Secretary of Defense that it was in the best interests of the United States to help their allies defeat an enemy they had not even known existed until a few days ago.

The strike force they'd hastily assembled with NATO was now within sight of their target, having crossed the three hundred miles from Iceland in a little over an hour.

'The Sixth Fleet should be there right about now, sir,' the Chief of Naval Operations said tersely.

Westwood felt Connelly stiffen next to him. He reached out and took her hand where it rested on her thigh. She startled and looked at him. He kept his gaze locked on the screen ahead.

Lily stirred in her sleep. She sat up, brushed her hair from her face, and blinked at the dark cell, wondering what had awoken her. That was when she felt it. Felt her.

Tomas's drowsy voice echoed in her head. *Lily?*

Lily's pulse accelerated. She closed her eyes and reached out with her mind, seeking the familiar consciousness that had just brushed against hers so briefly. It was several seconds before she sensed her once more.

Aunt Olivia.

She felt Tomas wake fully at her breathless words, their connection buzzing with a sudden burst of his energy.

You can hear her?

Not quite. But she's close.

Lily's eyes widened when she registered an echo in her aunt's consciousness. It was only as the link between their minds strengthened that she finally understood what it was she was sensing.

Navia.

Lily felt Tomas's jolt of shock.

You can—you can feel her too?

Ivan had told them what Victor had said about the reawakened souls. After witnessing Bastian and Crovir's rebirths, Lily had had no trouble believing him. She swallowed when she discerned the other ancient souls bearing down on them.

Yes. And not just her. Lily pulled back the covers and climbed off the bed. *It's time.*

'Found them.' Olivia opened her eyes and studied the dark mass looming on the horizon through the plane's cockpit window. 'They're on the thirteenth floor, in the basement of the main facility.'

Asgard twisted on his heels and headed into the aircraft's cavernous hold to tell the others.

Olivia's heart quickened as she reached out to Lily's faint consciousness. *Can you hear me?*

It was a moment before she heard her reply.

Yes.

Olivia swallowed, joy and relief flashing through her at her niece's voice. *We're coming for you.*

Lily's resolve resonated across their connection, so intense it raised goosebumps on Olivia's skin. *We'll be ready.*

CHAPTER THIRTY-SIX

ETHAN GLANCED FROM THE LUMINESCENT DIALS OF HIS DIVING watch to the shadowy ripples ten feet above him as he bobbed in the undercurrent. It was another minute before Howard's tense voice came over the sub-assault headset under his suit hood.

'Continuous loop recordings on the security cameras are set up. You guys have fifteen minutes, tops.'

Ethan signaled to Reynolds where he floated next to him and kicked up toward the surface. He emerged slowly from the icy waters, scanned the area, and drew up on a concrete side ledge.

By the time the Rangers had climbed out around him, he'd unlocked the watertight exit door in the south wall of the channel and twisted the opening wheel to expose an emergency tunnel. They crowded inside the underground passage, removed their rebreathers, and stripped out of their neoprene drysuits.

Cold air fogged in front of Ethan's face as he checked his gun and the suppressor attached to the muzzle.

Forty minutes had passed since they'd been dropped off in a fjord by an amphibious assault ship behind the cover of one of the uninhabited islands that dotted the eastern coastline of Greenland. They'd navigated five and a half miles of open water with the aid of free-flooding, wet submersibles and reached one of four access channels leading to the underground port without any incident.

'Go straight for one hundred feet, then turn right,' Howard said over the headset. 'You'll see another door after forty feet. This one opens onto the corridor that will take you to the security center.'

Though Howard and Eva had managed to identify and infiltrate the computer networks of the secret port and the weapons base, neither of them had been able to connect to the main research station. The only way to do this, they hoped, would be to access it from one of the secondary facilities.

'Number of unfriendlies in the immediate area?' Ethan said into his transmitter.

'Six within fifteen feet of that door.' Howard paused. 'The place is crawling with them. Be careful.'

Ethan took the lead and moved swiftly up the tunnel. He reached the junction Howard had indicated, headed into the side passage, and slowed when he saw what lay at the end.

'Shit.'

'What?' Reynolds said as he came up next to him.

Ethan indicated the door's opening mechanism. 'It's another locking wheel. They'll hear the damn thing the second it starts moving.'

'How many revolutions?' Howard asked over the headset.

'Two and a half,' Ethan said.

'Go slow.'

Ethan stared at the security camera in the corner of the ceiling. 'Seriously? That's your suggestion? Go slow?'

'Well, yeah,' Howard muttered.

Ethan sighed, holstered his gun, and placed his hands carefully on the wheel. He closed his eyes and sent a gentle, controlled wave of elemental energy through the door. They all held their breath when it unlocked with a soft click.

Ethan froze. Reynolds stiffened beside him.

'You're okay,' Howard said over the headset.

Ethan maintained a steady stream of elemental energy as he slowly twisted the wheel, eliminating friction from the rotating parts. It was a full minute before it completed its final turn. He grabbed the panel with Reynolds and carefully pulled it open.

A brightly lit, concrete passageway appeared on the other side.

They peered out before pulling back.

'I'll take the guys on the left,' Ethan murmured.

Reynolds nodded.

They stepped out silently into the passage with the rest of the Rangers, splitting up and moving toward the figures at either end. Ethan got within seven feet of the guards he was targeting before one of them turned and spotted him.

He shot the man in the chest, saw the round punch through his uniform, and crushed his gun and those of his two companions with a blast of elemental power. Bullets whizzed past him as the Rangers fired at the disarmed figures.

Fifteen seconds later, they had control of the corridor.

'We'd better secure these guys and leave them in the escape tunnel,' Ethan said as he observed the dead men. 'I don't know how many of them are Immortals. They could wake up again.'

Reynolds hesitated before nodding, his expression uncomfortable.

Howard's voice came over Ethan's earpiece. 'The security room is one hundred feet north and fifty feet east of your position. I count eight guys inside.'

They turned and headed in the direction he had indicated. Halfway to their target, they walked into a group of guards.

Ethan's pulse stuttered when he registered the empty looks on the faces of the five men who had just stepped out of a room ahead and to their left.

Super soldiers. No doubt about it.

'Go for head shots!' he barked at Reynolds as the figures reached for their weapons.

Gunfire exploded across the corridor.

Heat surged inside Ethan's chest and down his left arm as he raised his hand and released a barrier of elemental energy.

By the time the last fragmenting bullet had smashed into the invisible wall, he'd ground their enemies' weapons to a pulp. The super soldiers stared at the lumps of metal in their grasp, cast them to the ground, and charged wordlessly toward them.

Ethan snatched an EMP grenade from a pocket on his thigh and was about to depress the button when it was kicked out of his hand. He cursed, ducked beneath a powerful fist, and lunged toward where the device had fallen on the ground. His eyes widened when he caught a glimpse of the giant figures heading their way from the far end of the passage.

Ethan closed his fingers around the grenade, reached inside to the glimmering, pulsing source of his power, and felt the soul within him stir.

Conrad paused on the dimly lit staircase when he heard shots through the receiver in his ear. He signaled to Greaves and the group of Rangers behind him before peering over the railing to the shadowy drop below.

It had been eight minutes since they'd infiltrated the underground port via a submerged channel to the north and started making their way to the generator room. They'd emerged from an escape tunnel fifty feet from the access door they were targeting and were a quarter of the way down the stairs that would lead them to the basement of the facility.

Conrad's blood pounded steadily in his veins as he strained his ears. Bar the steady humming that made the metal steps vibrate under his feet, no other sound escaped from the level beneath them.

'What's happening?' he murmured into the transmitter pinned to his combat suit.

'Ethan and Reynolds came across a group of super soldiers on their way to the security center,' Howard replied over his earpiece. 'They're engaging them as we speak.'

Conrad frowned. 'I'm not hearing any alarms.'

'I disabled them.'

Conrad smiled faintly at that. 'We're almost at the generator room.' He was about to start down the steps when he paused again. 'How's Laura?'

'Heavily pregnant and as grumpy as a cave full of bears. *Ow!*'

Conrad swallowed a chuckle. 'Did she just smack you on the side of the head?'

'Yeah,' Howard muttered. 'How did you know?'

Conrad grinned. 'She does it to Anatole all the time when he's being an ass.'

'She says to tell you that she loves you. And if you die before she has this kid, she will follow you to hell and bring you back just so she can personally kill you herself.'

Conrad sobered up at that. 'I won't die.'

He motioned to the Rangers and headed silently down the stairs. Fifteen feet later, the outlook opened out to his left. He stopped on a landing and studied the giant space spread out below him.

Dome-shaped turbines and generators lined the floor of a murky cave. Rising at the far end was the faint outline of the concrete containment unit housing the facility's nuclear reactor. A maze of platforms, walkways, and pipes connected the elements of the power plant.

Fifty feet ahead and to the right, light spilled through the glass observation windows of a control room built into the wall of the cave.

Conrad closed the last twenty feet to the ground with the Rangers in tow and ducked into the shadow of an overhead gangway. They made their way silently through the gloom toward the source of the light, their weapons in hand.

Hairs rose on the back of Conrad's nape as he passed an aisle next to a turbine. He saw movement out of the corner of his left eye, dropped to the ground, and raised his gun as he rolled and came up on one knee. A figure stepped out of the narrow space and punched Greaves hard in the solar plexus. The Ranger grunted as he flew backward and crashed into three of his companions, taking them to the ground.

Conrad pulled the trigger of his semi-automatic, saw his silent bullets smash into the super soldier's liquid-armor suit, and snatched an EMP grenade from a pouch at his waist. Pain exploded in his left loin. He gasped, lunged out of the way of the second super soldier's boot, and yanked his staff weapon from his back.

He jumped to his feet, sent a pulse of healing energy to the fresh contusion on his flank, and narrowed his eyes at the group of blank-faced men closing in around them. Motion captured his attention to the right.

Conrad's pulse spiked when he saw the hulking figures of five giant super soldiers approach from the direction of the control room. He twisted a ring on the staff and unsheathed his swords, heat building inside him as he focused his ungodly gift. Power flashed through him from the soul that now dwelled in his heart.

CHAPTER THIRTY-SEVEN

'Left turn coming up in twenty feet,' Eva said in Alexa's ear. 'The control room is fifty feet up the passage. There are two guards stationed outside.'

Alexa slipped the second Sig from the holster on her lower back and moved silently along the corridor, the Marines and the Freemasons at her side.

Thirty minutes had elapsed since they'd jumped out of the cargo hold of a C-130 Hercules and parachuted down to the ice under the streaming waves of the Aurora Borealis. They'd landed one mile from the weapons base and skied their way down the frozen slopes of a shallow elevation toward the hulking, dome-shaped roof of the structure projecting from the plain below.

It had not taken long to locate the air vent Eva had identified as an access point. By the time they had crawled through the ventilation ducts and reached the second level, the AI had taken control of the facility's security cameras.

Alexa slowed when she neared the junction and motioned to the men with her. They froze against the concrete wall.

She stepped out into the adjoining passage, let out a soft whistle, and raised her guns. The guards framing the doorway ahead never saw the bullets leave the suppressors on the Sigs.

By the time they hit the ground, their vacant eyes staring sightlessly beneath the bullet wounds in the middle of their foreheads, Alexa was already running, the Marines and the Freemasons following in her steps.

A figure came out of the control room as they closed in on it. Alexa recognized the man's combat suit as he reached for the automatic rifle looped around his chest, his motions lightning fast.

She holstered the Sigs, jumped, and locked her legs around his waist. The super soldier lowered his weapon and reached for her throat as she twisted violently and brought them both to the ground with a scissor kick.

He slammed into the concrete, the rifle clattering noisily out of his grasp, his fingers falling from her flesh. Alexa rose into a low crouch, blocked the knee heading for her head, and saw four blank-faced figures in liquid-armor suits step out of the control room.

'Do it!' she barked at one of the Marines.

She snatched her sais from their sheaths and leapt out of reach of the fallen super soldier as he lunged toward her. She straightened, deflected the swirl of fists that came her way from two more attackers, and caught a glimpse of the Marine punching the button of an EMP grenade. The transmitter went dead in her ear.

Alexa dove beneath a deadly blow and drove a sai up into a super soldier's chest. Satisfaction tore through her as the blade cleaved through the deactivated combat suit and sank into his heart. She cut the man's throat with the second sai before slicing another super soldier across the gut.

Movement ahead caught her eye.

'Oh shit,' muttered one of the Freemasons. He stared at the colossal figures moving down the passage toward them.

Heat bloomed in the center of Alexa's chest. She lobbed two flash bombs inside the control room and felt the ferocious energy burst forth and flood her veins, hardening her limbs and focusing her senses.

The ground trembled and shook beneath her feet as she turned to face the giant super soldiers, the power of the soul residing inside her resonating through her very core and fusing with her own. A savage smile curved her lips.

ZACHARY PEERED OVER THE EDGE OF A CRATE AND STUDIED THE layout of the warehouse.

'That's a lot of hardware,' murmured the US Army Special Forces lieutenant next to him. They stared at the helicopters, tanks, and armored vehicles lining the vast space below. 'You weren't joking when you said this guy wants to start a war.'

'The people with me have been fighting him and his allies for a long time,' Zachary said.

The lieutenant hesitated. 'By people, you mean that hot, scary chick headed for the control room with the Marines?'

Zachary smiled faintly. He examined the bridge cranes and walkways crisscrossing the space above them. 'That hot, scary chick is my wife.'

The lieutenant blinked. 'Wow. You have bigger balls than me.' He observed the uniformed men stationed across the shadowy chamber. 'Those the—super soldiers we were warned about?'

'Some of them are,' Zachary said. 'We won't know until we engage them.'

The lieutenant frowned. 'The way this place is laid out, they'll see us the moment we're on the ground.'

'I have an idea.'

The lieutenant followed Zachary's gaze to the roof. He raised an eyebrow. 'That could work.'

They had disposed of some dozen men before a burst of gunfire sounded in the middle of the warehouse, giving away their presence.

Zachary steeled himself when he saw a Special Forces soldier fall from where he had been fast-roping to the ground behind a guard fifty feet to his right. Bullets whizzed around him. He clung to his rope and looked down. An armed figure stepped out of an aisle between two rows of Apache attack helicopters twenty feet ahead.

Zachary cursed, swung violently to the side, and dropped rapidly, the thick cord humming between his gloved hand and thighs as he fired back. A cacophony of shots exploded around the warehouse as the Special Forces soldiers engaged the rest of the enemy.

He released the rope when he was still six feet from the ground, arched his body through the air, and struck the guard in the chest with his shoulder as he landed. They tumbled to the ground and lurched to a stop next to the front wheel of a Humvee, their guns clattering beneath the undercarriage.

Zachary felt a blow glance off his hip, grabbed his attacker's ankle as he lunged under the vehicle to grab his automatic rifle, and yanked sharply. The guard cursed and rolled onto his back before kicking at him.

Zachary blocked the boot with his hand, slipped his broadsword from the scabbard at his back, and stabbed the man in the left thigh. The blade slipped through the guard's uniform, pierced his leg, and wedged itself an inch into the concrete beneath his limb. He cried out and cursed where he lay pinned to the floor.

'I know this has gotta be hurting like a bitch, but can I say how pleased I am right now that you're not wearing one of those liquid-armor suits?' Zachary commented brightly as he climbed to his feet. 'I mean, seriously. Talk about unsporting.'

A shadow engulfed him from behind.

The guard's lips twisted into a mocking grimace as he looked up past Zachary's shoulder.

Zachary twisted to the side. A large fist blurred an inch past his cheek and smashed into the door of the Humvee. His stomach dropped when he saw the dent and knuckle prints it left in its wake.

He looked over his shoulder, saw the giant super soldier, and clasped the handle of his sword.

A hand closed on the back of his neck.

Zachary gasped as he was lifted off his feet and rammed violently into the side of the Humvee. The guard screamed beneath him, blood gushing out of his open wound where the blade had escaped his flesh.

Zachary sagged against the vehicle and shook his head dazedly. He gritted his teeth and tightened his hold on his weapon as the super soldier grabbed his shoulder and spun him around. Air left his lips in a guttural choke when his attacker punched him in the gut. The super soldier switched his grip to Zachary's throat and raised him off the ground once more.

Movement flashed behind the giant. A figure in saffron robes darted through the air, a jō staff spinning in its hands.

The super soldier grunted as a series of powerful blows landed on his back, arms, and legs. He released Zachary and turned to face his new adversary.

Zachary stumbled as he hit the ground feet first.

He regained his balance and smiled fiercely at the young man standing to the super soldier's right.

'Anzan.'

The brother of the monk who once saved Zachary's life and who had become one of his and Alexa's most cherished friends grinned at him briefly before locking stares with the super soldier once more.

The giant moved.

Anzan deflected his furious attack, his movements nimble as he danced across the ground, always a hairbreadth from the super soldier's deadly hits.

Zachary headed toward them, his broadsword in hand. He swung the blade at the giant's back and scowled when it struck the combat uniform and juddered in his grip.

The giant twisted around and backhanded him across the face.

Stars exploded across Zachary's vision as he sailed off his feet and slammed into the back of an armored vehicle. He groaned, shook his head lightly to clear the ringing in his ears, and straightened.

Alarm flooded him when he saw the giant land a blow on Anzan.

The monk gasped as the super soldier knocked the jō staff out of his hands and rammed his fist into his gut. He clenched his jaw and raised his arms to block the vicious punch heading for his skull.

The giant blinked and froze. His head swiveled slowly sideways.

He stared from the blade that had impaled his forearm through the sleeve of his combat suit to Zachary's savage smirk. His vacant gaze moved to the device in Zachary's grip.

'I don't think so, asshole,' Zachary growled.

He dropped the EMP grenade, clutched his broadsword in both hands, and yanked it out of the giant's flesh before driving it into his chest.

The super soldier grunted as the blade carved through his uniform and entered his body.

Zachary withdrew his weapon, inhaled sharply, and ducked beneath the giant's swinging fist. He moved back and joined Anzan as the latter retrieved his staff weapon from the ground.

'He's a tough bastard to kill, isn't he?' Zachary said as they faced the super soldier.

'As my brother used to say, he is a most savvy opponent,' Anzan murmured.

Zachary stared. 'Seriously, Yonten used to say that?'

Anzan pulled a face. 'We think he drank a lot of bad yak milk when he was a child.'

Zachary studied their glassy-faced opponent. Though the EMP device had disabled the giant's liquid-armor suit, it appeared to have had less of an effect on his neural implant compared to the other super soldiers Ethan and the others had faced in Nevada.

Zachary held the broadsword in a white-knuckled grip and dug his heels into the ground, the energy of the warrior prince whose spirit he had inherited soaring inside him and filling his bloodstream.

There's no way I'm dying this time. He glanced at the fierce young monk who stood at his side. *And neither will he.*

CHAPTER THIRTY-EIGHT

IVAN STARTLED WHEN THE CELL DOOR CRASHED OPEN. THOUGH he had anticipated what was about to happen, he still stared, dumbfounded, at the three figures framed in the opening.

Lily and Tomas Soul's faces reflected a depth of maturity he had not expected to see in children their age. But more than the fact that they seemed older and wiser than their physical appearance would imply, it was the determination in their eyes and the absolute power he felt emanating from their bodies that sent a shiver of awe down his spine.

Standing behind them, his blue gaze startlingly similar to that of the little girl before him, was King Bastian. The older Immortal watched Ivan silently, his expression inscrutable.

'Come,' Lily said.

Surprise jolted Ivan. Barely half a day had passed since he'd awakened in Vlado's research facility and started communicating with Lily in his mind. It was the first time he was actually hearing her voice in person.

It was as soft and serene as it had sounded in his head.

He hesitated before dipping his chin.

Fifty minutes ago, Lily had woken him up and warned him of the events about to unfold. When she had communicated what she had perceived from her psychic contact with Olivia Ashkarov regarding the vast troops on their way to confront Vlado's army, Ivan had struggled to believe her. For Lucas Soul and his cousins and allies to have assembled so many humans and Immortals to assist them in their mission at such short notice seemed practically impossible.

You don't know our family and friends very well, do you?

For a moment, Ivan had wondered whether the little girl was being ironic. It hadn't taken long to realize she was genuinely curious.

No, I do not.

Tomas spoke then, his amused tone strangely adult-like. *They are pretty determined. And as stubborn as they come.*

What Lily had said next had left Ivan reeling in shock.

We're going to do what?!

Lily had repeated her statement. *We're going to break out of here and go up to the labs. We have to stop what Vlado and his scientists are doing.*

Tomas's voice had come again. *And we have to help the others when they get here.*

Ivan had stared blindly at the wall, bewildered.

He'd glanced from the camera in the corner of the cell to the electrified exit.

But how?

Leave that to us.

Ivan cast a final look at the room where he'd been kept prisoner and headed out the door.

A warm feeling washed down his left arm and right hand as

he followed the children and the king up a concrete corridor. He blinked and slowed to a stop.

The burn mark on his palm had disappeared, as had the ache from his broken limb.

'Was that you?' Ivan said, stunned.

Lily glanced at him over her shoulder and nodded.

'But—but I thought Conrad Greene had to physically touch someone to heal them!'

'We don't have to,' Tomas said.

LUCAS LOWERED HIMSELF CAREFULLY OUT OF THE OPENING IN THE ventilation pipe and dropped into the emergency exit tunnel. He landed softly on his feet and scanned both ends of the somber passage before signaling to the figures above him.

Reid, Anatole, and a troop of Bastian Hunters joined him in the tunnel.

'Have Alexa and Ethan connected their devices to those networks yet?' Lucas murmured into his transmitter as he unsheathed his katana.

It was a couple of seconds before Jordan replied. 'That's a negative. They've actively engaged the enemy and have triggered their EMP grenades. We lost all communication with their teams and access to those two stations' security cameras twelve minutes ago. They'll have to physically reboot the systems before Eva, Howard, and I can get in again.'

Lucas's heart plummeted.

Eva's analysis of the structure of the three facilities had revealed they would likely be resistant to a large, external EMP discharge. With this in mind, they had decided to arm themselves with EMP grenades to deal with the problem of the liquid-armor suits. They had planned to use them at the very last moment, when they were face to face with the super soldiers. They had known they would knock out every electrical circuit around them once they did so, including their own communication devices.

Though Lucas would have preferred access to the research base's security cameras to navigate the level they had just infiltrated, he knew roughly from the GPR and infra-red images they had studied in the last few hours where their target was. By his estimation, they still had two hundred and seventy feet to go before they reached it.

Reid laid a hand on his shoulder.

'They can do this,' he said quietly. 'Trust in them.'

Lucas swallowed and nodded. 'I do. I just hope they're okay.'

They headed fifty feet east along the tunnel, turned, and came to a steel door.

Lucas removed a small, explosive device from a pouch on his combat uniform and placed it on the lock.

'Once this goes off, they're gonna know we're here,' he warned.

Anatole bared his teeth in a cheerful grin. 'Let the fun times begin!'

Reid sighed. 'I worry about how much you enjoy these life-and-death situations.'

Several of the Bastian Hunters muttered their agreement as they retraced their steps and crouched in the adjoining passage.

Lucas glanced around grimly as he lowered himself next to them. 'Remember our primary objective. We have to take control of that command post.'

He took a deep breath and detonated the bomb.

❄

VLADO BOLTED UPRIGHT AT THE SOUND OF THE ALARM. HE yanked back the bed covers and reached for the phone on the nightstand just as it rang, the sound muted by the shrill blare echoing across the room.

'Sir, we're under attack!' barked one of the Crovir Immortals in charge of the research facility's security. 'There's been an explosion on Level One, near the command post. We have intruders in the warehouse on that floor too and we've lost contact with the port and the weapons base. The cameras on Level Thirteen have also gone offline!'

Vlado scowled and climbed off the bed. He tucked the handset between his ear and shoulder and headed rapidly for the closet.

'Do we know the identity of our attackers?' he said darkly as he shrugged into a custom-made, liquid-armor, combat suit.

'We believe they are the Immortals related to the children we captured on the island. The rest of them appear to be human soldiers and Bastian Hunters.'

Vlado holstered a gun, slipped a knife into a sheath on his thigh, and walked over to the bed. He hesitated before grabbing the polished sword resting on metal brackets above the headboard. He strapped it to his back and opened the drawer of the nightstand.

'Have the jet ready for evacuation.' He removed a rectangular device from inside the drawer and pocketed it. 'And mobilize all the super soldiers. They are to engage the enemy and kill them on sight.'

Vlado ended the call, grabbed his satellite cell phone, and turned just as the door opened.

Jessica Wu stared at him from the threshold, her face pale.

'You know what to do,' he said.

She swallowed before nodding, her expression determined.

Vlado exited his quarters and made for Crovir's rooms at the other end of the floor while Wu headed off toward the elevators. He passed the soldiers he'd assigned to the older king's guard and found him sheathing a pair of ancient swords that had graced the wall of the dining hall.

'I take it by that infernal noise that something has happened?' Crovir said blithely.

Vlado nodded stiffly. 'Yes. Come with me.'

'Where are we going?' the king said as they left his chambers.

'To the secondary command post.'

Vlado's mind dwelled briefly on the prisoners on the thirteenth floor. He knew it was likely the children who had disabled the security cameras down there.

Whatever they're up to will have to wait for now.

Olivia frowned at the super soldiers. She had already suppressed the consciousness of the Immortals and half-breeds in the warehouse and those within a hundred-foot radius of her location on the first level of the research complex. The only ones left standing were the vacant-faced figures confronting them across the depot packed with armored vehicles and military hardware.

'Are you getting through?' Madeleine shouted from where she, Anna, and a group of Bastian Hunters engaged two super soldiers on her left.

'I need more time!'

Olivia blocked a blow to her head with her sword, clenched her teeth, and pushed at the elastic barriers she could sense around the super soldiers' minds.

They had already detonated an EMP grenade and gotten through the men's liquid-armor suits with their blades and guns. Still, the super soldiers remained standing, their hardened bodies absorbing what would otherwise be deadly injuries.

Asgard stepped in front of her and deflected the knife heading for her chest. 'I'll buy you a couple of minutes!'

Olivia nodded, conscious of the second battle raging in the command post at the opposite end of the facility, where Lucas, Reid, and Anatole had gone.

Are you ready?

Navia's reply resonated in her head. *Yes.*

Olivia's knuckles whitened as she focused on the energy in the shimmering contours of her heart and fused it with the power of the soul inside her. It was easier this time around.

Gasps echoed across the warehouse as she released the violent psychic wave.

Having done her best to protect the minds of her kin and their allies, Olivia was relieved to see them still standing as the echoes of the blast reverberated around the warehouse. Elation flashed through her when she felt the super soldiers' mental shields stretch and snap under the force of her assault. She inhaled raggedly and forced her way inside their minds.

They shuddered and fell a moment later, their bodies collapsing as she shut down their brains. The sound of fighting ceased around them.

'You did it,' Madeleine said weakly, staring at the unconscious figures on the ground.

Asgard stiffened next to Olivia. Her stomach twisted as she followed his gaze to a doorway on the other side of the warehouse. She gripped her blade in her hands and turned to face the group of giant super soldiers walking toward them.

CHAPTER THIRTY-NINE

THE ARMOR-PLATED DOOR BURST OPEN AND SMASHED ONTO THE floor of the room on the other side.

Tomas stepped inside the lab he and Lily had been taken to the day after they had been captured and brought to the facility. He glanced at the glass wall to the right. It had been replaced, the polished surface reflecting their images once more. This time, he sensed no one behind it. He headed across the floor to the concealed opening where the super soldiers had first appeared, Lily at his side.

'Where are we going?' Ivan asked.

'To save them,' Lily said.

Tomas placed his hand on the hidden panel, located the lock, and manipulated it with a small surge of elemental energy. The door swung open soundlessly a second later.

Ivan's puzzled gaze moved from Lily to the shadowy space before them. 'Save whom?'

'The children.'

Tomas took the lead and headed into the decontamination

room. They passed an airlock chamber, a set of interconnected labs, and finally came to another large, steel door.

Ivan frowned. 'I don't understand.'

'You will soon,' Tomas said.

He placed his hands against the metal. Lily mimicked him and closed her eyes.

'They are many,' she murmured.

Tomas swallowed and nodded. He could sense it clearly now, the strange collection of consciousness he and Lily had felt before. Minds that were similar to but not quite the same as those of the super soldiers. Young, immature beings who did not possess the mental shields of their older peers and had not yet been indoctrinated into the mindless violence and unquestioning obedience that was meant to be their fate.

They knew what these creatures were.

Tomas stiffened when he detected the others around them.

Lily removed her hands from the steel panel and turned to Ivan and King Bastian. 'There are super soldiers on the other side of this door. Stay behind us.'

The two Immortals glanced at each other warily before narrowing their eyes.

'You cannot truly expect us—' the king started.

'We're not going to let you—' Ivan said.

'You have no weapons,' Lily interrupted.

'And these men are beyond anything you've ever faced before,' Tomas added. 'Please. We will do this faster if we don't have to worry about you.'

Ivan hesitated for several seconds before finally grumbling his acquiescence. King Bastian dipped his chin reluctantly a moment later.

Tomas looked at Lily and read the resolve in her gaze. 'Ready?'

She nodded, her expression hardening.

Power surged inside him, flashing waves of golden light that streamed through his veins and filled him with heat. He detected the same violent pulses rising in his twin where she stood beside him.

Tomas concentrated his elemental energy into his palms and let go.

The steel door buckled inward before ripping from its hinges. It soared some fifteen feet through the air, crashed onto the floor of a cavernous space, and skidded to a stop at the base of a glass tank in a shower of sparks.

'What the—?' Ivan whispered hoarsely.

He stared, aghast, at the structures filling the gloomy chamber and the tiny figures floating inside. Shadows shifted at the edges of the enormous lab.

Tomas stepped across the threshold with Lily and studied the giant super soldiers headed their way. Among them were the four men who had nearly overpowered them that first day.

'Together,' Lily said in a voice of steel.

Tomas glanced at his sister and nodded.

They linked fingers and raised their free hands.

Ivan and King Bastian gasped and dropped to their knees under the elemental and psychokinetic storm that suddenly engulfed the chamber.

Tomas drew a shuddering breath when his energy merged with Lily's. A dizzying thrill shot through him as he felt his powers amplify and expand. It was like that first time all over again, when they had fought to save one another in the lab. He sensed Lily's abilities similarly escalating.

The super soldiers stopped in their tracks.

❄

A WINDOW BLINKED INTO LIFE ON THE MONITOR TO THE LEFT. Howard startled and leaned toward it. Camera feeds started populating the screen next to the dark satellite images.

'They—they did it!' Laura said hoarsely beside him.

Howard's pulse accelerated as another window flashed open on the monitor to the right. It was filled with a second array of feeds.

'Jordan, Eva, are you seeing this?' he said between numb lips.

'Yes,' Jordan replied on the Sumava link, his eyes bright with excitement.

Their elation faded when they finally registered the scenes of devastation being transmitted from the security cameras inside the underground port and the weapons base. Though they knew the battles had been taking place, they had been unable to see any signs of the conflict from the satellite imaging of the nocturnal landscape.

'Bloody hellfire,' Dimitri murmured.

Victor scowled on the video link from Vienna.

Laura rose awkwardly to her feet.

'Are those—?'

Acid burned the back of Howard's throat as he gazed at the still figures visible through the smoke and fire dotting the underground complexes. It was several seconds before he saw movement on one of the cameras.

Howard's heart struck up a rapid tempo against his ribs as he zoomed in on the feed.

A figure in a black combat uniform stepped over a body in the security room of the weapons base and headed over to a computer. He removed something from a pouch at his waist, plugged it into one of the ports, and started working the keyboard.

Howard jumped when a call rang through the speakers in

the bunker. He swiped his fingers on the track pad and held his breath as a new window popped up on the main monitor.

'This is US Army Special Forces Lieutenant Malcolm Henderson,' the man in the security room said briskly on the video link. He dabbed at the trickle of blood coursing from his split lip. 'Your friends said to give you a buzz.'

'Where are they?' Alarm raised the pitch of Laura's voice. 'Are they okay?'

Henderson dipped his chin. 'They're fine, ma'am. They're on their way to the main research facility as we speak. We'll be following them once the rest of the cavalry arrives from the Sixth Fleet to help us secure the prisoners here and at the underground station on the coast.'

Relief flooded Howard. 'Ethan and Conrad managed to seize the port?'

Henderson raised an eyebrow. 'You mean the Power Ranger and the Snake Guy? Yeah, they did. Snake Guy took care of some of my injured men before he and the Power Ranger left with the scary chick and the guy with the broadsword. They should be getting there anytime now, along with their troops.' He glanced to his right. 'I've connected your device to the mainframe. Don't know whether it's working.'

Jordan had handed Asgard two USB keys to give to Ethan and Alexa for their mission. He'd placed the devices inside Faraday bags to protect them from the effects of the EMP grenades they would inevitably have to use against the super soldiers.

Eva's voice came over the video link from Sumava. 'I'm in the research facility's network. We'll have visual shortly.'

'Thanks,' Howard said to Henderson.

The lieutenant grunted and disconnected. A third set of

camera feeds flashed across the central monitor seconds later. Howard's stomach plummeted.

'Oh God,' Laura whimpered.

Howard reached out and took her hand blindly, his gaze riveted to the unholy battle playing out across multiple levels through the main research facility, where humans and Immortals clashed against an army of super soldiers.

'It's okay.' Howard swallowed. 'They—they'll be—'

'No,' Laura moaned. 'My water's just broke!'

Howard turned. His jaw dropped when he saw the wetness coursing down Laura's legs and followed it to the darkening patch on the floor.

'Shit.'

Laura winced, bit her lip, and doubled over, an agonizing groan leaving her throat. Her nails dug into Howard's hand.

'Laura! Are you okay?' Victor called out stiffly across the video link.

'Do I look okay, Victor?' Laura snarled.

Pain drained the color from her face in the next instant. She cried out and sat down heavily in the chair.

'I—I'll call an ambulance!' Howard twisted on his heels and reached for his cell.

'There's no time!' Laura's panicked gaze moved to the blood soaking the bottom of her dress. 'This kid is coming and I'm bleeding. We need to get him out, *now!*'

Howard grabbed the internal phone, cursed as he fumbled and dropped it, and snatched it off the floor. 'Rosa, I need you in the bunker! And bring towels! Yeah, it's the baby!' He paused and scowled. 'What the hell would we need a drink for?' A grimace twisted his lips a couple of seconds later. 'Oh. Sure.' He glanced from the laboring woman glaring at him to the bloody scenes being projected from the other side of the planet. 'I could do with a Scotch right about now.'

CHAPTER FORTY

JESSICA WU STRODE BRISKLY BETWEEN ROWS OF GLASS TANKS, fingers dancing on the screen of her tablet. The scientists stationed in the lab hurried after her, their eyes wide with alarm and fear.

'These men aren't ready for this!' one of them said. 'They have yet to complete the maturation process.'

'I don't care about that,' Wu snapped. 'We are under attack right now and we need them to be operational.'

'But we won't have time to battle-test them,' another scientist said in a low voice. 'You need to stop—'

Wu stopped abruptly, whirled around, and jabbed a finger in the man's chest. *'You have the audacity to dictate what I can and cannot do?!'*

The scientist blanched and hunched his shoulders. 'N—no. I'm just concerned about—'

'I am the one who created these soldiers.' Wu straightened and glared at the group of silent men and women watching her warily. 'They *will* execute the function and duties I brought them into this world to perform!'

Beeps sounded around them as the water levels inside the tanks started to drop, the chemical-rich fluid draining through the sluices at the bottom. The monitors attached to the life pods showed steadily rising vital signs as the super soldiers inside them started to awaken.

A crash sounded from the direction of the lab's main entrance. It was followed by a shocked scream. Wu frowned and headed rapidly up the aisle. She turned the corner, gasped, and staggered to a stop.

Lily and Tomas Soul stepped over the buckled, steel panel of the door they had ripped out of the wall. Visible in the passage behind them were Ivan Vlašic and King Bastian.

The two Immortals were not alone.

Rage burned through Wu when she saw the hordes of small, half-naked figures wrapped in blankets.

The children!

Her fury escalated as alarms started going off across the lab. She glanced at the closest tanks and swore. The computers and life monitors were frozen, the super soldiers' revival process disabled by whatever unearthly powers Lily and Tomas Soul were wielding.

Wu snatched the gun at her waist and pointed it at the two figures walking steadily toward her. White fog filled her mind a second after her finger found the trigger. The sound of the shot leaving the muzzle of the pistol reached her dimly as she collapsed to the floor.

The last thing she saw before darkness claimed her was the bullet smashing into an invisible force ten feet from Tomas Soul and dropping harmlessly to the ground.

IVAN KEPT ONE ARM AROUND THE SHIVERING CHILDREN CLOSEST to him and held a sleeping baby to his chest. He looked at King Bastian, who was cradling another infant. Others were in the arms of the hundreds of silent figures crowding the corridor behind them.

Footsteps sounded from inside the lab. Lily and Tomas emerged from the shadowy depths of the chamber. Ivan swallowed.

He knew he would never forget what he had witnessed them do for as long as he lived.

The unholy powers they had unleashed on the level below. The brutal display of force and the utter fearlessness they had shown in the face of the monstrous creatures who had opposed them. The psychic outburst that had nearly robbed him and King Bastian of consciousness as they crouched on the floor, battered by the tempest of unearthly energies roaring through the lab where the super soldier children and embryos slept inside their prisons.

It was after they had defeated their enemy that Ivan had seen the other side of their terrifying abilities.

The tenderness in Lily's eyes as she started awakening the innocent creatures inside the tanks. The compassion on Tomas's face as he wrapped a blanket around the first boy, one who stood five inches taller than him.

It was thanks to their calming psychic influence that the confusion and fear those children had experienced upon their revival had abated. It was also because of the twins' guidance that the newly liberated prisoners had helped them rescue their peers from the other life pods.

Lily's sorrow had filled the chamber when she had gazed at the small creatures they had discovered at the back of the lab, her emotions saturating the air to such an extent that Ivan had found himself choking back tears. There was little they could do to save the hundreds of unformed embryos and fetuses inside the tiny tanks crowding the rear wall, nor the scores of others who failed to wake up in the larger tanks. It was with reluctance and a rare expression of anger that she had turned off their life support.

Ivan startled when she stepped out of the lab and spoke.

'There's an emergency exit at the end of this corridor.' Lily indicated the north end of the passage. 'It leads to an elevator that will take you to the fifth floor. Beyond it, you'll find stairs that go all the way up to the outside of this facility. There's a building housing snow vehicles some thirty feet from where you'll emerge.'

Tomas glanced at the children and the babies.

'Take them and leave,' he told Ivan and King Bastian quietly. 'Go west, until you reach a crescent-shaped ridge. Wait for us there.'

King Bastian stiffened at the little boy's words. Ivan blinked and gaped.

'What—what are you talking about?' he spluttered. 'We're leaving together!'

Lily shook her head, a sad smile curving her lips. 'No. There is much for us to do, still.'

Tomas glanced at the ceiling. They could hear distant explosions from the upper levels of the structure.

'Our family and our friends need us,' he said.

Ivan's heart thundered in his chest as he watched them, frustration burning through him. Even though he was the leader of a race of Immortals, he had never felt so powerless in his life as he did in this moment.

He crouched down to their level. 'I—'

Lily moved toward him and touched his face. 'It will be okay.' She pressed her lips to his skin.

Ivan blinked at the warmth of her touch and felt a strange peace sweep through him.

Lily stepped over to King Bastian. He leaned down and she kissed his cheek. Surprise widened his eyes when she hooked her arms around his neck and hugged him tightly.

'Goodbye for now, King,' she said tremulously.

King Bastian straightened and stared at her, a strange expression on his face. A silent moment passed between the little girl and the ancient Immortal.

'Thank you,' the king finally said. 'For all that you have done. And all that you will do.' He bowed his head.

Lily nodded and bowed back. A noise came from the south end of the corridor. They turned and watched the figures heading toward them.

'Go,' Tomas said, his voice hardening. 'Now.'

Ivan hesitated before following King Bastian. They led the children swiftly down the passage and soon reached a turn.

Ivan stopped. 'I really don't think we—'

'They will be alright, child of Crovir,' King Bastian said calmly.

'How can you know that?' Ivan said, his fingers tightening on the infant in his arms.

'Can you not tell?' King Bastian cast a final glance at the two small figures outside the lab, his expression a mixture of sadness and hope. 'They are both of this world and another. One beyond the understanding of men like you and me.'

Ivan clenched his jaw and took one last look at Lily and Tomas Soul where they stood facing the horde of giant super soldiers closing in on them. He twisted on his heels and headed after the king, his heart heavy with guilt and anger.

CHAPTER FORTY-ONE

VLADO SCOWLED AS HE SCRUTINIZED THE CAMERA FEEDS ON THE flat-screen monitor on the wall.

Their enemy had reached the sixth level of the facility.

'How? How the hell are they beating the super soldiers?' He glared at the Crovir Immortals who formed part of his security team. 'Did Storm generate another lightning strike?'

'No, sir. But they're using EMP grenades to disable the liquid-armor suits.'

Vlado gritted his teeth and leaned his hands on the workstation of the secondary command post on Level Eight. Crovir stood silently beside him, his pale eyes impassive as he watched the battle playing out on the screen.

'Still,' Vlado said, 'even without that armor, our men should be able to—'

'It's her, sir.' The Immortal who had spoken zoomed in on a camera on the fifth level. 'It's Olivia Ashkarov. She's already knocked out every Immortal and half-breed she's come across since she entered the complex. It looks like she's doing the same thing to the super soldiers.'

Something twisted painfully inside Vlado's chest as he regarded the woman responsible for his father's murder.

She's here!

Blood splattered Olivia Ashkarov's combat uniform as she wielded her sword, the blade cutting ruthlessly into the flesh of the enemy before her, her expression cold and focused. At her side were Asgard Godard, Madeleine Black, and Anna Soul.

Although Vlado had learned what had happened in Mongolia, he had refused to believe Ashkarov was solely responsible for the fate of the super soldiers stationed there.

'We've bioengineered our army to be resistant to psychic attacks like hers. There's no way—'

'Your men are correct, Vlado,' Crovir said quietly.

Vlado stilled, his gaze swiveling back to the monitor. His stomach dropped when he saw a group of giant super soldiers appear before Ashkarov. Lines furrowed her brow as she raised a hand toward them. They faltered and swayed before dropping to the floor, their weapons falling from their grasp.

It was as if she'd flipped a switch inside their heads.

Impossible!

Fury filled Vlado as he watched her step over the unconscious men. He whirled around, unsheathed the sword that had belonged to his father, and headed for the exit.

'Take King Crovir to the escape tunnel and wait for me!' he barked at his men.

CROVIR WATCHED VLADO STORM OUT OF THE COMMAND POST.

Although he was angry at what was unfolding in the facility and felt nothing but contempt for the enemy who had dared thwart the plans he and the descendant of his son Kronos had been concocting, he was surprised at how much calmer he felt compared to the younger man.

I wonder. Is it because I have lived longer than him and seen more death and destruction in my lifetimes than he ever will?

'If you would like to come with us, sir,' one of the Immortals said, distracting him from his thoughts.

Crovir dipped his chin and was turning to follow his escort when something caught his attention.

He froze, his eyes riveted to the top right corner of the monitor on the wall. 'Where is that?'

The guard's eyes widened when he registered what had captured Crovir's gaze. 'That's on Level Five, sir.'

Crovir frowned. 'Show me how to get there.'

'BEHIND YOU!' ANATOLE SHOUTED.

Lucas ducked, felt a knife hum a couple of inches above his head, and drove the wakizashi into the chest of the super soldier at his back. The man grunted, his expression vacant. Lucas twisted on his heels and slashed his throat with the katana. The super soldier thudded to the ground.

'That was close,' Reid said several feet to his left.

Blood and sweat streamed down the former Marine's face and his chest heaved.

Lucas scanned the armory, tension humming in his veins. Although they had overpowered the men in the command post on Level One, the super soldier army was proving to be as formidable a force to deal with as they'd anticipated it would be. The human troops still standing at their side were visibly tiring and even the Bastian Hunters were not immune to the devastating fighting power of the bioengineered monsters they kept coming up against.

Much to Lucas's frustration, the enemy's numbers had increased exponentially the farther down the facility they went and they had been unable to descend beyond their current location on the seventh floor.

A figure charged at him from the right. Lucas steeled himself, blocked the rapid blows arcing toward his head and chest, and side-kicked the super soldier in the abdomen. The man slumped for a second.

It was all Lucas needed to drive the katana through his heart.

A choking noise brought his head around. Alarm stabbed through him. One of the giants had grasped Reid by the head and was lifting him into the air.

Anatole scowled, took a running jump, and drove his knee in the super soldier's right loin. The giant's free fist connected brutally with the Immortal's chest as he dropped back down toward the floor. A grunt left Anatole's throat as he sailed toward a wall fifteen feet away. He smashed into it, his skull cracking against the concrete.

Lucas yanked his sword out of the chest of the dying man at the end of his blade and headed resolutely for Reid and the giant. He swooped beneath the super soldier's swinging punch and brought the katana up toward his rib cage.

The giant cast Reid violently aside and blocked the blade inches from his body, grasping the razor-edged sword with his bare hand. He turned to face Lucas, blood pouring through his fist. Lucas glimpsed the blow coming from his right, leapt backward, and cursed when he stumbled over a body on the ground. Movement blurred below him.

Air locked painfully in his throat when the giant's knee made contact with his stomach. Lucas doubled over, twisted out of the way of a second kick, and gasped when his attacker's fingers closed around his windpipe. The super soldier knocked the swords out of his hands and hoisted him up.

Lucas choked as his feet left the ground. He grappled with the giant's unyielding wrist, folded his knees to his chest, and kicked him hard in the gut.

He might as well have hit a wall for all the reaction his attacker showed.

The giant lifted him higher before bringing him down savagely to the ground.

Black spots exploded in front of Lucas's eyes as his back struck the concrete. The giant followed him to the floor and closed his other hand around his throat.

Lucas bucked and heaved, a buzzing noise rising in his skull. He reached out blindly for his fallen swords as he struggled for air. Reid staggered into view from behind the super soldier, a gun in hand. The blasts of the shots reached Lucas dimly.

His fingers found the handle of the wakizashi. He brought the sword up and stabbed the super soldier in the heart.

The giant froze and blinked. He looked down at where the blade had entered his body, stared at Lucas blankly, and tightened his hold on his throat.

The buzzing sound filled Lucas's world. Darkness swamped his vision.

Then the pressure around his neck eased.

Air whistled in and out of his swollen windpipe as he gasped and took deep, shuddering breaths.

The giant gazed dully at his hands, which were slowly

uncurling from around Lucas's throat. Muscles bulged in his arms and neck as he attempted to resist the unholy force moving his body against his will.

'Miss us?' someone shouted.

Relief flooded Lucas when he beheld Conrad, Ethan, and Zachary approaching with a troop of human soldiers, Freemasons, and monks.

Ethan narrowed his eyes at the super soldier above Lucas. He flexed the fingers of his left hand and moved his arm in a sweeping motion.

The giant soared off Lucas and plowed into the concrete wall Anatole had hit.

The Immortal had been raising himself slowly from the ground. He startled, his gaze riveted to the bloodied figure a few feet from him.

'Well, that ain't pretty.' Anatole grimaced at Ethan. 'And, hey, a heads up would be great next time.'

Someone loomed over Lucas where he lay on his back.

'You look like shit,' Alexa stated bluntly.

Lucas smiled faintly and took her hand. She yanked him up onto his feet.

'It's good to see you.' He glanced from her to the others. 'I take it this means—'

'We've secured the other facilities,' Conrad confirmed with a brisk nod.

Zachary's face lit up. 'Looks like the rest of the cavalry made it too.'

Lucas followed his gaze to the far side of the armory. A thrill rushed through him. Anna was walking through a doorway with Olivia, Asgard, and Madeleine, a contingent of Bastian Hunters and human soldiers in tow.

A pair of freight elevators slid open eighteen feet to their right.

Lucas's pulse stuttered as a swarm of giant super soldiers exited the steel cabins.

CHAPTER FORTY-TWO

Ivan leaned over the metal banister and peered up the stairwell.

'Only two floors to go,' he said encouragingly.

He smiled tightly at the children spread out over the levels beneath him and the Immortal bringing up the rear of their ragtag group.

Ivan took the hand of the little girl next to him as he continued climbing the steps, an infant in his other arm. The child's fingers twitched in his grip at the distant clamor of gunshots and explosions echoing up the concrete shaft from the battle raging inside the facility.

Ivan's thoughts went to the two children he had abandoned near the bottom of the structure. He glanced at the girl beside him.

The least I can do for them is help these creatures they so desperately wanted to save.

The final landing came into view twenty feet above him.

Relief flooded Ivan. The exit was a short distance beyond it.

A loud bang resonated in the stairwell, startling him. The girl flinched beside him. Ivan stopped and looked over the railing. He stiffened.

A man stood on the third landing, a sword in hand. A door swung closed behind him.

He was tall and dressed in a similar fashion to King Bastian, the hem of his antiquated robes brushing the floor. His pale eyes shifted briefly to the children and Ivan before focusing on the king behind them.

A chill ran down Ivan's spine. He knew instinctively he was looking at the Immortal whose race he was currently the leader of.

King Bastian handed the infant in his arms to one of the older children. 'Take him and go.'

The boy hesitated before nodding. He held the baby close to his chest and herded the younger children around him up the stairs.

King Bastian turned to face King Crovir.

'This is between you and me, brother,' he said calmly.

King Crovir frowned. 'Indeed, brother.'

He removed a second sword from his waist and tossed it at King Bastian. The latter caught the blade expertly in one hand.

Ivan glanced at the exit, his heart slamming against his ribs.

'Leave, child of Crovir,' King Bastian said softly. He unsheathed the sword and grasped the handle in a double-handed grip, his gaze never leaving his brother's face. 'I entrust the fate of these young ones to you.'

Ivan cast a final glance at the Immortals on the landing beneath him before gritting his teeth and starting up the final steps, the children at his heels.

❄

ALEXA BLOCKED A SWIRL OF FISTS WITH HER SAI DAGGERS. 'WE'RE not getting anywhere fighting like this! We have to do this together!'

Lucas and Conrad nodded, sweat beading on their faces and blood dripping off the edges of their blades. They regrouped in the middle of the armory with Ethan and Zachary, Reid and Anatole bringing up the rear with their allies.

At the opposite end of the floor, on the other side of a sea of super soldiers, Olivia and Asgard were engaged in a brutal battle with the giants, Anna, Madeleine, and their comrades at their side.

Alexa swooped beneath a high kick, stabbed her attacker in the heart and throat, and studied the layout of the battlefield.

'Ethan, you and I should take point. Conrad, Lucas, you flank us.' She narrowed her eyes. 'We have to break through this crowd and join up with Olivia and Asgard's troops. Our best chance of defeating them is for all of us to work together in formation.'

Ethan's elemental power brushed against Alexa when he came up beside her. Just as she could feel Mila's life force buzzing in her veins, so could Alexa sense Jared's presence in the potent pulses surging across her skin from the man standing a couple of feet away.

Alexa tightened her grip on her sais. Heat rose inside her chest and spread through her limbs, bringing with it a flood of unearthly strength. The ground shook beneath her feet as the ungodly force overflowed and radiated from her body.

She exchanged glances with Ethan, Conrad, and Lucas.

In that moment, a flutter of memories echoed through her from Mila. Of hundreds of battles similarly fought, in distant lands and under strange skies, in times long gone. Of a connection between warriors who had navigated centuries of conflict imposed upon them by their fathers and kings. Of an eternity of devotion and affection between siblings and cousins in the face of constant strife and adversity. Of a bond between kin that had seen them through the most challenging and epic war they had ever fought, one that had seen the end of their Immortal reign and the beginning of the era of men.

Ethan's eyes glittered intensely as he studied the army before them, his gaze lingering on the far side of the armory and his soulmate. 'Are you ready?'

There was an echo in his voice from the soul who now lived inside him.

Alexa smiled fiercely.

'Yes,' she and Mila replied.

OLIVIA SWOOPED BENEATH A VICIOUS PUNCH. SHE DEFLECTED THE next blow with her sword and blasted the super soldier attacking her with a wave of elemental energy.

She sensed Ethan and her cousins' powers surging on the other side of the warehouse as they plowed into the mass of super soldiers separating them.

'We can't keep this up much longer!' Asgard said grimly a short distance to her left.

Olivia glanced in the direction of his gaze. A group of Marines and Bastian Hunters had been driven to the ground by three giant super soldiers some twenty feet behind them.

Navia's voice resonated inside her mind. *He is right. The men fighting with you are beyond exhausted. We need to finish this. Soon.*

Olivia dipped her chin. Just as she had done innumerable times in the past hour, she sought out the shimmering lines of power enclosing her heart and drew upon their unholy energy, the soul inside her lending her her strength once more.

Dozens of super soldiers collapsed as she discharged another brutal psychic assault that tore through the barriers of their minds and shut down their consciousness.

Olivia felt the spirits of the human soldiers and Immortals around her rally, their resolve strengthening despite the ceaseless onslaught of the unnatural army they battled against. She clenched her jaw and steeled herself for another psychic blast.

A sword hummed past her head and sliced away a lock of her hair.

VLADO FROWNED AS THE WOMAN LEAPT OUT OF THE WAY OF HIS next strike.

He brought his father's blade up and around once more. Satisfaction rushed through him when the wicked edge carved a crimson line across the flesh of her arm.

Pain flashed briefly in Olivia Ashkarov's eyes. It was replaced by a gleam of determination.

Pressure surged against Vlado's skull.

He glared at her in the face of her psychic attack. 'You will not defeat me!'

His fingers tightened on the handle of the sword and he aimed it at her once more.

Sparks erupted between them when their blades clashed.

She stared at him from the other side of their kissing swords, surprise dawning on her face.

'You are Jonah Krondike's son.'

Vlado blinked. He was certain she had not broken through his mental shields.

Lines furrowed her brow. 'You have his eyes.'

Vlado's pulse spiked, anger filling him with every beat of his heart. He pressed down with his sword and snarled. She grunted, her knees buckling under the sheer physical strength of his attack.

A heavy weight gripped his temples. Her eyes widened.

'You are like them!' she said hoarsely, horror tainting her voice as she glanced at the giant super soldiers around them.

Vlado felt the rigid walls protecting his mind waver under her assault. He took a shallow breath and concentrated on slowing his heartbeat, like Jessica Wu had taught him. It was a moment before he felt it.

A power that was his own. One created by a century of endless experiments and augmented by the drugs Jessica Wu had invented especially for him. A shudder raced across his skin as his body changed, his limbs hardening and filling with a deadly force.

'Not quite!' he sneered.

The sword blurred in Vlado's hands as he attacked again. She gasped and countered, her blade juddering in her hands under the violent impact. A thrill of excitement darted through him when his blade found the flesh of her left thigh. She winced and stumbled.

Vlado brought the sword up toward her heart.

Metal clanged before the blade could sink between her ribs.

Vlado froze. He turned his head slowly and stared into the blazing eyes of Asgard Godard, the older man's knuckles white on the handle of the arming sword with which he'd blocked the fatal swing.

Rage erupted inside Vlado. He growled, twisted on his heels, and brought his father's blade round toward the man who had dared challenge him.

A third psychic wave pressed against his skull as his blade clashed with Godard's.

Redness descended across Vlado's vision. He stepped up his attack, a roar of fury leaving his throat.

Godard blocked the first four strikes. The fifth found the skin of his left arm. The sixth sliced a red line across his abdomen.

The seventh pierced his heart.

CHAPTER FORTY-THREE

Lily faltered and closed her eyes briefly as the agonizing pain tore through her.

Tomas stumbled at her side, his anguish echoing across their connection.

She clenched her teeth and glared at the super soldier army standing in front of the command post on Level Eight.

We have to get to them!

Numbness bloomed in the center of Asgard's chest.

Madeleine screamed somewhere on his left.

He stared at the man in front of him and gripped the blade buried in his heart. He yanked it out of his flesh with a grunt, the sword cutting into his hands.

Olivia's eyes widened in incomprehension. It took a couple of heartbeats for her to register what had just transpired. Blood dripped from Asgard's palms where he held the blade that had impaled him.

Horror filled her. The soul inside her trembled.

'Noooooo!'

Olivia's scream of outrage washed over Ethan. He blinked and looked around wildly, his gaze seeking the woman both he and Jared loved.

For a moment, he could not understand what he was seeing.

A tortured howl sounded from the figure beside him. The floor cracked around Alexa as she charged through the super soldiers, her eyes glittering with anguish and rage.

He followed in her steps, his kin at his side.

Vlado whipped the sword out of Godard's grip and brought it up to slash his neck.

The blade shook violently as it struck an invisible force inches from Godard's skin.

Vlado looked past the Immortal to the woman behind him. Fear quickened his pulse.

Olivia Ashkarov's eyes glowed with a most terrible light. She raised a hand, her fingers trembling.

Vlado gasped as the sword twisted and crumpled in his grasp, the metal folding in on itself as if it were paper. Coldness filled his skull. He stumbled back, turned, and melted into the crowd of super soldiers.

❄

MADELEINE CAUGHT ASGARD BEFORE HE COLLAPSED. SHE wrapped her arms around him and lowered him awkwardly to the ground, her heart and that of the soul within her breaking and turning to ash inside her chest. She pressed her hands to his wound, tears blurring her vision.

Anna and Olivia dropped to their knees next to them, their tormented expressions mirroring the agony tearing her apart.

'Why?' Olivia said brokenly. 'You shouldn't have—'

Asgard raised bloodied fingers and pressed them against Olivia's lips while Anna gently explored the cut on his body.

'Don't say that,' he said hoarsely.

Asgard blinked as Madeleine's hot tears fell on his face. His eyes darkened as he turned his head and met her gaze, his look filled with so much love her breath locked in her throat.

He stroked her cheek. 'It's okay.'

Madeleine scowled and shook her head. 'No, it's not!'

Anna stiffened. She was trying to stem the crimson tide staining the floor beneath Asgard. Color drained from her face when she finally registered the truth in Madeleine's eyes.

Olivia froze, her expression crumbling.

'No,' she whispered.

'Yes!' Madeleine sobbed. 'This is—this will be his seventeenth—'

Anna twisted, her gaze frantically searching the battleground.

'*Conrad!*' she screamed.

The ground trembled under them. The sea of fighting figures parted ahead, the super soldiers falling under the invisible forces battering them. Ethan and Alexa came into view.

'I'm here!' Conrad shouted.

He emerged from behind them with Lucas and Zachary.

'There's still time!' Anna told Conrad as they slid to a stop and dropped to the floor beside Asgard. 'His body's gone into shock but I think you can still heal him!'

She lifted her hands from Asgard's chest. Blood pulsed and flowed from the cut.

Conrad pressed his fingers to the wound while Alexa and Ethan kept the super soldiers at bay around them. Lucas gripped Asgard's hand tightly, his face full of emotion.

Asgard gasped and shuddered as Conrad's healing energy entered his body. Sweat pooled and dripped down Conrad's face. He closed his eyes and clenched his jaw.

Asgard wrapped his fingers around Conrad's left wrist. 'I'm too far gone for that.'

Conrad grunted and blinked his eyes open.

He scowled. 'I can still give you a piece of my soul!'

Asgard looked over at Alexa and Ethan where they stood battling their enemy. 'No, you need to find the children.' He frowned at Conrad, Olivia, and Lucas. 'Promise me! That you will find them first!'

Lucas hesitated before nodding reluctantly. His tormented gaze moved to Anna and Zachary. 'Stay with him.'

They nodded, their faces full of sorrow.

Madeleine stared unblinkingly into Asgard's eyes as his niece and nephews rose to their feet and joined the fray.

He smiled at her. 'You died before me, in the past.'

Madeleine choked back tears and rubbed her face angrily, not wanting to miss her last moments with the man who had claimed her heart in this life and the one she had lived before. Anna laid trembling fingers on her shoulder.

'Did it suck as much as this does right now?' Madeleine said tremulously.

Asgard gasped and chuckled. 'Yes.'

A raspy cough left his throat.

He wrenched his gaze from her face and stared at the Immortals fighting around them. 'Look at them. Aren't they glorious?'

Madeleine bit her lip and glanced at the indomitable figures who had encircled them, protecting them from the epic battle raging across the seventh floor. 'That they are.'

Madeleine stiffened as the body in her arms went limp. She looked down at Asgard in time to see his eyes flutter closed and his lips part on his final breath.

The marked souls shuddered as their bond with Romerus shattered and dissolved and the one whom he dwelled inside passed from this world.

They opened their mouths and howled, their agony and fury resonating through the bodies of the men and women they now lived within.

Fire exploded inside Olivia's chest, her cousins' and her soulmate's cries echoing the scream of rage on her lips. The golden lines around her heart bloomed and expanded as Navia merged her soul with hers, filling her blood and her body with all of her power. Heat flowed through her and with it came an unholy radiance that danced along her skin.

The same light fluttered over the marked Immortals around

her, their bodies resonating with their own formidable energy, which melded with that of the ancient souls inside them.

MADELEINE GASPED AS THE TERRIBLE PRESSURE ERUPTED AND forced her to the ground. The Immortals and humans helping them fell around her. Reid and Anatole staggered and dropped to their knees on her right, their bodies similarly unable to withstand the savage storm raging across the armory. Even Anna and Zachary bowed under the tempest.

Madeleine clenched her teeth and hunkered down over Asgard. She lifted her head to witness the incredible scene unfolding before her eyes and was filled with awe.

ALEXA MOVED ACROSS THE FLOOR, THE POWER THRUMMING through her so forcefully that her teeth vibrated in her jaw, Mila's fury a river of fire in her blood and bones.

The world shivered and shook as she and her cousins carved a deadly path through the enemy before them, their skin shimmering with an uncanny brightness, their bodies consumed by the blazing energy burning inside them.

Olivia struck first, her psychokinetic blasts driving scores of super soldiers to their knees. The ones who did not fall faltered and froze under Ethan's elemental energy. Lucas and Alexa weaved and twisted through the overpowered men, their blades entering their enemies' hearts and the pulse points in their necks in lightning-fast moves. Conrad moved alongside them with his double-bladed spear and simultaneously healed any injuries they suffered at the hands of their enemy, his fleeting touches reenergizing them as he mended their bruises and cuts.

They advanced as one, their movements flawless and seamlessly coordinated. They had decimated a third of the super soldier army when they saw him.

The reborn souls and the Immortals they dwelled in froze for a moment when they finally spotted the man they had been seeking. Sixty feet ahead, Vlado Krall stood inside a thick ring of super soldiers. They started toward him, their steps accelerating as they plowed through the masses separating them.

A crack appeared in the east wall of the armory.

Lucas lurched and slowed as violent tremors shook the chamber.

The fracture widened and multiplied until the entire surface became a giant jigsaw.

A twenty-foot section of the wall exploded in the next moment. Lumps of concrete the size of his head flew inward and slammed into the super soldiers gathered at that end of the floor.

More super soldiers came into view through the jagged opening. Lucas blinked.

The giants were moving backward, boots skidding and scraping across the ground, muscles bulging in their limbs and necks as they strained against the invisible force pushing at them.

A gasp left Olivia's lips. Fierce joy filled her face as she studied the strange phenomenon with bright eyes. Lucas's heart stuttered when he finally spotted what she had sensed.

The sea of super soldiers parted.

There, advancing inside the room with unwavering steps, their eyes and skin alight with a terrible glow, pulses of breathtaking energy pounding out of their tiny bodies, were Lily and Tomas.

CHAPTER FORTY-FOUR

LAURA BIT HER LIP AND GROANED AS THE CONTRACTION TORE through her. She knew something was wrong from the amount of blood she was losing. Howard and Rosa knelt on the floor between her legs, their faces pale. Rosa stiffened.

Laura's heart twisted at the sight of the fear that flashed in her eyes. 'What?'

'He's breech,' Rosa said between pinched lips.

Laura dropped her head back on Bernard's lap and panted.

'He wasn't meant to be!' she gasped. 'Seriously, this kid's not even born yet and he's already causing trouble, just like his damn father!'

'And his mother,' Howard muttered.

Laura cut her eyes to him before looking at the workstation to her left. She could only see the top of the monitors from where she lay on the floor of the bunker.

'Eva, what's happening over there?' she barked.

'Do you really wish to know that at this moment in time?'

the AI replied. 'You appear to be in a lot of discomfort. Maybe you should—'

'Eva, I swear to God, not only will I ground this kid for life if he doesn't get his ass out of me soon, I'll ground you too, AI or not, if you do not answer my question *right now!*'

A muffled snort sounded in the diplomatic pause that followed.

'I know that was you, Jordan!' Laura snapped.

'The satellites are picking up quake activity over the primary site,' Eva said reluctantly.

Howard's head snapped around. 'What?'

Victor swore across the video call from Vienna. 'I have to go. We have Crovir Hunters surrounding our headquarters.'

RIPPLES MOVED ACROSS THE LANDSCAPE. IVAN STEERED THE SNOW vehicle around a bump in the ice and glanced in the side mirror. His breath faltered when he looked past the trucks he was towing to the pale, camouflaged dome of the main research facility half a mile behind.

Snow and ice trembled and danced at its base as it shook.

He swallowed and peered ahead to the west, dawn painting vivid streaks of pink across the sky at his back. A ridge appeared in the distance.

Ivan clenched his jaw and floored the accelerator. The children in the vehicle's cabin held onto their seats and the sleeping infants in their arms.

THE SWORD HUMMED PAST BASTIAN'S HEAD. HE STUMBLED INTO the wall of the stairwell and narrowly blocked the next blow.

Crovir sneered on the other side of their clashing blades and pressed into him. 'I was always the better fighter of the two of us, brother!'

Bastian gritted his teeth, his knuckles whitening on the handle of the sword as he resisted Crovir. He snarled and shoved him back toward the banister.

Crovir narrowed his eyes, slid the edge of his sword along Bastian's in a shower of sparks, and slipped out of the way.

Bastian stumbled. He gasped as he found himself leaning precariously over the railing. Motion blurred to his right. He missed the swinging blade by a hairbreadth.

Crovir swore as his sword clanged against the metal banister. Bastian twisted on his heels and deflected his strikes once more.

Sorrow surged through him when he glimpsed the deadly gleam in Crovir's eyes. He recalled another fight then, one that had taken place in another land and time, when he had been bested by his older brother in the final battle of their former lives.

He truly means to kill me this time.

Faces fluttered across his inner vision. His father Romerus, who had died at the hands of Crovir. His niece Mila, who had been accused of a crime she did not commit and been forced to stain her hands with her father's blood in order to stop his madness. Lily and Tomas Soul, who had been taken by force from their home by one of Crovir's descendants intent on returning the old king to his throne and the empire of the Immortals to its former glory.

Resolve suddenly flooded Bastian. By engaging Crovir in a

fight, he had hoped to buy Ivan Vlašic and the children they had been trying to save time to escape. He knew he had achieved that goal. There was only one thing left to do.

This. This is for me, and for Mila and Romerus.

Bastian tightened his grip on his sword and started attacking his older brother in earnest. Surprise flared across Crovir's face.

Their blades met over and over again while violent tremors shook the underground structure, and dust and chunks of concrete rained down around them.

A BURST OF HAPPINESS OVERSHADOWED THE MISERY AND FURY IN Lily's heart when she saw her father and sensed her mother's presence at the other end of the armory. At their sides were the rest of her family and their friends.

Emotion choked her throat as she realized how many Immortals and humans had perished to get to them and stop the man who had started all of this. Tomas's power intensified beside her, his rage eclipsing his brief rush of joy and sadness. She followed his gaze to where Vlado Krall stood inside a deep circle of super soldiers eighty feet to their right.

He stared from them to the marked Immortals trying to reach him, his eyes full of anger and fear.

Lily moved with Tomas at her side. Their cadence remained steady as they made their way across the chamber, never slowing, nor faltering.

The super soldiers fell before and around them, minds shutting down and bodies toppling to the ground under a powerful wave of psychokinetic energy.

They focused on Vlado Krall's mental shields when they got closer to him.

Tomas frowned. *His mind is...different. Something's changed.*

Lily stared. Her twin was right. She could sense a strange force resonating inside Krall, one she had not felt before. It was dark. Man-made. Dangerous.

Tomas shivered when she reached across their bond and dipped into the blazing source of his powers. He opened up and met her halfway once he grasped her intent.

Forty feet ahead and to their left, Olivia stilled and looked their way. Understanding dawned on her face. She frowned and nodded once.

Lily stretched out her consciousness to her aunt's, drew on the ungodly energy glimmering around her heart, and clenched her jaw.

This stops now.

The three of them took a deep breath and let go.

Vlado Krall screamed as a dreadful pressure gripped his head. He clutched at his temples and choked on his breath as pain tore through him, filling his vision with red spots.

He was vaguely aware of the super soldiers encircling him collapsing like dominoes, their giant bodies hitting the floor with dull thuds. He stumbled back several steps and looked around, gaze frantically searching for an escape route, his reason fleeing as icy fingers clawed at the walls protecting his consciousness.

Vlado froze in the next instant, his heart lurching madly against his ribs as he struggled to grasp what he was seeing.

His entire army was falling.

He blinked, shook his head dazedly, and watched the last super soldiers drop like dead weights to his right.

Vlado stared at the figures left standing in the armory. Five across the floor from him and two smaller ones to his left.

For the first time in his Immortal life, he could taste defeat. Jonah Krondike's face rose before his eyes. Rage exploded inside him.

He scowled. *I will not go down without a fight!*

A voice echoed inside the confines of his head. *You will not die as easily as him.*

Vlado stiffened and turned to stare at Lily Soul. All it took was one look at her deadly expression for him to know it was her words he had just heard, and become bitterly aware that she had breached the barriers protecting his consciousness.

The howl of outrage building inside him was cut off abruptly by an invisible force. Unseen bands wrapped around his body and brought him down to his knees.

Vlado wheezed and fought for breath against the vise-like chain around his neck. There was movement in front of him. He clenched his teeth and slowly lifted his head, muscles straining as he resisted the unholy powers holding him hostage.

Alexa King reached him first, her daggers singing in her hands as she crossed the blades across his throat and slashed his flesh.

Conrad Greene came next, his spear spinning in his grip as he twisted around him and stabbed the base of his spine.

Lucas Soul was the final one to come up to him. He paused for a moment, his eyes full of fire, before impaling his heart with his sword.

Coldness swamped Vlado as Soul yanked the blade out of his chest. He crumpled slowly onto his side and glimpsed the reddening pool staining the ground beneath his body. Sound faded. The formidable figures before him blurred as his heart fluttered and slowed, each struggling beat sending forth waves of darkness that encroached across his vision until there was no more left to see.

CHAPTER FORTY-FIVE

THE SILENCE, WHEN IT CAME, WAS SUDDEN, AND ALL THE MORE shocking in its intensity.

A shudder raced through Lucas as he stared at the dead man before him. The unearthly power flowing inside his veins gradually faded. He dropped his blades, twisted on his heels, and headed for his children.

They met him halfway and leapt into his arms, their cries of *"Daddy!"* the sweetest sound he had ever heard. Intense joy flooded him as he held their warm bodies to his chest and kissed their faces.

'Dad, I can't breathe,' Tomas said with a choked chuckle.

Lucas grimaced and loosened his hold. 'Sorry.'

He lowered them carefully to the ground, his gaze shifting briefly to the fallen army strewn across the armory. He swallowed and studied his children for a long time, his mind full of conflicting emotions.

'That was—incredible,' he said finally.

Tomas grinned. 'It was pretty cool.'

Footsteps sounded behind Lucas. Alexa walked up to Tomas and ruffled his hair.

'Pretty cool is an understatement, kid,' she said gruffly.

'It was fu—freaking amazing is what it was,' Ethan stated bluntly.

'Yeah,' Conrad muttered with a smile.

Olivia knelt in front of Lily and Tomas and hugged them, tears streaming down her face. 'I'm glad you're safe.'

They embraced her just as fiercely.

'Thank you for lending us your strength,' Lily said.

Olivia nodded shakily and pressed her lips to her brow.

Groans sounded as the Immortals and humans who had been robbed of consciousness by the violent storm of supernatural energies that had been unleashed inside the armory started to awaken.

Lily and Tomas sobered when Zachary approached from the left, Asgard's body in his arms and Anna and Madeleine at his side. Reid and Anatole followed in their steps, their shock reflected on the faces of the men and women waking up around them.

Anna rushed to Lily and Tomas and closed her arms around them.

Conrad moved toward Zachary and the still figure in his hold.

'No,' Lily said.

He stopped and frowned at her over his shoulder, puzzled. 'But I need to—'

Tomas shook his head, his expression resolute. 'There is no time for that right now.'

He and Lily glanced at the cracks in the ceiling and the walls. Tremors shook the chamber and the distant crash of collapsing concrete echoed above them.

'This place is going to come down any moment now,' Lily said. 'We have to get everyone away from here.'

A man covered in dust headed across the floor toward them, blood trickling down the side of his head.

'Not that I'm ungrateful at being alive or anything,' Reynolds said dully, 'but what the hell just happened?'

THEY WERE NEARLY ON THE FIFTH FLOOR WHEN THEY FELT them.

Alexa's feet froze to the ground amid the tide of humans and Immortals surging rapidly for the exits. Ethan faltered beside her, his back stiffening and his gaze swinging to follow hers as she looked to the right.

Zachary slowed up ahead and looked over his shoulder. 'Alexa?'

Alexa turned and headed for a door at the other end of the concourse, her heart thundering in her chest, her body moving of its own volition. Fire licked the birthmark on her nape, the sensation eerily familiar. It was a couple of seconds before she realized Lucas, Olivia, and Conrad had fallen into step with her and Ethan, their faces reflecting the same conflicting feelings flooding her.

'Where are you going?' Anna called out behind them, panic lacing her voice.

'It's okay, Mom,' Lily said. 'They have…to do this.'

THEY MOVED AGAINST THE FLOW OF BODIES, UNHEEDING OF THE ground trembling beneath their feet and the fissures spreading

through the underground structure, the crowd parting unconsciously before them.

Shivers danced along flesh that did not belong to them as they shuddered under the weight of centuries of emotion and the memory of a battle that had torn them apart.

A FRACTURE SNAKED DOWN THE WALL NEXT TO THE DOOR WHEN they were ten feet from it. It expanded rapidly until it framed the opening.

Olivia gasped when the wall caved outward, taking the doorway with it. A yawning pit replaced it.

The sound of clashing blades echoed dimly above the rush of blood in her ears as she stepped to the edge of the drop with the others.

HAIRS ROSE ON THE BACK OF BASTIAN'S NECK. HE STILLED, HIS sword freezing against Crovir's as an uncanny feeling washed across his skin. Crovir stiffened where he stood opposite him, his knuckles blanching on the handle of his motionless blade, his eyes locked on something above them. Blood drained from his face and fear widened his pupils.

Bastian looked over his shoulder. His heart lurched painfully inside his chest at the sight that met his gaze.

One floor up, on the opposite side of a gaping chasm and what remained of the unstable stairwell, five figures stood staring down at them.

'Father,' one of them said tremulously, her green eyes glinting with unshed tears.

'Navia,' Bastian whispered.

He straightened and swallowed convulsively as he beheld his and Crovir's children, his gaze hungrily roaming their at once familiar and yet unknown faces, taking in every old and fresh detail, imprinting them in his mind forever more.

An animal sound escaped Crovir. He backed against the wall, his petrified gaze frozen on his last-born child.

THERE SHOULD HAVE BEEN RAGE. THERE SHOULD HAVE BEEN hate. Yet, in that timeless moment of remembrance, the only emotions that filled Alexa's heart to bursting from the soul within her were sorrow and regret. And love. Love for the one who had given her life.

Hands closed around hers. She glanced sideways and saw tears shimmer in the others' eyes as they stood with their fingers linked and beheld the kings.

A violent tremor shook the stairwell. Dust clouded the air as cracks tore through the walls of the shaft.

'Father!' Olivia screamed, fear coloring her voice.

A wave of psychokinetic energy burst forth from her body just as Ethan moved, his own hand rising to project the elemental power pulsing from his core.

'No!' Bastian shouted, alarmed. 'You cannot save us!'

They froze as one. Alexa's pulse stuttered.

'Go! Now! While you still have time!' Bastian said.

Crovir blinked and stared at his brother.

A tremulous smile curved Bastian's lips as he studied the five of them.

'Live.' His smile grew fierce. 'You have much left to fight for, so you must live.'

'Father,' Conrad said brokenly.

Bastian's eyes burned brightly. 'Now, go!'

THEY MADE IT OUT WITH SECONDS TO SPARE AND FOUND THE others loading their injured and unconscious into the snow vehicles and trucks they had found outside.

Anna rushed toward them. 'Are you alright? What hap—?'

The rest of her words were drowned out as the facility finally caved in. The earth shook and rumbled for long minutes under fountaining clouds of snow and ice. When the billows settled, they revealed a crater where the research complex once stood.

Tears trembled on Lily's eyelashes. 'The kings.'

Tomas reached out and took her hand, his eyes dark with sorrow.

The color drained from Olivia's face in the next instant. Her gaze swung from the crater before them, to the north and east.

Ethan frowned and stepped toward her.

'Livvy?' He froze, his face pale. 'Shit.'

'What's wrong?' Lucas said tensely.

A muscle jumped in Ethan's jaw as Olivia turned and looked at them, horror painted across her features. She had projected her thoughts to him across their bond.

'Vlado Krall had a remote control on him,' he said stiffly. 'He activated it an hour ago.'

Reid scowled. 'That doesn't sound good.'

Conrad turned and narrowed his eyes at Olivia. 'What did it do?'

'It started timers on four nuclear devices,' she replied shakily.

Reynolds paled. '*What?!*'

'Three are located next to the reactors powering the facilities. They should detonate deep enough underground not to affect us,' Ethan said, staring blindly at his soulmate. 'It was Vlado Krall's last resort to ensure that his and Jonah Krondike's work never fell into the hands of any enemy who managed to defeat them.'

Lucas clenched his teeth. 'And the fourth device?'

Olivia looked east again. 'It's in a concealed cabin four miles from here. It's the only one above ground.' She stared at them. 'Krall meant for it to kill anything on the surface in a thirty-mile radius of its location. We have eighteen minutes until they all go off.'

Anatole swore colorfully.

Conrad glanced between Ethan and Olivia. 'Can you—?'

Ethan shook his head, frustration burning in his eyes. 'No. The detonators are foolproof.'

Reynolds twisted on his heels. 'Peters, we got any communication devices we protected from the EMPs?'

Peters slipped a Faraday bag out of a pouch at his waist and removed a satellite phone from inside it.

'Call the Sixth Fleet and tell them to scram. We have four nukes going off imminently, three subsurface and one above. Get them to give the Government of Denmark a heads-up.' Reynolds looked south, grimacing at the explosion of shocked cries that erupted from the soldiers and Immortals within hearing distance of his command. 'See if they can spare helicopters and a ship to meet us—'

'No. We have to go west.'

Reynolds turned and stared at Lily. 'What?'

He glanced in the direction she indicated. 'But, there's nothing—'

'Our only chance of survival depends on us reaching that ridge,' Tomas said. He pointed at an elevation in the distance.

Reynolds's perplexed gaze moved around their group before focusing on Lily and Tomas once more. 'Why? What's behind that ridge?'

'It's where Ivan and the children are,' Lily said steadily. 'And it's where we'll stop it.'

Olivia inhaled sharply and pressed her hands to her mouth.

Alexa glanced from Lily to Olivia. 'Stop what?'

'The fourth explosion,' Olivia mumbled. She gazed blindly at Lily and Tomas, wonderment dawning in her eyes.

Zachary headed over from the vehicle where Madeleine sat with Asgard in her arms.

'What's going on?' he said with a frown.

The sky darkened above them.

The crows came in a giant flock, silent but for the rustling of their feathers as their wings thrummed the air. They circled above the crater where the research facility once stood before diving inside.

Another flock appeared to the north and a third to the east.

IT TOOK TEN MINUTES FOR THE FIRST VEHICLES TO REACH THE crescent-shaped ridge. In the sheltered basin beyond, waiting inside a snow vehicle and five trucks, were Ivan Vlašic and several hundred children and infants.

'I've got him in front of me,' Lucas said briskly.

He stepped down from the cabin of the snow vehicle, walked over to Ivan, and tossed the satellite phone at him.

Ivan caught the phone with a puzzled stare before bringing it to his ear. 'Hello?' He dipped his chin at Lily and Tomas as they climbed out after Lucas, Anna at their side. 'Victor?' He listened for a moment, a scowl darkening his features. 'She did *what?!*' He exhaled loudly and pinched his forehead. 'Okay, give me a second. I'll call her.' He muttered something under his breath, disconnected, and dialed a number.

'Sylviana, it's Ivan.' He clenched his teeth. 'Never mind where the hell I am, I want you and the Crovir First Council to stand down right now. The Bas—' he faltered for a second, a pained expression flashing in his eyes, '—the Bastians had nothing to do with my disappearance. It was Vlado all along.' He sighed. 'Yes, Victor was right. No, I am not lying, nor do I have a gun pointed at my head right now. Now, do as you're told, goddammit! And FYI, I'm holding you personally responsible for whatever damage has been inflicted on the Bastian First Council headquarters!' He abruptly ended the call, a vein throbbing in his forehead.

'Subordinates, huh,' Anatole muttered with a grimace.

Ivan studied the scores of trucks and snow vehicles riding up and over the elevation past them before looking at Lily and Tomas. 'What's happening?'

THEY STOOD WITH THEIR HANDS LINKED IN A LINE ON THE RIDGE, the vehicles arranged in a thick wedge in the depression behind and below them.

'Hey, does this remind you of anything?' Alexa asked Olivia.

Olivia's lips curved slightly. 'The battle at Eridug?' She glanced at Alexa where she stood to her right. 'There were eleven of us then.'

Alexa smiled faintly. 'Some of them are with us right now.'

Sadness flashed through Olivia. She could sense Navia's

grief inside her heart. The time for them to part would soon be upon them.

'Aunt Olivia, I know you're scared,' Lily said after a moment on her left.

Olivia stiffened and looked down at her.

'What happened at Yuma was your rage,' Lily said. 'This—' she glanced over her shoulder before staring up at Olivia, '—this is your love and everything that you are.'

Olivia bit her lip. Her fear of the terrible psychokinetic storm she had unleashed at that time, the storm that had killed Jonah Krondike, had been at the forefront of her mind once more. Relief filled her at Lily's words and her warm expression. It was followed by a sudden resolve.

There was something she still needed to do. Something she had waited too long for.

She looked beyond Lily to the end of their chain on the far left. 'Ethan?'

He turned and gazed at her, his eyes full of so much love it choked her. 'Yeah?'

Olivia smiled tremulously, tears blurring her vision. 'Will you ask me again?'

Confusion flashed across his handsome face. Then he grinned, looked ahead to the east, and took a deep breath. 'Olivia Ashkarov, will you marry me?'

Olivia sniffed and followed his gaze to the horizon. 'Yes, I will.'

'Well, congratulations,' Conrad said drily where he stood on the other side of Alexa. 'It's a bit of a shame you two waited until the end of the world to get your shit together.'

Lucas chuckled to Ethan's right.

Lily froze. Her eyes widened.

Tomas blinked.

'Oh,' he murmured, his eyes sparkling.

'Uncle Conrad?' Lily breathed.

Conrad tensed and gazed at her. 'Yes?'

'Aunt Laura just gave birth to your son,' Lily said with a dazzling smile.

Conrad sagged next to Alexa. She grasped his hand tightly.

'Are they—?'

'They're fine,' Lily said. 'He's big and healthy. And loud.'

Conrad gulped. 'We were going to call him—'

'William,' Tomas said. He grinned. 'He's going to be my best friend and one of the greatest healers and warriors this world will ever see.' His smile faded slightly. He sighed. 'He's also going to be a gigantic pain in my butt.'

Lucas glanced at Alexa over Tomas's head.

'I think swearwords are allowed under present circumstances,' she said with a shrug.

Lucas swallowed a grin and nodded.

CHAPTER FORTY-SIX

SLIVERS OF SNOW FLUTTERED ACROSS THE FINGERS OF LIGHT piercing the gloom high above.

Bastian gazed at the distant rays and shifted awkwardly in the narrow gap where he had become wedged, slabs of concrete and debris piled high around him.

It had been some time since the structure had collapsed. He had broken his legs during the fall to the bottom of the stairwell. He could barely feel them now, the pain fading as the blood supply to his swollen limbs was slowly cut off.

A muffled cough sounded below him.

Bastian looked down to where Crovir lay with his head on his lap. The wound he had inflicted on his older brother's chest had stopped bleeding a while back.

'I never thought it would end like this,' Crovir rasped.

Bastian studied him, puzzled.

'Our dream,' Crovir continued in a weak voice. 'The one we had all those moons ago, before we built our empire.'

Bastian smiled faintly. 'You mean…for the two of us to rule this world?'

Crovir nodded and winced.

'Hush,' Bastian murmured. 'You will only make your injuries worse.'

Silence descended around them.

'You could have escaped,' Crovir said suddenly. 'After you stabbed me. You had a chance to get out.' He hesitated. 'Why did you not?'

Bastian stared into the pale gaze beneath him for timeless seconds.

'Because you are my brother,' he said finally. 'I did not leave you then, nor will I leave you now.'

Crovir blinked rapidly, a wet film forming across his eyes.

'You are a sentimental old fool,' he said throatily.

Bastian grinned. He tensed a second later.

Goodbye, King.

Bastian relaxed when he recognized Lily Soul's sorrow-filled voice inside his head.

Goodbye, child.

Bastian knew that he and Crovir had but moments left. Lily had predicted this end for them when she last bade him farewell, before he and Ivan had taken the children and left, and told him so in his mind.

He folded his arms around the man on his lap and gently kissed his brow. 'Be at peace, brother.'

Crovir grabbed his hand and squeezed it tightly.

THE CROWS FLED AS ONE, BLACK CLOUDS THAT DWINDLED RAPIDLY into the azure sky from the three facilities.

'Get ready,' Lily said.

Alexa took a deep breath and focused inward, to the source of her unearthly gifts. Heat erupted inside her heart. It flowed through her veins and warmed her flesh and bones.

She felt the same explosive energy burst inside Conrad and Olivia where they stood on either side of her, and through everyone else along their chain.

Fire seared the trishula birthmark at the back of Alexa's neck. From it poured the very essence of Mila's power, a potent force almost identical yet subtly different to hers. With it came all of the ancient warrior's memories, thoughts, and feelings. Tears pooled in Alexa's eyes at the enormous weight of the centuries of emotions.

Conrad and Olivia's fingers dug into her palms, their breathing ragged.

Alexa knew without looking that all of them were going through the same heartrending experience. She gasped when Mila's soul fused completely with hers. An unholy radiance burst into life along her skin and throughout the bodies of her cousins once more as their powers exploded.

MADELEINE SAT ON THE ICE BEHIND ONE OF THE SNOW VEHICLES, Asgard in her arms. Zachary and Anna stilled at her side, their gazes similarly riveted to the incredible figures on the crest of land ahead of them.

A golden light shimmered and danced around the seven Immortals, the brightest halos concentrated on the two children in the middle of the chain.

Standing behind them, so faint she thought she was imagining them, were six ethereal forms.

Sadness bloomed inside Madeleine, so sharp and sudden she choked on a silent sob. Tears blurred her vision as she experienced the heartbreaking sorrow of the soul inside her.

Anna took her hand, her eyes gleaming with tears of her own.

They knew then that they were looking at the original six Immortals. The ones who had revived inside the bodies of their marked descendants. The ones who had once risen against their own fathers in order to forge a different path for mankind and their own kin, in an epic war that history had long since forgotten.

Brightness bloomed on the horizon.

LILY AND TOMAS DREW ON THE FORMIDABLE ENERGIES OF THE Immortals beside them and raised their linked hands toward the searing ball of light rising toward the sky.

'Up,' Tomas whispered.

THE FLASH OF THE FOURTH NUCLEAR DETONATION WAS VISIBLE from the International Space Station where it orbited the Earth. What the astronauts witnessed next defied all known laws of gravity and physics.

Although the initial fireball created shock waves and ripples in the Earth's atmosphere, the mushroom cloud and sequential condensation rings never formed. Instead, most of the blast was concentrated into a rising funnel that dispersed its explosive power and radioactive material into outer space.

THE GROUND TREMBLED VIOLENTLY BENEATH TOMAS'S FEET AS HE watched the wall of ice and rock head toward them in a thunderous roar ahead of the firestorm.

The first wave of elemental and psychokinetic energy he and Lily had created had curtailed the devastating explosion by encircling it and channeling its cataclysmic force in the only direction it could go. Up, toward the sky.

There was little they could do to completely stop the effects of the blast at ground level and the destruction of the thick ice sheet and rock beneath it.

Sweat beaded on Tomas's forehead. He clenched his teeth and felt Lily's fingers bite into his palm. They inhaled, focused the combined powers of all seven of them once more, and released the second wave.

Olivia gasped and dropped to her knees. Ethan and Conrad folded a moment later.

Although Alexa and Lucas sagged at their sides, they managed to stay upright by the barest thread.

LUCAS'S ENTIRE BEING THROBBED AND TINGLED WITH SO MUCH power it nearly drove him to the ground. He blinked, his heart stuttering at what he was seeing.

The wall of ice and debris stopped half a mile from where they stood. He watched, mesmerized, as it soared higher and higher, curving along the massive bubble of elemental and psychokinetic energy it had crashed into, its angry howl muted to a faint rumble.

Twilight covered the land as it arched above and around the ridge. It took less than thirty seconds for the dome to form.

In that moment, Lucas felt the sudden agony of loss.

The two souls who had been his constant companions for the last three days were gone.

DEAFENING SILENCE DESCENDED AROUND THEM. MADELEINE blinked and slowly opened her eyes, blood pounding inside her skull.

Zachary uncurled his arms from where he had wrapped them over her and Anna's heads and took a shuddering breath. It froze on his lips in the next instant.

Anna gasped.

Madeleine followed their gazes to the sky. Or where the sky should have been.

Instead of azure, all she saw was whiteness. It took a few seconds for her to register that she was looking at a vault some one mile high.

'Is that—ice?' Anna said hoarsely.

Murmurs rose around them as humans and Immortals alike gaped at the incredible phenomenon, stunned that they were still alive and unharmed.

Something fluttered past Madeleine's face. She put her hand out and watched a snowflake land on her palm. Flurries formed above her head as more snow started to fall.

That was when she felt it. The absence of the soul that had been reborn inside her.

Footsteps crunched in the ice up ahead. Madeleine looked down and stared at the seven Immortals walking toward them through a film of tears.

❄

Conrad knelt by Madeleine and gently helped her lay Asgard on the ground between them. Shivers still shook the Healer's body, no doubt an aftermath of the incredible forces that had filled him only moments past.

'Are you sure?' she said.

He nodded and blinked back tears.

He could no longer sense Rafael inside him. He hadn't realized how much the reborn soul of his ancestor had come to mean to him in the three short days they had spent together until he was no longer there. He could read the same sadness in the eyes of his cousins, Zachary, and Madeleine.

Conrad took a ragged breath, laid his hands on Asgard's chest, and closed his eyes. He had just started to focus on the unearthly lines of energy surrounding his heart when someone touched his shoulder.

'No.' Lily lowered herself beside him and moved his hands aside. 'Let me do it.'

Conrad stared at her, nonplussed.

'Lily?' Anna said, her face pale as she exchanged a troubled look with Lucas.

Lily smiled at her father and mother. 'It's okay.'

She placed her hands on Asgard's body, a tiny frown furrowing her brow.

Conrad blinked. Shock flared through him when he grasped what he was feeling under his fingertips where they still lay on Asgard's chest.

'Conrad?' Alexa said in a low voice.

Olivia's knees slowly buckled beneath her. Tears streamed unchecked down her cheeks as she stared from Lily to Asgard. Ethan inhaled sharply and gripped her shoulder, his face turning to ash as whatever Olivia had felt was communicated to him across their bond.

'What's going on?' Madeleine said, her eyes wide with apprehension.

Conrad swallowed past the sudden lump in his throat. 'Seventeen. She's giving him back all of his seventeen lives!'

Panic washed across Anna's face. She took a step toward Lily. Tomas grabbed her hand.

'She'll be fine.' He dipped his chin at his mother. 'Trust me.'

Conrad's breath locked in his throat. He stared blindly at his fingers where they rested on Asgard's chest, unable to comprehend what it was he was sensing now.

'More.' His gaze switched to Lily's face. 'There are more than seventeen lives. I can't—' He faltered, his pulse racing as he finally grasped what was happening.

The new golden lines around Asgard's heart were multiplying faster than he could count them.

A shudder ran through the body beneath his hands.

Conrad looked up in time to see Asgard's eyes slam open. He gasped and bolted upright, his fingers rising to clutch Lily's where they still lay over his heart.

'Immortality,' Olivia whispered.

Conrad exchanged a stunned glance with her. He hesitated before nodding his agreement.

Alexa dropped to her knees in the rapidly building snowdrift, tears glittering in her eyes. 'You mean—?'

'He is a true Immortal now,' Olivia mumbled. 'Like Lily and Tomas, and Lucas and Anna.'

Asgard blinked and looked around dazedly before staring at Lily. 'What happened?'

Madeleine broke down and cried, her sobs echoing in the silence around them.

EPILOGUE

November 2017. Balthazar Island, Pacific Ocean.

Glass trembled and hummed violently. The windows vibrated in their frames. Bob startled and ran out of the room before peeking his head around the doorframe, bushy tail swinging hesitantly. Anna winced.

'Jesus, does that kid have a pair of lungs on him,' Ethan muttered.

He was seated at the kitchen island, his index fingers rammed inside his ears.

Olivia grinned on the stool beside him.

William Rafael Hartwell-Greene opened his mouth and let out another explosive shriek before shoving aside the bottle Conrad was holding to his lips.

Rapid footsteps sounded on the stairs. Laura skidded to a stop in the doorway next to the golden retriever, her hair still wet from the shower, her clothes disheveled. Alexa, Zachary, and Reid followed leisurely behind her.

'What the hell is going on?' Laura snapped.

Conrad sighed and indicated their son with a jerk of his head. 'He won't take his milk.'

Laura's shoulders drooped. 'Again?'

'Let me try,' Anna murmured.

She took the baby from Conrad's arms, walked over to a chair by the patio doors, and rocked him gently as she brought the bottle to his mouth. Will studied her with a calculated stare, reached up, and yanked sharply on her hair.

'Ow,' Anna said with a chuckle. A gasp left her lips as he folded his chubby legs to his chest and booted the bottle to the floor.

'Wow,' Reid said in mock admiration. 'Three months old and he's already perfected a double-front-flying kick.'

'Your son's a regular terror,' Ethan told Conrad and Laura bluntly.

'Ha ha,' Laura said with a scowl.

Conrad grimaced.

The front door opened. Madeleine and Asgard strolled into the hallway with Lucas and Tomas, fishing rods in hand.

'We heard the screaming from the water,' Madeleine said.

'I think he scared the fish,' Asgard said gruffly. 'Not a single damn one of them would bite.'

Lucas swallowed a bark of laughter. Tomas grinned.

A lighthearted feeling swept over Anna as she gazed lovingly at the people around her.

Thirteen weeks had passed since the events in Greenland.

Defying all scientific explanation, the one-mile-wide dome of ice and rock that had formed around the protective bubble Lily and Tomas had created with the help of Lucas and their cousins still stood and remained visible from space. It had taken a blast of elemental energy from Ethan and Tomas to create a break in the west wall large enough for them to pass through in their vehicles and meet with the soldiers who had been coming to their rescue.

Although everyone had feared that the snow that had drifted down on them following the detonation would be rife with radioactive debris, no trace of radiation had been found in the air above and around the impact zone by the International Atomic Energy Agency and the World Health Organization, something no one could fathom.

It was Lily who had revealed the reason why days later. 'Most of it followed the path of the primary blast into space. Tomas and I destroyed whatever was left over.'

Anna had stared at her children for a stunned moment.

'What?' Lucas had said hoarsely.

They'd still been at their apartment in Boston at the time.

Tomas had nodded. 'It's just as Lily said.' He'd glanced at his sister. 'It's like healing. Instead of flesh and bone, we cured the air.'

As she had lain in Lucas's arms in bed that night, Anna had turned to him and finally voiced her concern. 'There are still so many things I don't understand.'

Lucas had regarded her for a moment before pressing a soft kiss to her mouth. 'I think that's something the scientist in you is just going to have to come to terms with.'

A new era of previously inconceivable cooperation between the Bastians and the Crovirs had started following Greenland and the embarrassing Immortal war that had almost erupted. Victor and Ivan were even talking about merging their councils, something which Dimitri found intensely amusing. He had teased both men mercilessly about it when they had visited him in Sumava and had started to take bets as to who would lead a unified Immortal Council. It turned out Ivan was as much a fan of chess as Victor and Dimitri were, and even defeated Eva during a game that had seen Jordan sulk for an entire week.

Anna and the others' esteem for the Crovir leader had only grown after Lily and Tomas had related what had happened while they had been prisoners in the facility. As for the children and babies Ivan had helped rescue, they had all been taken into care by the Immortal societies.

It had taken twelve weeks for Anna and Lucas to rebuild their home on the island with Ethan and Conrad's help. Today was the first time everyone had returned to visit the new house.

'Where's Lily?' Alexa said presently.

'She went for a walk,' Tomas said.

'She was headed for the beach near the lab,' Asgard added.

Anna gazed fondly at her uncle. The fact that he was now a true Immortal like Lucas and herself had come as an utter shock to him when he had woken after his seventeenth death.

'But—but what about Lily's lives?!' he'd said, aghast.

'She is a true Immortal still,' Conrad had explained. 'And it looks like she can gift her immortality.'

Asgard had remained pensive for a long time after that. Anna knew he had been thinking of Madeleine. That he would outlive her was obviously a subject of much anguish for him.

Anna swallowed a secret smile. What she had not told him or the others yet was what Lily and Tomas had said to her and Lucas a few nights ago.

An unholy sound exploded across the kitchen, startling everyone. Anna stiffened and stared at the crying infant in her arms.

Tomas walked over to the chair. 'Can I?'

Anna glanced at Conrad and Laura. They shrugged.

She rose and passed the baby to her son.

Tomas took the seat and the bottle from her.

Will gazed wide-eyed at Tomas. He closed his lips around the teat and drank greedily, his blue eyes fixed unblinkingly on the older boy.

'Holy cow,' Ethan said, breaking the stunned silence. He pointed at Tomas and looked at Olivia. 'When we have kids, he can be their official nanny.'

Olivia blushed.

Tomas stiffened. Will giggled.

Anna bit her lip; there was a wet patch spreading on Tomas's T-shirt.

Laura's face fell. 'Did he just pee on you?'

Tomas sighed and observed the chuckling baby and the growing blotch morosely. 'And so it begins.'

SAND AND DIRT PUFFED AROUND ALEXA'S FEET AS SHE HEADED for the north beach.

A strange peace had descended on her and Zachary's lives since the events in Greenland. This despite the fact that they both sorely missed the souls that had been with them for such a fleeting time. Though three months had passed since the explosion, there were days when Alexa felt that Mila was still there, living in the space behind her eyes and inside her heart.

'They stayed for as long as they were needed,' Lily had explained while they were making their way back to Iceland on a transport helicopter following their rescue. 'To do what they couldn't do all those years ago. To see their fathers return to ash.'

Alexa knew the grief she had experienced since was not just

her burden to carry. She could glimpse the same sorrow in the others' eyes. It was truly as if a part of them had died. A fragment of their soul they had never even realized had always been there.

She passed Anna's lab. The trees cleared up ahead. Beyond them, surf rolled off the dazzling, green Pacific Ocean and crashed gently onto a white beach.

Lily stood at the edge of the water. She was not alone.

Alexa stiffened when she saw the figure her niece was talking to.

The man was tall and dressed in short boots, gray jeans, a white T-shirt, and a brown, leather jacket. A hoodie covered his head and obscured his face.

There was a crow on his left shoulder.

Alexa clenched her teeth and broke into a run, conscious she'd left her guns and sais at the house.

The man and the crow turned their heads and looked straight at her.

A memory slammed through Alexa's consciousness and brought her to a staggering halt, her feet inexplicably freezing to the ground. A memory of the night Mila had stumbled upon the dreadful sight of Crovir slaying Romerus.

She recalled the warm breeze and the incredible pressure Mila had sensed beside her as Romerus had taken his last breaths, and her instinct that something else had been present in the citadel with them that night.

Something beyond her understanding.

Something otherworldly.

The same powerful feeling washed over Alexa as she stared into the silver eyes of the man at Lily's side and met the fathomless gaze of the crow on his shoulder.

The man's lips curved in a faint smile as he studied her. He dipped his chin in a silent greeting, murmured something to the little girl, and turned on his heels. Gold flashed under his jacket and in the wings of the crow as they headed east along the beach.

Alexa took a ragged breath and found that she could move again. She closed the distance between herself and Lily rapidly.

'Who was that?' she asked.

Lily gazed after the man's fading figure before looking at her solemnly.

'His name is Uriel,' she said quietly. 'Romerus knew him as… Ury'an. The crow is Arael.'

Their names danced through Alexa's consciousness, silver tunes of power.

'You don't have to be afraid of them,' Lily said. She flopped down on the sand and sat cross-legged facing the sea. 'They're our friends.'

Alexa hesitated before lowering herself beside her. She looked east.

The man and the crow had disappeared.

'What did they want?'

Lily was quiet for some time. She started tracing a pattern in the sand with her finger. 'To warn me,' she said finally. 'About the visions I had when Tomas and I were still in the facility.'

Alexa regarded her niece for a moment. She sensed that whatever those visions had been, she wasn't quite ready to talk about them yet.

Lily suddenly grinned. 'Tomas says Will peed on him. And he pooped on Uncle Zachary when he was having his bottom changed.'

Alexa smiled.

'He wants to know what you thought of him,' Lily said after a while.

Alexa stared east along the beach once more. There was no trace of the man and crow who had vanished in that direction.

'He is…formidable,' she said after a thoughtful pause.

Her answer seemed to satisfy Lily. A comfortable silence fell between them. Alexa closed her eyes and turned her face to the sun, basking in the warm rays heating her skin.

'I will. If he asks me,' Lily said.

Alexa's pulse jumped. She lowered her head and turned to stare at her niece, her breath catching in her throat. 'How did you—?'

The question died on her lips. Alexa swallowed and looked out to sea. The treacherous thought that had occupied her every waking moment since Lily had made Asgard a true Immortal sprung to the forefront of her mind once more.

'If Uncle Zachary wants to be an Immortal, I, or Tomas, will grant him his wish,' Lily said.

Tears slowly pooled in Alexa's eyes as she gazed over the ocean. She reached out and grasped the little girl's hand.

'Thank you,' she whispered after some time.

Lily wrapped her fingers tightly around hers. 'It won't be long now.'

Alexa looked at her, puzzled.

'The day he holds her in his arms for the first time, he will come to one of us,' Lily said.

Alexa's heart struck up a wild tempo against her ribs at the expression on her niece's face.

'Holds who?' she breathed.

Lily lowered her head to Alexa's lap and touched her taut belly gently. 'Your daughter, Mila.'

Air locked in Alexa's throat. This time, the tears spilled over and blurred her vision.

She blinked them away until she could see Lily again. 'You mean…I'm—?'

'Yes.' Lily grinned up at her. 'I can't wait to meet her, you know. She and I will be the best of friends.'

Alexa pressed her hands to her face then, a low sob leaving her lips at the incredible happiness surging through her heart and overflowing her soul.

'I love you, Aunt Alexa,' Lily said softly.

Alexa wiped her tears away and smiled at the little girl in her lap. 'I love you too, Lily.'

Lily's expression slowly sobered. She sat up and started tracing patterns in the sand again. It took a moment for Alexa to realize she was drawing symbols. Five of them she recognized. They were the birthmarks she and her cousins possessed.

The others were new to her.

'Tomas and I spoke to Mom and Dad a few days ago. About how we can make all of you true Immortals.'

Alexa waited in silence, knowing there was more to come.

'It will happen,' Lily said. 'At some stage or another in the next few decades. It has to.'

Alexa startled at her grim tone. 'Why?'

Lily folded her legs to her chest and crossed her arms atop her knees. 'What we did to stop that explosion? The energies we projected? It sent ripples around the world that will awaken the others.'

Alexa stared at Lily, her heart thundering in her chest. 'What others?'

'The ones whose gifts have stayed dormant in their bloodlines up till now. Humans and…things that do not yet know who or what they are.' Lily turned and looked gravely at Alexa. 'You see, Uriel was not the only divine being who came to Earth. Others did too, after him.' She looked out to sea again. 'Creatures of light and darkness.'

Alexa listened, blood roaring in her ears and shock reverberating through her very core, as Lily spoke of what Uriel had told her and of the visions she had had.

Of the challenge laid before an Archangel by his Creator. Of the future the Archangel had wished to carve for humans and the creations fashioned by his master. Of the ones who would join ranks with Immortals and Angels in the future. Of the battles that still lay ahead. Of the End of Days and the war to end all wars.

'Our future allies will have their own destinies to fulfill.' Lily frowned faintly. 'However much we will want to help them, we must not do so. How they handle the challenges that will come their way will be their own test, just as everything that has happened since Crovir and Bastian became Immortals has been our trial.'

Alexa's pulse raced as she tried to digest the incredible things Lily had just revealed to her.

She recalled what Dimitri had said about the Order of the Three Spears, the sect created by the Lotus-born Second Buddha to preserve the secret of the existence of the Immortals. She remembered what he had said about the first Immortal Rinpoche had met and how he had been convinced the creature was of divine lineage.

She also remembered what Olivia had said when she and Ethan had first met them in Sumava all those years ago, about how all of them had been touched by a higher power, Lily and Tomas most of all.

Alexa took a shallow breath. 'That's a lot to take in.'

'It is,' Lily murmured.

Alexa glanced to the east again. 'Will he be there, at...the End of Days?'

Lily nodded. 'Uriel is the oldest and wisest of all the Archangels. He is also their greatest warrior. He will be our general.'

Alexa followed her niece's gaze to the horizon once more.

'What happens?' she said after a while. 'If we win the war?'

A breathtaking smile lit up Lily's face.

THE END

AFTERWORD

I hope you've enjoyed this final, epic chapter in the Seventeen series. For those of you who wondered why Origins preceded Destiny rather than being the first book in the series, I believe Destiny answers that question. The impact of this story is so much more because of the journey I took you on during Origins in early 2017. The tale of the original Immortals is still fresh in your mind, as is the emotional ride of their adventures. That their journey did not truly end in Origins I hope came as a pleasant surprise.

I never meant to write a spin-off series from Seventeen. Destiny was going to end with Lily telling Alexa about all the battles that were still to come, battles that would be fought by an Immortal-human army. But so many of you asked for a continuation of the Seventeen world that I just had to write it. And I've had so much fun with this second series.

Legion is different from Seventeen. When the Immortals feature in it, it's in a peripheral role only. There is less science and technology, and more myth and fantasy. There is also plenty of humor; these guys and girls are super dry.

Get the first book Blood and Bones and start a brand new adventure today!

If you liked Destiny, I would be really grateful if you could consider leaving a review on Goodreads or on the store where you purchased it. Reviews help readers like you find my books and I truly appreciate your honest opinions about my stories.

Make sure to sign up to my store newsletter for special deals on my books and new release alerts. Or you can sign up to my author newsletter to get upcoming release notifications, sneak peeks, and giveaways.

FACTS AND FICTIONS

Now, for one of my favorite parts of writing my books. Here are the facts and fictions behind the story.

Frangibles

Frangibles, or fragmenting bullets, are factual. These are bullets that split into multiple projectiles after hitting their targets. What should be one deadly projectile turns into several lethal shards as the eight trocars in the nose of the 9mm bullet open up and shred through anything they come into contact with, including, yes, your organs. Frangibles are also known as RIP bullets. Not Rest in Peace, although that would be highly applicable in this context, but rather, Radically Invasive Projectile. Whoever thought that acronym up will laugh all the way to their grave. Once thought to be the bullets of the future, frangibles are very much the bullets of the now and are in active use by various special armed forces around the world, including the UK's SAS as of 2017.

When I was researching what dangerous new ammo to give the bad guys in Destiny, I also came across three more "bullets of the future" that, quite frankly, made my eyes pop and my jaw drop.

MIB or Multiple Impact Bullet, is another type of fragmenting bullet, except this one doesn't fragment on impact but before, giving a wider zone of destruction. Why just go for the stomach when you can hit the liver and the spleen at the same time.

EXACTO or Extreme Accuracy Tasked Ordnance, is a self-steering sniper bullet that increases the hit rate of difficult long distance shots. EXACTO literally tracks moving targets in mid-air and can even accelerate. They were first field tested by DARPA in 2015 but have yet to be deployed on active missions. I think.

The final type of bullet is still very much experimental. That's the laser-guided bullet, which will boast steerable fins instead of conventional rifling and contain a smart chip that can steer it and make up to thirty trajectory corrections per second, all under the control of an optical sensor in its nose.

Pacific Missile Range Facility, Barking Sands, Kauai

The US Navy's Barking Sands facility is factual. Classed as the world's largest instrumental multi-environmental range, capable of providing complex and realistic training scenarios involving surface, subsurface, air, and space, PMRF is a missile testing and training facility for the US military and is heavily used by NASA and defense contractors like Lockheed Martin. PMRF plays an active role in RIMPAC, the world's largest maritime exercise and the setting for one of my favorite action movies, Battleship. In *Destiny,* I used PMRF for one very specific reason. It was the only military facility capable of facilitating a C-17 Globemaster III on its runway on Kauai.

WMRD, US Army Research Lab, Aberdeen Proving Ground

The Weapons and Materials Research Directorate of the US Army Research Lab is factual and is indeed based at the Aberdeen Proving Ground in Maryland. The aim of WMRD is to improve and enhance the lethality and survivability of the weapons systems used by the US military. Simply put, they make deadlier, faster bullets, and also make stronger ballistic vests/barriers capable of sustaining impacts from those deadly, fast bullets. And not just bullets. WMRD's field of scope encompasses researching the materials and technologies applicable to armor, armaments, missiles, ground vehicles, and helicopters, as well as an individual soldier's hardware. In *Destiny*, I have a WMRD scientist work out the components of the new metal the bad guys use to make their lethal bullets. More about that new metal later.

Nano film tracker

Although the nano film tracker Vlado Krall places on Dimitri Reznak's AMEX card is fictional, the science behind the water-resistant, liquid, thermoelectric element isn't. I based it on a technology called Power Felt, which is effectively a thermoelectric device that converts body heat into an electric current. Power Felt was much talked about in 2012 but never made it to market. Other technologies and materials based on the principle of piezoelectricity (the ability of a solid material to accumulate or generate an electric charge in response to a mechanical stress or stimulus) have been in R&D phase since, including a mobile device nanogenerator film capable of turning mechanical vibration into electricity (so, jiggle your phone and it charges itself), and even piezoelectric floors capable of harvesting the kinetic energy of walking pedestrians and turn it into electricity (look up power generating floors in train stations in Japan).

Missing submarines

The mysterious case of the four submarines that went

missing in 1968 is scarily factual. When I was trying to decide how I could get the bad guys stolen nuclear materials to build their reactors in Greenland, I thought the best way to do this would be to fake the disappearance of a few nuclear subs. The hairs literally rose on my arms when I actually started researching this subject and came across the 1968 missing subs.

The American Skipjack-class sub that went missing in the Atlantic was the USS Scorpion. The Russian Golf II-class ballistic missile sub that went missing in the Pacific was the K-129. The modified British T-Class sub commissioned by the Israelis that went missing in the Mediterranean was the INS Dakar, formally the Totem. The Daphné-class French sub that also went missing in the Mediterranean was the Minerve. There are many theories out there about what happened to these subs. Go read up on them. You'll be pleased to know that none, thankfully, involved Immortals or suspicious individuals named Krall.

Super soldiers

I already alluded to the concept of super soldiers in Legacy and wrote about it in the Facts and Fictions section of the book's back matter. In addition to bionanotechnology used to recombine human and Immortal DNA, and the use of performance enhancing drugs and strict physical training regimes and psychological conditioning to prepare super soldiers for battle, I added several more technologies to the super soldiers in *Destiny*.

First, bioengineering from the cellular level up. Whereas the super soldiers in Legacy were human soldiers and Immortals who either volunteered or were tricked into joining the Yuma program, the ones in *Destiny* were conceived and grown in a lab, their DNA put together with extreme precision from cellular conception. This makes them deadlier as they have none of the limitations of the original super soldiers.

Second, the use of nanotechnology and nanorobots at a cellular level. This makes the super soldiers highly adaptable to all sorts of environments and stresses, with the nanorobots being able to accelerate tissue repair, control blood flow to vital organs in critical injuries, and maintain a perfect homeostatic environment inside the super soldiers' bodies by regulating their organ function. Imagine a soldier with a life threatening liver or spleen injury or even head injury on the field; with nanotechnology on board, his body will instinctively be able to reduce and control shock, pain, and minimize permanent injury by a careful balance of hormones, chemicals, blood flow, and the autonomic nervous system. This technology is already in experimental phase by DARPA under its IVN (In Vivo Nanoplatforms) program. In Israel, a company called Nanoretina is developing an artificial bio-retina composed of nanoparticles that can restore sight in under an hour.

Third, the use of neurotechnology. Closed-loop neural implants like the ones Anna discovers in the super soldiers' brains and spines is not the stuff of the future but very much in experimental phase under DARPA's BRAIN program and by the Israeli's BIRD foundation. By using neuromodulation and neural augmentation, these devices can assess the state of your health and literally fix you from the inside out by sending nerve stimulation to your organs to control and modify their function. The biggest areas of research right now in neurotechnology are for diseases like strokes, spinal injuries, Parkinson's, Alzheimer's, and even ADHD.

In *Destiny*, I have Jessica Wu go further and use the neural implants to manipulate the emotions, free will, and pain thresholds of the super soldiers, enabling them to fight beyond the physical limits of their bodies. Cue the cackling of other evil, James Bond-type baddies the world over.

Liquid-armor tactical suits

The liquid-armor tactical suits featured in *Destiny* are very much factual. The use of nanorobots in said suits is entirely fictional. For now. Here's how liquid armor suits work.

Take some Kevlar. Soak it in a shear-thickening fluid (STF), which behaves like a solid when it encounters mechanical stress or shear. In other words, it moves like a liquid until an object strikes it. Then it hardens, in milliseconds. The science behind it goes something like this.

Shear thickening fluid is a colloid, so it's made of tiny particles suspended in liquid. Those particles normally repel each other, hence they float easily in the liquid. But a sudden impact overcomes the repulsive forces and suddenly those particles get super friendly with one another and stick to each other like glue. Or form hydroclusters, the correct scientific terminology. When the energy from the impact dissipates, the particles resume the hate part of their love-hate relationship and repel each other again. So, treat them nice and they stay liquid. Bitch slap them (or in military terms, shoot at them) and they turn solid enough to stop a bullet.

The other liquid that can reinforce Kevlar is magnetorheological (MR) fluid. Nope, nothing to do with the X-Men. And try saying that word really fast. MR fluids are basically oils that contain iron particles. Again, take some Kevlar and soak it in MR fluid. Expose it to a magnetic field and the iron particles in the liquid line up like a Roman infantry unit in phalanx formation, all vim, vigor, and as hard as diamonds. In the case of an MR liquid armor suit, it's not the impact of the bullet that would turn it into an impenetrable fortress of doom. It would be a switch that would activate tiny electric circuits inside the suit, thereby generating mini magnetic fields.

These are all currently under research by such types as our old friends at the US Army Research Lab and MIT.

I also considered giving the bad guys military exoskeletons like the one from DARPA's Warrior Web program, the Sarcos/Raytheon's XOS2, and the Ekso Bionics/Lockheed Martin's HULC, but decided I was venturing way too close into Iron Man territory. And nobody wants another smart-mouthed, billionaire playboy in Seventeen (I'm looking at you Howard Orson Rodney Titus).

Lightning and EMP devices

The electromagnetic pulse or EMP technology used in *Destiny* is factual. EMP is a short burst electromagnetic energy of natural or man-made cause that can disrupt or damage electronic equipment, as well as large scale physical objects such as buildings if it's huge enough. The biggest natural EMP that could hit the Earth would originate from the Sun in the form of a solar magnetic flare. The biggest and most destructive man-made EMPs that could affect the Earth would be high altitude nuclear explosions or non-nuclear EMP weapons. A lightning strike is indeed a natural form of EMP. The Nevada scene was one of my favorites of the entire book and nicknaming Ethan the Ultimate Power Ranger was a given. The EMP grenades our Immortals and their allies use against the bad guys are in developmental phase. As for the Faraday pouches in the final battle, those are factual too. Go look up homemade Faraday cages. You will never look at aluminum foil and metal trash cans the same way again.

Can an EMP disable a real liquid-armor suit? Probably not.

I theorized that the EMP would definitely destroy the nanorobots in the super soldiers' suits, but as to whether it could disrupt the chemistry of the shear-thickening or magnetorheological fluid is anyone's guess.

Uranium City, REEs, and HEAs

Uranium City is factual. No, seriously, go look it up. It's a community that was set-up in the 1950s around the thriving Cold War uranium mines of the times and expanded rapidly in the 1960s and 70s. Once the last mine closed in the 1980s, the population dropped dramatically and now less than one hundred people live in what is effectively a large ghost town on the shores of Lake Athabasca.

The fictional mine that Lucas and the others infiltrate in *Destiny* is based on the geographically isolated Hoidas Lake Rare Earth Project, thirty miles north of Uranium City. Hoidas Lake is one of North America's most significant and promising Rare Earth Element (REE) sites currently in development along a vein system known as the JAK Zone.

Rare Earth Elements have a large range of applications, from magnets, hybrid vehicles' electric motors, military vehicles and weapons components, super conductors and lasers, to LED light bulbs, X-ray machines, PET scans, and mobile devices. The largest producer of REE in the world before it got shut down in the 1980s was indeed the Mountain Pass Rare Earth Mine Priya Chatterjee mentions in *Destiny*. China is undoubtedly the biggest player in the world right now when it comes to large scale REE production and has been since the start of this century, with its Bayan Obo mine being its greatest natural resource. Australia, Russia, India, and Brazil are next in the top producing REE countries in the world, but their output is still dwarfed ten times over by the Chinese.

When I started thinking of the bad ass weapons I could give the super soldier army in *Destiny*, I knew I needed to put in a clue that Lucas and the others could use to eventually trace where Vlado Krall's base was. That clue was the metal used to make the frangible bullets I talk about above. REEs were identified as one of the groups of technology metals critical for the US civilian and military industries even as far back as a decade ago. Not only are they used in their pure forms for all the applications listed above, but they are potential vital components of High Entropy Alloys (HEAs), effectively new metals with the combined abilities of all their primary constituents and more, like Priya Chatterjee tells Lucas and the gang in *Destiny*. The spark plasma sintering technology mentioned in *Destiny* is factual and is a method of super heating elements to just below their melting point to enable them to bond at an atomic level, thereby creating a new material that is denser, more compact, and has improved tensile strength, electrical, and thermal conductivity. It's how ceramics are made.

IONDS

IONDS, the Integrated Operational Nuclear Detection System Howard and Jordan use to trace the nuclear signals of the missing submarines, is factual. It started life as Project Vela in the 1960s, a space-based military system consisting of twelve satellites able to detect nuclear explosions in the Earth's atmosphere and in space, and also gather data on natural sources of space radiation. It was an essential component of Nuclear MASINT (Measurement and Signature Intelligence) at the time. Nuclear MASINT falls under the more broad-based umbrella of intelligence gathering (the other intelligence gathering methods I've used in the Seventeen series and in the

Division Eight series are HUMINT, GEOINT, and SIGINT). Over time, the program was also used to monitor nuclear tests and EMP events on Earth. Navstar satellites were introduced in the 1980s and the whole thing is now known as IONDS.

The extra electro-optical devices I place on the IONDS satellites to detect the presence of nuclear radiation at a constant low level on Earth is purely fictional. I'm pretty sure someone is working on this somewhere in real life.

NUCLEAR EXPLOSION

I wrote the final scenes of *DESTINY* over a year ago, well before I finished Origins. The picture of those seven Immortals standing on a ridge and facing that explosion was etched in my mind from that time onward. So was the scene where the scientists on the International Space Station witnessed the fourth detonation. For me, this was the best way to explain the epic nature of what Lily and Tomas achieved.

A nuclear explosion consists of four phases. The flash and fireball of the initial detonation, which consists of an intense bright flash of light that can temporarily or permanently blind people up to fifty miles away, immediate heat radiation that can set fire to material up to eight miles away and burn people within a six to ten-mile radius, and deadly X-ray pulses that can kill up to two miles away. The second phase is the explosive nuclear blast which destroys and kills everything in its path within a two-mile radius and can injure people and cause damage to structures up to ten to twenty miles away; this second phase is accompanied by hurricane-strength winds. The third phase is the firestorm which is augmented by breaking gas mains and the winds of the blast; not only does the firestorm kill and destroy everything in its path, it also uses up all the oxygen in the area, causing death by suffocation. The fourth phase is radiation fallout and widespread contamination of all living and inert matter in the fallout zone, which can be several miles initially but can extend to hundreds of miles if one factors in winds. For example, the Chernobyl nuclear reactor explosion caused contamination as far out as Sweden and Norway.

The first phase of a nuclear explosion, the flash and fireball, is accompanied by the mushroom cloud or cap of the explosion, which is formed of smoke, debris, and condensation vapor. This occurs in all kinds of powerful explosions, not just nuclear; volcanic eruptions also give rise to mushroom clouds. Alongside this mushroom cloud will be a series of short-lived clouds called Wilson clouds. These take the shape of rings that form above and around the mushroom cap. They are effectively areas of rapid condensation that form in the atmosphere as a result of the initial explosion, which produces a shock wave of compressed air. In the wake of the compressed air, the atmospheric pressure drops, forming low-pressure zones around the mushroom cloud. This results in the cooling and condensation of water in the atmosphere, hence the clouds. Once the pressure in the atmosphere equalizes again, the clouds dissipate as the water evaporates once more.

In *Destiny*, the mushroom cloud and condensation rings that accompany the first phase of a nuclear explosion never formed. That's because Lily and Tomas create a wave of elemental and psychokinetic energy that literally wraps around the flash and fireball and propels it into outer space at super sonic speed, thereby dispersing over fifty percent of its kinetic energy. Since they cannot prevent the effects of the second phase, which is the blast at ground level, the only way they can save everyone on that ridge is to protect them under a dome of their combined energies, like the bubble they created on the island to protect Lucas and Anna from those RPGs. The wall of ice and rock generated by the nuclear blast literally skirts over and around this bubble, resulting in a solid dome when the debris cools down.

I thought it made for a pretty cool finale.

I hope you enjoyed this science and technology lesson. Check out the Extras section of the website for more research info from the series at www.adstarrling.com

BOOKS BY A.D. STARRLING

Seventeen Novels

Hunted

Warrior

Empire

Legacy

Origins

Destiny

Seventeen Short Stories

First Death

Dancing Blades

The Meeting

The Warrior Monk

The Hunger

The Bank Job

Legion

Blood and Bones

Fire and Earth

Awakening

Forsaken

Hallowed Ground

Heir

Legion

Witch Queen

The Darkest Night

Rites of Passage

Of Flames and Crows

Midnight Witch

A Fury of Shadows

Witch Queen

Division Eight

Mission:Black

Mission: Armor

Mission:Anaconda

Miscellaneous

Void - A Sci-fi Horror Short Story

The Other Side of the Wall - A Horror Short Story

ABOUT A.D. STARRLING

Visit Shop AD Starrling and buy all of AD's ebooks, paperbacks, hardbacks, audiobooks, and exclusive special edition print books direct.

Want to know about AD Starrling's upcoming releases? Sign up to her author newsletter for new release alerts, sneak peeks, giveaways, and more.

Follow AD Starrling on Amazon.

Join AD's reader group on Facebook
The Seventeen Club.

Check out this link to find out more about A.D. Starrling
Linktr.ee/AD_Starrling.